Sandra Rose lives in Australia and has a love for family and writing. She has an enduring interest in larger social and political concerns with particular focus upon matters of justice and equity. Sandra has worked in both the tertiary and welfare fields for a number of years and her academic studies in social and political sciences, centred around welfare and politics, led to her success in attaining a PhD in sociology and political science. She dotes upon her animals and relaxes by writing and crocheting garments for animals and her many grandchildren.

This book is dedicated to my dear husband, Glenn, who has been nothing but supportive of my writing enterprises, and my children and grandchildren whom I love more than life.

Sandra Rose

# A Selfish Endeavour

AUSTIN MACAULEY PUBLISHERS™
LONDON • CAMBRIDGE • NEW YORK • SHARJAH

A CIP catalogue record for this title is available from the British Library.

ISBN 9781035831623 (Paperback)
ISBN 9781035850402 (ePub e-book)

www.austinmacauley.com

First Published 2024
Austin Macauley Publishers Ltd®
1 Canada Square
Canary Wharf
London
E14 5AA

Again, I would like to mention my husband, Glenn, for being a very patient and thorough editor of this book, and for his constant encouragement.

# Chapter 1

As he listened to her, he could hardly believe what was coming out of her mouth, after everything they had talked about in the not too distant past. She may as well have been spewing forth black bile; he was so shocked. He looked at his feet, clad in brown leather, stark against white tiles, in a vain attempt to hide his face from her for a few seconds.

'So, what do you think...it's a great opportunity, eh?'

She was, as usual, blissfully unaware of his deep-seated feelings. Her voice, full of delight for the seemingly delicious but yet to be tasted future, made it very clear to him that she was not going to listen to a word he said.

'Umm, yeah sounds great, but...' was all he could manage, a response to her inflated enthusiasm reflecting the growing resentment building up inside of him. He turned and took the lid off the saucepan. Their dinner simmered quietly, letting out the occasional puff of steam: there was something he wanted, but dared not say. The ramifications would be incalculable.

As a way to deflect, he pushed the contents of the pan around with disinterest as she went on about the fantastic opportunity she had. He no longer wished to put anything of himself into the preparation of the meal. He felt that food should be cooked with love, or at least in good humour so that it was infused with positive vibes, which he thought made it taste better. He had been known to leave restaurants in the past if he heard any argument coming from the kitchen. Now he was afraid the dinner had absorbed his disappointment, his anger; it would be tasteless. The chicken and onion aroma made him gag.

When she had arrived home, he had been relaxed and happy; she saw that as soon as she walked in the door. But now, his hunched shoulders displayed to her more of his hurt feelings than she would have wanted to see. This morning, they had planned for a nice dinner. She knew that he wanted to talk about having a baby. In turn, he had gathered a few little extras to make their night extra special. They had the house looking great. It wasn't a big house, but it was enough for three; she had conceded this point to him on many occasions. Was she ready? She didn't think so, but she knew he was.

Their marriage had trundled along nicely for a few years. Now, he wanted more than anything to complete the rosy picture with a baby, another person to love and to share in their love. She wanted to stall that event for a few more years, and with this news, she thought he would understand, but he wasn't responding to it in the way she had hoped. Of course, she had expected it, a mood, some form of pushback, but it still made her bloody mad. She had been given a great opportunity, out of the blue, and he was, well, ditching it—his total lack of anything that even seemed like enthusiasm annoyed her. He could at least be proud of the fact that she had been hand-picked for something she had only ever dreamt of. Staring at his back, she plunged a water cracker into the runny avocado dip that sat in sickly glory on the white breakfast bench. She bit down so hard that it cracked loudly in her mouth. She waited with growing impatience for a response that did not come.

'I'll go and phone mum. At least she will be happy for me.'

Leaving the room, she chewed on what was left of the cracker. Phoebe knew from experience that she could talk him around to her way of thinking. However, the total silence worried her. She preferred it when they yelled at each other. That was nearly always followed with make-up sex; silence was a road not travelled all that often. She did not know where it would lead—she hoped but was doubtful that it would end up in bed, and she would get her way.

Her footsteps on the tiles echoed as she moved down the hall, and the sound resonated like bullets aimed at his head. She picked up the phone from the cradle which adorned the white antique hall table. His late mother had given it to them as a wedding present: something to be passed down to the next generation and the next.

'Hi mum, guess what...' the bedroom door slammed shut.

In the kitchen, Mic turned the gas off and leant against the new oak kitchen cupboards for support, leaving the dinner to cool. His bottom felt the protrusion of the mouldings that formed the bench top. The cabinets had only been installed a week ago, replacing the 1950's décor. He could've lived with it; she couldn't stand it. He was just getting used to where everything was, including the new height of the cupboards. He would, however, never get used to the cold-water tap that continued to drip regardless of the new tap fixtures.

'Shut up,' he yelled in frustration. His head throbbed. He tried to think fast. She was pushing him to make some comment—a comment he knew would cement the rest of their lives. This issue had been simmering, just like dinner, for a very long time.

He picked up the glass of red wine he had poured for himself before he started cooking. Next to it on the kitchen bench, he noticed the Cabanossi had not fared well in the heat. It looked pale and slimy against the white plate on which it sat forgotten. His stomach lurched at the sight of it. He hadn't felt physically sick since he had been on the rotor at Luna Park another lifetime ago. Life was easy then. They were both happy and looked forward to starting a family. He walked over to the dining room table and sat down. His head fell into his hands as he listened to the mumbling emanating from behind the closed bedroom door.

'That's right, mum, what do you think?' She had the phone balanced between her ear and her shoulder as she removed her sweaty work clothes. Her black skirt was proving to be a little problematic. 'Mum, just hold on a second, will you.' Throwing the phone on the disheveled bed, she quickly undid her skirt. It slid over her tan stockings and shoeless feet to transform into a little pool of black on the white-carpeted floor. White was the predominant colour in the house, one that Mic insisted would not go well with kids, and again she didn't listen. Her skirt would be kicked out of the way or tripped over later in the night. She found the phone again.

'What? Oh, he will. He will understand eventually. It is such a good opportunity, such a good…Yeah, he is sulking a little but mum, you know how hard I have been working towards this, don't you? What do you mean? What? That I shouldn't take the job if he doesn't…mum…yes, I know he likes it…mum…yeah…kids, not yet. Look, mum, I have to go. See you. Yes, yes, I will. Bye.'

'For God's sake.' The phone was thrown onto the bed again. Her mother always made her blaspheme, a remnant of guilt left over from her semi-religious childhood. She fished around for her summer pajamas under the bedclothes. She needed a plan. Plans were good. By the time she found her pajamas and slippers, she was more than just uptight. She was angry that there was to be a battle to get what she wanted. She would give him an ultimatum. It was risky; she knew after speaking to her mother that nobody would back her. Her family always took his side.

'So much for blood is thicker than water crap,' she whispered, all the more determined to go through with her plan.

'This has got to work,' she said to herself as she put on a floaty floral blue dressing gown and sprayed herself with expensive perfume. She looked feminine and smelt fantastic. Opening the bedroom door, she composed herself. It was not going to be easy convincing him. She needed to start the debate in the right frame of mind. After a couple of deep breaths, she found him sitting at the dining room table staring at a glass of wine with his head resting awkwardly on his right hand.

'All right, so it means moving to Canberra, so what? You can get a new job.'

She stood behind him and playfully massaged his head. 'It wouldn't be as hot, well, not like here.' She glanced at the broken air conditioner hanging uselessly on the lounge room wall. Something they had not got around to fixing after all the renovation work – the heat did not help the situation, and it was still only late spring.

'Don't.'

'What?'

'Don't do that!' He shook his head free of her hands and pulled his chair closer to the table. 'Getting a new job will not be that easy.'

She was hurt and just a little concerned that he had shied away from her touch. She walked around the table and sat with a hefty bump on the chair opposite him. She stared at her fingers, examining them for dirt and chips. When there was no response, she cleaned her nails with a toothpick plucked from the little red glass toothpick holder that always adorned the pinewood table whether they had visitors or not. Both sat without speaking.

Soon the silence got to him. He felt compelled to say something, but he knew he must be mindful not to come across as condescending as she hated that more than she hated hypocrites and fish stew.

He looked up at her with pain stabbing his heart. 'You know I am proud of you, Pheebs. You deserve the job with all the hard work that you have put in. But I thought we had already talked about this? About how we both felt? That it's best if you look for work here and not miles away. It's just, well, it's just that I thought we agreed that we would try very hard not to move. We're happy here, aren't we?'

'You might be.' The verbal jab struck him hard. He looked down at the table once more. It was becoming his place of refuge in this fight. He knew he was defeated. In fact, he knew that before the fight had even started. Hands clasped, he unconsciously knocked them on the tabletop.

'I know, sweetheart, I know,' she sought to soothe his anger by placing her hands softly on top of his to stop the knocking. She knew he didn't want to move away from the area. His family was here, the work he enjoyed, and especially the people he worked with every day. They had spoken of the possibility of her having to move for work, but they had both agreed that she would work locally. At the time, she had not envisioned the type of opportunity that had just presented itself. Then, she was more than happy to agree not to move. But now, she wanted this job more than she had wanted anything else in her life. How often do you get headhunted for a job you thought you could only dream about scoring?

She looked at him, his brown hair sticking up a little at the front. She knew he had run his fingers through it in frustration, probably while she was in the bedroom on the phone to her mother. His face was a little haggard, a mixture of the long day at work, the rush to get dinner ready, the sudden revelation she had made, plus the three-day growth. His powder blue eyes were lost on his rather large round face. She loved him, she was sure, but this job, this opportunity, this was something that she could just not let go of. At this very moment, she felt that maybe she didn't love him quite enough for that, not right now anyway. That thought scared her. She needed him to respond with some flexibility and a real consideration for what they needed to do as a couple.

'Mic?'

'What?'

'Will you listen to me?' She implored.

'Okay, as long as you agree to listen to me, deal?'

'Deal.'

She knew that one of them would have to give in. But she wasn't going to be the one. Maybe they had married too young. They hadn't had the time to find out who they were, and what they wanted. She could tell he was watching her, breathing her in, hoping that she loved him.

'Look, Mic, before you start, know one thing, I love you, and together we can work around this. I could commute. We could see each other at weekends.'

'Oh great,' he said, pulling his hands out of her grip. 'You're not even interested in my opinion, are you?' He stared at her. She gave no verbal response,

only a shake of her shoulders.

'No, I didn't think so.'

'I was only trying to give us options.'

'No, you weren't. You were trying to get me to agree to what you want, for fuck's sake.'

'Oh, grow up!' She yelled, regretting it as soon as she said it. 'Mic, I'm sorry, I'm sorry…I didn't mean it. I…' She reached out across the table, but he pulled his arm away.

'Yes, you did. You meant it. You think I'm not good enough for you anymore; not smart enough with your high flying university education!'

'Don't be silly. I am not going to get into your insecurities. I wish you would believe me when I say I love you. It's not the end of the world if I commute. Please think about it.'

'I have, and I have an option for you,' he said in pain and anger. 'If you take this job, our marriage is over!'

She sat in stunned silence. She had always imagined that she would be the one to end the marriage if it came to it. But, she had never expected this, not from Mic.

She took a few seconds to compose herself before she replied, 'You mean that you're not even going to try and give it a go, just give up? That's it. Over. Don't you think you are overreacting just a little?'

'No, I don't,' he said. He was annoyed that he had to give her such a stark ultimatum, but it was only to shock her into understanding the depths of his feelings in regards to her plans.

He had hoped that the tactic would work. Scare her a little. But now, he knew it was only going to make things worse. 'It's not me that has given up,' he muttered.

'Now, don't you lay this on me. It's you who won't move. It's you who thinks your life here with your friends in this pokey little house is more important than our marriage.'

'Pokey? You don't like this house?' he exclaimed. He had spent the best part of six months redecorating, making it look modern and cheerful. She said she loved what he had done. Now she calls it pokey? His tactic had fallen on the floor and straight through it. They both sat staring at their laps, shocked, unsure of what to say next. He took a sip of wine, fuming that she was so stubborn, and that he had walked into a situation he would find impossible to get out of anytime soon. In turn, out of frustration, she threw the toothpick she had in her hand to the end of the table in an attempt to break the stalemate. It worked. He stood up, took a deep breath and decided to tell her exactly how *she* felt.

'You're just not interested anymore, are you? And be bloody truthful for God's sake.'

'What do you mean?' She looked up at him.

'You're not interested in marriage anymore.' His voice was a little high due to his frustration. 'You put off having kids. You spend most of your time at uni or work. You never cook, and the house always resembles the local bloody tip.' He had tidied up the lounge room and cooked dinner.

She couldn't argue with him, but she couldn't resist muttering under her breath, 'Sorry for not being wifely.'

He ignored her, and in a softer voice, added,

'The reason I decorated the house was that I hoped it would motivate you, you know to help me keep it clean, maybe think about having kids.' They both worked hard. He did his fair share; all he wanted was for her to focus more on their domestic life rather than her constant preoccupation with theories and policies and to at least think about the possibility of having kids sooner rather than later.

He walked around the table and stood behind her. He looked down at the top of her head. He didn't want to watch the expression on her face when he told her a few home truths.

'You know we hardly ever get asked out by our friends anymore. Have you noticed that?'

He placed both hands on the back of her chair; he felt that it was a better option than her shoulders right now. Close contact would be inappropriate and very difficult. He would either shake her or pull her close. Neither would do, not now, maybe not ever.

'What has that got to do with this?'

'Don't you see?' he said, deflated and sorrowful. She shook her head.

Her glossy auburn hair waved between her shoulders. He almost couldn't bear it. He was going to lose her.

'They think I'm a poor bastard having to listen to you go on all the time about politics, women's rights, and God knows what else. They're so sick of you that they won't ask us out as a couple anymore. I've had to resort to going for a drink with my mates when you're out.'

She sat and said nothing. He needed another drink, and that meant a new bottle of wine to be opened and consumed. He went to the kitchen to get one.

She, on the other hand, was thinking about what he had just said. She felt her anger rising. How dare they be so condescending, so bloody patronising. She was only trying to better herself. They couldn't hack it. She stood up abruptly, scratching the brushwood floor with the feet of the chair as she did so.

'Well, well,' she shouted, 'I am amazed by how threatened men are about a little conversation about real life, things that matter instead of the football results or the price of a schooner or how big the boobs are on the girl at the bar with the low-cut top.' She had a habit of using her hands to get her point across; she cupped her small breasts with them. 'You can have your friends. I'm sick of them.' She clenched and unclenched her hands as she watched him looking for a bottle of red wine in the little fridge that rattled every half hour.

He slammed the bottle of wine onto the kitchen bench. Then, holding onto it tight, he retorted like an eight-year-old, 'They're all sick of you. And so am I!'

So this was the truth. He was sick of her. Or was it that he was sick of her because she wanted to make something of herself? What did he want? For her to ride along with him for the rest of his life like there was nothing out there to achieve? A future full of beer, BBQ's and footy—no bloody way. Her face turned ashen.

He was at her elbow. 'I'm sorry, love; I didn't mean for that to come out as badly as it did...to say that.'

She pushed past him, stopping halfway down the hall. Keeping her back to him, she yelled, 'How many times do I have to tell you; you don't put red wine in the bloody fridge.' For the second time that night, the same door slammed shut on him.

In all honesty, he didn't want the wine; he put the bottle back in the wine rack, not the fridge. He only drank wine because she did, and he always tried to please her.

He went to the laundry fridge to get a beer. He slumped into his old favourite armchair, stretched out his long legs clad in slightly worn work jeans and sculled the beer nearly in one go. He sought solace in the view by looking out of the large glass sliding door. The palm trees swayed in the breeze, and the street lights did their best to light the road for the nighttime traffic. For a while, he could hear her moving around, opening and shutting draws, banging cupboards.

Eventually, the noise stopped, and all was quiet.

Well into the night, he picked up the empty beer bottles, six in all, threw them into the bin along with dinner, which was long forgotten. He slept fitfully on the lounge with the glass doors open and his jeans discarded on the floor alongside his boots. He tried to convince himself that the heat was to blame for their argument. In the cool of the morning, everything would be okay.

# Chapter 2

Phoebe didn't sleep well. She was unsettled due to the nagging decision she would have to make: her marriage, or a new, fabulous, only in her wildest dreams kind of job? She felt terrible. She knew deep down that her marriage would not take precedence, and she felt guilty because of it. She only managed a few hours of much-needed rest just as dawn approached. She was snoozing when a knock came at the bedroom door. She glanced at the clock; it was eight in the morning. Dropping her head back on her pillow, she responded to the knock. 'Yeah?'

'Pheebs, I've made you some breakfast. Hurry up, or it will get cold.' She was a little put out that he had gone to the trouble.

'I'll be a minute,' she said tersely. She really didn't want him to be nice. She wanted him to be angry; it would be easier to leave. Kindness at the moment was not in her plan, her mood was too sombre, and she had made up her mind. She was going.

'Okay.'

He knew from her tone she was not happy. So he left to brew coffee. Stretching, she slid to the side of the bed. Her feet touched the floor. Her hair was all over the place. She looked for her dressing gown with one eye open. In the ensuite, she peed, splashed her face and patted her cheeks, and her colour returned. She made her way to the kitchen.

The smell of a full cooked breakfast greeted her in the hall: fried eggs, bacon, sausage, and tomato, topped off with fresh Jamaican coffee that was huffing and puffing its way to perfection.

‘Mic, why have you bothered?’ Her voice had an early morning raspy quality to it. He loved it when she sounded like that, ‘…I’m, I am not really in the mood for all this.’

‘Just thought we could fill up after last night, we didn’t eat dinner, and I thought you would be hungry; I know I sure am.’ He was too optimistic for his own good.

‘Yes, but,’ she waved her right hand over the frying pan, ‘we usually have this type of thing when…’ She stopped as she looked at him blankly.

‘You mean we usually have this type of breakfast on a relaxing Sunday morning. I take it you’re not relaxed at the moment?’ He smiled at her.

‘Are you?’ She retorted, defiant against his good humour. She sat with a thud on a stool at the kitchen bench. He turned his attention to the coffee in silence. The aroma overwhelmed the kitchen, blotting out the smell of the fried food.

With a steaming cup of extra strong coffee before them both, he ventured to try and explain himself. She looked at him. He still had on last night’s top matched only with a pair of undies, his usual dress code on a relaxed morning. He could have at least dressed, put some shorts on or something. She didn’t know why it annoyed her right at that very moment, but it did.

‘You know Pheebs; I really didn’t mean what I said last night. I was angry. I’m sorry.’ He gulped coffee; it scalded his throat a little; he waited for her reaction.

She sipped on her hot drink, her hands a little shaky, waiting for the caffeine to penetrate her nerve endings.

‘Mic, It doesn’t matter,’ the coffee had restored her voice but had not changed her mind. ‘You and I both know that I want this job and you don’t want to move. If you come with me, you will be unhappy, and if I stay, I will be unhappy. So I will leave, and you will stay. And you’re right. It’s about time I faced up to how

I feel. It's me that should be sorry, and I am. But I have to do this. I just have to. I won't be happy if I don't.'

She put her cup down on the bench and placed both hands around it, tracing the rim of her cup with her right forefinger. The bone china hummed like a cat being stroked. The noise was calming, almost hypnotising; she went into a stare, she wanted out, and she knew it. It had taken her a while to understand, but now she did. The job offer had made it clear; she wasn't happy. She loved him but was no longer 'in love' with him. She knew he was looking at her intently, waiting for her to say something else, to backtrack, to say she really didn't mean it. He waited, but she didn't say anything.

This was an opportunity of a lifetime. Not only had she been headhunted, but she had also landed the job of her dreams. She was going to be an advisor on womens' issues to the next Prime Minister. He didn't want to move. He could easily; he was an electrician, he could work anywhere.

On the other hand, she had spent a good seven years getting a degree including honours: she wanted this job, and Canberra was the only place she could be. It offered an opportunity, it was the heartland of politics, and he was not going to spoil it. Nobody was going to ruin it. But the thing that shocked her most was a growing realisation that she really didn't want him to come. She wanted to go on her own. She had never lived on her own, being totally independent. She was just sorry that it had taken her so long to realise it and to cause so much hurt as she chased her dream.

He interrupted her internal voice, 'I suppose it will be no use if I beg you to stay?'

'No.' The bone china cup, with its pretty blue butterflies, was the one he had bought her for special occasions. Why he had made her coffee in it this morning, she could only guess, maybe he knew, deep down in the pit of his soul, that it was to be a memorable day in their marriage—the beginning of the end: she pushed it aside.

'Okay.' He tried to sound positive. He didn't want her to know the full extent of his pain. 'I wish you all the best in your new life. Enjoy.'

He picked up his wallet and his car keys on his way to the front door, the one he had just painted in her favourite shade of eggshell blue. He stood still for a minute and asked, 'can you be gone before I get back?'

'Yes…I have booked an afternoon flight to Canberra.'

He was not surprised that she was already organised to go. It proved to him that no matter what he said, she was going to leave, and it hurt.

'Fine. Ring me when you arrive. I just want to know you got there safely. Okay?'

'Okay.' She felt her heart leap a little at that comment, he still cared deeply, and she had just ripped his heart out. A tear rolled down her cheek as he left.

Phoebe sat for a while staring at the second untouched meal he had made in two days going cold. Finally, she picked up both plates, combined the contents of the two onto one, covered it in glad wrap and put it in the fridge for him to eat later in the day. Although she knew she would be better off putting it in the bin, he wouldn't eat a meal that was the last one they would have shared as husband and wife.

She needed to organise a taxi and let Canberra know she was on her way. They had wanted her a day or two earlier, but she had to explain that due to some family commitments, she wouldn't be able to make it for a least a week, but as it turned out, she would be there a few days early.

# Chapter 3

Canberra can be cold, no matter what time of the year. This late spring day was no exception.

The corridors that penetrated deep into Parliament House held a decidedly frosty atmosphere, and not just because of the weather. The government was in trouble. It faced political oblivion in the upcoming election. The opposition was gaining ground as the days and weeks flew by. An early morning meeting of all available government MPs had been arranged. Chastisement, deflection and trivial matters filled the sunny room with gloom and desperation. Those seated at the large round table dominating the room had their attention averted by a loud and angry outburst.

'I don't know what the hell he is playing at.' The Prime Minister, elderly and well past his time in high office, was feeling pressure not only from the new 'golden boy' of the opposition but from some of his very own party members. The Minister for Health, Ian Markey, a close friend, short, stout with greying hair and matching beard, often failed to read him correctly and made mistakes in soothing the PM's tangled nerves.

'Look, Jim, if it helps in any way, polls don't mean a thing. You and I both know that. Anything can happen in four months, earthquakes, terror, floods, a day in politics and all that stuff. Just promise them tax cuts or something else they want, and they will vote for us no questions asked, you'll see.'

'What the fuck do I care what they want? It's what I want that matters!' As the PM yelled, he looked him straight in the eye. Ian jumped back in his chair and peered over his brown-rimmed glasses, shocked by the outburst in front of others. He thought it was disloyalty to him and their friendship on a grand scale. He didn't care how stressed he was about the election; there was no need to bring him down in such a public manner.

The PM's fist hit the desk. There was only one person who could calm the nerves of the Prime Minister, his chief of staff; a recent arrival to middle age, only marginally ambitious and not too easily rattled by the political to-ing and fro-ing of Canberra. He viewed the electorate with contempt, couldn't care less about what they thought. His job and lifestyle were all that mattered. Keeping the Prime Minister happy was just one of the rather tedious obligations he took in his stride.

'Now, Jim, you may not care what they want, but I know exactly what they want—you. Nothing more, nothing less.'

Usually, the chief of staff does not attend meetings with elected officials. Josh, however, was always on standby. Generally loitering outside the door where meetings were being held so that if the shit hit the fan, which was most of the time, he could swan in, calm the situation and take some control of his charge but not today;

'What are you talking about Josh?'

'They want the PM of the last six years to go out and show his face and shake hands. At the moment, they think the new guy will be good for them but come Election Day, they will want you. You have given them stability, jobs, and a future. All you have to do is show your face, remind them of who you are and what you stand for. The polls are showing a blip, an aberration. Like I said, nothing more, nothing less.'

Everyone in that room knew their ship was, in all probability, sunk. It would be an even worse situation if Josh was not around to bring a semblance of order in these dark political days. They knew, if it weren't for Josh, they would have capsized as a government years ago. And for that, they were grateful to him, which was largely why he was granted many privileges not given to previous Chiefs of Staff.

The PM had another random thought pop into his head. 'What was that bastard thinking?'

'Who, the Leader of the Opposition?' The Minister for Water and Resources chimed in.

'No, bloody Lassie! I was talking about the Minister for Social Security. Who the hell do you think? Where does he think he is, the House of Commons? He can't object to any of our changes, which he does all the time, in parliament. He must toe the party line—well, if he wants to belong to this party, the bloody little prick, he better not keep showing me up. Thank God I'm not the British Prime Minister. I couldn't stand my party having a go at me as well as the morons on the opposite bench…I…I can't stand the arse wipe. I am the Prime Minister; he listens to me.'

Josh scouted the room and was relieved that the minister he was talking about was not at the meeting. Probably out on the hustings, trying to get his electorate to vote for him again. Times were indeed tough, politically speaking. He knew what the PM said would get back to him, and he made a mental note to be prepared for the maligned minister to lose his front bench job, and if by chance, they did win the election, to polish a back bench seat for him. He, of course, would recommend a replacement. That would be fun. Nothing gave him more pleasure than seeing ministers grovel.

Later that night, the PM sat in the middle of a large leather lounge that monopolised one side of his Canberra office. He looked tired and in need of a holiday, but that was out of the question. The hard work of the election loomed almost unbearably in front of him. Josh looked at him; against his better nature, he felt a little sorry for the older man, but only a little. Here was a man trapped by his need for power—no matter what the cost, even to the detriment of his health and his long-suffering family. He was a grandfather, but no one in the house had yet to meet his grandchildren. Maybe Ian, but other than that, family and work were kept separate.

As far as Josh was concerned, he was a basket case, chasing something he would never catch. Josh had seen him change in many ways over the years. He had grown harder, more resolute in his determination to gain all the records that could possibly be obtained by holding a very long tenure.

Physically, he had become old quickly, which wasn't unusual for Prime Ministers and Presidents. His once thick brown hair was now replaced with a mat of silver that covered his head. His face, once open and honest, had fixed itself into a look of permanent defensiveness; eyebrows draw together over piercing brown eyes; mouth and jaw set hard against any criticism of his leadership.

'Would you like me to make you a drink, sir?' Josh was adept at becoming subservient on demand.

'Just the usual, if you don't mind.' The PM started railing about another minister, Josh didn't quite catch which one, but he was being called a nitwit and a hairy goat for some reason. He went over to the drinks cabinet leaving the PM to ruminate about the day on his own. He was just getting out the ice for the scotch when his mobile phone rang. He left the office to take the call in the adjoining corridor in semi-darkness. Security had done the rounds, turned off all the main lighting, and it was well past 1 AM.

'Hello.'

'Josh, my boy, how are you?'

'Fine.' He recognised the voice. 'What are you up to, Pete?' he said guardedly.

'Well, I was just thinking about when I become PM in a few months. Polls are looking good, but well, you know how it looks for the poor old bugger. Look, I will need a great chief of staff, and you came to mind.'

Josh couldn't believe what he had just heard.

'Say that again.'

'You heard me the first time. You will soon be out of a job. Now, I am in the club, and I want you to come and have a drink with me as soon as you're done putting your baby to bed, understand? I won't take no for an answer. When you hear me out and calculate your pay increase, I can't imagine why you would say no. I'm on a recruitment drive. Seeking the best, you are top of my list.'

'But I am the opposition, Pete. I am a Liberal Chief of Staff...I...'

'Don't give me that crap. I know you don't have any real political affiliations. To you, it is just a job, and so you are just the person I am looking for. I have already found my policy adviser for women's issues, poached from a regional council, bit of a looker, and just finished a first-class honours degree. Hopefully, she's not too stubborn. Just out of uni, so probably easy to mould into the Canberra way of thinking. It is a plus that she is also a bit of eye candy. Just what I need, she will look great on TV.' There was silence for a second or so. Josh did not know what to say. Pete broke the silence. 'Oh, and Josh, I know the ladies can't resist you but keep your hands off this one, married, unfortunately. See you in an hour.' He hung up.

Josh couldn't believe what he had just heard. He looked at his phone to reassure himself that the conversation had just taken place. Pete wanted him onboard! He must be confident of a win; otherwise, he would never be so cocky. It sounded okay, the same job but with a different boss. Pete was right; changing colours didn't matter to him. Politicians were all tarred with the same brush, and it was basically a loyalty issue, of which he had none. A political tart he could be called, a thought that made him smirk. Anyway, he was tired of looking after the old boy. He had been putting out feelers for a new position. If he was honest with himself, he was secretly worried they would lose the election. It wasn't looking at all good. However, he would have to be damn sure of an opposition win. The PM would never forgive him, and neither would the party.

'Josh, where's my drink?' The PM's voice echoed down the hall and broke his train of thought.

'Shit,' he mumbled under his breath. 'Sorry, sir, just a wrong number.' Josh quickly made up a drink and handed it to the PM at the same time asking: 'Sir, would you mind if I left now, I have some paperwork to finish.'

'What?' After a few minutes of grumbling and protest, he realised Josh was not going to change his mind. 'Okay, but see you bright and early in the morning.'

Bloody hell, Josh thought to himself, when do these people sleep.

Josh returned to his office. In his ensuite, he brushed his sleek black hair with his small comb and checked for any bits of food that may have lodged in his teeth.

He grumbled to himself, 'doesn't that man know how to rest? See you early in the morning, yeah right.' He stepped back from the mirror and brushed down his expensive Italian suit. It made him look long and lean. He grinned at the mirror. It was true; all the ladies did fancy him.

# Chapter 4

On the plane at cruising level, Phoebe watched white fluffy clouds whizz by as a pretty young cabin crew member gave out tea, coffee, and drinks and food for those who had preordered; no one was interested in buying anything from her as the trip was only a short one. Mesmerised by the outside of the cabin, she told herself that she had outgrown Mic and his friends. All they did was sit in pubs and clubs and drink all weekend. She conveniently forgot about just how hard they worked during the week, but you tend not to let positives influence the negatives when seeking to justify the actions you are taking that will cause a lot of hurt. She caught a glimpse of the ground as she thought about how she couldn't have a decent conversation with any of them. As far as they were concerned, she had become an obnoxious cultural elite, a latté leftie. On the other hand, she just wanted to be with people she felt she could talk to about things that she thought mattered, and in their circle of friends, people with any sort of sophisticated understanding were few and far between. No, she was sure she was doing the right thing. She was moving onward and upward.

'Tea, Coffee, or would you like to purchase a drink?' The beautiful cabin crew member was leaning over her. 'Er...no thanks.'

As the drinks trolley rattled past, Phoebe could see Mic in her mind's eye; he would be in the pub telling his friends that she had gone. She knew very well how they would all react. They would show him great sympathy, but behind his back, they would be high-fiving each other and buying endless rounds of beer. Suddenly the pilot announced that they would be landing in the next 20 minutes. It was a rather chilly fifteen degrees due to the slight breeze coming from the south. Regardless, it was a beautiful sunny day that greeted her as she stepped off the plane to start her new life in Canberra. She took a deep breath and walked, head held high, along the tarmac and into the strange new world that awaited her. Phoebe knew someone was picking her up, but she wasn't exactly sure who that would be. She had been instructed to wait in the baggage area; somebody would meet her and deliver her to her new place of employment. She hadn't brought a warm coat with her. She had forgotten entirely about the weather down south. It was late spring, and she was frozen. She only had a thin brown jacket hanging onto her slight frame, and whoever was picking her up was late. She grew anxious. Looking around, she couldn't see anyone that was looking for her. Soon everyone else from her plane was gone, and she was left waiting for she didn't know who.

Fifteen minutes had passed when she saw what looked like a government car pulling up outside. The huge glass windows of the terminal allowed her to see the driver get out and open the back door. She thought it must be someone of importance because it is a rare thing to park right in front of any airport terminal. She watched intently as a man immaculately dressed, tall and, as was readily apparent, very, very handsome, and quite disconcertingly so emerged from the dark interior. He looked the epitome of professionalism and elegance. Was he the one who was picking her up? He moved towards her, all smiles and confidence. She gulped as he held his hand out to greet her.

'You must be Phoebe. So sorry I'm late,' he said in an accent that almost mimicked someone from the upper middle classes of those hailing from the high tea set in England. 'I will explain in the car. Please hurry; I don't want to be here when the next influx of passengers turns up. Please let my driver take your bags.' The driver gave her a sideways glance and took her bags without speaking. His peaked hat hid a smirk as he bent down to pick up her bags. This is not what she expected. She thought a shuttle bus of some sort or at most an Uber would be waiting. She felt uneasy; it was all a little too official.

'Please forgive me. I haven't introduced myself yet, I'm Josh, Josh Peterson.'

'Pleased to meet you,' she said in reply, feeling a little like a fish out of water.

'And you are?'

'Ohhh, Phoebe, Phoebe Walters. Nice to meet you.'

'Well, come along, let's get in the car, and I can fill you in on all the gory details.'

Excuse me?' she said.

'Wait till we get in the car. Don't want to be overheard by any plebs who may be loitering around in the background, let's go.'

'Did he just say, plebs?' she thought. No, she must have heard him wrong.

He grinned, and she smiled back. But what did he just say?

Once in the car, he relaxed. She could tell because he let out a long, drawn out sigh.

'Nobody can hear us now,' he said relieved, and straightened himself up. The windows of the car were heavily tinted. From the outside, you would have a tough time seeing who was within. He obviously didn't want anyone to see them. While the driver stored her luggage, Josh looked at her intently. His brown eyes seemed to penetrate her clothes, unsettling her, and she shifted herself into a more protective position, bringing her shoulder nearest to him forward. He grinned.

No one sat up front with the driver apparently.

'Now, Phoebe, first of all, we need to take a little drive, and I will tell you how we currently stand as far as the election goes.

It is not long now till we give the voting public a say, even if it is only a token say in how the country is run. As far as the polls indicate, we are sure to win.' He paused, but only for a second.

'But like anything in life, nothing is guaranteed, and it is possible that the current PM will be re-elected. But not probable. Believe me, I wouldn't be putting myself through this if I wasn't very sure of the result. But, nothing, as you will learn, is certain in politics, and time such as in the 24-hour clock is irrelevant. However, I am not a gambling man. I like to be sure of things. That is why I would never make a good politician. They bet on the electorate liking them, which hardly ever happens. Oh, unless you are a Hawke or a Howard, or indeed dare I say a Rudd…Disaster.' He rolled his rather large brown eyes.

The car pulled out into a roundabout. At the same time, Josh turned and looked out of his side window, and she saw his profile. He was indeed very handsome, a nose straight and pleasing, black hair squeaky clean and well-cut framing his face neatly, which showed off his perfectly shaped ears. He knew she was looking at him; she knew that he knew he was handsome. His eyes darted back to her. She looked away quickly, a little embarrassed. She didn't want him to think she was staring at him like some love-struck teenager.

'What I am going to tell you, you may find rather confusing, but here it goes. I am currently employed as chief of staff to both the PM and the Leader of the Opposition.' He waited for her reaction. All she could do was look a little puzzled.

'That is why I was keen to get out of the airport quickly. The fewer questions asked, the better. Around here, you have to be on your guard at all times, especially when an election is looming.' He gave her another few minutes to take the information in.

‘I don’t understand. How can you be working for both sides? At once? Isn’t that a conflict of interest, is that even allowed?’

‘A conflict for who?’ He teased. ‘Certainly not me. It is very much in my interest. And as you will surely find out, all’s fair in love and war, as the saying goes.’ Her brow creased. ‘Concerned?’ He asked. He knew that if she were indeed disturbed by this revelation, she would need to be brought around. Inducements worked every time. He just needed to find out her tipping point and test the water as Pete had said to do.

‘Now let me explain,’ he said as he looked at her intently. ‘I have been working for the PM for more years than I care to remember. He, in my book, has had his day. I was thinking of moving on anyway. At the same time, Pete, Leader of the Opposition, as you know – and your new boss – rang me and asked me to join his team. Being the pragmatist that I am, I would not agree to it outright due to the small chance that the PM might win the next election yet again. He’s a slippery bugger, and I didn’t want to leave myself open to accusations of betrayal if he did. So I will still work for the PM until he is toppled off his throne, and when Pete is sworn in, I will change offices—or just move up the corridor, so to speak. In the meantime, I do a few silly things for Pete beforehand, such as picking you up. It’s like a test, you see, loyalty and all that. But if the PM wins, I stay put. Now, the crux of the matter is, will you be happy with this arrangement because if you are not, then this is your chance to say goodbye, get back on a plane and forget all about us down here, but if you agree, then welcome to Canberra and the many perks of being in league with the Pollies.’

She was frowning. Unsure of what to say. This was not at all what she had been expecting.

'Oh, and if you leave and blab about this little arrangement, you will find yourself in the middle of a shit fight with the government, and your career will be over before it even began. Do you comprehend what I have just said?'

The driver glanced at her in the rear vision mirror. She wondered if they were sworn to secrecy from all they would hear while they went about their work. She hoped so. She moved in her seat, uncomfortable and feeling hemmed in. She wanted to throw up. Instead of taking a lifestyle change, she had jumped into a hornet's nest. But still, she was a little dubious, maybe this was the trick, seeking to find out if she had the guts to stay. She hadn't even been in the government car for twenty minutes, and she had already been given an ultimatum. They don't give you time to settle into this crap, she thought. She sank further down into the leather seat. If it was true, she had thrown away her marriage for subterfuge and dishonesty; but she couldn't go back. She would look stupid.

She hated looking stupid. Josh wasn't letting on that this was a joke or trick. He sat staring at her, waiting for her response. It must be true, she would stay and accept the situation unsavoury as it was; it was the only option. This was her first real introduction to political life. Never in her life had she felt so nauseatingly stuck. Suddenly, out of the depths of despair and anxiety due to what had just transpired, an idea struck her. She sat back up and looked at the charming man challengingly.

'This change you were speaking about; does that include a change in your views? Are you leaning towards the opposition's stance on various topics, like education, welfare, the environment?'

'Sweetheart,' he replied condescendingly, shaking his head and smirking. Her fingernails dug into her palms. He went on, 'listen, I don't know what you have been reading, but both parties have exactly the same intention; to abandon society to the market and the corporations. There are no citizens anymore, only people who spend most of their weekends in a mall buying cheap shit to be thrown out in a matter of weeks. Policy advisors like you spend your days advising them on the best way of delivering non-information and making our intentions seem legitimate. My job, as chief of staff, is to keep everyone happy, especially the PM. That means only letting those who support the PM have access to him. I manage his day-to-day affairs in such a way that he looks good. Give him a drink when he needs it, and mollycoddle him most of the time. The press secretary, who you will meet, tells the public what it doesn't need to know via, you know, smoke and mirrors and so forth. We let them think that they are informed. Public happy, Pollies happy, easily done, no big deal.' He sniffed. 'We are all on the same side, after all, the side of power. Oh, and I will just add that I don't hold any ideologies close. Just as long as I am paid and left to my own devices after work, I don't care what goes on in the power dome.'

'But I came here hoping to make a difference!' She spoke too fast and immediately regretted what she had said. She thought she sounded like some idealistic dingbat. She was annoyed as she watched him look out the window; a grin slanted across his face.

'Didn't we all darling, didn't we all. Now, are you in, or are you on the next plane out with your tail between your legs followed by a bad media story?'

'What?' She said, alarmed. 'But I thought if I went back and didn't say anything, then I wouldn't face a backlash.'

He goaded her with his face. Blackmail! It added insult to injury. Her thoughts raced. The family, what would they think? If anything was said on the news, they would believe it and not her. She was sure of that. She would never get a job, and all her education would be for nothing. With all the positivity that she could, she thought that like-minded people would be working here wanting to do great things? Not everyone could be as fatalistic, so ruined by the power of being – well, in power. Maybe it wasn't as bad as he made out? It couldn't be. She refused to believe it. This was a test that she needed to pass, but even if it wasn't, she would stay and find out for herself. She would never know if she didn't at least try. She made up her mind. She wanted to make a difference, that's what she came to do, and bloody hell she would. What else could she do? She couldn't go home, especially not now. Not until she had won. Then those back home would see that she had made the right choice!

'I'm in,' she said.

'Good girl,' Josh growled with an attitude of confidence that told her he knew she would.

Sitting back in her seat, looking straight ahead with her heart pounding, the smell of the squeaky-clean interior filled her nose and made it itch. It was very stuffy inside the car. She pushed down on the button for her window, which created turbulence inside the car's confines. Josh looked at her angrily as his hair ruffled in the draft. He always arrived at Parliament House well-groomed; he never put his window down. He didn't say anything; he let her get over the initial shock of the realities of politics 'Canberra style' and the uphill battle she was going to face.

Suddenly, Parliament House loomed into their line of sight. Majestic, it lay shimmering brightly in the late afternoon sun, its white walls pure against the green grass slopes on its sides. She could see the newly erected walls that stopped people climbing up and running down the green slopes. This latest addition was to the dismay of many school children and mothers and fathers who visited. She wondered about them and how many were happy and confident in their government; she couldn't help but think the wall was a statement on the modern political era.

# Chapter 5

'How do you think the new girl will settle in, Josh?' Pete was scribbling in his notebook and didn't bother looking up while he spoke. Josh was settled on the biggest lounge that occupied the rather elegant but untidy office. Pete pored over the day's news regarding the upcoming election and noted down anything that caught his eye. Fortunately, for all involved, it was looking grim for the PM.

'Oh...I'm not sure. She was a little put out when I told her the score, but she likes her office.' Josh looked over the top of the newspaper that had occupied his attention for the last half an hour or so. There was no reaction from Pete. He was so damned sure of himself and arrogant. It was really annoying. Josh didn't realise that people saw him in the same light. He shifted uneasily in his seat. He was aware that Phoebe's appointment was only a political manoeuvre. An attractive woman, married or not, was always a vote catcher, especially if she was present at press conferences, meeting women at women's groups and the like. All she needed to do was give the impression that women in the electorate were essential to Pete in his capacity as P.M.

'She'll come around, they all do. But I tell you what.' Pete put down his pen and leant back in his chair. 'I'll listen to her, make her think she is making a difference like she wants and then...well...'

'And then, well, what?' Josh looked squarely at Pete; a small grin on his face thinly veiling his distaste for the man.

'I'll do just as I want.' Josh hoped that was just about her work and nothing else.

'Don't you always?' Pete winked in reply.

A knock at the door interrupted them. Josh jerked his head in the direction of the ensuite as he stood up to let Pete know he didn't want to be seen.

'Come in,' Pete said.

'Sorry to interrupt.' The Minister for Women's issues entered. A lady in her forties, rather thin and dull, in a black suit, but with an eager and pleasing face, walked and stood in front of Pete's table.

Pete stood towering over her and extended a hand. 'Eleanor, how lovely to see you. Would you like a cup of tea?' Pete went to pick up his phone, but the minister stopped him.

'No, no, thanks. Good to see you as well, Pete. Look, I just popped in...'

'Of course, you want to meet the new adviser for women. I will see if Danielle can sort out a meeting...'

'...well, yes, that would be nice, but I just came to let you know that I have heard from the 'women against low pay rates' lobby group, and they have stated that if you promise to bring in the changes you spoke to them about, you could count on their votes for sure. Good, eh?'

'Never doubted it. Thanks for letting me know.'

He sat back down as a way of dismissing her. But Eleanor only fidgeted a little and brushed a stray brown hair off her well-dressed shoulder. She didn't make any attempt to leave.

'Is there something else?' He looked up; she was supposed to leave.

'Well, yes,' she said nervously. 'I need to go home for a while. My youngest is ill and wants me to return for a visit. I know it means I won't be able to meet the new girl, but I will make sure I catch up with her when I come back. Do you mind?'

Pete looked at her for a second. His face hardened, and his lips thinned. She could have just come out and said when she first came into his office, but no, she had to try and play him. He wasn't impressed and felt like ripping strips off her, but he caught himself just in time. It would be impolitic to get any of his ministers offside at this point. He needed a stable and robust group of ministers with their full support. He would make sure she regretted trying to make nice and then asking for a favour. People who beat around the bush annoyed the hell out of him.

'No, of course not. You go and don't think of this place for a few days.'

'Thanks, Pete.' Her voice echoed her relief. She knew it was the wrong time to go, with the run-up to the election, new staff and all. 'Well, I'll get going. Thanks again.'

'Coast is clear, Josh.'

Josh walked back into the office, went over to the window and stood looking out. Protected by the two-way blinds, no one could see him from the outside.

'What a slacko, leaving you at a time like this.' He looked back at Pete.

'Bloody women. I don't know why we have to have them here at all.'

'You don't mean that do you?' Josh was taken aback. He had not realised that Pete was so extremely sexist. He knew most of the men in Canberra accepted women as part of the new terms of political life, himself included. Of course, many would be happier if they stayed in their place, but to hear it verbalised by this man, who was so powerful, made him a little uneasy. He felt for sure trouble would be brewing if it became public knowledge. He reminded himself that as Pete's future chief of staff in office, he needed to curb some of his views or make sure they never become known to the general public.

'I, on the other hand, like having them around,' Josh said as he eyed a young woman in the courtyard outside. 'The younger ones anyway, gives me something to look at in this God-awful dreary place.'

'Don't tell me you have got your eye on the new girl?'

Josh thrust his hands in his pockets and rocked back and forth in his shoes, wondering how the hell Pete jumped to that conclusion; he looked at him.

'Now Pete, you know I never kiss and tell.'

Pete shook his head and laughed. 'You're a dark horse, Josh. I just can't make you out.'

'Good, and hopefully you never will, for both our sakes.'

'Josh, have you introduced Phoebe to any of the other policy advisors?'

'No.'

'Why not?'

'Pete, I can't have every Tom, Dick or Harry knowing that I am working for you now, can I? We only told Phoebe to get a reaction, to see if she would be a player in the game.'

Even as Josh said this, he was not so sure she would be. 'Sorry mate, I clean forgot. I'll get my PA to arrange it.'

'Thanks, that's a good idea.' Josh was sarcastic in his reply. It went over Pete's head. Pete had forgotten entirely that his PA and Josh had history. Even if he did remember, he wouldn't have given a toss.

'Bloody hell, she will have to rearrange a few things until that woman comes back.' He wrote a note to himself so he would remember.

Once finished, he leant back on his chair. 'Has she managed to get into her apartment yet?'

'She should have access by this afternoon. She stayed in a motel last night.'

'Well, she has had a day to settle in, and tomorrow, she is thrown in at the deep end.'

'Yikes!' Josh knew what that was like.

'Listen, Pete, I have got to go. The PM will be looking for me shortly.'

'Okay…Gin and tonic time?'

'Oh no, more like scotch and coke time, haha.'

Before Josh left the room, he picked up the paper he had been reading and threw it onto Pete's desk: 'Hail the new PM.'

Pete picked it up. As he read the headlines, he smiled. It wouldn't be long now, and he would be king of all he surveyed.

# Chapter 6

It had been a very long day. Phoebe had been hanging around the hotel for someone to arrive and give her keys to her apartment. Finally, at 4 o'clock that afternoon, she let herself in. It had been a trying few days. Her argument with Mic, a rather shocking introduction to political life and the feeling she had been left alone to fend for herself, she was very close to hopping on the next plane home. But here she was, inside a very bland and half-empty apartment. There was a bed with a somewhat soft mattress, a sombre grey lounge, tables and chairs, a TV and of course, there was a fridge that rattled and a rather dirty looking oven. She was surprised to see a new looking washing machine in the laundry. She had been told that this apartment was used as a stopgap measure until the 'newie' found an apartment of their own. She had about six weeks to find somewhere else.

She stood in the middle of the lounge room and looked around in disbelief. Her shoulders hunched over a little more as she noticed the old wooden windows were in desperate need of cleaning.

'Welcome to Canberra,' she said softly to herself.

She yearned for a cup of tea, forgetting that to have a cup of tea, she needed to go shopping. She headed for the kitchen where the empty fridge stood guard over the 1950's orange décor. There was not even a comforting bottle of milk in there.

'Oh shit,' was her depleted response when she realised that a cup of tea would not be next on her agenda.

A knock at her front door diverted her attention.

Surprised to have a visitor, she sang out 'coming.' She checked her clothes, some jeans and a pale pink sweater, to make sure she looked okay. She swung the front door open and stood facing a woman who looked around sixty. She had on the typical 'Canberra suit,' which was always dark in colour and very sharp, maybe even starchy looking, teamed with a shirt; in this case, it was brilliant white. Before Phoebe had time to say hello, the unexpected visitor said:

'Hidy ho. My name is Jean, and I am one of a pool of secretaries that work for Pete. You might even say I am the head honcho. Anyway, he sent me over with a few things to help you settle in. I hope you don't mind my interruption?'

'No, no...of course not. Come in, come in.' Phoebe was a little taken aback by the sudden appearance of this woman who she had never set eyes on before. She was, however, grateful for the supplies.

Jean picked up the box of goodies that she had placed on the front step before knocking at the door. With a puff or two, she carried it to the kitchen table and put it down carefully. Phoebe followed.

'You seem to know your way around.' Phoebe quipped as a joke as the apartment was tiny.

'Oh yes, I have been welcoming people into this apartment for many years.' Her face had a welcoming tone to it which was aided by being a little plump.

It was devoid of wrinkles, and she had an attractive peach and cream complexion. Her searching green eyes looked around the apartment, turning into slits as she took in the amount of dust sitting on top of some of the furnishings and fittings.

'Those cleaning contractors have a lot to answer for. I'll ring them in the morning. Now, I bet you could do with a lovely cup of tea, am I right?'

'You sure are.'

'Well, you go and put the kettle on. It is in the cupboard by the stove, and I will dig out of this box all that we need. Tim tams are my favourite biscuit. I hope they are yours as well?'

Phoebe was doing as she had been instructed, and Jean watched her out of the corner of her eye. A cup of tea and some kind words were usually enough for the story to come out. She worked assiduously towards creating the right environment, so this would happen.

As usual, when she poured the hot water into the teapot, she tried to guess the story behind each person's arrival. For Phoebe, it must have something to do with her marriage, and she was confident that all was not well. No one had mentioned the husband, or when he may arrive—no one, and she knew full well, Phoebe was married. She took notice of how pretty Phoebe was as she arranged biscuits on a plain white plate. She was sure; if she were right, the husband must be heartbroken. She couldn't help but feel a little excited at the prospect of endless gossip. If it came to be irrevocably broken, the marriage that is, she knew Phoebe wouldn't be left on the shelf for too long. Not in this town; the hookups are what keep the place functioning.

The kettle boiled, and the tea was poured. The cups were strategically positioned on the table, ready for the inevitable outpouring of sentiment. Jean sat with her back towards the setting sun. She didn't want to miss one facial expression on the new girl's face, which in her opinion, said much more than words. Oh, how she loved her job.

'Well, my dear, I bet you have had a hectic few days?' She said as she handed the plate of chocolate biscuits back to Phoebe.

'Yes, yes I have.' Phoebe was cautious. This woman reminded her of another, a neighbour from a few houses down the road from where she and Mic lived, or she used to, lovely and sweet-natured, but wanting to know everything so she could top up on stuff to tell other people for weeks on end. The next question proved her intuition to be spot on.

'Is your husband coming down soon?' Jean got straight to the point.

'No.' Short and blunt.

Jean knew it. Not many marriages survived the career change, the Canberra change. She didn't want to smirk, but it was difficult.

'Oh,' Jean replied as she stirred the tea.

'Anyway,' Phoebe changed the subject. 'Tell me about Pete. What's he like? I mean as a boss.'

'Oh, you know, he is pretty good, doesn't yell, remembers my birthday and is very good towards his family; I'll give him that.'

'Funny, he doesn't come across as the family type. Like, I know he is married and all that, it's just that he, I can't put it into words; he just doesn't seem fatherly. I mean, he is very career orientated, and well, you don't see much of his wife and kids on the news or anything…'

'Oh, he does spend an awful amount of time at work, a terrible amount, but then he has his wife to do all the domestic stuff…' Jean looked at her square in the eye '…doesn't he?'

'Touché,' thought Phoebe. This woman is good.

'And what about you, Jean, are you married?'

'My first husband died a few years back,' she motioned to Phoebe as she was going to commiserate, 'and I have since remarried quite happily. I have three grandkids, Sophie, 10, Amy, 7 and Will, 4, and of course, my daughter and her husband in Belconnen, Louise, and Paul. We visit most weekends. My husband Barry doesn't have children of his own, so my grandkids make up for it.'

They spent a further half an hour in conversation, in which Phoebe had to keep guiding her off the subject of marriage, particularly hers, and onto her grandchildren. Most of the biscuits were gone by the time the conversation finished.

Finally, Phoebe was able to shut the front door behind her. She foraged around the box to see what else it held and found a TV dinner and some small bottles of shampoo, conditioner and bubble bath. A long soak would be heaven. As she ran the water and undressed, she heard a noise from the direction of the lounge. She found an old sheet lying on the laundry floor and wrapped it around herself. On entering the room, nothing was different. It was not until she turned around and looked at the front door that she noticed it. A small piece of paper had been pushed under the door. It was folded over, and her name was clearly visible on one side. She picked it up. It was a note from Josh.

# Chapter 7

The following day, Josh was busy trying to allay the fears of the PM who was at his residence, sick in bed. Time was precious. The PM needed to get up and make himself visible. The state of his health was being raked over and over in the papers. They were saying he was too old and unfit to lead, that it was about time the old man handed the reins to young blood.

'Fuck that,' he said as he threw the iPad he had been reading aside and tried to clamber out of bed, 'get my clothes ready, Josh…JOSH!' He fell back onto the pillows exhausted; he could hardly sit up in bed, let alone get dressed.

'Don't worry, sir, you'll be fine in a few days. The deputy leader can take over some of your responsibilities for you.' Josh was trying to get the PM to stay in bed, not only for his own sake but for his as well. He didn't feel like mopping up the mess that would follow in the PM's sick and paranoid wake. Josh knew it would be good if the old man did get out. Indeed, it would cement his loss. He just wasn't in the mood for drama. But as soon as he mentioned the deputy, he regretted it. Not only did the PM despise his deputy, but he was also terribly jealous of him. He had what the PM didn't: youth, robust health and charisma. On many occasions, especially parliamentary dinners, when both were under the influence of a little too much free alcohol, Josh was always on hand to intervene to quell the fiery atmosphere between the two. He still managed to salvage each sticky situation with a few pacifying words, being adept at knowing what those with shallow egos wanted to hear. That is why Pete wanted him on his side of the political divide. He was a great pacifier.

'That's just what that scumbag will want, now help me up!' The PM summoned all his strength to lurch himself at Josh, who caught him before he fell onto the bedside table and knocked a rather expensive lamp on the floor.

'Get me my tablets.' The PM yelled, 'leave it alone'. Josh stood up quickly and helped him to the bathroom. He gave the PM his tablets and waited just outside the bathroom door.

'They have got to pay more money for this shit,' he grumbled to himself as he sat on a red velvet chair waiting for a summons. He had another reason for wanting the PM to stay in bed today. It was going to be busy. He knew for sure that he would run into Phoebe at some stage. He thought it would be best if it didn't happen while he was in the company of the PM, it would be all somewhat awkward. It wouldn't be long, and he would be in his new job, safe for a while until he made up his mind what to do with the rest of his life. He was now more than ready to fly off. He often dreamt about travelling the world, drinking whiskey at a bar on a beach somewhere soaked in sunlight and watching pretty girls walk up and down a long promenade. 'One-day Josh, one day,' he promised himself as he listened to the strained bodily functions of the PM and the results being flushed away.

At around the same time that morning, Phoebe called a taxi to take her to work. As she climbed in, she made a pact that whatever happened, no matter what, she would stay true to herself and what she believed.

'Where to?' The taxi driver said as she sidled into her seat. 'Parliament House, please.'

She checked her black leather bag for keys, make-up, and phone. She had not had any calls during the night. Not that she was expecting any. She sighed. Eventually, the gentle hum of the car relaxed her, and she took in the scenery. She was surprised by how little traffic there was on the streets. A tall, well-dressed man flashed past, and he reminded her of Josh and the note he had sent so secretly in the night:

*See you tomorrow. Remember: you don't know me. Burn note. J.*

There was such an air of intrigue about the whole situation that it actually made her laugh.

The taxi driver thought she had said something to him.

'Yes, love?'

She didn't know what to say, so she said the first thing that came to mind.

'Much in the way of crime around here?'

'Not on the streets love,' was his cheeky reply. Phoebe nodded her head and grinned.

After what seemed only a few minutes, she was outside Parliament House.

She suddenly felt rather small and out of her depth. This was the place she had always wanted to work. It was a dream. However, as she stood on the precipice of the rest of her life, it felt more like a nightmare. 'Come on, come on.' She took a deep breath, straightened up her clothes, smoothed her hair and walked towards security.

'Oh hello, Phoebe,' Jean called out as Phoebe walked by her desk on her way to her office.

'Hello Jean,' she replied, maybe a little too curtly. Jean ignored it.

'You managed to get your security pass okay then? No trouble?' Phoebe was forced to stop and reply.

'Everything was fine. Thanks.'

'You're welcome. Would you like me to bring you some coffee or tea?'

Phoebe softened. 'I think I will have some coffee this morning, milk, no sugar, thank you.' She gave her a small smile.

'Okay, no problem, I will bring it in shortly.' 'Thanks.'

Phoebe told herself that she must not be so ready to assume a defensive position as she resumed her path. It would leave her isolated, and she needed to have people on her side if she was going to survive in this place. She put her bag down on her desk and looked out of her internal window that faced the corridor and the other administrative offices.

Jean was busy talking to others who were hidden behind a wall constructed of a huge pane of tinted glass that Phoebe couldn't see through. She was sure, however, that they could see out. Jean had her head popped through the half-opened door situated a little to the left of her desk that occupied the space just in front of the wall. Phoebe could see Jean's head popping up and down, talking a hundred miles an hour to whoever worked behind the wall. Phoebe was sure Jean had primed them about her arrival and the morning pleasantries were a ploy to keep her still long enough for them all to have a good look and form their own conclusions about her. They were probably all aware that her husband was not coming to join her. Phoebe reminded herself never to tell Jean anything she didn't want to be repeated.

Phoebe shut the door and pulled down the little cream blind that adorned its small window. She needed alone time to look around and acquaint herself with her new work environment. There was a filing cabinet in one corner, a bookcase in the other, and a rather dull but functional desk in the middle. On top of it sat a phone, a computer terminal, a standard office clock. What looked like grey polyester carpet filled the floor space and on the wall opposite her desk a rather uninspiring picture of a kitten hanging onto a branch of a tree before it presumably plummeted to the ground with the caption 'hang in there.' How apt, she thought.

She did love the view from her external window. Outside was a very pretty little garden in a Japanese style that inspired a sense of tranquility. Even though other offices surrounded this garden, the green oasis in the centre was a pleasant distraction. She was sure she would spend time when thinking, looking out and being inspired by this little patch of oriental greenery.

A knock at the door forced her out of her thoughts.

'Come in.' Phoebe turned to see Jean carrying a tray with a plunger coffee maker full of coffee, a cup and what looked like a freshly baked scone, some jam, and butter.

'Wow that looks good.'

'Yes, we have a lovely canteen down the way. They make freshly baked goodies every day. Why do you think I am so large, eh?'

Phoebe grinned and said:

'That coffee smells good. I think I'll like working here.' 'I'll just put it on your desk, shall I?'

Phoebe nodded and quickly put her bag on the floor.

'When you are ready for lunch I will take you and show you where the canteen is. Unless you want to go now?'

'No, no, lunchtime will be fine.'

'Okay. Everyone eats there, even the PM at times. You haven't met him yet, I suppose?'

'No, I haven't, but I am looking forward to it.' Jean grinned, or was it a smirk?

'Okay. Let me know if there is anything else you would like.'

'I will.'

'Do you want me to close the door?' 'Yes, please.'

The room was silent again but bursting with the aroma of the fresh coffee. It felt like maybe, just maybe, everything would be okay. And the events of the last day or two that had put her on edge were just an aberration, compounded by nerves and uncertainty. She absorbed herself in reading some papers that had been left for her to go over, and very soon, it was time for lunch. Jean knocked on her door again.

Jean reassured Phoebe as they headed towards the canteen, that she would introduce her to the rest of the employees, the mysterious people behind the wall, after lunch. Phoebe agreed that it would be a good idea. After a rather long five-minute walk down many corridors, a café or canteen as Jean called it appeared in front of them.

'Here we are.'

They entered a rather large eating area that was only half-filled. All the people were in Canberra suits sitting around tables deep in conversation. As they made their way towards the counter, a few suits looked in their direction, but there was no one Phoebe recognised, not even from TV, which disappointed her a little.

They ordered.

'Would you like me to have lunch with you today so that you're not Nigel?'

'Pardon?' Phoebe said: 'Nigel? Nigel, who?'

'Oh sorry, it's an expression my grandkids use for someone who is on their own, like, has no friends.'

'Oh, yes, yes, I have heard that before.'

'I mean, so that you're not on your own for lunch.'

Phoebe laughed.

'Yes, that would be nice.'

They sat at a smartly polished table, exactly like every other table in the room and waited for their lunch in idle chitchat about the office.

Lunch arrived. They had both ordered Turkish bread with chicken, avocado, and salad on an oversized plate and a cappuccino to wash it all down.

'Wow, I can't get over the size of the meals,' Phoebe said before she tucked in. Jean was already attacking the Turkish bread and just smiled back at Phoebe with her eyes.

Some of the other eaters left their tables. Phoebe watched a particular party of people get up and leave their table as Jean was filling her in on who they were and who they worked for.

Suddenly, in the doorway was the PM. Phoebe had seen him many times on TV and given him a piece of her mind as well, not that he could hear her. In person, however, he seemed smaller, and he looked terrible. Behind him was the unmistakably resplendent figure of Josh. He was manoeuvring the PM towards a table in the corner, where they wouldn't be noticed. The PM, however, was having none of it. He pulled away from Josh, and Phoebe could see that a few faces in the room had to constrain a laugh. She thought how sad it was that this leader was reduced to what would seem to be a petulant child when not in front of the cameras and protected by the confines of Parliament House. Josh gave up. He followed the PM to the table he wanted to sit at. Unfortunately for both Phoebe and Josh, it meant they would be in the uncomfortable position of confronting each other face to face as the PM headed straight towards them.

Phoebe looked the other way, and Josh kept his eyes averted. They were headed straight past, and it seemed disaster was averted, but then Jean stood up and said:

'Hello, Prime Minister, how are you today?'

Phoebe bit down on her bottom lip; for some reason, she found the situation a little funny.

Josh froze.

'Hello, my dear.' The PM only had a slight recognition of who Jean could be. He knew that she was one of the girls that worked for Pete.

‘Who is this?’ He asked in his usually gruff manner as he indicated towards Phoebe.

Phoebe stood up.

‘This is Phoebe. She is Pete’s new policy advisor on women’s issues.’

‘Ha, since when did Pete care about women?’

He held out his hand. Phoebe took it. Josh still didn’t look in her direction.

The PM, however, forced his hand. ‘This is Josh, my chief of staff and policy advisor on practically everything.’

Josh turned and nodded. His face was stern as he tried to hide how uncomfortable he felt.

‘Hello,’ Phoebe said. Josh noticed she had a twinkle in her eye. He couldn’t believe she was enjoying watching him suffer. He wondered if it was a mistake to have let her in on his deception.

Josh walked on. ‘See you, ladies, later.’

But the PM wasn’t finished. He had been looking at Phoebe as if she was an alien. ‘Hey, I know what he is up to! Sex appeal, the sly bastard. He wants to show off beautiful women to get more votes. The bastard, well my sweet, you have been conned, mark my words, he doesn’t give a rat’s arse about women…Ha.’

Josh pulled the PM away. Phoebe was shocked. What had just happened? What the hell. God, this place was…Jean tried to play it down by stating that the PM was past it and didn’t know what he was talking about most of the time. Phoebe was no longer hungry, and she excused herself and went back to her office. Jean, however, was not going to let her lunch go to waste. There was still one full piece of Turkish left on her plate.

At their table, Josh felt like hammering the PM, but he constrained himself.

‘Boy, is that new policy advisor a looker or what?’

Josh glanced over in Phoebe's direction. Phoebe was gone, and Jean was just finishing up. There was something about Phoebe that annoyed him. He couldn't understand it, but she really made him feel uneasy. He was glad she had left.

Once they returned from the café, Jean introduced her to the women behind the wall. Phoebe learned that each and everyone in the office had a crush on Josh. They couldn't believe that Phoebe did not find anything attractive about him. They all knew she was lying and made jokes about it. Phoebe returned to her office. She was both appalled and intrigued by everything that went on here. She had never worked in such a place.

# Chapter 8

'Come on for shit's sake, or we'll be late.'

'Okay, okay, I'm coming,' Mic replied.

He was going out with his mates for the night. Jamie, a long-time school friend, was sent to pick him up. But he was getting somewhat irritated by the fact that they hadn't left the house.

The phone rang.

'You answer that, and I swear to God I will go without you.' Mic looked at the phone and decided it was best to let it go. 'Look, whoever it is will leave a message, okay?'

'Okay,' he agreed and headed into the night.

Phoebe threw her mobile on the desk. It had been a long day, and nearly everyone else had gone. She had wanted to do some reading and catching up. The many meetings during the day had left little time for anything else. The election was only weeks away. She had wanted to talk to Mic just to see how he was doing and hear what he had been up to—to listen to a friendly voice. He was, however, proving very hard to track down.

Suddenly, there was a very quiet knock on Phoebe's office door. Whoever it was, was going to enter, she stood up and readied herself.

'Security.' The guard stuck his head in.

'Just checking if everything is okay love, is it?'

'Yes, yes, just fine. I will be leaving shortly. Is that alright?'

'Yes, just let me know if you want an escort to your car.'

'Fine, yes, I will let you know,' Phoebe replied. The security guard shook his rather ample chin and shut the door. He was a pleasant fellow, proud of his work and his three kids. He showed photos of them to everyone who he successfully ambushed throughout his shift, and Phoebe was no exception.

He closed the door and was gone as quickly as he came. She let out some of her angst.

'Bloody hell Mic, where the hell are you?'

She threw files into her briefcase with a violence that wasn't warranted, but it did help alleviate some of her pent-up stress and frustration.

She found the one thing that she hated most about being in Canberra was the loneliness. It tore at her. After just six weeks, she found herself talking to almost anyone who listened when she went shopping. Sometimes they purposefully ignored her, but she spoke anyway. This was strange for her as she was generally quite reserved, but when in a shop or a mall, the temptation to speak overwhelmed her, and she found herself prattling on about the most ridiculous things to complete strangers.

She never said anything of importance, just rattled on about the weather, how big her feet were getting or what she had decided to have for dinner. Worse were the reactions from the people she would run into from time to time when she needed food or a new pair of stockings. They avoided her by slavishly serving others who had ventured into the shop.

Was this the effect Canberra had on people, or was it just her? She understood that many people who worked here didn't live in the centre of Canberra, but the other suburbs and most weekends—it was like a ghost town. Many were married and had full lives of their own or didn't want to introduce her to their husbands because she was a 'looker'. Many women were not confident of bringing home an unattached attractive female and introducing her to their midlife husbands.

There was only so much reading of policy issues that one could do in a day: fun and adventure beckoned. She wanted to have a good laugh and a drink. No, she needed to have a good laugh and a drink, and for that, you need other people. What grated her most was the fact that Mic was probably out with his mates doing just that. She couldn't believe it, but she was starting to miss her nights out with him and his stupid mates. Instead, she faced boredom and blank walls on the weekends. Saturday afternoon rolled around soon enough, and Phoebe was on the lounge watching what she thought was a dead boring show about women and ageing. 'Grow up,' she said as one woman complained bitterly about wrinkles being over the hill at the grand old age of twenty-nine.

She went to the fridge and looked in. Not much there for dinner, well nothing that caught her fancy. The women on TV were now in a restaurant enjoying a very delicious meal, laughing and having, in general, a perfect time.

'Why not?' Phoebe asked herself.

'Why can't I go out to dinner by myself?'

The idea perked her up a little. She would be able to do herself up a bit and go out in search of a restaurant that looked friendly and had good food.

'Why not indeed?'

She jumped in the shower and felt reasonably happy. She had something to look forward to, and not just another night watching some stupid show on the box and falling asleep on the hard lounge. She had tried to talk to Mic a few times during the day. As usual, he was hard to get hold of, or he didn't have time to talk. She was starting to get the feeling he was trying to give her a hint about what she wasn't sure about. Maybe he was moving on? But was she?

Tomorrow at least, she would have something positive to say to her mother when she rang her and not just the same old same old. Her mother was always on her back; she had done the wrong thing, moved away, left her husband, blah blah blah blah blah…and sometimes during the long lonely weekends, she felt maybe she had. But no, she would remind herself, this was a new beginning. She was going to make her own destiny, whatever that may be. Going out on her own was the first step to self-determination. She looked at herself in the mirror. She was getting a little worried about the fact that she was getting older, but tonight she gave herself a break, 'not bad, not bad my girl.'

She became apprehensive as she picked up her bag, ready to head out. In the past, she always had friends, Mic or family to go out with. 'What the hell am I doing?' She sat on her bed, deflated and stared at her reflection in the wardrobe mirror. She looked good, was intelligent, had a good job and was friendly, but going out alone seemed to her to be in the sphere of the psychotic loner, geek or 'Nigel' as Jean had said. The very thought of it terrified her. She desperately wanted and needed to go out, but she was scared to death.

'Come on, come on. What the hell am I doing?' She reapplied her lipstick with a very shaky hand. She looked at herself again.

'Just go.'

She called a cab and spent all the time waiting for it convincing herself that nobody would care if she was on her own, and anyway, what did it matter to anyone else? What did they care? Like really?

A slight Italian accent greeted her as she slid into the back seat. 'Where would you like to go?'

He waited for her response.

She didn't know. Now she felt foolish. She should have had a place in mind.

The cab driver turned to look at her, hoping that would jog her memory.

She stared at him. He had adorable brown eyes which narrowed when he asked:

'Do you know where you want to go?' 'No, not really, but I do know what I want.'

'And what would that be?' he stated with a cheeky grin on his young face.

She smiled, not missing his meaning, 'I want a really nice restaurant that is friendly, where I won't be noticed eating on my own. Do you know any like that?'

He pulled a face pretending he was disappointed but said, 'my cousin has an Italian place not far from here. Dimly lit eating booths, very private, beautiful place and the best food, good food.' He smiled.

'That sounds fantastic.' 'Okay, here we go.'

After some banter and a quick trip through the city, he dropped her off in front of a very ornate Italian looking building; white columns with red, white and green awnings. He told her as she got out of his rather dirty taxi to make sure to tell the waitress that she knew Tony. He assured her she would get the best service.

Inside it was warm and intimate, pretty to a point but not beautiful, no. It was the kind of place she would have come with Mic on a special occasion. One deep breath later and she could smell garlic and an array of aromatic herbs. Her stomach rumbled a little in response. She waited for the waitress to seat her. As she did, she concentrated on watching a pile of dishes being delivered to the noisy kitchen in the rear of the building. This distracted her so she would not think about being in a restaurant on her own.

She thought about leaving just as the waitress caught sight of her and indicated that she wouldn't be long. Some of the other customers noticed and looked over at her. She changed the position in which she was standing as a way of trying to hide her 'aloneness'. She nodded with a sly smile in reply.

'Sorry to keep you, we are a little busy, you know. You have a reservation?' Her Italian accent was slightly stronger than the taxi driver's.

'A reservation? Oh no, no I don't. Will that matter? I know Tony.'

'Ha, everyone that catches a cab knows Tony. No, it doesn't matter. Er, are you solo, or are you expecting somebody?'

There, the inevitable question. Phoebe looked at the waitress, straight in her Mediterranean brown eyes. Glancing at her overly arched but beautifully manicured eyebrow, she said, 'Yes, I am dining alone.'

'Bene su di voi,' was her response as she turned on her heel and led Phoebe behind a wall at the far end of the restaurant. They were soon in a small room partitioned off from the main eating area. There were a few empty tables. Phoebe was given her pick.

'This one will do nicely,' grateful to the waitress for her consideration, which she had not expected at all.

'Would you like a drink?' 'Lemonade would be great.'

'Buono.' With a wink, the waitress was gone.

Once she was alone, Phoebe took in her surroundings. The place seemed to be a satire of all things Italian right down to its red and white checked tablecloths. The candleholders were made of old wine bottles, and fake bunches of garlic adorned the walls. But it had something that a lot of other nicer, more expensive places didn't—a feeling of being welcome.

'One lemonade and one magazine so you don't go mad talking to yourself.'

A Woman's Weekly landed on the table alongside a rather large and frosty glass of lemonade.

'Ready to order?' Phoebe hadn't seen the menu on the table.

'Oh, no…sorry, I haven't even looked at the menu. Do you mind if I take a little longer?'

'No, I have nothing better to do but to wait for you. You go right ahead and take your time.'

Phoebe knew she was pulling her leg as the waitress laughed as she disappeared to serve others in the restaurant. Even though she was alone, she found that she was enjoying the experience. There was a nice cold glass of lemonade, a magazine to read, a tacky restaurant decor which provided atmosphere, and to top it all off, a lovely meal to look forward to. She could very quickly get used to having time to herself out of the confines of the house and the interruptions at work.

Soon, she heard voices heading her way. The waitress was having a joke with someone whose voice was very familiar. She waited to see where they would end up. Much to her disappointment, they came into her little oasis.

'There you go Mr. Ryan, your usual seat.'

The waitress looked at Phoebe apologetically, almost as if she was saying that the man's arrival was unexpected.

Mr. Ryan took his seat, he hadn't taken too much notice of the woman sitting opposite, but he felt a little uncomfortable; someone was staring. He looked over, and Phoebe blurted out;

'Josh! What are you doing here?'

'Having dinner, much like you I assume,' he said in his usual cool, calm manner.

'Well, yes, I felt like having dinner out, and this place was suggested…' She was so embarrassed to be found by him in this situation.

'On your own?' He asked as he looked around the room, trying to conceal a small smile.

'Yes,' came her defensive reply.

'Well, I don't see why we shouldn't make a night of it, eh?' He weaved his way towards her table. She couldn't help but notice the movement of his hips as he did so. She had no time to say no, anyway. How could they both sit opposite each other and have dinner alone, like strangers? She felt her freedom snatched away and resentful that he had taken it. She hid her magazine under her seat; he would accuse her of hypocrisy if he had seen it. It was what she considered a trashy woman's mag that she had told him she hated not long after they met.

'So…?' She asked as a question.

He took the hint. 'This is my favourite place to eat and escape the crowd. It is not too pretentious, and it has a quirky atmosphere, don't you think?'

'Well, yes, I will have to agree with you there.' 'Finally,' he replied.

'What?'

'We agree on something,' he smiled.

She smiled back in spite of herself as she tried not to think about how captivating his face was.

Just at that moment, the waitress came around the corner and was surprised to see them seated together. She took their orders.

Josh was going to have garlic bread, veal scaloppini followed by ice cream and a cappuccino. Phoebe wanted no entrée, but she would have lasagna and some gelato to follow.

Josh ordered a bottle of what he told her was 'very nice red wine,' with two glasses.

The waitress begrudgingly left them to it; she couldn't believe how quickly the pretty lady had managed to 'pull' Mr Ryan. She had been trying for the last 12 months but with no luck. She headed into the kitchen with the orders and a side dish of malicious gossip.

To the surprise of both Josh and Phoebe, the Chef brought out Josh's garlic bread. He set the dish down in an elaborate and somewhat intrusive manner. Phoebe could feel his breath over her shoulder. He had a good look at her and smiled as if he was privy to some secret they shared. She tried to smile but felt hemmed in until he stood back, wiped his hands down his white apron and brushed the thick fringe of his slightly fat face and said, 'enjoy, godere, godere' seemingly with his whole body.

He took his large frame back to the kitchen and told the waitress that the 'woman' was a looker, and it was no wonder Mr Ryan wanted her. The waitress glared at him as he continued where he had left off, decorating a ham and prawn pizza. She felt she was a looker too, much better than that intruder. She took pride in her highly teased and sprayed hair and her rather lovely nails that she managed to keep even though she was a waitress.

But this said more about her ability to get out of the washing up than of her skills at balancing both hard work and good grooming.

'What is your entrée like?'

'Well, as far as garlic bread goes, it is great. Are you sure you don't want some?'

'Positive.' She was trying to limit her carb intake, and as she had ordered lasagna, she thought bread would overload her system. Her stomach had been playing up, and she had a suspicion that she may have a touch of coeliac. Well, that's what Dr Google said it probably was. She wasn't positive, but cutting back couldn't hurt.

Phoebe watched him while he enjoyed his bread. He was a puzzle. Most of the time, he infuriated her. His lack of passion for politics, his lack of determination to make changes to the lives of those the government-which she felt they could if they worked together with their boss -all made her all somewhat dismissive of him. But there was something, something else, which drew her in; he was mysterious and very private, almost to the point of ridiculousness. She was sure if he knew about the rumours going around about him, he would be furious.

He looked at her; he knew she was watching him. 'So you have heard the rumours?'

'What?' She was shocked as it was like he was reading her mind.

'Come on. I know that anyone who works at the prison for longer than two days gets to hear some concocted story about my past.'

'Concocted, is it?' 'Yes.'

'Then tell me the truth.'

At that moment, the wine turned up. Josh was grateful for the intrusion. 'Ah, Gia, just what is needed. A good drink.'

'Glad to help.' She poured a glass of wine for Josh and set the bottle down before Phoebe to let her know she would have to pour her own. She left.

'Funny,' Phoebe said, 'she was really nice to me when I came in. I wonder what I have done to her.'

'Oh, it's not you, sweetie, it's me. She likes it best when I eat alone.'

'I should have known, another Josh conquest.'

'No, not a conquest, a pretender who would like to be a conquest.'

'And, may I ask why she is not a conquest?'

'Well, the truth is, I fancy the food here more than her, and I don't want relationships to get in the way of my being welcome. While I don't touch her, her brothers will not kill me, and I can continue to enjoy their cooking.'

Gia walked past the partition that separated them from the rest of the restaurant on her way to the kitchen. Josh caught a glimpse of her.

'Salute,' he said. She ignored him.

'So, come on, tell me the truth about your past. I can then set the record straight in the office.'

'No, I don't want you to do that. I'd rather they have their own version than to know the truth. Drink up girl, I don't want to drink the whole bottle on my own.' They enjoyed the wine for a few minutes in silence until the waitress brought their mains.

'Ah, thanks Gia.' 'That's okay Joshy boy.'

'Thanks,' said Phoebe, trying to constrain a smile. Gia turned her back on Phoebe.

Phoebe looked at Josh, and he had a look on his face that said, 'yes, I know I am gorgeous, and no, I am not interested.' She could understand Gia. If she was brutally honest with herself, she had to admit that he was a very handsome man, probably the most handsome she had ever seen. However, the most attractive thing about him was his ability to remain aloof. He kept everyone guessing.

If he did have a lady friend, no one knew about her or saw her, which made many women think that he was in much need of a woman's touch.

But it seemed to Phoebe that Josh was happy to be on his own or at least to give the impression that he was. But it led to much gossip and innuendo, which she had enjoyed hearing about, but she was starting to doubt the foundation on which all the gossip was built. Josh didn't help matters either by not refuting or setting the record straight, and she scolded herself for listening to any of it. She was the first one to get upset by idle talk. But it was all so intriguing. She made a mental note not to get involved in that very distraction anymore.

She sat back on her chair, sipping her wine, looking at him while he ate. She wished he would open up to her, but she knew he wouldn't. And why should he? She had spent most of her time in Canberra trying to make him feel uncomfortable. Why should he trust her?

'Not hungry?' He had noticed that she had neglected her meal while she was deep in thought.

'Not very,' she lied.

'Come on, you have hardly eaten a thing.' He pointed his fork at her meal just like her father did when she was a little girl.

'What is it about men, always telling women what to do, what to eat, what to wear?'

She put her wine down on the table and looked at him.

'Where did that come from?' he said, but it didn't stop him devouring his veal.

She changed the subject. She didn't like talking about her father, he was dead, and that was that.

'Josh?'

'Yes,' he said after he had drained his wine glass. 'Why are you here, in Canberra?'

'Oh no, you're not going to go all philosophical on me, are you?' He was pouring himself another drink. He offered her the wine bottle, but she refused with a shake of her head. Her hair caught the light. He noticed.

'Well?' She was determined to get an answer and not one bound up in mystery and half-truths.

'I could ask you the same thing.'

She squinted back at him and remained silent. He knew she wanted an answer, so he gave it to her, even if he knew it would not be what she wanted to hear.

'Money.'

'Money?' She was taken aback. 'That's all your job means to you? Money?'

He lifted his shoulders and grinned, looking like he had been caught out doing something that he shouldn't. 'It's as simple as that.'

'I don't believe you,' She said and poured herself another glass of wine. This man would drive any woman to drink.

'You must have had aspirations and dreams. Surely, you must have had something when you started?'

'Oh, I had something when I started.' 'What?'

'Youth.'

'Oh come on, you're not that old, and anyhow I still don't believe you. You came here just like me, trying to do something that you thought worthwhile. What happened?'

'Oh nothing happened to me, darling, but it's no use fighting the monkeys that run the ship. Come on, you have been here long enough to realise that this place isn't for the benefit of the populace. It's about holding on to the job as long as you can so that your nice fat super payout gets bigger with every passing day. You get your name in the record books, and you help your mates—the ones with the bananas.'

'So you are saying you did come here hoping to help make a difference?'

'Look, they churn out idealists every day from a university somewhere. You soon realise, however, that the real world isn't made up of idealists but pragmatists. Those with the most money have the most power. Power helps. If you don't have it, you're stuffed. I decided to be on the side of the ones with links to immense money, and therefore power—the politicians. If I fight against them to try and even out the balance of the rich making policy via the politicians to suit themselves, then where does that leave me? Nowhere. At least here I know what I have got—a job. An income, food in my stomach which if you haven't noticed is getting very expensive, and you are wasting yours.'

'Is it that hopeless? I think together we could change things, just a little.'

'Haha, no, no we can't. Now eat your meal and stop wishing for the impossible…please, otherwise you will give me indigestion.'

She finished eating while he watched. He wished that she wouldn't make him overthink what his job meant to him. It was bad enough just trying to get through each day without analysing his own very existence within the madness.

'Would you like a coffee?'

'No thanks. I think I will go home. It's been nice.' She was tired.

'Okay. I will call you a cab.' He reached for his phone and ordered two cabs. As they left their table, she felt the eyes of Gia burning holes into her back.

They both stood at the bar, waiting in silence to be driven home. Josh, forever the gentleman, let her take the first cab that arrived. She said goodbye and saw Gia's eyes light up when she realised they were going home in separate cabs. Gia yelled an exuberant 'adios' to Phoebe as she left the restaurant. Once in the back of the cab, Phoebe noticed Gia wasting no time in cornering Josh who was laughing at her upturned face. Phoebe wondered what it was Gia was telling him. She felt slightly sorry for her. Josh was a hard man to pin down, and Phoebe knew that women who fell for him were probably in for an uphill battle to gain his affections. She chuckled to herself. Honestly she did feel a bit sorry for Gia.

# Chapter 9

A couple of days later, Phoebe noticed that most secretarial staff were missing from their seats just after morning tea. On further investigation, she found that they were all crowded into the room behind the wall, some spilling through the doorway. She ventured out of her office to have a look.

Maybe it was a travelling salesperson selling perfume or some other sort of fun. She needed a light-hearted distraction from the rubbish that Pete had given her to work on. After all, he would, in all probability, not use it for anything but to keep her busy. As she neared the women blocking the door, she was surprised to hear her name mentioned. Stifled giggles arose from the crowd.

One of the women closest to her gave her an apologetic look like a schoolchild caught red-handed stealing something off the teacher's desk. More giggles – she pushed her way into the room. A woman she had never seen before was holding court in the centre of the room. She had her back to Phoebe, and everyone facing her just stared over her shoulder at the new arrival. The women knew that something was going on and turned around slowly. She didn't seem surprised by Phoebe's appearance; in fact, Phoebe felt she was rather pleased that she had shown up.

'Well, well, here she is. We were just talking about you,' she said without any embarrassment or discomfort at all.

'And why, may I ask, am I the talking point?' Phoebe was slightly annoyed that they had been discussing her, seemingly making her into a joke.

The woman had on the standard Canberra uniform, except for her shoes, which were strappy, silver and far too high to be comfortable for work. Her face was hard, like she was angry most of the time, giving her an air of permanent dissatisfaction. She seemed to say through her face that no matter how well life could be going, it could be going a lot better. Her hair was wiry, parted in the middle down to her shoulders and bleached blonde. Her eyes held very little in the way of warmth. Phoebe disliked her straight away.

'Well, you seem to have got what every other woman wants, and you have only been here, well, a very short time, compared to everyone else. Tell me, what is your secret?' She whispered to her like they were the only two in the room.

'What do you mean? What have I got? What secret?'

Just as the woman was about to reply, Jean jumped up and headed towards Phoebe.

'Now, now Phoebe, all this, well, it's all just a little bit of harmless fun, that's all.' Jean looked into Phoebe's eyes trying to plead with her not to lose her temper.

'Fun at my expense.' Phoebe was bitter about being the focus of a game. She felt betrayed.

'Funny, seems like she's the one that has been having all the fun.' The woman said.

Phoebe looked at her. 'Who the hell do you think you are?' Everyone in the room sucked in a deep breath. Jean grabbed her arm.

'Who are you?' Phoebe demanded, ignoring Jean's efforts to diffuse the situation.

'Tell her, Jean.' The woman said.

'Now Phoebe, she, she is Pete's PA, personal assistant, Danielle. It is a wonder you haven't met her yet. Jean smiled slightly, highly embarrassed that Phoebe had ended up in this torturous situation.

'Yes, sorry, but we've been a bit busy, haven't we? I have been on holiday, but you, you have been playing the femme fatale, shall we say.' The woman smirked at Phoebe.

'I don't know what you are talking about.' Phoebe decided to leave and ignored the interloper.

'Just glad to know you like Italian food. After all, it is the food of love, isn't it?' Phoebe turned to face the other women. 'Or is that Greek? Anyway, it doesn't matter does it, Phoebe?' Danielle then cocked her head to the side and continued, 'you don't need food when you have love, do you?'

'Look, I don't know what your game is, and I am also very sure I have no idea what you are talking about.'

'No?'

'No,' Phoebe replied adamantly. She would not let this woman get the better of her.

'Oh well, if you want to keep all the details to yourself, go ahead. But I genuinely think that in future, if you want to keep your affairs secret, make sure you eat out of town. Boy, I wonder what your husband would think?'

Phoebe stood dumbfounded. Was she referring to her inadvertent dinner with Josh? What had he said? Why had he said anything? Male ego? Did he want the others to think he hadn't lost his touch? Or that she was an easy pickup?

'Well?' Danielle wanted her to bite back. She was angry that Phoebe would not own up to anything. Phoebe, however, just stood staring at the floor. Jean grabbed at her again, but she threw her off for the second time. Phoebe looked around the room and then directly at Jean, who was having trouble keeping tears in check. Suddenly she turned quickly on her heels and went back to her office, slamming the door in anger and frustration.

'Ooooops,' said Danielle in response to the slamming door. 'Did I say something wrong?' No one giggled. The spiteful scene had drained all the fun out of the air. All were a little deflated and ashamed of their role in helping Danielle, who they all knew was spiteful, in embarrassing Phoebe, who they all rather liked. They returned to their desks to mindlessly churn out the copious amounts of paperwork that needed signing or review.

'I think you should get back to your office now, don't you, Danielle?' Jean stated, wishing she had never got herself involved in the drama.

She knew Danielle was wicked, and she had been drawn in rather effortlessly, of which she felt largely ashamed, and it showed on her face.

'What's the matter, Jean? Have I upset a favourite?' Jean ignored her and set about tidying her desk.

'Tchh,' Danielle left, obviously not pleased. Jean heard her heading back to her own office, or to what was called either the vipers den or the snake pit and sighed with relief. Danielle had risen professionally very quickly. Everyone knew that she thrived in the backstabbing environment of politics; it got her out of bed in the mornings. As for the women, the rest of the day was spent in silence; only Jean's occasional sniffles could be heard over the click and hum of the machinations of the daily grind in the office.

Phoebe recovered by late afternoon, well enough to leave a devastatingly brutal message on Josh's message bank. Once finished, she threw her mobile onto her desk and walked over to the window. Outside in the garden, it was still and peaceful in stark contrast to her racing pulse. The green of the shrubs and the trees eventually led her to slow her breathing.

Closing her eyes, she took a deep breath. 'What the hell was he thinking?' She thought it was typical of him to brag, but the point was, he had nothing, absolutely nothing at all to brag about.

'Shit,' she exhaled and leant towards the window, her hands spread out on either side of her body to hold her up. Looking at the floor and the dust on the skirting board, she groaned. 'What the hell am I doing?' Self-doubt crept in. An event like this could open up a crater of self-criticism. Her working-class sensitivity regarding whether she was good enough for such a position never took long to rear its head and wallop her, wallop her hard. Her self-doubt informed her that she had jumped into this job rather than walked. It was proving harder and harder to stay confident, let alone focused on work when all this personal crap got in the way. She felt she had landed in la-la land and not the city where the Federal Government governed her country. Standing back up straight, she stood and stared out the window for a very long time.

# Chapter 10

Everyone in the bland meeting room heard Josh's phone ring. Josh fumbled, trying in vain to turn it off.

'Leave it will you!'

The PM hated it when mobiles rang in the middle of a meeting. A minute later, all recognised the message-received tone on Josh's phone.

'Josh, will you turn off your bloody phone!' The PM glared. Josh just nodded his assent, but was a little surprised to see the message was from Phoebe.

The meeting continued. After all, it was a crucial meeting; all had to figure out how to dodge protesters who were sure to try and ruin the annual gala dinner that they were all looking forward to later in the week. Most importantly, they had to look like they were not trying to avoid them and were happy for the populace to engage in their democratic right to voice their concerns.

'What the bloody hell do they want me to do anyway?' The PM spurted out angrily, which took everyone by surprise. One minister chipped in.

'Well, they are all worried sir, you know, about the new benefit reforms; apparently, some people are going hungry...'

All looked at the culprit. Everyone else realised it was a rhetorical question. The PM hissed at him through pursed lips. He didn't believe, not for one minute, that anyone was going hungry, especially when there were such things as a gala dinner to look forward to.

Josh checked the message while the rest of them discussed what might be on the menu. It left him reeling. What was she ranting about? Bragging, bragging to who? And about what?

'She's lost it already,' he mumbled under his breath. The PM looked at him. 'Want to share it with us, Josh?'

'Sorry PM, nothing to worry about.' Josh tried to turn his attention to the meeting but soon found himself wondering again. What the hell she was going on about?

Everyone rose to leave. 'Well Josh, glad you could physically make the meeting. That was good of you.' The PM was by his side.

'Are you sure you are up to this for another term of office? There's not somewhere else you would like to be?'

'Well, yes sir, I am, and no, no there's not.' 'Yes, but do you really want to do it?'

Josh was taken aback. Did the PM know something about his plans for the future?

'Well, yes sir, I do.'

'Then at least start looking a little interested at the meetings.'

The PM turned to mumble an array of profanities aimed at Josh as he left the room, followed by various sycophants. Josh wanted to say that he had no hope in hell of winning the election but held his tongue. This was especially hard for him as the PM's true believers, who were lower down the pecking order than Josh, looked down their noses at him as they passed by. Josh knew they were all waiting for their turn to be the PM's lackey. They were like vultures waiting for death. 'They can have it,' he thought to himself, 'with pleasure.'

Josh wanted to get to the bottom of the voice-mail before he did anything else. Phoebe, sick of waiting for Josh to reply, eventually picked up her phone from the desk, packed up her bag and left the office for the rest of the day. She hadn't had time to see the sights of Canberra, so needing a change of scene, she decided that the rest of the day would be spent in a park or a bar. She hailed a taxi and asked to be taken to the nearest place she could get a drink. It just so happened that it was a bar that presented itself as the first of her options. She went in. The place was practically empty; an old man sat in one corner watching the weekend re-run of the footy, and a couple of hopefuls in ties and jackets sat at a little table in the middle of the room planning how to sell their product to their next unsuspecting customer.

'What can I get you?' The barman asked while pouring the old man another beer.

Phoebe didn't know, so she resorted to ordering Verdelho, which she always did. She wasn't very imaginative when it came to ordering drinks. Her range only stretched as far as four white wines and two reds.

'Just the house Verdelho, thanks. And make it a large one.'

'Only have house Moselle, that okay?'

'Err,' her stomach lurched a little. She remembered a queasy night spent in a club toilet, desperately drunk on Moselle. She didn't drink it now, but...

'Oh, okay, anything will do.' Desperate times call for desperate measures. 'Don't think, just drink.'

She took a few sips, surprised by the sweetness, and was happy to have a glass or two, the events of over 20 years ago forgotten. She took a look around. It was a place devoid of comfort, not much in the way of welcoming pictures, ornaments or cushions. No, this place was for real hard-drinking and little else. It was perfect. She swallowed another mouthful. Mic, she wondered, what was he up to? Rummaging through her bag for her phone, she thought she would give him a call. Having a chat would be good. She found it hidden under her diary, but suddenly she stopped. 'Don't be stupid,' she berated herself, 'not a good time to call. The last thing I want is for him to think that I am not having a good time or God forbid not coping,' she mumbled this to herself as she dropped her phone back into her bag.

'Another?'

'Yes please, why not.'

The bartender smiled at her as he poured. 'Hard day?'

'Don't even go there.'

'Well, there is still plenty of time for it to get better.' She half-smiled back.

He backed off. He had learned discretion during his time serving the army of disgruntled people. He knew when someone wanted to talk and when they just wanted to drown their sorrows.

She mellowed as the wine took effect and traced the engravings that decorated the tabletop with her sharpest fingernail. She read it out loud; Trudy and Wayne forever, Tracy loves Paul. She wondered if the hopeful scribbling had worked out for the authors. What was it about men? Why did they always want to try and make women feel intimidated? And what is it with other women joining in the game? To her that was treason. Her thoughts meandered around her head.

'Ya bastard ref! What the hell do you think ya are doing?' The old man yelled at the T.V screen. Phoebe jumped at the unexpected outburst.

'Hey, Fred, that's enough old man.'

'Yeah, yeah,' he replied, apparently used to being told off by the bar staff.

The bartender looked at Phoebe. He was happy to note that she didn't seem to mind the old man's outburst, even though it had made her jump. But she was distracted, this time by a message on her phone.

'Bloody Josh,' she said out loud. On slamming the phone on the table, the barman caught her eye, 'give me another one, will you?'

'Sure.'

Her wine arrived, and she drank it down quickly, which in turn made her light-headed, and she swayed a little on her seat. She threw up a little in her throat as the memory of being very drunk on this type of wine returned.

'Hey, hey, you want to walk out of here, don't ya?' The bartender did not want to put another drunk in a taxi.

'Oh God,' she whimpered, 'do you have coffee?' 'What type—latte, cappa…'

'just black and strong.'

'Okay.'

She drank what she could only describe as the worst coffee she had ever tasted. Black, sweet, sharp and bitter all at once, but it did the job, and she felt her head clear a little of the alcohol-induced haze that she was quickly heading towards.

'Aghh, ya mongrel,' yelled the old man again; this time, his raised voice sent a sharp pain through her head.

'Shut up, Fred! Another coffee love?' The barman asked.

'No, no, oh God no…I think I need some air.' Phoebe got up off her seat, wobbled a little but managed to walk outside without tripping or running into anything or anyone. Once outside, the fresh air made her feel violently ill. She held onto the pub wall and told herself to 'hold it down girl,' the feeling soon passed. A combination of stress, anger, drinks, and lousy coffee took their toll. She knew she had to get home, the sun was almost ready to set, and it was getting cold. She had totally lost track of time.

The taxi drew up in front of her apartment with a sudden jerk. The driver knew she was a little under the weather, and he didn't feel like cleaning up after anyone. She paid him and no sooner had she planted her second foot on the ground and shut the taxi door when he sped off, not waiting to see if she had made a mistake with the address.

Josh watched her walk or what he would more accurately call 'stagger' down the path towards him. He had been waiting for her for around half an hour.

'There you are,' he said pretty drily. 'What the hell have you been drinking?'

'Go away,' she gritted her teeth at him while she fumbled for the front door key.

'Go away? I will not. Not until I find out what the matter is. For goodness sake, you're losing the plot, and you have only been here five minutes.'

'Feels like an eternity. What type of madhouse is it in Canberra? I am tired—so just go away, please Josh, go away.'

He grabbed the wrist in which she held her keys. He pulled them from her grasp and let them both into the apartment. He pushed her into the kitchen and made her sit at the small dining table as he busied himself preparing coffee. Neither said a word while the kettle warmed and eventually boiled.

'Drink this.'

She did as he told her. She wanted a clear head so she could say to him exactly what he needed to be told.

'You know,' she finally stated, 'I gave up my marriage for this lame excuse of a job. I walked away from a man who adored me just to have it all blow up in my face.'

Josh didn't respond. He looked out the window, watching the tail lights of passing cars flash by, thoughts racing around his head.

'I studied hard to make something of myself. Now, my husband has someone else, who my mother tells me weekly, he is besotted with. My family thinks I am a job snob because I wasn't happy as a working-class girl. Oh no, I can just hear them—who the hell does she think she is with letters after her name and a high-flying career? You know I haven't spoken to my brother or sister for ages. They thought I moved out of my circle when I started uni. Shit. I can't be who I am 'cause I am not happy pretending to be something I am not just to make everyone else happy. And I am fast losing out on who I want to be because of the bloody politics of this damn place!'

Josh had heard this sort of thing before. Canberra and ambitious women usually collided, and it wasn't Canberra that suffered.

Ironically, the females of the human race always came off second to her—the city.

'Well, aren't you going to explain yourself? After all, you are the main reason why I feel so shit.'

'Sorry, but I have no idea what you mean. What am I supposed to have bragged about?' She could not read his face; he looked vacant.

'You're good. No wonder you've survived in this place,' she responded, almost as if resigned to the fact she was beaten.

'Honestly, Phoebe, I have no idea. Could you please tell me what is going on?'

'That God-awful woman, the one that works for Pete.' 'Danielle?'

'Yes, that's her.' 'What about her?'

Josh was uneasy, and he wanted to warn Phoebe to be careful. 'That woman is like Medusa. She has a head for everything that goes on. She is to be avoided at all costs.'

Phoebe sighed, 'She thinks that something is going on between us. Someone told her about our meeting at the restaurant the other night. That someone could only have been you, Josh.' She stood to face him, a little wobbly on her feet.

'Well, my dear, you are mistaken. I have no reason to talk to that woman. She has caused me enough grief. In fact, I would not tell her anything even if I had no one else to tell.'

The venom in his voice surprised her – her next question was voiced with a little less anger, but she was still on edge.

'Well, who the hell did? It sure wasn't me?' Phoebe moved towards Josh and was just about to point at him, but he grabbed her elbow and pulled her close and stared down into her eyes. For a minute, he was lost, transfixed by them.

'Let me go,' she struggled to free herself; he obeyed. He turned and leant on the kitchen bench, noticing the scratches from years of abuse by those who didn't use cutting boards. He hadn't had a feeling pass through him like this for many years. He had kept himself away from women, especially attractive women. They only bought grief to your door. But it was unmistakable; she had moved him, and he didn't know what to do.

'Josh, Josh.' She tapped him on the shoulder, surprised by what had just happened. He excused himself and abruptly left. He couldn't stay, not now; he needed to get out, get away from her as fast as possible.

'Josh, don't you walk away from me, I haven't finished…' But he was gone.

'Shit,' was the only thing left for her to say.

# Chapter 11

'Josh, where the hell is my coat? I have a press conference in half an hour—JOSH!'

'Coming.' Josh was hoping and praying to whatever god was listening that they would soon make the week come to an end. The run-up week to Election Day was always hell, but this one was proving to be especially dangerous. The PM was looking defeat squarely in the face, but losing wasn't a word he had in his dictionary.

'Where is my policy speech? Ohhh, for fuck's sake!'

'Here it is,' Josh handed it over politely. It was quickly snatched out of his hand by the PM, who was sweating profusely. 'Hanky sir.' Josh held out a very colourful one which in turn was also snatched violently out of his well-manicured hand.

'Josh, sit...stay and listen to this and tell me if it makes sense. Sit, sit.' Josh was just about to place himself by the window; at least he could daydream while watching the trees that dotted the courtyard outside sway in the breeze.

'No, not there. I need your undivided attention. Sit behind my desk, and I will read it to you from here, go on sit, sit.'

Josh did as he was told, and on the way, he picked up a ruler that lay by the art deco green desk lamp. He felt like being mischievous, so he rapped it a few times on the desk. He was the teacher, the PM, the inept student, very much in trouble if his speech was not up to scratch. Josh imagined giving him a good six across the palm of his puny right hand. Whack! Whack! However, the PM didn't get involved with the role-playing, and Josh was left to smirk at his own internal thoughts.

‘Now, as you all know, I am very concerned about…’ Josh was soon lost in his own thoughts, or as it turned out, only one thought, Phoebe. He hadn’t seen her since that night in her apartment, which now seemed a long time ago, but it was just a few weeks. He had tried to put her out of his mind, but he couldn’t.

And if the PM loses the election, as everyone expected, except the PM, he would be thrown into close working proximity with her. They would, in all probability, be working within a few feet of each other. He wished he hadn’t promised Pete his backing if he won. He wished he had frightened her off the first time he had met her. He should have been more convincing about life in this city, told her it had the tendency to chew you up and spit you out. But she was stubborn. He had found that out all right, but maybe if he had been a little meaner, or perhaps if he wasn’t so damn good looking…

‘Well, Josh, what do you think the punters will make of that, eh? Not bad. Promise them everything but give them nothing. They all fall for it ‘the public.’ Most haven’t got the brains to work their way out of a wet paper bag, and we let them vote!’

Josh was still lost in thought.

‘Ohhh, for God’s sake Josh. You haven’t heard a word I have said! I don’t know what has got into you lately, but if you have been sucked into believing all that bullshit about us losing the election, then you can go to hell with the rest of ’em.’

‘Of course not, sir. I was just running over what you said to me in my head, believe me—’

‘Oh shut up, will you? You’re just as bad as the other arse lickers in this place.’

The PM checked his appearance in the mirror and left.

'Thank you, thank you so very much for all your years of undying loyalty,' Josh mumbled to himself as the door of the office slammed shut on him and his defunct ruler.

***

'Bloody Josh, answer the phone.' Pete was holed up in his office and wanted some insider information about the PM. He wanted to know how he was faring under the stress of looming political defeat, not because he was concerned, he just wanted to gloat.

No luck. He wondered if Josh was losing his nerve. He had, after all, been the PM's lackey for a long time.

'If that bastard turns on me, he will be toast,' he said to himself as he poured himself a stiff drink. He had to face the press soon over some dimwit minister contradicting him on an important policy he had made public that morning.

***

Josh hadn't lost his nerve, just his head and what worried him more was that he was in danger of losing his heart. He walked the corridors of power lost in thought. Not for a long time had he had feelings for a woman, and that was what they were, he had to admit, even if he hated to; he had feelings. He had been hurt, badly hurt, and he had sworn never to get involved seriously with anyone again. He had two choices, ignore how he felt or run with it. The second option scared the hell out of him. But it would be hard to ignore. He couldn't risk it again, deception, lies, loss, could he?

Josh went back to his office; he had better pick up his mobile, which he had deliberately left behind. The PM was bound to be having a hissy fit somewhere. He noticed he had eight missed calls, three from the PM, four from Pete and one, surprisingly, from Phoebe. He bit his lip. Who to ring first? He decided on Pete.

'Josh, been trying to get you for a while. What are you up to buddy, you and the little guy?'

'Not right now Pete, come on mate.'

'Oh, why not? Not holding up too well, eh?' 'I guess.'

'Oh come on, he must be running around like a jackrabbit, yelling and screaming, hahaha.'

He was, but Josh didn't want Pete to know. 'Well, at the moment, I think he is having lunch.'

'Your loyalty to the end is admirable Josh. I hope you will do the same for me once I am PM, but you can stop trying to protect him from me now; we both know he is politically what you and I would both call toast.'

Josh was annoyed at Pete's self-assurance.

'Pete, what can I do for you?'

'Well, I need you to come up with a good policy on equal opportunity, you know, how women want equal pay—all that crap.'

'Why not ask Phoebe? That is the reason you employed her, wasn't it? And it's not in my job description. I am chief of staff, not a policy advisor.'

'Yes and No.'

'What do you mean by that?'

'Well, you have to have a woman who seems to write policy, but we both know men rewrite it, don't we? Why not just jump straight to the man?'

'I don't think Phoebe would see it that way.'

‘Tough. Oh, come on, just a soundbite, something imaginative. You’re up to that. I know you used to do policy in the long distant past.’

‘I’ll ask Phoebe.’

‘Stuff you, Josh, are you going soft or what? Forget it. I will get someone else to do it.’

Pete hung up.

Josh rang Phoebe.

‘Finally!’ She said when she answered her phone. She had been impatient waiting for him to ring. ‘Look,’ she started before Josh had time to utter a word. ‘I want to know if you have found out anything about the other night – you know – who spread the rumour? If it wasn’t you, then who the bloody hell was it?’

‘Phoebe, just what type of work are you doing for Pete?’ ‘What?’ She was taken aback by the question.

‘What do you do all day?’ ‘What type of question is that?’

‘Just look at what you are doing and think about what it is you are doing in this place.’

He hung up. He didn’t have the energy for another fight.

Phoebe looked at her phone for a second and wondered what he was going on about. If he was trying to dodge her question, he had better think again. She would get to the bottom of all this rubbish.

As she put her mobile in her bag, she looked over at her desk and the papers piled there. What had she actually achieved since she started work here? She had read over copious numbers of policies and made suggestions as to how they could be reworded, but what else? She hadn’t written or given any advice on anything substantial other than to point out the best place to get a takeaway and that bit of information she had given to a new secretary. She sat down heavily on her chair.

'Bugger.' Now he had her wondering. Was he trying to make her as dissatisfied with work as he was? Suddenly she felt an overwhelming desire for home, for Mic and her old life. Before she got into the shower, Phoebe decided she would ring him in the morning. First, however, she rang her mother to try and find out what was going on in his life. There was a bit of gossip going around that he had broken off with his girlfriend, but she couldn't be sure. Her mother, she was certain, would tell her this in the hope that they would get back together.

'Hi, mum.'

'Oh Phoebe, I am glad you have rung. I was just telling your aunt that you were interested in what Mic is up to, and she...'

'Mum, why did you say that? Just because I wanted to know how he was going the last time I rung doesn't mean anything...'

'I know you, Phoebe, always want your cake and eat it too.' 'Why do I bother with you at all?'

'Well, if that is the way you feel, I will hang up.'

'Look, mum, I rang to see how you are.' She didn't dare mention Mic now. 'Work is really getting on top of me at the moment and...'

'Thought it would.' 'Mum are you well?' 'Yes, very.'

'Good, I'll ring you later in the week.' She hung up.

Why couldn't she just mind her own business and be a little understanding rather than always trying to find fault?

'Go back to your daytime TV and gossip mags and leave my life alone,' she mumbled to herself.

She was resigned to the fact that she would never change. She hopped in the shower. It would help wash away the strain of the last few weeks.

While drying herself in the bathroom, draped in only a thin towel, she heard the doorbell ring.

'Who the hell could that be at this time at night,' she mumbled, angry at being disturbed from a precious time of self-pity.

'Josh!' She exclaimed as she looked out the window. He was waiting patiently in the cold; she stood for a millisecond longer than necessary, admiring his frame.

Finally, she opened the door and let him in. He walked straight past her into the lounge room and stood looking at the floor.

She stood behind him forgetting her only apparel was a towel.

'Phoebe,' he finally muttered, 'I am sorry that I didn't get you to go back on that bloody plane you flew here on. This place is soul-destroying, and I should have made you go back home to your husband and forget about your grand vision of public service.'

He turned to face her. At that very moment, she wished he had succeeded also.

'Josh, it's not your fault the way things have turned out. I just…' He moved towards her. She took a step back.

'Phoebe,' his voice wavered.

He looked vulnerable; she didn't like him this way. He was always so confident and sure of himself.

'Josh, what's the matter? What?'

He took another step towards her; this time, she stood still.

He placed his hands on her bare shoulders and muttered, 'You.'

Before she knew what was going on, his mouth was on hers.

She didn't resist. His mouth was soft and inviting, and she found herself enjoying the taste of his lips. She realised that her towel was ready to fall, she didn't try to stop it.

The towel slipped to the floor. Suddenly Josh pushed her away. He dropped his hands to his sides while looking at her, splendidly naked before him.

'I'm sorry Phoebe,' he said in a heavy voice. 'I am so, so sorry.' He turned on his heel and headed for the front door. Phoebe grabbed at his arm and tried to pull him back around to face her.

'Josh?'

He pulled away, and he dared not look back. He left without another word.

Phoebe stood still for a while, staring after him. She was stunned, not only by his blatant display of affection towards her but by her own reaction. She was, before Josh turned up, going to ring Mic and test the waters with the somewhat tentative hope that he would have her back. But who was she kidding? How did she really feel? Lost was probably the best way to describe it; lost and alone.

She looked at the floor and realised that she had actually wanted to be naked in front of him.

'Shit,' she said as she scooped the towel off the floor and put it

back around her.

'What must he think?' She sat on the lounge. What was going to happen now? How could she face him at work? How could she go back home? She couldn't do either. She sat for a very long time, her thoughts buzzing around a brain that was preparing to deliver a massive headache. Finally, she went to the cupboard and poured herself a rather large red wine. Regardless, red wine or no red wine, she wouldn't get much sleep.

***

The following day her mother rang.

'Yes, mum. What do you want?' She only just managed this greeting through a head recovering from a little too much red wine and the remnants of a thunderous headache.

'Charmed, I am sure. Glad to hear how happy you are for me to ring you.'

'Mum, I need to get to work.'

'Well, I am just ringing to let you know that Mic had an accident, and he is in hospital with a broken leg and a few fractures, not sure where though.'

'A broken leg? Oh my God? Is he okay?'

'No, he has a broken leg. I think as you are still his wife, you should get back here and visit him.'

'Mum, you know election week is coming up, and I am needed down here. I am sure he is all right. Anyway, he has his new girlfriend. I am very sure she doesn't want me pushing my nose into their business.'

'What do you mean, 'their business?' He is your husband; he is YOUR business.'

'Mum.'

'Just as I thought, you always put your work first and family second. No  wonder you haven't had any kids yet.'

'Do you have to ring up and spoil my day? Do you do it intentionally?'

'You do that all by yourself.'

Her mother hung up.

***

'Phoebe, Phoebe.' Jean was looking for her when she arrived.

'Phoebe, Pete has a photo shoot this morning, and he wants you in the background of the photo. Please hurry, he has rung me twice already looking for you.'

'Okay, Jean calm down. I will be there as soon as I can.'

Phoebe dropped her bag in her office, closed the door behind her, and stopped in front of Jean's desk.

'You need to go to the front of the building to the grassy bit, you know it.'

'That will take me a least 10 minutes to get there.'

'Run!'

Phoebe took off her high heels and started running. She had to run around all the people in the corridors and try not to mess herself up too much as she was going to be photographed.

'At last,' she thought, a little recognition.

She headed outside. From the doorway, she could see a crowd. In the middle were many cameras. She headed that way. Soon she could hear Pete's laugh and voice arise from the crowd. They giggled. She had to hand it to him; he charmed the press, especially the female journalists. Not many could sidestep his manufactured charm.

Pushing her way through the throng, she got a distinct impression that they had finished. The cameras were not being held up but rested on the sides of the photographers. He gave her a half-hearted wave and headed back inside.

'Pete,' she yelled again. He ignored her.

She grabbed the arm of a photographer. 'Excuse me, was anyone else in the photos with the opposition leader?'

'Yeah, we grabbed a few women who were walking past.' 'Who were they?'

'Look, love, you will have to ask him. He seemed to know them. I only take the photos.'

She was standing among the press in her stockings. She quickly put her shoes back on.

'I knew this was going to be a crap day.' She headed back to her office. A sweet bun and a coffee from the canteen would help, or so she thought.

'Phoebe, Phoebe.' She heard Jean calling again as she opened her office door. 'Just wanted to let you know that your mobile phone has rung a few times. In your rush, you left it behind.'

'Thanks, Jean. Oh, Jean, you couldn't do me a favour, could you?'

'Be glad to.'

'Could you get me a coffee and a bun from the canteen?'

'Sure,' she replied without hesitation, still wanting to make up to Phoebe for the embarrassment she suffered at the hands of Danielle.

'Oh, Jean.'

'Yes?'

'Where has Pete gone?'

'Pete? I'll just check his dairy.'

Phoebe waited by her door patiently as Jean searched her computer screen for Pete's schedule.

'Well, it says here that he is off to Queensland to talk to a woman's group who want him to do something about better pay. He is meeting up with the local M.P who is a woman.'

'Typical,' Phoebe shut her door and sat at her desk. Not once had he mentioned this to her. She had several ideas as to how to tackle the issue, and not once had he asked her to comment. She was, after all, supposed to be his advisor on women's issues.

She picked up her mobile and reviewed her missed calls. She rang 101 to receive her voice mail messages; she had two. To her utter surprise, it was her sister Sarah.

‘Phoebe, I know I am the last person who you expect to call you. Can you please ring me back? Mum is upset with your attitude, and she has begged me to talk to you. So if you ring and I talk to you, I can tell her I at least tried to talk some sense into you.’

The next message was short and sweet and again from Sarah. ‘Hurry up.’

Phoebe could hear the children in the background. Good old Sarah. She was a real earth mother; she pictured her with a child on each hip and a broom under her arm. She would love the fact that their mother was disappointed in her, yet again.

Her mobile ended up back in her bag and turned off. She didn’t need a family feud to add to the mix of the day’s events. She sat back on her chair, contemplating another day with little to do but fiddle around on the computer. A knock at her door heralded the arrival of her refreshments and not a moment too soon.

# Chapter 12

The day dragged on; finally, Phoebe decided she would go home. Pete obviously didn't want her around during the run-up to the election. He had made that quite clear. However, she couldn't resist checking with one of the girls in the office to see if he had penciled her in for anything. She still held on to a largely unfulfilled optimism, but it was slowly being subsumed into feelings of worthlessness.

'No, Phoebe, sorry. He is on the road most of the week. But wait, no, he has a list of those invited to a pre-election party in his office the evening before the election. You're on that list!' She said this to Phoebe as if she was a child who had not been invited to a much anticipated birthday party, but she had been asked to go shopping with her Nan instead.

'Great.' Phoebe replied sarcastically. 'I can't wait for that.'

'Neither can I,' said the young girl earnestly, obviously new to the job and still a little star-struck.

'So I take it all the girls are invited?'

'Well, yes we are…' The young girl was a little put out that Phoebe was being so, well, dismissive of her excitement as she watched the older women turn away.

'See you then.' As Phoebe walked out, she arranged a flight out of town via her mobile.

Back at her flat, she had time to reflect. Why was she really heading home? No one had said they wanted her to go back. She thought, however, that it may be good to go and see how she really felt, not only about Mic but also about her job. She was sure that Mic would take her back. She was very sure about it. But she needed to see how she felt. Anyway, a little breathing space would be good and being by the sea would be perfect. She would book herself into a hotel once she got there. She liked to be spontaneous, and she wanted to be able to escape once the inevitable questions from her family became a little too much to bear.

There was no way in hell she would stay at her mother's. Anyway, she had become very used to her own company, which was a little sad, she thought.

As she stepped off the plane, the roar of overhead jets added another layer of noise to the airport environment. Her head pounded. She remembered, however, as she waited for her luggage, that she didn't tell anyone she was coming. 'Good.' She would have time to look around, get her bearings and think about where she was.

Hailing a cab out of the front of the airport was easy. Trying to keep up the conversation with the garrulous taxi driver was hard. She wished as she swallowed a couple of Panadol that he would just shut up and let her look out the window at familiar surroundings in peace.

'Where are you going, love?' He finally asked; they were now in Hunter Street.

'Oh, just a nice hotel. What one would you recommend?'

'Well, all I know is that a lot of my customers go to the Novatel. It's right on the beach.'

'Yes, I know the one you mean. Could you drop me there?'
'Sure, have you got a reservation?'

'No, but that shouldn't be a problem, should it?'

'Don't know love, never done anything like that myself, but I will wait if you like, just in case.'

'Okay, good idea.'

The first thing that hit her as she got out of the taxi was the smell of the salty air. As pointed out by her taxi driver, the hotel had the privilege of being right across the road from the beach. She hadn't been this close to the coast for many months. The air sure smells good.

Canberra air just wasn't the same; it was fresh and cool, but not salty, nothing like sea air. There was no problem getting a room, and she waved her good Samaritan taxi driver goodbye. He left with a toot, toot, of his horn. Once in her room, she wasn't sure what she should do.

The view from her window was breathtaking. It is not until you are away from a place for some time that you appreciate it all the more on your return. Many people she knew in Canberra turned up their noses when she mentioned that she was from Newcastle.

'Is it nicer now BHP has gone?'

She would reply that it had always been nice even with the steelworks. Now, looking out the window at the crystal clear waves hitting the shore, she was happy she always stood up for the old steel town. It deserved it. Newcastle beach was just as nice as anywhere else, and today it was the best place in the world.

'Well, I just might go for a stroll downtown and see how much the old place has changed.'

She made her way past Customs House and the Royal, but it was not the same since the earthquake. Bright new apartments now overshadowed the older buildings. Further down the road, she found the mall was not much different, still a little quiet. She walked further down Hunter Street. It was also a mix of brand new apartments and old run-down buildings, a result of both the earthquake and more recent 'Pasha Bulka' floods. She thought that Newcastle was resilient, it had seen its fair share of disasters, but she wondered how much more the people who lived here could endure. Novocastrians seemed to take it all in their stride. She felt a tang of pride, she was from this place, and it felt good.

On her way past the 'Ducks Nuts', a popular local pub, a man suddenly appeared from its dimly lit depths straight into her path. 'Phoebe, is that you?'

She was taken aback. She hadn't expected to see anyone she knew, although that was probably wishful thinking. Newcastle, after all, was a city that was, in reality, a large country town. You were sure to run into someone you knew as you navigated its long main street. She was taken aback, annoyed. Everyone she was trying to avoid would find out that she was in town. The biggest sin would be that she hadn't bothered to let anyone know. Great.

'Yes, yes, it is you. How the hell are ya?' 'Gary, how are you?'

'What you up to? You visiting your mum? I bet she is pleased to see ya, eh?'

'Yeah.' She was uncomfortable. Gary was one of Mic's best friends, one of the guys that always tried to avoid her, as Mic had informed her.

'I tell ya, Mic is doing really well.' He offered this information unsolicited. 'He and his new Mrs are getting on great guns, really good. Hope ya job suits.' She got his underlying intent. It went something like this; was her job really worth her marriage? Mic is happy, so stay away. Mic's new girl is much nicer than you, so fuck off!'

'How is it all going by the way?' It sounded to her as if there was a hint of skepticism in his voice, like he was hoping she was miserable and wanting Mic back, but it was all way, way too late. She wasn't going to give him the satisfaction of telling him how deeply dissatisfied she was with her job and just about everything in her life.

'I am very happy in my position. The job is everything I had ever hoped.'

'Great, great,' he said, somewhat disappointed that she seemed okay but not entirely convinced. 'Say hi to your mum for me.'

'I will. Bye.'

'See ya.'

He headed across the road to his car while she wondered how many drinks he had had. She waved as he pulled out into the traffic, and then she made her way back to her hotel. She didn't want to bump into anyone else from the past. To her annoyance, she had left her mobile in her room, and now she would have to let people know she was in town. Town being what everyone called the city. Her first task when she got there was to ring her mum. There would be hell to pay if she didn't let her know before someone else did. She would have to walk briskly to beat the jungle drums.

Back in her room, she found her phone had a message for her. She rang 101.

It was Josh.

'Phoebe, where the bloody hell are you? We need to talk. I really need to see you. I am not kidding, making it up or mucking you around, or any other type of nuisance you can imagine. Please, could we meet tonight at the Italian?'

She drew in her breath. The last time she had been with him on her own, he had kissed her and then left abruptly, leaving her in a state of shock. She didn't have time to respond and was left feeling rather confused, if not a little annoyed. But when she replayed the message, she could hear strong emotion in his voice. It trembled slightly. She knew that something was up and that he needed her. Now, instead of enjoying Newcastle and the salty air, she felt stuck and hemmed in by the past as this jaunt had quickly turned into a problem. She knew what she wanted but was not sure how she could make it happen.

She sat and looked out the window to collect her thoughts. Why was she really here? Had she secretly hoped that Mic's relationship had broken down? Obviously, it hadn't. Gary had let her know that. However, she wasn't that upset by the news, which was not unexpected, so why stay? She didn't want to see her mother. She would just go on and on about leaving Mic and working and not having kids, on and on. She decided in that second that she would go back to Canberra and see what Josh wanted. Her heart pounded. She couldn't pack the few things that she had taken out of her overnight back quick enough.

She went downstairs to check out, exactly 2 hours after checking in. This amused some of the staff. It was obvious they were trying not to giggle, and one or two of them were biting their lips at this bizarre woman.

However, one of the staff remained composed and asked, 'Are you sure? You have only just checked in.'

'Of course, I am. And could you please see if there are any available seats to Canberra out of Williamtown airport within the next hour, oh and order me a cab.' The girl taking the orders glared at her. Phoebe's tone of voice was bordering on condescending. Phoebe realised, 'Please,' she added to keep her on her side, but it was a little too late for that.

'Certainly, please take a seat while I try and get you out of here,' came the dry response.

She was in luck, the girl informed her, there was a seat out, but it wouldn't be until 7 o'clock the next morning.

'I wanted it for tonight.'

'I have tried, but that is the only flight to Canberra within the next 24 hours out of Williamtown. I can try Sydney for you if you like.'

'No, no, that won't be necessary, thanks…' She had no choice but to wait. Sydney was out of the question. She was irritated. It meant that her dinner with Josh would have to be put off until the following night. She rang, hoping he would understand. He didn't answer, so she left him a message explaining where she was and how she couldn't get back until the following day. She hated playing telephone tag.

'Excuse me. I suppose you will still be needing your room now?' The question said condescendingly, meant to make her feel silly. She ignored the obvious intent and responded appropriately.

'Yes, I will.'

'Could you also book me a taxi for 5.45 AM for Williamtown airport?'

'Certainly.'

She had never in her life been so happy to see a place and to leave within such a short space of time. She could only put it down to one thing: Josh. The trip to see Mic was really just a pretence so she could find out how she really felt about him once and for all. It had made her realise that her old life was just that, her old life. No matter what, she was now well into a journey she never thought she would be on. But on it, she was. Her agitation about being stuck and not being able to get back to Canberra, back to him, told her she was well and truly over Mic; but did Josh feel the same? She ordered room service, a burger and fries and to follow apple pie and cream. The bar fridge was soon raided. And one overpriced bottle of wine later, she was fast asleep.

She slept soundly for a short time, but vivid dreams made her restless. In them, she was kissing Mic, or so she thought, but when she drew back from the embrace, it was actually Josh. She moved forward to kiss him, but he pulled back, turning away and running down a dimly lit corridor that looked both familiar and threatening. Ultimately, she was left all alone in a room that seemed to be closing in around her. She called out, but all had left. Suddenly, Pete appeared. He was angry, yelling at her. Veins were sticking out on his head, and his eyes were bulging. She covered her ears and tried to flee. But she ended up not being able to run. He was catching up to her. She turned in fright and saw he was being followed by faceless women in suits. They bore down on her as she crumpled to the floor. Her hands came up to her ears, and she screamed silently. As she did, the figure of Pete and the woman disappeared, replaced by her mother.

'What are you doing, Phoebe?' She said. 'What in the world are you doing?'

She felt herself falling into an abyss, but before she reached the bottom, she woke up.

OHHH God, she mumbled–disorientated, it took her a few seconds to work out where she was as she sat up and shook her head. The slightly dated decor brought it suddenly back to her. She sat for a few seconds remembering the dream and the events of the previous day. The bedside clock registered 3 AM. She was thirsty. She got up and poured herself some cool water. From her window, she could see the blackness of the ocean with its eerie foam waves washing up on the shore. Beach lights highlighted a lone person sleeping on the sand surrounded by sea mist not far from the concrete path that circled the curve of the beach. Too much drink, she presumed. At least, she hoped that was the reason for the lifelessness of the body. Only two hours left to sleep, and she would have to get ready. Was it worth it? TV seemed a better alternative. She surfed the channels one by one. Each was showing hour-long infomercials, which can only be described as excruciating, boring, and banal.

So much for quality TV—forced through lack of choice to watch the benefits of a product that makes you suddenly look like a movie star, she dozed off.

RIINNNNNNGGGGG. It was 5 O'clock. She showered, and as she was dressing, the in house phone rang.

'Yes.'

'Your Taxi is here.'

'Oh, thanks, tell them I will be as quick as possible.' 'Okay.'

'Thanks.'

The taxi was 15 minutes early. Never mind. She dressed in record time, checked her room and left.

Once back in Canberra, she dropped her stuff back at her flat and went to her office. She hoped that she could meet up with Josh during the day.

Any thoughts of sneaking into her office, however, were dashed. 'Phoebe, Phoebe, Sorry love but I have an important letter for you from the assets team. Look, I don't want to interfere, but I think it is probably about your flat. They don't like anyone staying on too long, and you have been there now for a while, quite over the time allocated...'

'Yes, thank you, Jean. I am well aware of how long I have been there.' She wasn't and the call to leave the flat, as dreary and uninviting as it was, was just another problem to climb over.

A little taken aback by Phoebe's abrupt reply, Jean handed her the letter. She shoved it under her arm and marched off into her office. Jean felt a pang in her chest. She still thought Phoebe was angry with her for the ambush she had walked into. But for Phoebe nothing, but nothing mattered at the moment but Josh. She tried his mobile. No answer. Throwing her phone on her desk, she decided to walk to his office. Something for which she would have to find a good excuse; she didn't want to raise suspicion, although it was a little late for that. Winding her way through the maze of corridors and doors, she passed the cafe. The first into work were still sitting around enjoying their breakfast. The coffee smelt divine. She promised herself one on her way back. Josh's office was near the PM's. Luckily she had her ID with her. A couple of security guards checked her out but then waved her on. She knocked at his door. Feeling both excited by the anticipation of seeing him and anxious because this was a really silly idea. Fortunately, by the time she realised he wasn't there, rationality set in. She walked away quickly so as not to be seen by anyone else. However, she was unaware of the eyes watching her from the one-sided window that graced the wall opposite Josh's office.

Danielle made a note of the time and date. Something was going on between this pair, and it wasn't purely professional. Even so, why would they have a working relationship? She worked for the opposition. Josh was up to something, and she was damned sure she would find out what. It would be Friday night in a couple of days, and the pre-election drinks would provide an excellent platform for her to question him. It would be interesting to see how the PM would react. He hated secrets and innuendo, and those two, she was sure, had plenty of that.

Phoebe made good on her promise to herself. She ordered a large soy latte, sat in the furthest corner of the room and tried to put all thoughts out of her head; work, Josh, her mum, and sister, just about everything. The only thing she wanted to think of was the smell of her coffee. But just as she was finishing off the last remnants of it, a voice over her shoulder broke her concentration and filled her with dread.

'Well, Phoebe, I haven't seen you in a long time.' Phoebe put her cup down and resisted the temptation to throw what was left in her face.

'No, I have been very busy, you know, helping to run the country and not the office gossip mill.' The thing that bugged Phoebe most about Danielle was that she never raised her voice. She never seemed to be bothered by anything anyone said to her, whether it was vindictive or not.

'Well,' Danielle said, 'that is because, unlike the rest of us, you have nothing to gossip about.' With that comment, Danielle turned on her very sharp heels and left. Phoebe went straight back to worrying. Had she seen her? What the hell was she thinking? She must ring Josh and tell him what she had done. He would not be pleased. Bloody hell, why didn't she just wait until the cover of night?

Back in her office, she read the inconvenient letter:

*To the occupant, we are writing to remind you that your stay at these premises is now due to come to an end. Your present place of residence was provided on a temporary basis of which you would have been informed. Could you please arrange to find your own accommodation AS SOON AS POSSIBLE. New arrangements need to be made by the middle of next week, which is viewed as an appropriate time frame to make a move.*

*Regards*

*Co-coordinator Assets Team.*

She threw the letter in the bin. She thought they didn't need to be rude about it. She was starting to wonder why she came back. Her phone rang. It was Josh. 'Phoebe, I missed your call this morning because I was out walking and didn't take my phone with me. Are you all right?'

'Yes, I'm fine, but Josh, I think I have given Danielle some more ammunition to use against us.'

He shifted in his seat. 'What have you done?'

'Something very silly. I went to your office. I thought you would be there. Josh, I know it was silly, but I needed to see you. Danielle saw me, or I think she did. She followed me to the canteen…Josh?' Josh was quiet on the other end of the phone. 'Josh, Josh, are you still there?'

Josh knew that Phoebe's image would also have been caught on the security cameras surrounding his and the PM's office. It wasn't a capital offence, but it would confirm the rumours flying around this place faster than a cheetah on steroids. More fodder for the fire.

'Yes, I am still here.'

'And Josh, I have to move out by next week.' 'Ohh great.'

By the time she had hung up, they had made arrangements to meet at the Italian restaurant at seven that night. Josh had also promised to help her find a place to live. She still didn't feel better. The only thing that would help was chocolate. Something that had nuts, caramel, marshmallows, just about anything that you could stuff into a chocolate bar and into your mouth in one go.

'Jean, Jean.'

'Coming.' Jean had been chatting to the girls behind the wall and quickly turned and left the conversation midstream when she heard her name. She knew Phoebe was a little uptight, upset even, so she didn't want to keep her waiting.

'Yes, yes…coming…' She found her pacing her office floor, shoulders hunched and hair looking more windswept than office preened.

The one thing that Phoebe really disliked about Jean was her ability to be very kind, both in word and action but then take secret glee in the gossip that circulated the building. Jean had especially liked the rumours about the young, pretty secretary, who had only been in her job for a very short while but had managed to catch the eye of a very nice up and coming professional. Not long after starting her job, they were engaged and planned to head overseas for a very long vacation before they married. Well, the first thing that went around quicker than a spinning top was the belief that she had purposely fallen pregnant.

There was bleating and pounding about how devious this was and how she had, in all probability, ruined this young man's career. Heading overseas indeed, she had left work early so as not to show off her growing belly. It was also alleged that the young man's parents were quite upset by it all and told him in no uncertain terms what a fool he was. However, all of these delicious rumours were proved wrong when the young girl in question came into the offices a few weeks later, without a pregnant belly, to say goodbye to the gossip gorged workmates she was very fond of.

'Jean, I need a chocolate.' 'Yes, that would be nice.'

'I mean, could you get me one?'

'They have them at the…' But before she could finish, Phoebe interjected.

'I am aware of that Jean, but I would…I mean, could you do me the favour of going and getting me one? I am really busy at the moment.'

Jeans eyes roamed the room. There was no papers or policy documents on her desk, only her mobile phone. Something was up.

A little put out at being reduced to running errands all the time, she responded calmly, as she didn't want to give her anything else to be mad at her about.

'Okay, no worries. What type would you like?'

'One that has the works, you know nuts, caramel, coconut.'

'Back in a tick then.'

Whatever was bothering her, it was worse than she had first thought. Jean knew from self-experience that the higher the calorie intake, the worse the problem. There was something very amiss, and it wasn't just to do with her accommodation or the run-in with Danielle. Whatever it was, she was determined to find out.

With her mouth full of chocolate, Phoebe took a call from Pete,

'Listen, you do know about the pre-election drinks? We are all meeting in the senate board room. Everyone who is on my team is to be there. No excuses. The election is only a few days away, and I want to start celebrating. All the polls are calling a landslide. Soon, my dear, you will be working for the leader of the country. Does that turn you on or what?'

Phoebe nearly choked on a nut. What the hell? She chose to ignore his last comment and just accept the offer of drinks. She would not be able to get out of it even if she wanted to.

'Good girl, see you then.'

She had only just hung up on Pete when her mobile rang again. It was Josh. 'Are we on for tonight?'

'Tonight?' It had slipped her mind.

'Phoebe, I really need to talk to you.'

'Ohh, yeah, okay. Ahhh, Pete has just asked me to drinks to celebrate the—'

She cut in mid-word.

'The election?' She could almost feel Josh move in his seat. 'When?'

'The day after tomorrow. I know he has something on around 8 o'clock, so probably around nine, I suppose.'

'Hang it; I can't wait. It's lunchtime in half an hour. How about we meet at the café, Queens Terrace, on the other side of the building. It's a bit of a walk from my office and miles away from yours. If we meet there, we reduce the risk of being seen. Hang on. I have a call coming through.' He put her on hold while he took it.

Why he was in such a hurry to talk to her, she could not understand. Maybe it was to explain what a mistake it was the other night. But the way he had kissed her. Surely he must feel something to do what he did. But then again, he was a lady killer. Maybe he wanted to tell her that he really didn't have any feelings for her and that he had made a mistake. She hoped with all her heart that he wouldn't say that, but she had to be realistic; this was Josh, the most wanted but the most aloof man she had ever met.

'You won't believe who that was, Pheebs.' She liked the way he had shortened her name. It made their relationship seem a little bit more intimate. 'Only the future PM himself inviting me to his little drinks party. God, I hate the way that man is so sure of himself. I'm beginning to wish I hadn't signed on with him. I think I hate him more than the current PM.'

'Will you come?'

'I don't think so. Only Pete and you know of our little arrangement. If I turn up at his pre-celebration party, what would people say? Oh, I know, something like this; something is really going on. There is a rat in the ranks, and we were not just imagining it. If the PM does manage a victory, I can wave goodbye to any type of job in Canberra.'

'Josh?' He didn't respond but told her, 'I will see you at the cafe in 25 minutes.'

'Rightio then, okay.'

She threw the chocolate wrapper in the bin and wiped the few stray crumbs off her desktop. She noticed Jean hovering by her office door. She couldn't be sure if she heard her conversation with Josh or not. She hadn't really said anything that she could make any sense of.

'Can I help you, Jean?'

'Did you say something, Phoebe?'

Phoebe knew full well that she had heard her.

'Do you need something?'

'No, not at all. Just picking up a few bits and pieces from the carpet. Don't really know what it is, but it looked awful, so in the bin it goes.'

Phoebe couldn't see anything on the floor but knew Jean wanted something. She reminded her at that very moment of her mother. When she was younger, her mother would beat around the bush trying to find out what was going on in her life. She could never just ask her straight out. It was a little annoying, but it was something her mother got over, and now she hated it when she just poked her nose into her business.

'Oh, Phoebe, I hope you don't mind, but I did get a list from the local real estate with all the available rental properties. Do you want me to print it out or just email it to you?'

'Email will be fine Jean. Thanks for your concern.'

Jean walked back to her desk with the imaginary dirt clutched tightly in her hand.

'By the way, I am also popping out for lunch. Be back soon.'

'Lunch?'

'Yes, Jean, lunch.' Phoebe was annoyed at her inquisitive tone.

'Fine, fine.' Jean could only imagine what was going on as Phoebe rarely ate anything when she first arrived. Now she had not only had her hunting chocolate, but she was also going to eat lunch as well.

Jean fell into her old habit of putting two and two together and getting five. For her, it was obvious Phoebe was pregnant.

She had, after all, gone back to Newcastle for a visit. Not a long one, but enough to let her husband know the good news. She had been in Canberra for a few months, and well, she would be quite sure of it by now...

'Jean, Jean.' She was rocked out of her thoughts by Phoebe.

'Jean, how do I get to the other side of the building?'

'The other side of the building?' She was thrown by the question. 'Don't you just want to go to the local?' Phoebe shuffled her feet, annoyed by the question. 'Well, yes, but then I need to go to the other side of the building. Now could you tell me how to get there, please?'

'I'll do better than that. I will get you a map.'

'Thanks.'

As Jean looked through her top drawer, Phoebe heard her office phone ring, indicating an internal call. She chose to ignore it.

'Here you are, now I have marked where we are now. Where do you want to go?'

'To the other side,' replied Phoebe.

'But...who do you want to see?' As she said it, Jean could tell that Phoebe was not going to tell her. Pregnancy, of course, makes you a little emotional. 'Just follow the map, and it will get you there.'

'Good.' Phoebe took it and headed off. Jean's phone rang.

'Hello' was all the office protocol that Jean could muster as she answered. Her mind was working overtime trying to work out where Phoebe was going. It was Pete. 'Jean, I am trying to get Phoebe on the phone, she is not answering. Do you know where the bloody hell she is? Is she in her office?'

'No, but I will find out where she is and get back to you.'

'Tell her to get back to me ASAP.'

'Okay, I will.'

‘Sometimes I don’t know why I hired that woman.’ With that comment, he hung up.

Phoebe followed the path on the map for what seemed an eternity, but in reality, she was only 5 minutes late for her secret meeting with Josh. Weirdly, it was exciting, all these secret meetings and subterfuge. She had always been so straight, so upfront about things, especially relationships. Once she and Mic were married, every day was the same. Nothing altered much, except maybe his working hours. There were no undercurrents, nothing to keep from family and friends, no deceit. Now here she was having a secret affair with a very unreliable man. She thought she might be getting a little ahead of herself, classifying what she had with Josh as an affair. The kiss the other night, well, it was just that, a kiss. But what a kiss. But it may have doomed her relationship with Josh before it had even started. She couldn’t believe how much she wanted him. She was here to work, to pursue a career, one that she had longed for. But that had been a letdown so far. Josh, she felt, was the only thing that kept her here; otherwise, she would have left and started all over again somewhere else, somewhere where she knew no one.

Maybe selling something lovely, like clothes or shoes; an easier life seemed more and more inviting. It was amazing how quickly this job had turned her off from wanting to work in an office. She knew she was stressed; she was losing hair every time she brushed, and she was tired all the time. The job seemed to be making her sick.

# Chapter 13

When she finally found her way, he was sitting in the corner. He had not yet ordered, so she took it on herself to order for the both of them at the counter, a soy latte for her and a long black for him. Once she had done that, she joined him. However, the look on his face told her the news would not be good. She tried to lighten the atmosphere. 'Gee, this building is like a rat warren, filled with them too I'm afraid.' She hoped she would get what she was referring to and laugh.

He only lifted his head to look at her. What was he thinking? He looked immaculate as usual. His dark brown tie made his brown eyes seem deeper and more soul searching than they normally did. She sat down.

'Phoebe,' he started slowly. 'I have something to apologise for and something to tell you. But there is someone in the building who knows and will try to destroy us because of it.' All Phoebe heard was the word 'us'. Maybe she had been wrong. Maybe he did want her?

'First of all…' He broke off, the coffee arrived. Once they were alone again, he took up where he left off. 'First of all, I want to say how dreadfully sorry I am for the other night. It was wrong of me to take advantage of you like that.'

Phoebe tried to interject, but he stopped her by holding up his hand. 'But I want you to know that I don't regret it. You have made me feel again for the first time in a very long time. But to be honest, I am scared about it. You, I know, are a woman of integrity. It's funny, but I feel safe with you, and I haven't felt safe with anyone for a very long time.' This was almost a revelation to her. This was not the Josh she knew, strong, confident and removed from the everyday worries of mere mortals. What was going on? She was so stunned that it took her a few seconds to realise that he reciprocated her feelings. But she needed to tread carefully as he was still hurting over something that she knew nothing about. She decided to stay silent while he told her what he felt she needed to know.

'It is for this very reason that I am telling you why I have shied away from relationships for many, many years.' He sucked in his breath and exhaled slowly. He knew she would be shocked at what he was going to say, but he needed to tell her. He dropped the bomb, 'Danielle.'

The name didn't register with Phoebe straight away. 'Danielle, Danielle who?' It only took a slight raise of Josh's left eyebrow for it to hit her.

'You mean that bitch in the PMs Office?' He nodded. 'What has she got to do with you?' She said a little loudly, and he gestured to her to keep her voice down.

'Everything and nothing.'

'I'm not following you. What do you mean everything?'

'Phoebe this is hard for me to explain. Please, please just listen.' He shifted around, played with his coffee cup and took a deep breath. Phoebe leant in. She didn't want anyone overhearing him. This seemed unlikely, as they were very much alone in the dimly lit cafe.

'A long time ago, when I was in my early 20s, I was with Danielle.'

Phoebe nearly interjected with a 'what?' but refrained. She didn't want to stop him from talking.

'We met early in our careers. We both wanted to work here, in Canberra. She started as an undersecretary, and I was what you would call a jack of all trades. I was just out of uni doing a little bit of this and that. Not really sure what I wanted, but I knew I wanted something. Anyway, one thing led to another, and soon we were living together. Our jobs were going well, too well, especially for Danielle. She managed to gain several quick promotions, and I was settling into work at an MP's office.'

'One day, out of character, she took a few days off work. She said she wasn't well. I found out a month later that she had had an abortion. She hadn't even mentioned to me that she was pregnant. Instead, she kept it to herself and made the appropriate appointments. She told them at the clinic that the father was not on the scene and had the deed done, as neatly as that. I only found out about it when the clinic made a phone call to the flat. I happened to answer because I was off to a work dinner and had popped home to change. They didn't tell me what they wanted. I looked up the name of the clinic and put it all together. Instead of going to the dinner, I waited at home to confront her.'

He gulped his coffee. It was of little matter that it was now lukewarm. He needed to wet his dry throat. Phoebe was stunned. Her head spun; she had many questions but did not want to interrupt.

'Anyway, she eventually came home around midnight. In frustration, I had shredded one of our lounge pillows, so there was fluff all over the carpet.'

'What are you doing?' She asked. I noticed she was a little tipsy.

I said, 'I should be asking you what you have been up to.'

'She had no clue as to what I was referring to.' She took off her shoes and rubbed her feet.

'The Riverdale clinic rang', she stopped what she was doing and went into the kitchen. Josh shook his head. He was reliving his disbelief in front of her, and it tore at her heart.

Josh went on. 'She said...Oh, what did they want? She asked me this as if I was a fool. I couldn't speak.' Danielle replied 'Okay, I will get back to them. Do you want something to eat?' Josh's face was white as he relayed this information but he went on.

'No,' I replied. I followed her into the kitchen. I just had to ask – 'Have you had an abortion?' She stopped rummaging through the knife and fork drawer. It was the way that she replied that showed me the woman she was.'

'Yes, now do you want some toast?'

'I couldn't believe it. As cold as can be. Just as if I had asked her if she had dropped off the laundry. I couldn't do anything. I just stood looking at her.'

'Josh, don't pretend that you aren't pleased. What would we do with a baby? I certainly didn't want it.'

'I replied, you didn't even ask me if I did!'

Phoebe reached across the table and grabbed his arm. 'Oh Josh, I am so sorry.'

He looked up at her, 'Phoebe, as unreal as it may seem now, I did love her back then. I thought she loved me too. But she didn't. If she did, she would have told me about the baby. But her job, her career was more important than us, including our child.'

Phoebe sat back in her seat. This conversation seemed to remind her of the one she had with Mic. She hadn't had an abortion, but she didn't want kids with him. She wanted a career. She had robbed Mic of the children they would have had together. Did that make her as bad as Danielle?

No, she refused to believe her decision was as bad as hers. She hadn't totally destroyed a man. Mic had moved on, happily, so it seemed. But Danielle had destroyed Josh. Under his show of self-confidence lay a defeated man.

‘Josh.’ Phoebe purred his name. He leant across and grabbed her hand.

‘That is why Phoebe, that woman takes an interest in you. You see, she thought I was overreacting. Being silly about a little thing that hadn’t even grown arms. A blob of flesh, she called it. But to me, it was my child. She wanted us to stay together.

I think she thought we would be a formidable force in politics. But I couldn’t stay with her. I could hardly look at her anymore. I lost my motivation to work hard. I didn’t want to be a public servant anymore.’

‘But you are chief of staff.’

Josh gave a wry grin. ‘Only because I fell into it, so to speak. I stayed on because I couldn’t think of anything else to do. I met the PM at lunch, and he liked me, and eventually, he put me on.’

In actuality, it was Josh’s laidback style the PM liked.

He was good at negotiation and tactful. But most of all, the PM enjoyed Josh’s attention to his needs; his job really was to be chief molly coddler. This was the most important aspect of Josh’s suitability for the job.

‘I used to dream of running away and living a life of absolute selfishness, but I didn’t, and I don’t want to anymore, not since meeting you.’ Phoebe drew breath. She was about to say something, but Josh held up his hand to stop her; he hadn’t finished.

‘I never thought, after being so deceived by a woman, that I would ever want to put myself in a position for it to ever happen again. And to be honest, Phoebe, you have left a husband yourself for a career. But I can’t help how I feel. I even think that the future may hold something more than my complete emotional separation from the other half of the population.’

A cheerful waitress asking if they would like another coffee interrupted them. What remained in their cups, and Phoebe’s was almost full, was cold. They both declined; time was against them. Once the attendant left, Josh continued.

'I don't want to make a mistake, and I don't want to make you uncomfortable. You going to Newcastle made me realise that I don't like to think of you as being far away from me. But I know you went there to sort things out. So, tell me. Are you going back to hubby or not?'

Phoebe was stunned at this last admission. He had strong feelings for her and wanted a relationship.

'Josh, I didn't realise it at first, but I feel the same.' He gave her a wry smile at that revelation. 'My trip was, on the whole, an unmitigated disaster. I don't really know why I went. I knew my husband was happy with someone else, but I just needed to be sure of my feelings. Once you rang, all I could think of was being with you. So, whether it is a good or a bad thing, you may be stuck with me.'

He became very serious and looked her in the eye. 'This, whatever it is, must be kept a secret. People are already suspicious, and if we are to have any chance of a life, we must keep Danielle from finding out. Not only will she do everything she can to undermine what we might have, but she will also get us both fired.'

'You think she still loves you?' Phoebe asked.

'Not sure, probably not. It is more of the case that if she can't have me, no one else can. But she is deluded enough to think I would even give her the time of day. It has been hard enough having to work with her. Although I try not to be in the same room as her very often, I can't avoid it most of the time. Look, I must get back. The PM will be looking for me.'

They both got up and started to walk back to their respective offices. The corridors were pretty empty, so they could for a little while walk together, which they did in silence. Just as they walked past a ladies' restroom, Josh grabbed Phoebe's arm and pulled her inside. Pushing her against the entry wall, he held her at arm's length, looking deep into her eyes. He leant forward and kissed her. At first, his kiss was soft and searching, and then it grew strong and passionate. She reciprocated; she noticed that he smelt off cologne. His hands started to explore her body, and she wrapped her arms around his neck, pulling him closer. Suddenly a toilet flushed, and his mobile rang. He pulled away reluctantly, his breathing slightly laboured. Phoebe straightened herself up. They didn't want to be spotted by the toilet flusher, so they quickly left the small anteroom. Josh gave her a peck on the cheek and walked on ahead. Phoebe stood watching him. She couldn't believe it. He wanted her just as much as she wanted him. How she was going to keep it a secret, she didn't know. But what would be even harder to control would be her absolute hatred of Danielle. Not giving away her feelings or bringing up the past hurt she had inflicted on Josh would need all of the self-control she could muster. And muster it she would.

'Phoebe, Phoebe.' Jean called her as she walked to her office. That woman, she thought, was keeping tabs on her. 'Yes, Jean.'

'I have left some papers on your desk for you to look at, from some minister. And Pete was looking for you earlier. Could you give him a ring?'

Do I have to? Phoebe thought to herself. 'Yes, yes, thank you, Jean. I will get onto him.'

'Pete, Phoebe here. You were looking for me?'

'Yes, I was. You are a hard lady to track down. I hope you won't be as hard to grab…I mean to get hold of for the pre-election drinks.'

Drinks? Phoebe had forgotten all about the drinks. Her mind was so caught up in other things that the PM's double entendre went straight over her head.

'Yes, yes, sure. I will be there.'

'Good.' Pete drawled down the phone. 'I did have a minister that wanted your advice on something—you weren't around, so I sent over some paperwork for you to have a look at. Could you get it back to the minister ASAP with some ideas around...well I have forgotten, but you will see what it is when it gets to you.'

'Fine.'

'Bye.' And with that, he signed off. The rest of the afternoon was spent pretending she was going over the minister's papers. In reality, she was going over and over the conversation she had with Josh. It seemed that the afternoon flew by, and before she knew it, the admin staff were going home.

'Have a nice night Phoebe.' Jean said on her way out. 'Thanks.'

Phoebe wished she wasn't included in the cohort of those that had to attend dinners and drinks. She quite liked it when she first started; they broke up the monotony of being alone in a flat, night after night. But now, after attending, no—*enduring* them, she was more than happy to stay home. But the politics outside of the job was just as important as the paperwork and endless meetings. Sucking it up and playing by the rules was one of the un-stated requirements of anyone wanting to keep their job. There was a saying that you either played politics or you perished. Everything is political, even the colour of the toilets in the public areas.

Getting ready for drinks, Phoebe was less than enthusiastic to mingle with those she knew and those she didn't. Making small talk made her nervous. Anyway, she didn't have anything to wear, or so she thought and found it a chore to apply her makeup. To her surprise, a car horn sounded outside as a car had arrived to pick her up.

The driver knocked at the door and returned to the car. 'Hello,' she said as she got in. 'Who sent you?' The driver looked at her in the rear vision mirror, happy with what he saw, and said, 'I only get told where to go and who to pick up, and that is about it, and around here, its best that way.'

'Oh, okay.' Phoebe was a little curious but happy to be chauffeured around in comfort. She settled back and watched the world go by. She had concluded that Josh had arranged her lift. She wished he could be at the gathering but was well aware of the difficulties. There was no way he could turn up. Only a couple of days, and with the election over, and Pete as PM, maybe all would be different, maybe then they could come out in the open. She knew that all the women who threw themselves at Josh would hate her—Danielle, she had no idea how she would feel at her so-called conquest of what everyone thought was unattainable.

Everyone who was anyone in the opposition party was there. However, the only one Phoebe wanted to see was Josh, but that was not going to happen. She manoeuvred around the room. She had yet to meet most of those who were hanging onto their drink, smiling and nodding to each other, kings and queens of the world. None of them doubted the election result, and they were almost drowning in their own self-assurance. Phoebe didn't know anyone, largely due to Pete. He kept her hidden away, and that many had their own advisors and worked in their own little enclaves or kingdoms.

She noticed Jean holding court with the secretaries. They didn't impose themselves onto those they thought above them, and those above did not bother with them. The social classes didn't mix in the microcosm of politics in the House. Shame, she thought, maybe there would be a better understanding of the needs in society if it was more democratic. Instead, those with power mixed with those in power and those without knew their place. Jean saw Phoebe and waved. To Jean's unease, Phoebe made her way towards her group.

'Hi, Phoebe, enjoying yourself?' She asked nervously.

Phoebe sat down. 'I am not sure yet. What about you ladies?' Some of them moved uncomfortably in their seats. They didn't want an outsider crashing their intimate group. They couldn't comfortably talk about anyone and everyone if she sat and listened. She was, after all, their main target. It was half the fun of these evenings. A few nodded their heads in response. A waiter appeared, and all took a bubbly drink from the tray, Phoebe included, and he turned his back to get some more.

If Phoebe was going to buck up the courage to talk to anyone else, she felt she needed to be well lubricated. As she sat and drank, her thoughts kept going back to Josh. She wished more than anything that he was here. It would make it much more bearable. After a while, the group of secretaries realised Phoebe was there only for refuge. She had no interest in what they were saying. Happily, they continued to talk, but in more subdued tones about everyone in the packed room, and it wasn't a small room. They had hours of chatter ahead of them.

Half an hour and a few canapés later, Pete quieted the room. He wanted to thank all for coming and to thank them for helping him win the election. A chuckle went around the room, 'cocky bugger,' Phoebe thought. The election hadn't even taken place. Her phone rang. It was Josh. She excused herself and went and stood by the nearest wall. The group of yenta's watched her walk away and raised their eyebrows in unison. They could all easily guess who she was talking to.

'How are you bearing up?' Josh asked, concerned.

'Okay. But God isn't Pete up himself.'

'Is that a rhetorical question?'

She giggled. 'Thanks for arranging a lift for me. It was much appreciated.' She noticed Pete heading towards her out of the corner of her eye. 'Have to go.'

'Phoebe, what lift? Phoebe…'

'Ahhh, good to see you. Enjoying yourself?' 'Yes, I am,' she lied.

Pete looked her up and down. She was a looker. He wanted her, but he knew he must take his time with this one. She was not a pushover like the others.

'Did you get here okay?'

'Yes, thanks.' It took her a minute, but it soon dawned on her. 'You arranged the lift?'

'Think nothing of it, can't have beautiful women roaming around at night on their own now, can we? Especially after they have had a drink or two.'

She shifted uneasily from one foot to another as she mumbled her thanks. He moved in to kiss her on the cheek. His mouth lingered a little too long beside her ear. She could feel his warm breath, and she pulled back, so she was claiming her own space. He smirked and told her to mix with others, especially ministers who would help with her career. He would introduce her to them. She declined his 'kind' offer, but she was not feeling up to meeting new people.

'Would you mind if this pleasure was saved for another time?' He left her somewhat displeased but also a little excited about the chase. She was proving a hard nut to crack, but crack it he would. A waiter walked past her, and she grabbed a drink. Did Pete just make a pass at her? One thing for sure was that she no longer wanted to stay at this awful party. No one was really interested in her, the only one who was, wanted to bed her, so she left.

Once home, she called Josh. She wanted to be comforted by his voice. She wasn't going to tell him what had happened. Josh had placed himself in a very difficult position. If he argued with Pete, Pete would probably tell the PM about their little arrangement. Josh would lose his job, both of them would. But Josh didn't answer. Disappointed and feeling a little down, she would try and take her mind off things. It was still early in the night, and as she had nothing more interesting to do, she started packing. She didn't have much, so it didn't take long. Apartment hunting would be next on the agenda. She got out her laptop and started searching. This was a Godsend. It took her mind off everything for a while. After an hour or so, she had narrowed down her choices to a couple of apartments. The effects of the wine.

# Chapter 14

As soon as she opened the door, he grabbed her by the arms and pushed her onto the nearest wall. He kissed her hard, and she responded. Any pretence of guilt on her behalf, because she was still married, was washed away by his passion. Her jacket hit the floor, followed by her skirt. He soon followed, with his coat, shirt, shoes, and pants ripped off. He picked her up, carried her into the bedroom and threw her onto the bed.

There was an awkward moment when he struggled to undo her bra, but soon his mouth was on her breast. She gasped. She rubbed her hands through his hair as he explored both her nipples with his tongue. He was kissing her again. Slowly his hands produced such a feeling of lust that her lower back ached, and she could hardly wait for him to penetrate her. Finally, with a groan, he entered. Time almost stood still as waves of pleasure led to a long and protracted climax for both of them. Exhausted, he lay on her chest. They breathed heavily but with a profound sense of satisfaction. It was quite a few minutes before either of them could get their breath so they could speak.

'Wow, well, I wasn't expecting that tonight,' she whispered. 'I have thought of nothing else,' he replied.

She rolled over and leant on her elbow, looking at him intently for signs that he thought that he had had her as a conquest, like a smirk or a look of self-satisfaction.

She couldn't see any such expression, much to her relief.

She rolled onto her back, staring at the ceiling. 'Well, I have broken one of the Ten Commandments. Don't know how I feel about it either.'

'Are you referring to adultery?' he asked. 'Well, yes…I am.'

'Who did it first?' 'What do you mean?' 'You or him?'

'He did…Ohhhh, are you suggesting I use Prince Charles' escape clause? She did it first, so it is okay.'

'Well, if you want to put it that way. He broke his vows first. Once he has done it, you are free to do as you like as far as I am concerned. Besides, everyone has broken the commandments at some stage. Impossible to keep no matter how perfect you are. I, for sure, have broken most except for killing someone and believe me that has crossed my mind on numerous occasions.'

'Even you, Mr. Perfect…ha, ha,' she chuckled, mocking him for his high self-regard. He looked over at her with a cheeky grin.

'Did you enjoy it?' 'Yes.'

'Then be happy. How about drinks?'

'Do you want a coffee?'

Subject changed, a segue that any politician would be proud of.

'Not this time of night. So, how was it?' He pushed on.

'Fine, but boring. I think I hate having to mingle the most out of all the other things I hate about this job.' She looked over him, hoping he wouldn't see that she was hiding something.

'Me too,' he answered.

'I can't believe that. You always look like you are in your element, especially when the ladies are around. No, I don't believe you at all.' She tried to make light of the situation to cover her own somewhat flat-footed tracks.

'Believe me; it is all a charade. What did Shakespeare say? The world is a stage. I am just an outstanding actor. I really hate mixing. Believe me or not, no other ladies interest me. I would much rather be on my own or alone with you.'

That admission took her by surprise; she stared at the ceiling. Was this all going way too fast? The way she felt at that very moment, nothing in any previous relationship had ever felt so right. But there was the small matter of the nagging truth that she was still married and the man who had just bedded her, well he was a man with a troubled past, a very troubled past.

'Cat got your tongue?' He was a little put out that his declaration had resulted in reflective silence on her part.

'Um,' she responded.

'Cat got your tongue?' He said again, but a little more deliberately.

'No, not at all. I feel the same way. It's just that, well it has all been a little bit…'

'Quick?''Yes.'

'The sex, well I will try to…'

'Yes, no. You silly bugger. You know what I mean.'

Right at that moment, her thoughts about Josh's predicament crossed her mind.

'Josh, there is no chance that the PM will win, is there?'

'This is politics love, anything can happen.' He noticed her worried expression and sought to assuage her fear. 'But if I were a betting man, I would definitely put my money on Pete.'

'But what if the PM does win? Do you think Pete would tell him about your little arrangement? You would lose your job.'

'Yes and yes. But I am not a risk-taker, and as I said, I bet that Pete will win. Don't worry about things that haven't even happened yet. Let's enjoy the rest of the night and leave the office where it belongs, like a bad memory of yesterday.'

It had gone midnight. Josh had one thing on his mind now, and it wasn't sleeping.

They ate breakfast together the next morning, coffee and Vegemite on toast. But it could well have been Eggs Benedict with croissants; it was, they both said, the best breakfast they had had in a long while. Josh was upbeat about going to work. He was sure there would only be a few days left of pandering to the delinquent PM. Phoebe was less eager. Her day must entail avoiding Pete at all costs. She hoped it would be easy as he would be busy rustling up votes as it was the last few days of the campaign trail. She, however, was wrong.

Jean had left a note on her desk. It read:

*Sorry I am not here this morning, busy with posters. Pete wants you to fly to Perth with him. Meet at the airport at 3 PM. Take some clothes you're staying until after the election. He wants you there in his electorate when they announce the result.*

Phoebe went pale; the blood ran from her face. 'What the hell is he playing at?' Sitting down, she tapped her fingers on her desk. What to do? Go, or be sacked? Go and be pestered or stay and have no job. Pete would, in all probability, be expecting a little more than policy advice—not that he wanted that anyway. She began to question herself. Had he really made a pass? Had she imagined it? Urrrrgh! Why did everything boil down to sex? Why couldn't she go to work without being summed up as a 'nice piece'? Why did the worry of it take up more of her work time than it should? She went home to think; if she decided to go, she could have a bag packed ready to leave for Perth. If not, she would pack up the flat and leave Canberra forever.

The wind was blowing when she arrived at the airport. She was a little early. Pete had not arrived as yet. She mulled over her coffee and reflected on all that had happened. It had been a wild ride so far. If she had known the reality of politics in Canberra instead of holding a romantic vision of it, she would not, in all probability, be sitting in an airport drinking what could only be called mediocre coffee waiting to board a plane with an asshole.

Pete arrived in a flurry as photographers started to make a small mob in the foyer of the airport. No one bothered with her, after all, no one knew who she was. Phoebe got up and moved into a position where Pete could see her. She stood side by side with the mob. It was enlightening, the photographers clearly didn't like the future PM, and she had to stifle a laugh at the names they called him as they waited for him to walk by.

She was surprised to find that they had been given a private plane to fly to Perth and that she was the only one who was on board with him. What was he up to?

'So, where is everyone else?' She questioned him as they crossed the tarmac, a little nervous about the situation.

'Decided I needed a bit of a reprieve from the crowds. Let's say it's a well-deserved break before the real job is taken up.'

'And who gave you this plane to use?' She was really annoyed. He was so cocksure of himself and his ability to charm anyone who needed to be. Most PMs in waiting took a whole planeload of journalists. Not Pete, oh no, he had to show off and show her just how sure he was of himself. He would win, so why should he stick to a convention?'

'Isn't it a little bit of a conflict of interest?'

'What do you mean? You think I will give political favours to the one who was so generous?'

She looked out the window of the plane as it idled on the tarmac. She wanted this flight to be over. She knew one thing for sure. She wouldn't fly back with him on this plane. It was small, which meant they would spend the entire trip closer together than she would want to feel comfortable. She would repurchase her own ticket on a regular plane.

Pete was looking at a bottle of wine as he spoke to her, 'Well, I will say this, whoever it is will remain anonymous; therefore, you will not have to worry about it, okay. Sit back and relax, we have a long flight that will be filled with fine wine and food and, I am sure, a scintillating conversation.' She sucked in her breath as the engines roared to take them into the unknown.

Once they were allowed to take off their seatbelts, Pete asked the attentive stewardess to open the wine and provide a cheese platter. Phoebe could hardly believe it. It was as if they were on some sort of weird date, one she felt as if she had been tricked into; in reality, she had. Shame, in another reality, Phoebe would have enjoyed the experience of being on a private jet, but in this set of circumstances...no. All she wanted to do was to get off, and the sooner, the better. She sipped her wine. He passed her some cheese on a biscuit. She felt a lump in her throat. The smell of the cheese reminded her of the big fight with Mic that had led her to where she was now, 12 000 feet above the ground with a guy with the biggest ego she had ever met. She shook her head; she didn't want to eat. He popped it into his mouth instead. The crunching was enough to drive her crazy, and she drained her glass. He took this as a sign to pour her another. She didn't refuse. How many hours more? Too many as far as she was concerned. With the platter taken away, and the main meal being prepared, Pete looked at the side of her face. She had looked away from him the whole trip. This, however, was no deterrent. He had tamed stubborn women, some who he perceived to be a whole heap more so than her. She just needed a little bit of moulding; she would come round. The main meal arrived around 6 PM, three hours into the flight.

It looked absolutely delicious. Grilled chicken in mushroom and white wine sauce, sautéed potatoes, green beans, and honey drizzled carrots. Shame she wasn't hungry.

'Looks great.' Pete thanked the stewardess. Phoebe could only manage a half-hearted smile. She wouldn't eat it; it would be like giving in to this little setup.

'Well?' he queried, not hungry? She just shook her head. He ate. She, on the other hand, sat and wished the time away. If only…if only what?

If only she had stayed with Mic? No, she didn't want that. She felt too much for Josh. If only she hadn't taken this job, no, because again she wouldn't have even met Josh, she could not imagine life without him now. If only, if only, if only she weren't on this damn plane with this man, a man she knew was destined to have the country by the throat.

As they were preparing to land, Pete told her that he expected her to accompany him to his electorate and do some last-minute politicking. She, he assured her, would look good in the pictures, and she could be happy with the fact that she would be immortalised in print with the future Prime Minister on the day of his election, a grand tale for her grandkids. Great, she thought to herself. But she nodded her assent. They were quickly ushered to a waiting car. Pete took some calls, and she checked her phone for texts.

She realised that Josh didn't know where she was. She sent one word: 'Perth.'

She soon received his rather exasperated response 'What?' She sent back, 'Can't talk now will ring u tonight.'

The day dragged on. It was full of boasts, backslapping and self-aggrandisement. Pete was an insufferable bore. Phoebe walked behind him, smiling most of the day and trying to look at ease. But she was rather lousy at it. She could have screamed every time someone said to her what a great guy he was. She smiled through gritted teeth and agreed. From one school to the next, sporting club to shopping mall, the day was endless.

The next morning Josh downloaded ABC news hoping to get a glimpse of Pete on the last day of his campaign, and of course, Phoebe. He was busy seeing to the incumbent PM whose days were numbered literally to one. Everyone knew this of course, except the PM. We are doing really well, aren't we? Josh could only lie.

'Yes, PM We are.' He looked down at his phone on which he could see Pete waving and smiling; following not too far behind was Phoebe. Josh could tell from her body language that she wasn't having much fun. What the hell was he playing at? Why drag her across the country when he had hardly taken any notice of her since her arrival?

'Josh!'

'Yes.'

'I am getting out of the car here to make a little speech before we head to the club for dinner. What do you think?'

'Yes, good idea.' It really didn't matter what he did. 'Where are we?'

'I think we are at Eastwood School.' The PM left the car. Josh had told Phoebe where he was headed, but she had not mentioned Perth, not at all. He could not shake the feeling that Pete was up to something. It troubled him. He would never trust him, especially with Phoebe.

The results came in early. The hotel where they were staying and having election drinks erupted into wild applause and death-defying cheers of victory. Pete won by a landslide. Phoebe congratulated him, and he responded by grasping her hand, bringing it up to his mouth and kissing it slowly while looking deep into her eyes. She wanted to puke. A photographer quickly caught the scenario on camera, and it was uploaded onto a myriad of social networking sites with the caption—is the new PM in love? The full force of the political body moved to have an apology made under threat of a massive lawsuit. The wayward photographer issued a groveling apology. After all, as everyone knows, the newly minted PM is happily married. Not long after this debacle, Pete's wife was by his side, smiling and waving to show that they were indeed a happily married couple. It was a lesson learned by the PM to keep out of the way of photographers when embarking on seduction.

Even though the picture and the caption were soon taken down, Josh saw the image on Twitter. He wasn't happy. What the hell is going on? Phoebe was in Perth. But why? As an attractive sidekick for the PM? Why the hell was he kissing her hand, and so publicly? What was he playing at? From the look on Phoebe's face, she was not impressed by the gesture; at least he was thankful for that. He needed to talk to her, to find out that she was okay. What worried him most was the thought that Pete himself may have designs on Phoebe. If that were the case, he would tell him unequivocally that was not an option, not negotiable, and was definitely not something he would tolerate. His job would be lost, but that was something he could live with. He could not give up Phoebe, not now. Shit, shit, shit. He knew he would have to think about this. Not rush in. Why in the hell had he taken up his job offer? He could have a little cozy, albeit boring job with the coalition playing shadow puppets now if he hadn't.

As it was, Pete had him where he wanted him, and as it stood, Josh was in no man's land. The loser of the election had retreated to his home, entirely shocked that he had lost. Josh had to tell him that he no longer worked for him and then congratulate Pete.

Every nerve in his body was telling him to quit, stay as he was, but if he did that, he wouldn't be able to keep his eye on Pete and, in turn, Phoebe. He needed to talk to her, face to face, not over the phone. What to do? He sent her a text asking her to call him so they could make arrangements to meet. He couldn't go to work tomorrow. Where would he go? His old office or his new one? This situation had become way more complicated than he had ever expected. A drink, somewhere, somewhere where no one would recognise him. An out of town pub would provide a place where he could sit and wait for Phoebe to ring, in peace and alone. He found one and waited for her to call.

***

Election night was a long one. Phoebe finally fell into her hotel bed, exhausted and somewhat angry. Pete had proven himself to be a self-centred pain in the backside. Tomorrow she would book herself an ordinary plane ticket and get back to Josh. Together they needed to sort out what to do. Would they work for Pete or move on? What to do? Josh had held a position in the political to-ings and fro-ings in Canberra for many years. She, on the other hand, was a newcomer. It would be easy for her to leave. But she would be giving up on something she had strived for and had worked very hard to achieve. A tear rolled down her cheek, and she fell into a fitful sleep. Tomorrow was another day; hopefully, she would wake up with a better attitude towards life, love and the world in general.

***

He left the pub at closing time and tried to call a cab. One would be there in about half an hour. He started to walk towards the city. Josh tried to ring Phoebe again, but all he got was her voice mail. She had forgotten to ring him, and her phone was dead. He reasoned that she must be asleep. He wandered towards the cold streets of Canberra, having given up on the cab, waiting for her to call, but the call didn't come. The rest of the country may be celebrating the election, but he certainly wasn't and never would. Canberra was a lonely place on many nights, but it was especially so on this one. He even felt estranged from his familiar surroundings. There must be more to life than living in a political web that strangles those who see its real character. Tomorrow he had some critical decisions to make. Hopefully, the rising sun would help him to think clearly. He knew Phoebe would have just run out of puff. Election days were exhausting; she would ring. With that thought, he finally arrived at his flat and went to bed.

***

Phoebe woke early, looked around in a sleepy haze, not quite remembering where she was. It took a minute or two for her to remember that she was on the other side of the country and that Pete had won the election in a landslide. If he were obnoxious before, he would be doubly so now. She would get room service to break her hunger. She didn't want to go to the in-house restaurant; she was not up to seeing anyone, let alone anyone she might know or have to put up with. An omelet and strong black coffee, and to top it all off, a blackberry Danish. There was no way she was going to endure another long flight with Pete on a private plane. So she booked a seat on Jet star. Her plane didn't leave till 3 PM, so she had plenty of time to relax, stay in bed and just breathe. In any other circumstance, she may have enjoyed a luxury flight. It would be much better if it was with Josh, and they were heading to somewhere really nice.

She headed for the bathroom and looked in the mirror. Her eyes were a little blurry, so she splashed her face with cool water. Once dry, she noticed that her cheeks were dotted with small red marks, sort of like welts. She put it down to rub her face hard with the bath towel. She still felt tired. Breakfast arrived, and she had a long hot shower to relieve stress once she had had her fill. She plugged her phone in to charge, and just as she was thinking about phoning Josh, she received a text from her mother—Mic's girlfriend pregnant, he is over the moon. She stared at the message. It took a little while for it to sink in. Mic was going to be a dad. It was something he had always wanted. But she was not the mother; another woman had that opportunity, someone else was going to give him a child. Her emotions ebbed and flowed within seconds, happy for him but sad for herself. He was happy, and she wasn't. She hadn't wanted a baby. She had wanted a career, a career that she was desperately trying to make work. She did want a baby eventually, but not now and, as hard as it was to say, not Mic's.

Deep down, she was delighted that he was happy. She acknowledged that she wasn't, but it had nothing to do with her biological clock. She glanced at the text again. Her mother would not have sent it; she wasn't any good with anything other than making phone calls.

It was, in all probability, her sister, or even Mic himself. She knew her mother kept in contact with him. All she could manage in reply was a smiley face. She sat on the bed and sipped her coffee. She fell into a stare, looking out the window into the bright morning sky. She took a few minutes to concentrate on what was good about her life. There was only one thing: Josh. She went back for her phone and noticed all the missed calls he had made the previous night. A wry smile crossed her face. With him, they could conquer the situation, of that she was very sure—she put the text to the back of her mind but would send Mic something nice for the baby in due course.

***

It felt good to be back in Canberra. She couldn't say that she enjoyed flying as she liked to be in control or to at least see who was, but the flight back was far less stressful. She knew Josh was waiting for her. Back at her apartment, however, the reality of her situation hit home. The place was bare, not at all welcoming. She had almost forgotten that she had to move. Emptiness. The bare necessities were there, so she made herself a cup of tea and thought about letting Josh know she had arrived home. Her hands ached. As she waited for the kettle to boil, she opened and closed her hands, trying to alleviate the aching. She was still tired. She thought it might be best to go to bed rather than tell Josh she was home. It was late. That is just what she did.

***

7 AM, Josh is on the phone.

'Phoebe, I have been trying to ring you. Where have you been?' She could hear what he was saying, but she found it hard to respond. Deathly fatigue had hit her, and even speaking was proving to be almost impossible.

'Josh, sorry, I just don't feel too good. Can I ring you back?' She had forgotten all about the post-election meeting.

'Phoebe, what about the meeting? We both have to go. This is where the shit, will in all probability, hit the fan, and we both need to be there. I know you have had a few rough days but just try to make it in this morning. Please. Then take the afternoon off.'

'Okay.' Was all Phoebe could say in response to Josh pushing her to do something she just didn't want to do. In truth, he was a little concerned about her while she was away.

She hadn't rung, but considering how unwell she sounded, he knew that she would have gone to bed as soon as she arrived home. He just hoped that she could pull herself together for the meeting. He was worried that his job might not be forthcoming. Pete may not hold his pre-election promises. If he didn't, then Josh knew his future was in real jeopardy. Phoebe was the only other witness to this promise. He needed her to be there.

After she got off the phone, she dragged herself out of bed with a head clogged with fatigue. She could hardly think straight. Where was the coffee? She couldn't see it, but it was where it usually sat. She felt like someone had given her a drug. After a strong black coffee, she showered and looked through her bag of clothes for something to wear. Never had it been so hard to dress. Fingers and thumbs got in the way. Finally, she was able to call a taxi to take her to the meeting that she had apparently forgotten all about. She really wanted to go back to bed. She promised herself rest in the afternoon. She would sleep, and she was sure she would feel better in the morning. On stepping out of the taxi at Parliament House, she stood for a minute trying to garner the energy to walk to where the meeting was to be held. It actually took her a few minutes to think of where it was. She fought an overwhelming feeling of wanting to lie down on the grass just a few feet from where she stood. She imagined herself curled up in a little ball, enjoying the coolness of the outside air and the shade of the trees. She felt a little warm. Never in her life had she felt so tired as she did at that very moment. With great determination, she placed one foot in front of the other. She was not looking forward to seeing the new PM. Pete was not a man to be trifled with, and her actions on the plane had made him quite short and curt with her. He felt that no matter who you were, he deserved your unmitigated attention. A throwback from childhood, spoilt and much so, no matter what he wanted, his mother made sure he got it, be it attention, presents, cars, phones or food. If he wanted her, and she had a feeling he did, as she and Josh were an item, then they were goners. But the way she felt, she couldn't care less. The thought of laying in the shade was overwhelmingly more inviting than working in this place any longer—her dream job had turned into a nightmare.

She saw Josh just as he was about to enter the meeting room.

'Phoebe?' He called her name as a question as she looked terrible. She raised her hand in a limp gesture, which suggested she felt as bad as she looked. She also shook her head at him. She didn't want anyone to see them talking, not yet, not until their futures were certain. She went in first, and a minute later, Josh entered. Pete was at the head of the table waiting for staff members to turn up. He stood as Phoebe walked in and greeted her as if she was the most important person coming to the meeting. He did the same with Josh.

'Good to see you, Josh, my man. Told you I was a sure bet. You made the right decision. Sit. Sit, would you like some coffee?'

As he replied, with a 'yes please,' he could feel all eyes on him. Some even held their mouths wide open in disbelief. He was, for his part, trying with all his willpower not to look in Phoebe's direction.

'How about you Phoebe, coffee? Or would you like tea?'

'Coffee this morning for me, thanks.' She didn't look at him but at the floor. He looked over the top of her head as he made the orders. They waited for their drinks, and as they did, the stragglers rolled into the room. All of them saw Josh and looked surprised that he was at the meeting but tried not to let it show. They didn't want anything, even their facial expression to annoy the PM. Most discussed the election results in hushed tones as they waited for the demand to sit. The meeting was for staff such as Phoebe and other policy advisors—Josh was to be the new chief of staff, and his welcome by Pete was nothing less than astonishing. The rest of them were told that 'he' was their man and that nothing would get through to him, the PM, without Josh's approval. All stared at Josh, not quite believing what they were hearing. Pete rambled on about how he wanted things done, threatened anyone who was tempted to leak anything to the press. Talking to the press was his prerogative and no one else's unless he gave the go-ahead. Threateningly, he also stated that everything about them, what they were doing in their day-to-day work, life, their family and their love life was now his property, his concern—He would know everything about them. These were the rules, and if they didn't like it, they could choose to walk away—now.

Too many pollies and their staff members had crossed the line when it came to public trust—he would know what everyone was up to. No-one knew if that included surveillance; all would cover computer cameras with tape when they got to their office. They all stared at Pete, uncomfortable with what they had just heard. Did he mean it? They all supposed he did. Pete, satisfied that they understood, made his apologies. He had to go and decide on a caucus and who his MPs would be. Everyone knew he already had it arranged, but no one said anything. They just watched him leave in disbelief. Joy at the election win was now somewhat muted by the oppression and dictator-like tendencies displayed by the new leader. As they streamed out of the meeting room, Josh sent Phoebe a text; could she meet him in the staff canteen. They needed to talk, and they could do so there in relative isolation. Just as he sent his text, he received one. It was the former PM, and he wanted to speak to him a.s.a.p. Josh sent Phoebe another text putting off their meeting until just after lunch. It was going to be a long, arduous day. Phoebe read the text and didn't know if she would make it to lunch, never mind thinking about being around after it. She was just so dogged tired.

# Chapter 15

Josh knocked at his old master's office door. 'Come in' was the response. He entered. The now vanquished PM was sitting at his desk. As Josh neared, he could see the colour of the older man's face turn bright red. On reaching the desk, he just stood looking down at the top of his head. No words were forthcoming. It was like the diminutive politician was so angry his mind could not formulate the words needed to express it. Anger was probably too soft a word; acrimony, rage, vexation, hate, displeasure. No word was appropriate that fitted the situation or the wrath of the man in front of him.

Josh, in turn, shifted uncomfortably on his feet. He went to say something when a hand shot up to silence him. Josh drew in his breath, waiting for the explosion that was about to happen.

To his amazement, he was told to sit down, which he did, dutifully in the chair facing him. Silence. Josh was very uncomfortable; this was not what he had been expecting.

Both men looked at each other straight in the eye. 'Josh,' he said, face reddening, 'you and I have worked together for many years. I have thought of you as not only as my chief of staff but also my friend, and a very close one at that.' Josh looked at his shoes, shiny under the glare of the lights above; he could cope with angry outbursts but not a reminiscence of their past working life together. It was too much, but it continued. 'I always thought I could trust you, and I believed you had my best interests at heart. And as for the party, well…' both looked into space until his ex-boss let himself go. 'That is why I am incredulous that you have taken a position with that imbecile, who is now the PM, which grates me to admit and makes my bones ache.' Josh went to speak, but a tiny and defiant hand was held up again, which shut him up. Josh watched as his former boss regained some composure. 'All I can conclude from this is that you never had mine or the party's interests at heart or as your motivating factor in working for me. You only had your own self-interests at heart. You were very good at your job, but you were not loyal to the position you held, as obvious as it is to me now. You deceived me in a way I could never have imagined. You have lied, been secretive and come out of it shining brightly in a new job with the ruling party.

'You have proved yourself to be better at underhand dealings than any politician I know; well done.'

Josh was uncomfortable. He hated politicians, and to be labelled as one was an insult to his very being.

'Just let me say this, if your position with that creep ever falls flat, which I am inclined to believe it will, two egomaniacs cannot, for long, work together, you will never find another position in Canberra, or for that matter any state parliament or council chamber. You are done for in the public service, even as a street cleaner. So enjoy your time while you can. I don't have your back anymore. You have made a potent enemy, in fact, many enemies. I am sure in due course you will make yourself another one in Pete. Now get out of my office before I really let you know how I feel.' He left the room and shut the door. A loud crash on the other side of the door signaled a paperweight thrown just as he closed the door. Josh headed straight to the first place he could find scotch. He needed a very stiff drink.

***

With Pete busy and Josh away to meet his come-uppence, Phoebe decided to go see the doctor. She was sure it was the flu or something or other. A pill would cure-all. She didn't have time to be ill; Pete had thrown a lot of work her way. Some of which was surprisingly very interesting. An hour later and she was in the waiting room. She sent a message to Josh—can't make our meeting, let you know when we can meet up—OK, was the reply. He wasn't in the mood for texting; he was onto his fourth drink. He knew he should stop drinking and get to work on something, but he was feeling a bit adrift and needed to relax a little before heading into another lion's den.

The doctor was looking over her details as Phoebe looked around the room. It was neat and filled with all sorts of health-related material.

'Now, Phoebe, let me know how you have been feeling.'

'Well, my job is hectic. I am an advisor to the PM,' she expected him to be impressed, but he wasn't. Who in this town wasn't an advisor to the PM? She continued, 'and I am usually OK, but lately, I have been feeling exhausted, like, to the point of not wanting to get out of bed in the morning even though I have had a good night's sleep.'

'All right, any other symptoms you can think of? Aches and pains anywhere, periods OK?'

Phoebe thought about it for a minute, 'period's fine, but sometimes my hands hurt a little, a bit stiff. I find it hard at times to write with a pen for very long.'

'OK, let's check your temperature and blood pressure.' She looked at the doctor while he messed around doing what doctors do. Middle-aged, she guessed, married with grown kids. Polite but probably bored seeing people who are worried day after day, but getting on with it anyway. She liked to think she could read people.

'Blood pressure OK, but your temperature is slightly raised. I might send you off to get some blood taken, OK? Just to check if your tiredness could be because you lack iron or something like that.'

'Ohh. I thought I might just have the flu or something?'

'Well, apart from the temperature, you don't really have flu symptoms. As I said, it may just be low iron levels. Do your hands hurt now?'

'No. Not really.'

'I would suggest you go and get yourself some iron tablets while we wait for the blood to come back. Also, you do have a very demanding job. Any chance you can take a break?'

***

Back in her office, Phoebe scoffed at the doctor's advice to take a break. She had a huge black coffee in front of her and a pile of papers to look through. She pulled up the collection of documents and rested her head on them; she would take his advice and have a 10-minute snooze.

'Knock, knock,' Phoebe was out to it on her desk. She didn't hear the knocking.

'Knock, knock.' The door opened, it was Jean. Phoebe could barely look up.

'Sorry to interrupt, but you have a meeting in 10 minutes with some other advisors, you know, about the women's health thingy. I did tell you about it earlier, but you must have forgotten. Anyway, I have bought you in a fresh coffee.' Phoebe could feel saliva on the edges of her mouth and quickly wiped it away.

'God, what is the time, Jean?' '3 o'clock just about.'

‘What?’ Phoebe had been asleep on her desk for around 2 hours. ‘How did that happen?’

‘Phoebe, look, I know it’s none of my business, but you have been very busy lately; maybe some time off would help, blue skies, sand?’ She handed Phoebe her coffee.

‘Thanks.’ Phoebe knew the tiredness was more than just being busy from long hours and the stress of all the politics that came with the job. She was fighting exhaustion on a massive scale. It hit her when she least expected it like a tonne of bricks. She had never felt this tired in her entire life, and a week on the beach was not going to fix it. Here’s to hoping the results of her blood would show something that could be remedied quickly.

‘Who did you say I was meeting with?’

As Jean was going through the list of meeting attendees, Josh was recovering from his liquid lunch. Pete had already made some rather hard to fulfill demands, such as replacing his old car with a new luxury model that the plebs, as he put it, would not get too upset about.

He also wanted his stuff moved as quickly as possible into the Prime Minister’s Office—‘get that little runt out a.s.a.p.’ were his words. Following protocol was not his strong point. It was usual to let the defeated incumbent have a few weeks, even a month, to get over their loss and move their stuff out. Pete would have none of it; he wanted the office and the PM’s lodgings and nothing would stop him from claiming it all right away. He had the right to demand it. Good manners, as in the past, played no part in Pete’s political world.

Phoebe felt a little better for the sleep. She tidied herself up and headed off to her meeting. Why she had to get to know a group of women who were seeking to ingratiate themselves with the new PM, she would never know. Jean said they were from the ‘women against the hatred of women’ league. What the hell did that mean? And how had they managed to get a meeting this early in the piece? She was sure Pete set this up just to annoy her. It was not her job to meet and greet these people; she was his advisor on women's issues—issues that would make a difference, not his substitute for those he couldn't be bothered to see—women against the hatred of women league—what the...?

She smiled as best as she could when entering the room. Soon a yawn was stifled, which she tried to hold under her breath but failed. Opening her mouth wide and letting a long yawn out, she apologised to the group and made up a story of late nights working on some report or another. They all responded with thoughtful nods of their heads to let her know that they too, had a busy life filled with little else but trying to break down glass ceilings all over the country. If ever there was a stereotypical look to those deemed to be 'radical feminists', then the room was full of them. She suddenly felt a little too girly and pulled at the hem of her skirt and tried to make her lipstick less visible.

Sitting down at the extended meeting table, she settled in to listen to what they had to say. Her initial hesitancy turned to intrigue as she found herself very interested in their conversation. She was impressed. After the allotted hour, she thanked them all for coming and that she would pass on their thoughts and ideas to the PM. He had assured her he was very interested in anything to do with helping women meet the challenges of the modern world, including the rise of misogyny and the barriers in the workforce that still impeded them.

All of the attendees left quite pleased with themselves and very impressed with Phoebe. That wasn't so bad; Phoebe thought to herself as she went back to her office. In fact, they were very educated and articulate women. She scolded herself for being so affected by the way they dressed. Wasn't it a women's right to wear what they wanted? She would write up a report for Pete about the meeting. She was sure that if he gave his political support to some of the issues they had bought up, he would be a clear winner in gaining the confidence of the female populace. She noticed her hands throbbing and stiff as she sat down to type. It was getting on for 5.30—she would write the report tomorrow.

Josh was waiting for her when she arrived back at her flat. He had left work early as well. He was tired but not exhausted in the way Phoebe felt. A good sleep that night would fix him up. Phoebe felt like she could sleep for a couple of days and then some more. Most of her stuff was packed up as she was hoping to have word back the next day regarding a little apartment not far from where she was now.

'When do your blood results come back, Phoebe?'

She was making a cup of coffee for them both. 'In a day or two,' she mumbled. He sensed her fatigue.

'Hey, how about I get us something really nice to eat for dinner? What do you fancy? Pizza, Chicken, Thai, Chinese? You just tell me what you want, and I will get it. I want you to eat, and I don't want you cooking, now what do you want?'

'Josh, I am so tired I just want to sleep. I don't think I have the energy to eat.'

'No,' he said, as he took off his jacket, 'that is not going to happen, you must eat first.' He was on a roll, 'not eating will not help. In fact, it will help you sleep. Your stomach will be so busy digesting food; it will make you snoozy. How about I go and get something and surprise you—eh?'

She gave in. 'If you like.'

'Here, drink up your cup of coffee first.' Josh looked at her; she didn't look well to him. She looked a bit drawn, and her sparkle seemed to be missing. 'Phoebe, you have a bit of redness on your face. Is it a rash or something? Go and have a look in the bathroom mirror.'

She looked at herself. She had redness that crossed her nose, which spread down to her cheeks just under her eyes. She took a photo of it with her phone. She would show the doctor on her next visit; just as she finished taking the picture, Josh came into the bathroom. 'What do you think it is?'

'Probably nothing, a bit of sun, I suppose, but I will show the doctor the photo of it on my next visit.'

Josh returned with dinner; curry chicken dish and rice and fried ice cream with caramel sauce to top it off. Phoebe was asleep upon the lounge, her phone cast on the coffee table.

'Phoebe, I am back,' he struggled with the takeaway bags as he shut the door. 'I will dish up, and you really must eat something.'

She opened one eye to see what he had bought home. 'I am really tired Josh, I don't think…'

'Don't tell me that you are not going to eat this feast? I have navigated tribes of world-weary men and a group of girls on the prowl for a good time.' He noticed her phone on the table. 'Err, were you speaking on the phone?'

'Mum.'

'What did she want?'

'To tell me how well everyone is going and how she is always being taken here and there and everywhere by someone that is not me, basically.'

'Oh good for her, well a good curry will liven you up.' 'Doubt it.'

'Get up and eat.'

Phoebe hated to admit it, but she did feel better after the curry. Indian food was an old favourite. Her mind wandered back to when she was in Wales with Mic; oh so long ago now. It was bitterly cold, and they were both starving. They had never had an Indian meal before. Australia had no such thing as an Indian restaurant back then, not to her knowledge anyway. Feeling adventurous, they decided to give it a try. Well, they were overwhelmed not only by the interior of the restaurant but by the food. Never before had they experienced the colour, aromas, and textures that they had set before them. They spent more than three hours in that restaurant taking it all in. From then on, they had Indian food each week if they could afford it. They thought it was funny that they would fall in love with Indian food in such a place as Wales.

'Penny for them.' 'What?'

'A penny for your thoughts.'

'Oh, just thinking about when I first had Indian food.' 'Long story is it?'

'No, not at all,' she replied softly.

Josh left it at that. He noticed that she was becoming a bit reflective at times, like she was reassessing all that was going on in her life. He was starting to wonder if she was regretting their relationship. But, told himself, he would not pry. She would tell him what was going on when she was ready.

While they were eating, she realised that he would have had to go to a Chinese takeaway as well as Thai to get the food they were now enjoying.

'You spoil me,' she said. He nodded in agreement.

'Well, are we going to bed? I have a hell of a day tomorrow.' Josh was picking up the remnants of the meal to put in the fridge for a leftover treat tomorrow. 'Pete has already upset some of his ministers. He is not going to stick to one of his election promises, as they thought, giving pensioners free train travel once a year to a destination of choice anywhere in the country. Ha, those ministers practically won their seats on that.

Now they have to go and try and make him stick to it, or they will have a lot of explaining to do back in their electorates. I wish them well with all that. They all know what he is like, so not much sympathy there. Pete never makes political promises, only statements that may or may not be true, and then he can retract them. He argues that it is his ministers that turn what he says into promises, and he will not be turned. Slippery fellow, one of the best at deflecting what he is accused of saying into something completely different.'

Phoebe was staring at him while he rattled on. He noticed, and without rhyme or reason, he lurched into describing how to make a dry martini. He loved nothing more than imagining himself in his little cocktail bar on the beach, creating what he thought would amount to the world's best drinks. Everyone would travel the globe just to have one.

Phoebe was bemused but only half-listening. She also had a hard day ahead of her; meeting with the new women's minister. This one was very good friends with Danielle, so she knew she was in for a frosty reception no matter what else happened during the day.

***

Phoebe was busy in her office when Pete came in. She was surprised. She thought he had things to attend to in another state.

'Pete, to what do I owe this visit?'

'Not much, just checking up on my women's advisor…err, you're meeting with the women's minister today, aren't you?'

'Yes, why?'

'Just don't take anything she says too seriously. Women have it pretty good, and she just wants to make us men look bad. She is carrying on about more mummy time or some such rubbish, rich bitch stuff. Just humour her for me—Eh?'

'Tell her that I am all for it or whatever and that I will bring it up before cabinet shortly—just don't tell her how near. This one is feistier than the last one who was always lurking off to look after her children.'

Phoebe gritted her teeth. Pete had unceremoniously given the last minister the shove to the backbench. He wanted a woman to have no responsibilities other than the government. Families get in the way. No women graced the cabinet room in a political capacity. The only female to enter that hollowed turf was Danielle, who many thought outclassed all and sundry with her behind the scenes machinations.

'Oh, do I detect disapproval? You have it good, no reason to jeopardise your position, eh?'

'Just answer me this Pete. What is the point of giving anyone a Ministerial position if you don't listen to them regarding their portfolios?'

'Well, I have people like you to tell me what I need to know.'

'But you don't listen to us either.'

'Wow, we are a little edgy today. How about I take you to lunch, and we can talk it through? Meet at the trough at about 1.30?'

'No thanks, I am meeting someone else for lunch.'

'Well, if it's Josh, then I am afraid you're not. He has gone interstate for me and won't be back until tomorrow. Good luck with the minister and see you at 1.30.'

He left. Phoebe couldn't believe it. Josh hadn't let her know. She checked her phone, no messages or texts from him. What was Pete up to? And more importantly, why would he suggest Josh be her lunch date? He must know something about them; in fact, she was sure he did.

Her office phone rang. It was Jean. 'Phoebe I must tell you that the Minister for Women's Affairs is in the meeting room. Um, I think I should warn you that she has Danielle with her.' Phoebe hung up. Her head was aching, and her muscles and joints along with it. She didn't know if she would have the wits to be able to humour both of these women at the same time, especially Danielle, who was always looking for a weakness to exploit. It suddenly struck her: If Pete knew about her and Josh, it was Danielle who told him. This was going to be a fascinating meeting.

On her way there, Phoebe started to question why it should be such a big deal for people to know about her and Josh. Sure, she wasn't divorced as yet, but that was just a formality. Mic had moved on, very much so, and was happy. She couldn't claim to be happy, not due to Josh in any way, but due to her situation. Her dream job sucked, literally. She hated what she saw and knew of politics. It wasn't noble or selfless, which she had thought in her somewhat delusional days as a student. It was hostile, selfish and narcissistic. She had given up life with a good man for this crap. But deep down, she knew it would have ended up in divorce from Mic in the long run. She wasn't really sure why she knew that, but she did. She needed to spread her wings, and if it weren't for this job, something else would have intervened. Mic was more of a homebody, he liked his routine. As it was, Mic was happy, and she was glad for him. In a snap decision, she decided she didn't care any longer about people knowing about her and Josh. She hoped Josh felt the same. Just as she was about to enter the meeting room, she received a voicemail from him.

'I have been sent chasing my tail in Tasmania to see what Pete's factional buddies want to do about a logging contract. But

I think they have already made up their minds—don't think it is above board. Talk to you later.'

The factions ran the party and were, to her, an insidious rot that threatened the very heart of politics. It was the main reason Pete never listened to advisors or ministers. He was 'advised' by those who bequeathed him the premiership, and it was their wants and needs that were first and foremost, not those who voted for his government. It had taken her a little while to realise the power wielded by the factions. She was hoping to be able to undermine them but was still trying to work out how. On that happy thought, she braced herself and entered the viper room.

They were huddled around the coffee machine and didn't hear her come in. Their conversation had them so enthralled they had lost the ability to sense when there was an intrusion. For her part, Phoebe wondered if they were talking about some great policy or plans that the minister had made to make women's lives better. She knew better than that. They, were in fact, gossiping about her and Josh. Of course they were. Once they were aware of her presence which took at least two minutes, they turned towards her with what looked very much like smirks on their faces. Smirks Phoebe would have loved to wipe off with one quick smack.

'Hello, Phoebe,' drawled Danielle. 'We were just talking about you and Josh. How is the romance going?'

'Ha, Danielle, you have a very active imagination,' Phoebe replied, having decided when entering the room not to share anything with these two about her and Josh, in fact, nothing to do with her or any part of her life.

'Err, my dear, I don't imagine anything, I tend to know what is going on, and after all, it is my job to keep my ear to the ground, especially when it comes to romance and illicit affairs.'

Phoebe ignored her and held out her hand to the minister. 'Hello, nice to see you again, minister.'

'You too,' she replied as she looked Phoebe up and down. She didn't seem in the least put out that the little tete-a-tete she was having with Danielle was interrupted by the very subject of the topic.

'Well, I don't know about you, Minister, but I am far too busy for gossip, especially about myself. I am sure you have better things to do as well.' Out loud, the minister agreed with Phoebe, but she did enjoy the gossip; and this gossip was quite juicy. She was pleasantly surprised by Phoebe's directness, not something she had expected from what Danielle had said about her being largely wishy-washy. She had expected a wallflower type of person.

'Let's take a seat then, shall we.' Phoebe was not going to be bullied by anyone. 'Danielle?' Phoebe pulled out a chair for her to take a seat. The minister had sat down. Instead of taking up the offer, Danielle headed for the door.

'No thanks, like you, I have better things to do.' She wasn't going to win any point against Phoebe today. They listened to her heels click their way down the corridor. Rather belatedly, Phoebe said, 'Okay, bye.'

The minister thought it great fun to see these two women at each other's throats. She rather liked Phoebe and felt that the battle would not be as one-sided as she first suspected. Phoebe looked at her and nodded for her to commence whatever it was she was there for.

Phoebe had to listen to the minister as she talked about some focus group report she had reviewed. Phoebe had read it as well but had decided to throw it in the bin. Phoebe had read many of these so-called reports and focus group findings. Lots were based on pseudo-science and don't really mean anything much—

it's the methodology that counts, and some reports missed this bit or did it rather poorly. But many in Canberra took them seriously, as the minister was doing, primarily if the findings reflect some of their own firmly held beliefs or those of their electorate. Phoebe's heart sank as the minister interpreted the results, telling Phoebe what a good idea some rather low-value policy would be that could evolve from the findings. She made herself look interested.

'What a good idea, Minister, I am sure the PM will be very interested in this.' In actual fact, she knew for sure he wouldn't.

'Could you give me a copy of the report, and I can have a look at it?' She didn't want to acknowledge to the minister that she had already read it and thought it was tripe.

The minister handed her a hard copy. Yep, it was the very one she had dismissed out of hand. It suggested there was a need for middle-class women to get free time to be 'self-actualising'—whatever the hell that meant. They could only do this with more funding for childcare workers or for some type of place where children could be left so they could go off and have a massage or meditate. Phoebe was sure that was all that was needed in regards to women's rights, more middle-class welfare. She knew the minister was only upholding the views and wants of her rather affluent electorate. But even so, it highlighted the loss of collective welfare in the community to special needs welfare, even for those that didn't need it.

'Well, Phoebe,' the minister turned to face her as she headed for the door. 'You have surprised me. I had expected a bitch of a woman from Danielle's description of you. But you are a rather nice person, I think. All her dislike for you stems from her jealousy. You have caught yourself the uncatchable—one that Danielle let go. She will never forgive you for that. So watch out. She is a formidable foe. I keep her on the good side just for that very reason. Watch your back.' With that, the minister left the meeting room, mobile phone in hand.

'Wow.' Phoebe had not expected that. She stood dumbfounded for a minute, taking it all in; she was tired, dog-tired. With the report under her arm, she headed back to her office. As she passed a rather large bin, she dropped the report into it. She didn't have the strength to carry it all the way back to her office.

# Chapter 16

The next morning, Phoebe received a call from Josh. 'I am not liking this working for Pete business,' he said down the phone to her.

'No, neither am I,' she replied. There was a long silence. Both of them did not know what to say. Life was way too complicated. Their silence reflected the fact that they did not know how to make it less so.

As an afterthought, Phoebe asked, 'Where are you? Are you still in Tasmania?'

'Queensland?' 'What? Why?'

'I have asked myself that question many times this morning.'

'Who the hell are you meeting with this time?'

'Some joker from the business council up here, not sure who he represents. He wants to see if he can get government approval to put some God-awful development close to the Barrier Reef. I am doubtful, but he seems convinced our new PM is all for it. That I do believe. What's the Barrier Reef when there is a load of dodgy money to be made—eh? Just like what is the wilderness of Tasmania but a product to be bought and sold?

'Rrrrrr.' Phoebe's anger was audible. 'I tell you what; I think that half my problem is that I now know too much, and it wears me out. Any semblance of believing politics is for the people has been beaten out of me. I am exhausted.'

'Me too.'

Another long silence, Josh was the first to break it. 'Well, babe, I had better head off now. I will say this though, last night, I dreamt of a better world but still woke up in this one. It sort of bummed my morning.'

‘What? Beach fronts and bars?’ ‘No, just a better world.’

‘Ha, ha, ha. Josh, when I first met you, you were all for yourself and getting what you could out of a job. Be careful; you sound like you give a damn.’

‘Frankly, my dear, we can’t have that now, can we.’

‘No, we can’t. Ha, ha, ha. A very good comeback.’ ‘See you.’

He laughed.

‘Tomorrow?’

‘Hopefully. If Pete doesn’t send me to another part of the country to keep me out of the way. You know, I don’t think he cares about what I’m doing flying around the country. He wants me out of the way for other reasons.’ Phoebe didn’t respond. She didn’t want to think about what he was implying. He would explain when he came back.

Later that morning, Phoebe was sitting in her office reading over a policy measure that would benefit not only wealthy women but all women. She didn’t care if Pete looked at it or not, her job was to provide sound policy advice, and she just got on with it. She would put it on his desk, and he would probably do what she had done to the minister’s report—bin it!

She put down her pen and rubbed her hands. They ached. The typing and writing played havoc with them. Her only ring, a dress ring from her single days, would not budge. Her fingers looked like sausages, and they felt creaky when she clenched her fists.

‘Old age,’ she mumbled to herself. She was only in her early 30s so it was a rather self-defeating remark, but it was just how she felt. It was soon lunchtime, of which she was glad. Something nice to eat, something really naughty like fish and chips would do the trick and a few steaming hot coffees, a heart attack waiting to happen sort of lunch. Making her way to the pigpen, as she had come to call it, she saw Pete heading towards her with a couple of hangers-on tagging behind him.

'Well, hello, my dear, and what may I ask are you up to? Off to feed your face again, eh?'

She tried not to take offence at his rather weak attempt at humour.

'Well, gee Pete, yes you caught me.'

'You're looking a bit flushed. I take it you are excited to see me.' He gave a rather annoying little chuckle after saying it and turned to his companions to view their entertainment at his joke.

'No, I wouldn't say that, but I do feel sick and a little warm, make of that what you will. Where are you going?'

'I am off to a cabinet meeting; it's time to get the mob completely under my control. Aren't you glad you are not a government minister and have to put up with boring meetings?'

Phoebe just shook her head as he walked away. Yes, she was glad she didn't have to go and listen to policies not being discussed but rammed down throats. She was sure he just made stuff up as he went. His comment about her face made her detour to the toilets.

As she pushed the door to go into the toilets, two women brushed past and gave her a look as if to say to each there, 'that's her.' Was she being paranoid? Looking over her shoulder, she could see them talking and glancing at her, the door swung shut, and they were gone. Looking in the toilet mirror, she was shocked by her face. She had never seen anything like it before. Her nose was bright red and blotchy, and the blotchiness flowed down the sides of her nose and spread across her cheeks.

'God, I look terrible.' She leant in closer to the mirror. Touching it didn't help. It wasn't hot, it was just there. She hadn't brought her bag with her, so she couldn't powder her face to make it less noticeable. She stared for a few more minutes trying to think of what it could be. She was disturbed by someone coming into the toilets, so she looked down at her feet, turned and hurried back to her office. She would need to make another appointment to see the doctor yet again.

She needed some pampering. Just as she was picking up her phone, it rang.

'Phoebe?' She knew the voice.

'Yes, is that you, Mic?'

'Yes, Pheebs, look, I am sorry to tell you, but your mother is in hospital. Pheebs, she is not very well, not well at all.'

'Ohh, I...why are you telling me, and not my sister.'

'Pheebs, this is not the time to get into a sibling sniping match. She is not well, and I think you need to come and see her.'

'What hospital is she in?' 'The John.'

'Ok, I will be there as soon as I can.' 'Goodbye.'

'Mic, what is wrong with her...'

He was gone. She was dumbfounded. What was it with the people in her life? What was her sister thinking? Why had he rung and not someone else in the family? They were still married, but he had moved on and was expecting a baby, and she was with Josh, but none of them knew that. Well, it was about time her relationship with Josh was out in the open. It was the only good thing she had in her life, and she wanted people to know. She didn't want to go back to Newcastle and have everyone thinking that she was a lonely old biddy. Why did going home cause her so much distress?

Reality set in. She let Jean know she was heading back. She deflected all the questions aimed at finding out why, closed her office door and went home to pack. Once packed and a flight booked, she had time to phone Josh. No answer. A text would have to do.

Later that night, waiting for her flight at the airport, she received a call from Pete.

'Where are you going?'

'To Newcastle, my mother is unwell, and I need to see her.' She tried hard to hide her annoyance. He never bothered with her usually. Why was he so interested in her now?

'You should have let me know.' 'Sorry…'

'I'll let you go for two days, and then you need to come back. Ok?' 'What…?'

'Two days.' 'Pete…'

He hung up.

What was he up to? Why now? She didn't sign up for this rubbish. She wondered if she should just quit. Quit and go where? She couldn't go back to Newcastle; ridicule would await. Stay in Canberra and see what happens? Josh is in Canberra, so that is a bonus.

They would just both have to tough it out. No option. She booked her flight back, and just as she finished doing this, she heard the call to board.

She didn't know it, but Josh was landing as she was sitting in her seat to take off.

He had an urgent meeting with Pete, and he was a bit wary of what it could be about. Pete's demeanour since the election had turned from one of a likeable control freak to a rather unlikeable control freak. He had agreed to work for him for many reasons; his job with the last PM was under threat, he was tired of the old boy and needed a new set of faces, he thought Pete would be a better boss. Boy, was he wrong. He preferred the self-indulgent neediness of the last PM to the narcissistic braying of Pete.

Once in the airport terminal, he saw Phoebe's text. 'Shit.' He had just wanted to come home and spend the night with her in her new apartment. They hadn't had much time to enjoy it as yet. He liked it. He appreciated its charm, the wood fire, and its privacy. All he wanted was to be alone with her. The strength of his disappointment surprised him. He hadn't felt like this in a long while.

After Danielle, he had put up a shield, kept women at a distance, used them for sex and company when he needed it, but she had changed that. She had made him dependent on her. He needed her; he wanted her. But in all honesty, he didn't know if he liked the situation or not: he was a little crestfallen, so he went back to his place and drank some very expensive scotch in a very short time.

# Chapter 17

'Eerr...you said she was on death's door.' 'Well, she looked like it yesterday', Sarah replied.

'She certainly doesn't now.' Phoebe arrived at the hospital early the next morning, expecting to see her mother on her deathbed. Instead, she was complaining about the food and laughing at her grandchildren's antics. A nurse came in and asked if they could keep the children quiet. Her mother was not impressed. 'Bugger off,' she said as the nurse left the room, which in turn made the grandchildren laugh louder. Phoebe was annoyed.

'Sarah, I dropped everything and raced up here and...and so it seems, not much is wrong.'

'Trust you to say that. Phoebe, you can't say that there is nothing wrong. She is in hospital, and she did have a funny turn, you know.' Her sister's green eyes drilled into her as she said this. She was patronising her, and Phoebe was fuming.

'Oh, just shut up!'

'Now, girls,' her mother interjected. 'I am all right, so go and get on with whatever it is you both do. Well, I know what you do Sarah, but what do you do again, Pheebs?'

This was too much for Phoebe. She walked towards the door with all the intent and purpose of leaving and never coming back, no matter how sick or near death her nearest and dearest were. Her mother always did this. Divide and conquer. How was she ever going to have a good relationship with her sister when her mother always sought to undermine them. All through their childhoods, it was competition, derision, and delight at their bickering. But then she thought better of it. She wouldn't let her win, not anymore.

'Mum, I am going to get a coffee, and I will come back as soon as it is a little quieter in here, okay?' A nod of her head was the only indication that her mother had heard what she had said.

Phoebe indicated to her sister that she wanted to talk to her outside the raucous confines of the hospital room.

Sarah followed.

'Why did you get Mic to call me? Why couldn't you have rung and told me what was going on? Tell me the truth.'

'Well, I was busy, and he offered to call you. Didn't think it would be a big deal. He was here yesterday and thought I had better let you know. Honestly, Phoebe, she was terrible yesterday. The way you are carrying on, it's like you would do anything not to come, even with mum ill.'

'Don't say that.' Phoebe was taken aback by what she said and the weird fact that Mic visited her sick mother. It made her feel, well, she wasn't sure how she felt, but it didn't feel right.

'Well, you hardly visit or call. What do you think I would think? That you would drop all your important meetings and the like to run down here to visit a mother that you don't really like?'

Phoebe ignored the comment.

'Look, I'm tired and hungry. I am going to get a coffee and some food. I will stay with mum this morning, but then I am going home this afternoon. Okay?'

'What, to Canberra? Don't want to visit with the rest of your family here? You know, your nieces and nephews. Remember them?'

'Well, that would be great, but I have a job to get back to. And anyway, where is our illustrious brother in our time of need?'

Her sister just went for her throat: 'Oh, yeah, right, the job, mustn't let anything get in the way of the job.'

Phoebe's shoulders dropped as she said: 'See you later Sarah.'

Sarah shook her head and wondered what had gone wrong with Phoebe to make her so aloof and distant from them all. This was done with little insight into her own behaviour that helped to push her sister away. The sound of Phoebe's heels soon faded into the distance, and Sarah went back to her mother and the gaggle of noisy children.

Phoebe found a café downstairs, but it was packed. 'Damn, I just want a coffee and somewhere quiet to sit,' she thought to herself. She decided to stand in line and wait; the need for coffee overrode the compulsion to leave. She regretted it as soon as she spotted Mic and his new partner making their way around the corner, to see her mother presumably. This was going to be awkward.

Mic saw her and stopped and looked at his feet. He didn't know what to do. It amused her somewhat. She thought she would wait to see how he would respond. Next, he looked at his partner with a half-smile, grimace type of face as he tried to work out what to do; if he ignored her, he would feel bad, but if he said hello, he knew it would be awkward as hell. Phoebe saw the swollen belly of his girl and swallowed.

They came towards her. Phoebe gauged she must be about six months gone.

'Phoebe,' he said in a jovial but somewhat forced way.

'Hi, Mic, how are you?'

'Well, really well. Ohhh, this is, this is Tania.'

The two women looked at each other. Both are intrinsically curious. Both a little jolted to meet the other.

'Hello, Tania, nice to meet you.'

'So you're Phoebe; I've heard a lot about you.'

'Ha, all good, I hope.'

It was awkward.

'Well, yes as it goes, all good.'

'Sure,' Phoebe replied, knowing full well that this was a lie. 'Mic tells me you have an important job in Canberra.' 'Well, yes, I have a job, but no, it's not that important.'

'Not important? Mic interjected. 'So you left for an unimportant job?'

'Well…' Phoebe didn't expect that. Tania butted back in.

'You work with the PM; that sounds important to me.'

A change of subject was needed. 'So you're both here to see my mother I suppose?'

'Well, yes, we are. Have you seen her?'

'Yeah, she seems okay at the moment. You had me going yesterday when you rang. I thought she was on the way out.'

'Well, to be truthful, so did we. The doctors did some tests, and we should know what is going on in a few days.'

This was a little weird. It was her mother, but Mic and his new girlfriend knew more of what was going on with her than she did.

Phoebe didn't say anything. She was confused about the situation. Finally, she managed to mention the elephant in the room, so to speak, the baby.

'Congrats on the upcoming birth, happy for you both.'

Mic just nodded, but Tania started to talk about how excited they both were and how it was just too exciting, and they couldn't wait to meet the baby.

Mic and Phoebe exchanged glances. There was a lot of emotion on their faces as they looked at each other. All the hurt, the loss and the futility of their relationship. But there were still feelings; their glances gave that away, but nothing that would make either of them consider getting back together. It was the end. It was a relief for Phoebe. She could move on without a guilt shadow following her around the hallowed halls of Parliament House.

'Yes, can I help you?' They had been moving slowly towards the counter as they talked without realising it. Phoebe was the next to order.

'Look, we won't hold you up. You get your coffee.' Mic wanted to go.

'Okay, nice to meet you, Tania.'

'You too,' she replied. They left Phoebe staring at them as they walked up the long corridor arm in arm, chattering about the unexpected encounter with the past. She was handed her coffee. She paid for it and then something sweet she needed to relieve her stress. Sitting at a table away from the crowd, steaming coffee and a delightful cake in front of her, she felt weird, disjointed, disconnected. She wasn't sure how to express how she felt. Life was going on here, as usual. She didn't seem to be missed or needed. She felt like she had no connection with the place anymore. The coffee and cake helped to massage her feelings somewhat. She couldn't shake off the emotion of being external to those who should be closest. To top it all off, she liked Tania. She seemed nice. There was nothing pretentious or mean in her countenance, well, none that she picked up on anyway for such a brief encounter. After the last remnants of cream had been wiped off her face, she sat and stared at her half-empty coffee cup. Soon she was in some kind of hypnotic stare, which was only disturbed by the ringing of her phone. It was Josh.

'Hi.'

'Hi, you,' he responded. 'You sound tired.' 'Well, I feel everything at the moment.' 'What do you mean?'

'Not really sure what I mean. How is everything down south?'

'Well, I got a phone call from Pete. He is acting really strange at the moment. He seems to want to keep me at arm's length. He does not want me to make any suggestions or be involved in his day-to-day needs, or handle any issues that arise. He has another guy who seems to be doing my job unofficially; he turned up while I was on the goose chase all over the country. Now, it seems, I am to help out that new minister, you know, the one that was in the safe seat. Apparently, he is having a really hard time understanding his portfolio, and he wants me to spend a few weeks sorting him out. Not in my job description, but I will do it nevertheless.' He heard Phoebe let out a long breath.

'I am sorry sweet, how is your mum?'

'Oh, she is fine, I really don't know why I am here, and everyone seems to be getting on quite well without me.'

'When are you coming home?'

'This afternoon if possible.' She felt so out of it here that she didn't think twice about how Canberra was now home, not Newcastle.

'I am just about to go and say bye to mum. I was going to stay a bit longer, but I don't think I will. Then I will get on the next available flight. I really need to see you.'

'And me you. We will talk about everything when you get back over a huge glass of wine and maybe some Italian; what do you think?'

'Sounds good, see you soon.' 'Yep, see you.'

She waited until Mic and Tania were leaving. She waved them goodbye as they passed her in the corridor and then headed up to see her mother. She just hoped her mum was too tired after all the grandchildren's antics to make any remarks about how much of a failure she was by her last century standards and how Tania was a lucky girl to have Mic and a baby on the way. Oh, joy. She was wrong.

With her mother's words still ringing in her ears, she boarded the mid-afternoon flight back to Canberra. She settled down and ordered a drink as soon as she was able. She couldn't wait for the wine she looked forward to sharing with Josh. Just one, maybe two onboard drinks would be just enough to soothe her jagged nerves.

# Chapter 18

Josh was looking out the window of the new townhouse when Phoebe arrived in an Uber. He didn't know it was her at first as he didn't recognise the car, so she had a short time to study his face. He looked worried. She thought he looked like he had aged, but only a little. He still looked great, and she was looking forward to their night together as she walked up to the front door, and he opened it.

'Hi,' he murmured as he kissed her cold cheek. 'Hi, yourself. What's up?'

'What's not,' he responded.

She pulled him by his hand through the doorway. 'Let's get in and get a drink and tell me all about your day. I bet a box of chocolate-coated Krispy Kreme's that I can beat your day in regards to it being a disaster.'

'Umm, I bet you can't.'

He collapsed on the lounge while she put away her bags, freshened up, and found some clean glasses for the copious amounts of red wine she wanted to drink.

Putting a full glass in front of him, she sat and waited for him to take his first sip and tell her what had happened since she left on her own self-defeating journey.

'I don't know, I just don't know what I am going to do, or should do. Sorry, what we are going to do. I really don't.' He took a gulp of wine and put his glass down hard on the coffee table.

'What do you mean, what is going on?' He was about to tell her, but she interrupted him as she arranged herself on the lounge.

'And what do you mean, what are we going to do?' He waited for her to settle and said:

'This new guy is hanging around the entire time, talking to Pete in private, and basically blanking me out at every opportunity. I am not privy to anything, and I am the chief of staff. I am supposed to know what is going on at all times.'

'What's his name?'

'Well, that is a good question. I have not been formally introduced, but I think it is...James...John...no James, James, yes I am pretty sure.'

'James? Not heard of him.' She pulled her legs up underneath her and relaxed into the back of her seat.

'Well, that makes two of us. I have been from one side of the country to the next, and now I have to hang around that stupid MP for a few weeks. I know Pete is up to something. I think he set out to trap me. Right from the beginning, he set me up, one way or the other. Whether he won or lost the election, I was toast. Touché, you bastard.'

'What do you mean?'

'What do you mean? What do I mean? Can't you think of anything else to say?'

Phoebe knew Pete was ruthless, but she was at a loss about how he would have set him up or why. She took little notice of his outburst as he went on.

'Think about it. Pete asked me to be his chief of staff before he even won the election. Ok, ok, he won, to my great relief.' He took another big gulp of wine. 'But what if he had lost? He could have let everyone know about my defection. He had plenty of evidence. I would be out of a job and black banned from Canberra forever. No one likes a turncoat. As it stands, he won. I have a job. Or so he wanted me to believe. My job hinges on his goodwill. His goodwill is drying up, and so are my chances of hanging onto my job. He wants me gone. If that happens, I will not be able to work in any capacity in politics anywhere in Australia for a very long time—and well, it's all I know.' He looked deflated.

Phoebe was trying to take in what he had just said. She fidgeted and drank while he stared into space. Finally, she said, 'Okay. Why? What would be his motive? Why would he set out to undermine you like you think he has?'

'I have given this some thought over the last few days; plane travel allows you time to think. I guess it is because he is helping out an old friend.'

'What? Who?'

'Danielle, that's who.'

'Danielle? What has she got to do with it?' Phoebe was taken aback. Surely Danielle was old news? True, Danielle hated her, but why would he think that she had anything to do with his being set up for a fall? She had loved him once, if that counted for anything.

'I am not following...'

'Even though she did the dirty on me, she is a vindictive bitch. She doesn't want me to be happy. Ever! I have been working at a high level in this place for years; she only joined the higher ranks when Pete became opposition leader a few years back. I bet my bottom dollar she is behind this!'

Phoebe thought he was being irrational. There must be another explanation...she was trying hard to think of one.

She put a question to him, 'Why would Pete do anything she wanted, especially something as nasty as shunting you? You know Pete is only out for Pete.'

'They are kindred spirits. They revel in each other's darkest desires. She tells him how wonderful he is, and he reciprocates. They feed off each other. They are like two conjoined succubbi.

Bringing down someone for the other is fun and a show of loyalty. I bet they plotted this when he became the opposition leader. They set a trap, and I fell for it—if I lose my job, I can no longer work here. I am done. You are in danger too, I suspect. They know about us, I am sure. Anyone in my orbit will feel the wrath.'

Phoebe thought his take on things was a little exaggerated. She put it down to the fact that he was tired and stressed. Strange thoughts enter the mind when you are not feeling on top of things. She reached out to him, hoping that a little love and affection would soothe his soul. He was happy for her to stroke his head and give him little kisses on the cheek and forehead, but after a minute, he grabbed her hands and held them to his chest.

He looked at her directly and said, 'I have been made to look like a fool. I have been trapped by my own vanity. Pursued, told how I was needed, I was the best. I fell for the overtures, the sweet words. I was wooed into a trap, and now that trap is closing in.' He let go of her hands and stood up to gaze out the window into the cool, clear night. She looked at him confused and a little disconcerted. The Josh she knew had always been strong and afraid of no one. This Josh was turning into someone who was defeated before the fight had even begun.

Suddenly, he turned and looked down at her and stated, 'You know, I never thought that I cared for this job, this place. I always wanted to be somewhere else. But now that my back is being pushed further and further to the wall, I realise that I do like my job and being in this rotten, rat infested world of backstabbing and cheating. I don't know what else to do. I will fight them. I will not let them win.'

'Glad to hear it.' Phoebe said, somewhat relieved. 'Now, do you want to open another bott...?' He sat down next to her and stared intently into her face.

'Pheebs, if I am going to fight this, it might be best for you to separate yourself from me. I don't want my battles to impact you and your career. So I think we need to cool our relationship for now.'

'What? I'm not sure...why?' She didn't expect this.

'No, Josh, you are the only thing that keeps me going in this place. I will not let those bastards come between us.' She could feel her face flush. 'We will fight this together. My bloody career is a joke anyway. Let's just say that it hasn't turned out how I expected. If you go down, I will go with you.'

'I don't want you to do that for me, Phoebe. I really don't want us both to end up unemployed and unemployable.'

'Don't be silly. We can both get jobs somewhere else if we lose them here.'

He exhaled, 'Phoebe, I don't think you fully understand the implications of my, or what will *our* position be if we do fight and lose.'

'Ah, Josh, don't be so dramatic. How about a cup of coffee, it will help us think, and we can start planning our attack.'

'Don't be so flippant; it's serious. Okay, a cup of coffee would be great. But Phoebe, please, the political networks are vast and all-encompassing. Business is political, and politics is business. We won't get jobs in any company connected with the current administration or the last—or the one before that and indeed any future government!

'I can't believe no one would employ us,' she said as she rattled around in the cupboards getting out cups for coffee.

'You had better. Seriously Phoebe, you better be ready for the unemployment line if we can't resolve what I am very sure is happening.'

'Let's just wait and see, eh?' He heard the fridge door open. 'Ohh, shit. Black okay, the milk is off.'

'That will be fine.'

He started to go over his thoughts out loud once again.

'Josh, please, stop. I just want to enjoy this cup of coffee, and then I want to enjoy you, OK.'

'Sounds like a plan,' came the response with less enthusiasm than she would have liked.

'Don't sound so excited,' she scolded.

'Okay. I won't,' he said, as he managed the smallest of grins. 'Hey, do you want to tell me about your day? I am waiting to win the doughnuts.'

'No, I do not. I have had enough of today. I just want it to finish and to forget about most of it. How about we ditch the coffee and the planning and just go to bed?'

'You know what? That is the best plan you could have ever made. The doughnuts can wait till another day.'

'Well, let's say maybe 'til the morning?'

# Chapter 19

The next morning Josh was at his desk checking the list of meetings he had arranged for Pete to attend that day. While he was looking, something wasn't adding up. He checked and doubled checked, but some of the people showing up in Pete's diary didn't correlate to those he thought he had listed. One, in particular, caught his eye.

'What the hell?' He rang Pete's office. No answer.

The person Pete was to meet later in the day was political poison. He had warned the old PM to stay away, and he had. But Pete obviously did not take his advice. Worse still was that Pete had not included him in any sort of dialogue relating to the meeting. He would not be able to steer the conversation or at least debrief the PM about issues raised, and most importantly, perceived conflicts of interest.

Josh didn't have much time to act; he had to leave for a few days to help out the beleaguered MP he had been ordered to rescue. This meeting and stopping it, however, was so much more important. He rang Pete's mobile. He should be around as his first meeting of the day was scheduled for 10.30 AM. It was now 9.45 AM. He ran his fingers through his hair as he listened to the phone ring out and go to voicemail.

'Shit!'

He tried to ring again as he walked towards the PM's office. In the hall, he bumped into the treasurer. He was a tall, slim, blond man, and in Josh's estimation, of limited ability to do the job he had been given. Why Pete had chosen him to guide the country's economic future baffled him. But he knew that it was a strategic appointment. Pete never did anything without an underlying reason. Again, the motive remained a mystery for now. The treasurer was looking down his nose at Josh as he asked him if he knew where the PM was in his tailored North Shore voice.

'No,' Josh replied. 'But I am looking for him as well, as it happens. If you see him, could you tell him that I need to see him as soon as possible, and it is important, very, very important?'

'Well, as do I, and it is also very important, exceedingly so.'

The treasurer went on his way as Josh nodded his acquiescence. He was in no position to usurp the treasurer; he knew his place.

'Twat,' he mumbled under his breath. Josh watched him walk to Pete's door and knock. A voice emanated from the office that was not instantly recognisable to Josh. It shouted, 'Come in.'

'What the…!' Josh thought 'who could that be?' The former PM had wanted – no, *needed* – I'm to be in the meetings to back him up. Pete was a different kettle of fish. He wanted privacy. Therefore, Josh's position was not as secure, as he was not feared as the PM's trusted advisor or indeed a spy. Everything now seemed to be kept secret, and it appeared that there were shadowy players in the background who knew the secrets, and it made people edgy and defensive. His current emotional state was a testament to that already.

Josh waited patiently. He was intent on finding out who the voice in the PM's office belonged to. The treasurer, whether by need or in spite, took a very long time. He finally left at 10.20 AM, giving Josh a cursory look of disdain. Josh took no notice and knocked, hoping to see Pete next.

'Enter.' He did, and he was taken aback to see this James fellow sitting at the PM's desk. In shock, Josh stated that he needed to speak with the PM before his next scheduled meeting.

'Well,' came the drawn-out reply, 'you won't see him here. He is in town, at some fancy restaurant. Can't remember the name of it offhand. Problem?' At that moment, Josh wanted to slap the smug smirk off his face. He resisted, but it took all of his willpower to do so.

'Look, James,'

'Jamie, if you don't mind.'

'Sorry, Jamie, I don't have time to play silly buggers. I need to talk to the PM as soon as I can.

'Sorry.' He gave Josh a dismissive wave of his hand to signal that he wanted him to leave.

It was all Josh could do to not scream at the man sitting on the throne, presumably with his sights set on being the one who wields power. Josh felt sorry for him for a microsecond. He knew as well as anyone that no one shares power with Pete or has any chance of wrestling it from him. And who the hell calls themselves Jamie, especially a grown man? Defeated, he left.

As he raced down the corridor for a split second, he felt like running away. Far, far away. Out of breath, he leant against the nearest wall and thought of the long-forgotten dream of owning a bar somewhere warm and secluded. What happened to that; who knows? 'Think Josh, think…' his mind raced. He couldn't put coherent thoughts together. 'I need a drink.' He set out to find the nearest bar.

Someone was heading towards him and said, 'Excuse me'. He put his hand up to shut them up. He just didn't want to talk to anyone until he had had a scotch.

***

While Josh was ready to give up on everything, political Pete was having a great time. He was being wined and dined by the business elite. It was quite exciting. Nothing was too much or too expensive; the champagne flowed, as did the dodgy deals. Pete looked around in a self-satisfying manner that was becoming an ingrained part of his personality.

This was what politics was all about. Getting what you wanted. If anyone thought that politics was about the people, Pete felt that they were seriously deluded. No, he was just where he wanted to be. And no one would knock him off his perch, especially if he made the right contacts and built up his power base. He was sitting next to some compelling people in all walks of industrial and manufacturing life. And everyone, everyone was here to see to his needs and his wants. He was king. They all bowed down to him. He played them as pawns. He did what he wanted and to whom he wanted.

Josh crossed his mind. He felt little empathy for his position. He was not forceful or self-centred enough to make it in this town. He had outmanoeuvred him. He would soon be just another part of the flotsam and jetsam of the political game. He didn't feel sorry for him; it was his own fault for not playing the game well enough and for upsetting people along the way. He always felt that Josh thought too much of himself. In fact, he thought he was a little too arrogant about his looks. Although he was taking delight in the downfall of Josh, he didn't want to hurry the event as he was enjoying the spectacle. He downed another glass of champagne and decided to make Josh's descent a little slower and a lot more excruciating. Phoebe was to be the target, but he must get her on his side. She would be a prize for his expert political manoeuvring. It would make it all the more of a challenge, and why? Well, just for the fun of it, of course.

Later in the afternoon, back at the House, Phoebe ran into Danielle, or to be more specific, Danielle had run into her. The unexpected meeting had the effect of making Phoebe feel like she had been transported into a parallel universe; Danielle was being friendly. In fact, she was being very helpful. She had invited her to lunch and a chat. This was the universe of the sweet Danielle and not the bitch. It all seemed just a little surreal.

A late lunch, or what would be best described as afternoon tea, was set for 3.30 PM. As they chatted over chicken stuffed wraps and soy lattes, Phoebe felt uneasy but pleasantly surprised. Danielle, when she wanted, could actually be funny and interesting. It didn't matter what time of day it was, the café was always busy, and the noise made hearing her a little hard, but Phoebe got the gist of what she was saying.

Danielle talked about how it was when she started work here, she knew nothing of politics, and it took her a long time to settle into the hustle and bustle of the place. Josh had worked in Canberra for a very long time, and due to his experience and commitment over the years, he was very much valued by Pete.

'Oh,' Phoebe let slip because it was so at odds with what Josh thought of Pete's perception of him.

'What was that?' Danielle asked. Her perfectly manicured left eyebrow arched in interest at what was a spontaneous expression of Phoebe's confusion on the topic.

'Nothing, nothing at all. I am just glad to hear that Pete values Josh. I am sure Josh will be happy to know that.'

'I am sure Josh knows that already without having to be told.'

'Well, yes, yes I am sure.' Phoebe didn't know what to think. One minute Josh is saying Pete is out to get him, and the next, this woman, who is very close to Pete, is saying what an asset he is. Taking a sip of her latte gave her a second to think. She eyed Danielle up and down. She noticed that she had dyed her hair, and now it was a darker shade of blonde. It looked nicer on her, and it was not as ageing as the other colour she usually wore. Her hair was still very wiry; she would look even better with a good cut. Her clothes were immaculate, as always. Today she wore navy blue, matching jacket and skirt, with a crisp white shirt. Her shoes were very high and the same navy blue as her suit. Phoebe felt almost scruffy in comparison. She also noticed her earrings, diamond and a delicate little necklace sporting a bigger diamond. Yes, she carried herself well and presented herself as the ultimate professional.

Phoebe glanced over at the doorway of the café. She saw Josh walk in. He, in turn, noticed both of them sitting together. For a minute, he couldn't believe what he was seeing. Phoebe smiled, Danielle saw, she turned and looked at Josh and gave a half-hearted grin.

He threw his hands up in the air and mouthed to Phoebe, 'What the fuck?', turned and walked out. Phoebe was embarrassed by this turn of events. She was just about to make up some excuse for his behaviour when Danielle beat her to it.

'He thinks you are dining with the devil.'

'I don't, I am sorry...yes, I suppose he does.'

'Don't worry. Both of us will get him to see that I am not all bad. I have had to grow up a lot and leave the past to the past. We will make a good team, you and I. He will come to rely on us to support him in his position, as Pete has grand plans for him.'

'He does?' Phoebe felt it was hard to believe but hoped that it was true. She felt some relief wash over her.

'Yes, he does.' Danielle looked at her phone, a text from her office.

'Well, I have to go. See you soon, and thanks for the catch-up. I know we didn't get off to the best of starts, but I am sure we can get past that and work together from now on. After all, we are on the same political team, aren't we?' And with that, she was gone.

Phoebe sat totally bewildered. Had she been punked? Or was this for real? Ever the optimist, she opted for believing it was real, overlaid with a tiny bit of scepticism. But if it was real, then both she and Josh had little to worry about. Maybe Josh was just adjusting to his new role, and his interpretation of events was a bit misguided. She sighed, not from relief as such, but more contemplation. As she walked back to her office, she looked down at her own clothes. Drab brown pants and a light orange jumper gave her the look of an elderly librarian. She knew one thing for sure, if she was going to be working more closely with Danielle, she would need to upgrade her wardrobe.

***

Josh, as yet, had not come to her place as was usual on a Thursday night. Phoebe had sent one text after another since Josh had walked out of the café earlier in the day. He had not answered her. She knew he was mad, but she felt that he would have calmed down by now as women often do. No, he hadn't. That was obvious. On the way home, she had splashed out and bought extravagant ingredients to cook him one of his favourite meals; chilly crab cakes on a bed of fragrant couscous. It was a way of making it up to him for any offence he had taken to her consorting with the enemy, so to speak. She didn't know what to do with his dinner; she would eat hers in front of the TV—put his in the oven or fridge? The fridge won.

Soon after the news had delivered its daily menu of doom and gloom, she got a text:

Josh, 'What u doing?'

'Not much. Where r u?' 'Bar drinking.'

‘Come home dinner in the fridge.’ ‘What the H were u doing today?’ ‘Come home, and we can talk.’ ‘Okay, but not in the mood.’

‘OK, just eat.’ ‘OK’

She threw her phone on the coffee table and stared into space. How would she handle the coming confrontation with Josh? Was he overreacting, or was she being stupid and gullible? Wow, this town made you crazy one way or another. She wanted to survive it, so a strategy would be called for. How it would work and what form it would take was another matter. She needed to think on her feet. For starters, she decided that coffee with a few, maybe even a packet of Tim Tams, would sweeten him up. ‘But he hasn’t had his dinner, and he has been drinking,’ she said to herself. ‘Since when has that stopped him before?’ She forged ahead with her plan.

By the time he arrived via an Uber, the coffee table was adorned with the delights of freshly brewed coffee, sugar, milk and one of many frozen Tim Tam packets that resided in the freezer. She had never known a man to like chocolate biscuits so much. If they provided stress relief, and she knew that chocolate had been scientifically proven to be good for your mood – who was she to argue about it? She enjoyed the guilty pleasure herself more often than not.

She heard him knock. She stood, took a deep breath and went to open the door. On opening it, she noticed that his appearance was a little disheveled, but on the whole, he still looked amazingly handsome and chic. She often felt that comparatively, he was Adonis, and she was the Mona Lisa. No matter what he did, he never looked bad. Sometimes this annoyed her. She wished he would have a bad day, but he never did, and she could live with that. What she didn’t like was this new vulnerability that she was finding hard to deal with.

He came in and stood looking down at the coffee table and all the delights that it held.

'So you think caffeine and sweet biscuits are the solution?'

'No, but it will help soften the mood, don't you think?' 'I don't think...'

'Oh, come on. You can have your dinner later if you still want it. Sit, and I will pour you a coffee.'

She handed him a biscuit, and they both dipped it into their hot drink and held it for the required time for the end to melt just a little. Once the appropriate time had elapsed, they sucked on the other end of the biscuit from which the lovely, sweet, sticky filling flowed forth and gave them both an instant sugar hit. Heaven.

'Okay, I have to admit, I do feel a little better, but not much I should add. I am really confused as to why I find you in a friendly tete-a-tete with a woman that you hate and who is out to wreck my career.' It wasn't a question; it was a cold hard fact.

'I know, I know. I never thought that I would ever eat with her. But Danielle was so lovely to me earlier in the day, and I thought she wanted to make up, be nice. I try to find the good in others, but you think I am naïve, don't you?'

'Well, yes, I very much do. I remember not so long back when you said that woman needed to be avoided at all costs.'

'Yeah, I did. But I wasn't long in the job then, and I was nervous and uptight. I was angry with everyone, including dear old Jean. And she was a woman scorned who felt threatened by me. She's probably come to terms with it by now.'

'Like hell she has. What you have to remember is that this is Canberra. On the whole, people aren't nice or good. They're out for what they can get. And more often than not, they're after other people's heads. They will do it any way they can. They are two-faced. They will be lovely to you if it means getting something they want, even if it means the end for you. You need to be more aware of the political environment that you are in. Everything is political, you must remember that; there is always an ulterior motive for everything.'

'Does that description include us? Or are we the exception to the rule?'

She handed him another biscuit before he could answer, and they repeated the ritual again. As she did, she thought about what he had just said. Could it be true that everyone was only out for their own interests in this place? Surely not? Wasn't there someone that wanted what was best for the country? Was politics always just solely a selfish endeavour?'

He read her thoughts. 'Look, I am sorry to burst what was left of your bubble in regards to politics as a noble calling, but that concept is long gone. You have to watch your back at all times. Danielle doesn't care…'

She interrupted him, 'but she said Pete held you in high regard and valued you…'

'She said that to knock you off guard. She wants you to believe everything is okay, and that way, they can divide us. For what reason, I am not entirely sure, but I do know it means my downfall and yours if you are not careful. Don't you see?'

She licked the last remnants of chocolate off her fingers. 'Okay, okay, I will be more careful and not let them draw me in.' She could not help but think in some back recess of her mind that maybe Josh was just a little jaded and that he was indeed overreacting. But she would take his advice for now and be careful. What she needed to do was to be a little more in tune with the motives of others. She didn't know how she would work them out, but she would try her hardest just to keep one step ahead.

Coffee finished, and nearly a pack of biscuits later, she asked if he felt like the dinner she had made him. No, he didn't. But he did feel like going to bed. She was a little fatigued, and the bed was inviting. But he wasn't interested in sleep like she was. However, it didn't take him long to change her mind. And she was glad that he did.

The next morning, she felt a little more powerful. She knew she loved Josh, and he loved her; they were solid. She was good at her job, and she liked it 75%—no, that was too generous, maybe 60% of the time. She would make sure she manoeuvred with a heightened sense of awareness; she was not going to be drawn in so quickly. The only thing that weighed on her mind was her tiredness and her aching hands. She must get back to the doctor and find out why she is so tired all the time. Then she remembered that she hadn't managed to get the blood tests done that the doctor had suggested. She checked her diary, nothing much on the next day. She would do it tomorrow morning if she could find a pathology centre open on a Saturday morning. Apart from that chore, she was looking forward to the weekend, a time to relax and have some fun with Josh.

Her phone rang. It was Danielle. 'Hi Phoebe, Pete wants you to accompany him to Tasmania, leaving early tonight. There is a women's conference regarding getting women back into the workforce tomorrow, and he wants some female staff members, advisors and ministers to accompany him. He also wants you to outline some of the main issues facing women who want to work but find it hard to do so. You can do this on the plane flight down and have some ideas yourself, so get yourself informed and up to speed, okay?'

'I…I, this is rather quick, don't you think? I am…'

'Sorry about the short notice, I will send all the details to Jean, and she will update you on the schedule. See you there.'

Phoebe looked at her phone. She was both excited to be asked and disappointed that her weekend was ruined. She sat at her desk trying to work out if there was an underlying motive. It was last minute, but sometimes that's the way things are here. Other women were going, so it was not just her that was being inconvenienced. It was a conference in her area of expertise, so it was right that she should be asked. She couldn't really see any other option. It was important that she attend, and she was being asked for all the right reasons. She would let Josh know later as they were meeting for lunch. All morning was spent researching the significant issues impacting women getting back into the workforce after children and long absence from work. Of course, childcare and the resultant time lost due to it was top of the list. Jean brought her a coffee around 11.45 AM.

'Jean,' Phoebe was curious. 'Why do you work here?'

'Me? Well, let me see.' she squinted and looked thoughtful for a minute before she said, as a matter of fact, 'the money, why else?'

'Oh, come on, I know you love your job. There must be more in it for you other than the money.'

'No, no, really, it is the money,' Jean said with a broad smile on her face. 'Oh and the wonderful people, everyone is sooooo nice, haha.'

'Now you're pulling my leg.'

'Well, to be truthful, I do like my job, and besides, what else would I do? Sit around the house all day trying to find the last remaining cobweb to darken my doorstep?'

'Yeah, that would be fun.'

'What about you, Phoebe? Why do you work here?'

'Well, I hope to make a difference in the lives of women and to use my influence to make that happen and...'

'Good luck with that.' Jean retorted with a look that told Phoebe that she had heard it all before.

Phoebe thought she would change the topic. She didn't want to get into it too much at the moment, the whys and wherefores of why she was here. She needed to get herself ready for the trip to Tasmania. She had never been to the Apple Isle, and truth be known, she was a little excited to be going. Her weekend with Josh was forgotten as she thought of all the places she wanted to see. Port Arthur, the vast wilderness, Hobart and Salamanca with its sandstone buildings all came to mind. She had always been a little jealous of her sister going there for her honeymoon long before the tribe of kids arrived. Phoebe had not been able to afford to travel when she was younger due to low paid work and paying off a brand new expensive car she foolishly bought on a whim. Now her sister could not afford to travel, and she was going places for free, for work, even if it was limited to the confines of the country. But she always had her passport ready just in case an international gig came up. What could be better? She was especially pleased as she knew that there would be many people attending, and she wouldn't have to spend too much time in the company of the PM. Hopefully, they would go out somewhere nice for dinner as a group and let off some steam.

'How many days are we away for Jean?'

'Looks like two nights.'

'I will need to go early to pack some things. Gee, I wonder if everyone else is as rushed as me to get ready for this; talk about last minute.'

'Oh, this meeting has been planned for a while. I saw it on my calendar about three months ago. They must have included you at…here is your schedule.' With that, she walked out to 'grab' some lunch as she put it and asked if Phoebe wanted anything'

'No, no thanks.'

Jean could not have known how this information stabbed at Phoebe's heart. She lived in a world where she knew what went on but failed, at times, to grasp the politics of office dynamics and the fragile egos of the protagonists. Basically, Jean had just told her she was an afterthought, someone that they tagged on at the last minute: but why? She tried not to think it could be anything but an oversight, but in the back of her head, she couldn't help but think that there was a reason, in all probability, to make up numbers. Whatever it was, it made her feel unwanted and less valued. Well, if they did it for that reason, their nasty little ploy worked.

'Shit.' She had been excited about it, but this information made her feel less inclined to go. She didn't want to get infected by Josh's pessimism. She tried to look beyond the personalities and move forward. She calmed herself a little. She knew that she had a tendency to jump to conclusions about what others thought of her. She was often wrong. But this time, she felt that her instincts might not be too far off the mark. Were they trying to wear her down with their games? Now she had a decision to make, to go or not? Her mobile rang—it was Josh. It was 12.45 PM, and she was late for lunch.

She sighed. Was she taking on too much of what Josh had said and not thinking for herself? Maybe she was reading too much into it. She had been asked, albeit at short notice, but this was a positive step after all. She had been left out of meetings and the like before, and now she had been included. Surely this was a good sign that things were looking up? She grabbed her bag and made her mind up to go. All she worried about now, as she traversed the never-ending corridor to the pigpen, was how to tell Josh.

***

As she unpacked in her harbour-front hotel room later that evening, she thought about Josh's response to her news. He wasn't happy. Not only because their weekend together was ruined but also because she hadn't let him know earlier; why tell him today and not last week? He didn't understand why she had kept it from him, especially when they made arrangements for the weekend. She made up a response around totally forgetting, which he only half believed. She was aware that he knew anything like a trip away would have been a top priority and that she would've been over the moon to be going. But there was no way that she was going to tell him that the invitation was last minute. She knew for sure that he would read something devious into it, cause a fight, and beg her not to go. She glanced out the window at the water. They were staying in Salamanca, so a wish had come true. It was beautiful. The city lights reflected and bounced off the bay, and the ferries carried tourists to destinations unknown and mysterious to her. She wished Josh hadn't left in a huff. Anyhow, she wasn't going to let his mood upset this experience. A knock came at her door.

'Hello.'

'Hi Phoebe, its Pete. Just letting you know I am right next door. We are all going for a drink and some dinner downstairs if you'd like to join us. See you in about five.'

'Ohh, okay,' she replied to the voice behind the door. She hadn't realised he would be staying so close to her. She was hoping not to have to socialise with him at all on this trip.

'Ummm, see you downstairs,' she managed in a tone of disguised disappointment. He didn't give her time to open the door, and when she got to it, he and his security staff were gone. She wondered who he meant by 'we'. From what she could make out on the plane, there weren't that many of them who had come along for the meeting. She had expected a planeload of females ready to fly the banner for women. Disappointingly there wasn't that many. There was Danielle, of course, and a few female MPs, but that was about it. It certainly wasn't a large delegation, as she had been led to believe.

When her mobile rang, she was standing in front of the mirror deciding what to wear, either the blue skirt and white shirt or a suit. She didn't feel like talking to anyone right at that very moment, so she let it go to voicemail. One glance at her phone told her it was Josh. She would ring him in the morning.

She was not in the mood for another argument. She slipped on the slimming navy blue skirt and white shirt that showed off her figure, brushed her hair and refreshed her makeup. She looked great, and for a change, she felt good as well. Indeed, she felt as if she was, at last, in step with the world, instead of always fighting against it. The tiredness that had been dogging her seemed to have lifted, and she was ready to have a nice time. She was starving and couldn't wait to feast on some Tasmanian delights. Her phone rang again. This time it was her mother. She definitely did not want to talk to her, so she put her phone on silent, slipped it in her bag and headed downstairs.

***

'Gia, give me another drink.' Josh put his phone in his pocket. He was a little concerned that Phoebe had decided to ignore all the bad stuff that had gone on and to make out everything was fine. He knew it wasn't, but she still wanted to believe it was, and he knew why. She didn't want to give up on her dream. Gia handed him his whiskey. 'You okay, Mr Ryan?' He waved his hand as a way of saying yes; he didn't want to get into a conversation with her as he had other things on his mind. She left him alone, only for him to hear her talking to her brother in the kitchen at the top of her voice about him. He ignored her. No one else was in the restaurant, and as she was talking Italian, he didn't know what she was saying, but he could hear his name popping into the conversation as she went on. The only woman he was worried about right now was Phoebe, and she wasn't interested in talking to him.

He thought of his plan to escape it all, the politics, the backstabbing, the deception, and open a bar somewhere warm, far away, exotic and full of the smells of aromatic spices. His favourite childhood beach was in Sri Lanka. His family were well to do and went on international holidays each year; he, his mother and father and his little sister. They would stick a map of the world on the wall of their house and spin either him or his sister around in circles, blindfolded. Once they had stopped spinning, they would stick a pin in the map and hopefully, it would be somewhere where they all wanted to go. Most of the time, it was, primarily when it was his turn. His sister usually ended up somewhere in the middle of the Pacific Ocean, and they would have to decide on where to go that was close by.

This would undoubtedly lead to arguments which he won; his skill of winning debates was honed in this manner. As a result, they had been to several tiny islands that dotted the world, and they were beautiful, but he was very proud of the fact that he had been the one to land a pin strike on Sri Lanka. The beaches were beautiful, the smells out of this world, and the days long and hot. What if they could do that now? Him and Phoebe, just pick a place and go? Why couldn't they? Gia drew him out of these thoughts by putting a plate of garlic bread in front of him. He had been drinking all afternoon, and she wasn't keen on him getting drunk with little to eat to line his stomach. He hadn't realised just how hungry he was until he breathed in the garlicky, buttery goodness of the bread.

***

Phoebe found Pete and Danielle in the bar, next to the hotel restaurant. They were well away, drinking what looked like cocktails. Interestingly, very few people were there, so it seemed rather bare and just a little uninviting. Of those enjoying a drink, none were interested in the fact that the PM was amongst them. Maybe it was the two somewhat intimidating bodyguards the PM had trailing after him or the fact that most people couldn't care less about politics. She wasn't sure, but it just didn't sit right with her somehow.

As she walked towards them, Pete stood to greet her. Danielle just nodded her recognition.

'Welcome, welcome, my dear.'

Phoebe smiled nervously. Something wasn't right. Where were the others? 'Hello,' she managed, but her voice indicated that she was a little confused.

'Welcome to Tasmania. You know you have come to a wild place if it has devils living in it,' said Danielle in a dry, almost sarcastic manner.

Phoebe looked from one to the other. Something wasn't right. She wasn't quite sure what, but there was something in their manner that didn't seem to sit comfortably with her.

'What would you like to drink? You name it, and you can have it.' 'You must try the Bloody Mary; divine.'

‘Okay, maybe I will. Thanks, Danielle.’

Pete and Danielle chatted with each other while they waited for a new round of drinks to arrive. Phoebe noted that the bar was quite trendy, with corrugated iron walls, candles, lanterns, and mismatched furniture.

The small talk continued. Nothing was mentioned about meetings or why indeed they were all here. All they spoke about was the drinks and the fun they were going to have. The only thing that came up was the one press call they were going to have in the morning, and that was it.

‘Oh, I thought that we…’ She tried to interrupt.

‘You know what thinking does to you, Phoebe?’

‘What?’

‘Makes you boring. Now drink up.’ Pete put her drink in front of her, and she took a few sips—Danielle was right, it was delicious, and she quickly drank most of it down. As soon as she put her glass on the bar, another drink appeared in front of her. Pete looked on in amusement as she gulped it.

‘I might have my dinner in my room tonight. What about you, Danielle?’

‘Yes, me too. I am a little tired. How about you Phoebe?’ Phoebe raised her eyebrows and agreed, a little confused that there was no official dinner. What did she know?’

She was feeling very tired herself. As she stood listening to their banter, she grew increasingly tired. She wanted to call Josh but couldn’t remember where her phone was. She needed to go back upstairs. Her head was spinning. She had had too many Bloody Marys.

‘Um, I think I will head upstairs…’ she grabbed hold of a bar stool as she tried to make her way past.

‘Whoo, hang in there,’ said Pete as he winked at Danielle, who replied rather laconically, ‘I’ll be going, shall I, Pete?’

'Yep.'

He summoned his bodyguards over to help him get Phoebe upstairs.

Phoebe had no idea what was going on. She was very sleepy, and she let the men almost carry her to her room. She lay for a while on the bed in a state of drowsiness. The room spun around her. After a few minutes, she tried to get up but couldn't muster the energy to do so. It wasn't long before she realised that there was someone else in the room with her. They were on the phone. Her sight was blurred, but she was sure it was Pete. She couldn't make out what he was saying, his words were muffled, but he seemed to be in a good mood and talked animatedly to whoever was on the other end of the phone.

He hung up, and the next minute she could make out that he was standing over her. His clothes were missing. She tried to talk, but nothing would come out of her mouth. She felt him taking off her shoes, then her dress. Next, he began undoing the buttons on her shirt. She could feel his fingers brush her breasts as he made his way down from the top button towards her stomach. She tried to yell at him to stop. She was screaming, but nothing was coming out of her mouth. He pulled her head and shoulders up off the bed and removed her shirt; she tried to stop him, but it was almost as if she was paralysed. He bent forward and kissed the nape of her neck, and moved slowly up towards her ear. He put his hands around her and undid her bra very slowly and methodically. He pulled it off and lay her down again. His lips covered her right breast, and his other hand cupped her left. She was totally helpless and unable to stop the molestation. Next, he was pulling at her pants. His tongue made its way down towards her navel. Her pants were now on the floor; she was completely naked and completely helpless. He separated her legs and pulled her further down the bed. In his arrogance, he felt to see if she was ready for him, she wasn't, so he helped her along by lowering his head into her. She was now in a state of panic. Never had she felt so much anger and frustration and not been able to express it. Once he was satisfied with his efforts, he entered her, and as he did, he looked directly into her eyes and said that he was glad that she wasn't resisting, as he had known all along that this was what she really wanted.

The next thing he was off her and putting his clothes back on. She heard a knock at the door. 'Room service' – he had ordered room service like they were on a date or something. She saw him pour champagne into two glasses. He took a sip of his and put a drink next to her by the bed. He took whatever food was on the trolley and started to eat. He didn't offer her any. She finally managed to make a sort of grunting noise. He looked over.

'Don't worry. I will leave you some. I don't think you are quite up to it yet but give it another half hour or so, and we can have a drink together.' She stared at him and told herself that he would not get away with this. She would get him, and he would be sorry.

He must have read her mind as he said, 'You know, I have had other women accuse me of all sorts of things. Rape, sexual harassment, misogyny, none of them were able to prove a bloody thing because they all lied. They were ashamed of what they did, so they made up silly stories to cover their tracks. The media called them out as whores, and had the evidence to prove it.

'Josh, I know, is very keen on you, and you on him, but I could tell you wanted me just that much more. He likes his job, and so do you. This little get together was mutual—wasn't it? You had me carry you into your room and begged me to stay. I am sure there are witnesses to that.' He ate some chips as he let what he was telling her sink in.

She responded with eyes wide open in defiance. He was not worried; he did what he wanted. 'Oh, and you know your sister and her tribe of kids. Well, it would be a shame if she was to lose them to social services, wouldn't it? Her husband? Well, he has a good job, for the time being, doesn't he? I wonder how long that will last, eh? And who would pay the mortgage?'

His appetite sated through greed, vanity and sex, he decided he wanted a good night's sleep. He stood up, stretched and said his goodnights, planted a kiss on her forehead and left. She still couldn't move. She stared at the ceiling until she could feel her body move again.

Once she could sit up, she swung her legs around off the bed and sat with her head down, looking at the floor. A tear dropped onto the carpet, another on her foot. Finally, she could make her way to the bathroom. She looked at herself in the mirror. She could not believe what had just happened. But did it? It all seemed like a bad dream, but she knew it was real. Her clothes were dropped where he had pulled them off her, and her body ached from its misuse. She didn't know what to do next. She had just been raped. He had warned her of the consequences if she said anything. Anyway, who would believe her against the PM in a trial of disgraced women? She was in danger, and so was Josh and her sisters' family. She wanted to tell, to let people know what a bastard he was. But he had ways of making people shut up, and she was no exception. Leaning on the sink and staring hard at her reflection, hair a mess and mascara streaming down her face, she made the fateful decision to get into the shower.

# Chapter 20

The next morning Phoebe awoke to the sound of her alarm clock. It was 6.45 AM. She had no memory of setting it the night before. She didn't know why she had to get up so early. She stared at the ceiling for a while, trying to orientate herself. Her head was foggy, and for a little while, she drifted in and out of consciousness, through valleys of deep nothingness and then out again.

What suddenly reminded her of what happened the night before, she would never be able to say. She sat up in bed and put her hands to her mouth to stifle a cry of absolute horror and despair. Running to the bathroom, she leant over the toilet and threw up what amounted to be the remnants of the Bloody Mary she had enjoyed so much but now bitterly regretted drinking. Her crisp, clean nighty splattered with red dots, she fell back on her knees, utterly defeated. With her head hanging down, she wondered what to do next. What the hell was she going to do?

Time marched on as she stared at the toilet bowl, lost in deep thought, wondering if it was her fault. Had she invited him in? Had she made him feel she had wanted him? Her head was too cloudy to think straight, but the thought that he had put something in her drink, well, that was too much to comprehend. A Prime Minister, drugging a woman so he can have sex with her…no. It wasn't for sex; her thoughts cleared. It was for power. Of course. Pete was all about power and control. She realised that as hard as it might be to believe, she had been drugged and assaulted by the PM. It was just after 9 O'clock when she finally dragged herself off the floor of the bathroom, with much of what had happened to her remembered and grieved over. She recalled that there was a press call scheduled for 10.00 AM. She needed to think. So she filled the little kettle that sat on the sink with water from the bathroom tap; she needed to keep focused.

She knew the window of opportunity to go to the police had elapsed. She had showered and washed away much of the evidence—she checked in the mirror; she had no bruises or any type of outward physical signs that she had been raped. But what was she thinking?

As if the police could be told. They would never believe her. He had made threats not only to her but also to the people she loved; how would anyone believe that a sitting Prime Minister could be so ruthless and so utterly devoid of any moral compass. The easy way out would be to put the blame squarely on herself for putting herself in the situation in the first place. Then she could move on to a degree. If she hadn't been so stupid as to come in the first place, if she hadn't given Pete and Danielle the benefit of the doubt, if she hadn't drunk those Bloody Marys. If she had only listened to Josh! The list of things she shouldn't have done loomed large in her thoughts.

But she was fooling herself to cover for the horror of the situation. She knew who was to blame—he was! But what could she do? He held all the cards. Careers were at stake, and worst of all, her sister's family was in danger. She knew that if he were threatened, he would do anything to save himself. She knew he would follow through with his awful threats. This was beyond comprehension. It was like living in something Machiavelli would write. She knew politics would be rough but not down and out dirty, shameless and full of such unabated vengefulness, not in this day and age. She must play it smart. She must go along like she is okay, everything is fine, but think about what to do, how to get back at this man, how to make him pay for what he has done. She must become much more tactical and more conscious of the lies and deception that surround her. She must play the bloody game; adroitly, much better than the men.

The kettle boiled. At 9.45 AM, there was a knock on her door. It was Danielle. 'Hey, Phoebe, the car will be here in five minutes. Can you be downstairs in two?' Her voice was loud and clear through the door.

'Yep, sure,' Phoebe replied, her mouth tight as she said the words as full as confidence as she could muster. Danielle lingered by the door, not sure of the state Phoebe was actually in. Phoebe checked herself in the mirror; she looked good, if not a little sad around the eyes. Then she remembered her phone. It was in her bag, but she had forgotten she had put it on silence. There was a missed call from her mum and 6 missed calls from Josh. She didn't have the energy to talk to him at the moment, so she kept it on silent. She would talk to him after the press call. As Danielle made her way downstairs, she wondered what had really happened, if anything at all.

Josh was having his breakfast at his desk. He had not slept well through the night and, consequently, had slept through the morning alarm. He turned on the TV to watch the news. He knew his day would be shitty. He had a couple of senators coming to see him about something Pete had done, and as they didn't have the backbone to face Pete directly, they would take it out on him, and he would have to tell Pete what they were angry about, and he would, as usual, not give a shit. Coffee and a bacon sandwich would help him face it all. But as he ate, he thought about Phoebe. Why the hell hadn't she returned his calls?

Suddenly, breaking news interrupted the regular stream of stories: the PM was doing a press conference. 'Shit,' Josh mumbled to himself. He had forgotten all about that. Anyway,

Pete hadn't wanted his advice; he had told him he didn't need it as he had Phoebe with him, and if he needed anything from her, he would take it. Suddenly Phoebe was in view. Josh was uneasy about her appearance. She stood just to the left of the PM with the strangest expression on her face. He couldn't tell if she was upset, tired or having a meltdown. She also had a slight rash around her nose. 'A makeup mishap?' he questioned out loud. As Pete waffled on about the rights of women to access refuge and break free from domestic violence, Josh could not take his eyes off Phoebe. He knew something was wrong, very wrong. Because why the hell wouldn't she answer her phone?

Back in the car on her way to her hotel, she decided she would go back to Canberra straight away. She needed to put some distance between herself and Pete. She wouldn't tell him; she would just go. He wouldn't miss her. He had other women to amuse himself with. That stung; how could she suddenly be so callous as she knew most if not all the women in his orbit probably endured his attention rather than welcomed it. But she was in self-preservation mode and could not spend precious energy worrying about others, not now. She needed to worry about herself. She was so tired that she could hardly stay awake.

Once she arrived back at the hotel room that had been the scene of her nightmares, she threw herself and her bag on the bed. It would be easy to break down, to cry and to scream, to lose control. She bit her bottom lip, forcing herself not to do so. Her mind raced as she looked at the detail on the ceiling, swirly patterns of paint that had their heyday in the 70s but were coming back into fashion. She thought about Mic and the marriage she had left. She was not going to kid herself; she was content most of the time, mostly she felt safe. Her life was good, he was a great man, and they were doing well. So why wasn't it enough? She couldn't answer that right now because she was in danger of regret, an emotion that would not help her present situation. No matter if she did, he had moved on and had made a life for himself with a lovely woman who had given him what he had wanted most; a child.

'Bloody hell,' she mumbled. 'What am I going to do?' A tear trickled into her ear. She knew she must not break. No use in 'what ifs'. All that matters now is 'what is,' and what to do about it. She drew in a deep breath and went to the bathroom. Looking in the mirror, she noticed that she had a rash on her face that spread over the bridge of her nose and down onto its sides.

'Great, what now?' Then she remembered that she hadn't had the blood test she was going to have before the whole Tasmania thing. She will do it tomorrow. But now, she was tired. It was best to go to bed, get some rest and then make plans to return to Canberra later in the night. She was sure she could get a last-minute flight back. She put on a podcast to help lull her to sleep, and soon, she was slumbering, although a little restlessly. Her phone, still on silent in her bag, registered 15 missed calls from Josh. He too would have to wait.

***

'What the bloody hell have you been up to, Phoebe?' Josh was in a horrible mood on the other end of the phone. 'Well?'

Phoebe was just getting over the fact that it was the next day, 10 AM to be precise. She had had nearly one full day's sleep but was still so very tired she could hardly answer him.

'Josh, please...'

'Phoebe, I have been ringing you nonstop for over 24 hours. Why haven't you returned my calls? What has happened?'

'Nothing, what do you mean, what has happened?' She was alarmed. He had almost a sixth sense about things, and she was terrified that she would let something slip. He must not find out; she was sure he would kill Pete if he did.

'I saw you on TV yesterday. To be frank, Pheebs, you looked terrible.'

'Oh, thanks.'

'I am not going to lie. You looked out of sorts like you wanted to be anywhere else but there. Tell me what happened?'

Phoebe bit her lip, trying to think of something to say that would stop his interrogation. She closed her eyes tight and said,

'I wasn't feeling well, but I am all good now, nothing to worry about, all good.' Suddenly, she thought that if she put a little bit of truth in the lie, she would sound more convincing. 'To tell you the truth, I do feel tired most of the time. I am going to see a doctor when I get back. Have a checkup. Probably just need a tonic, as my mother would say.' She managed a half-hearted laugh.

Josh didn't say anything. He was sure she was not telling him the full story. With a furrowed brow, he asked,

'Why didn't you answer your phone?'

'Well,' she cleared her throat, 'I put it on silent 'cause my mother was ringing all the time, and I didn't want to talk to her. I put my phone in my bag and forgot about it.'

'Why put it on silent? Why not just let it ring?'

'You know my mum Josh. Once she decides she wants to talk to me, then she will keep ringing until I do.'

'Umph' was his reply.

'By the way, I'm coming home today.'

'Why? I thought this conference thing or whatever it is was for at least another day. I wasn't expecting you till tomorrow. Oh, and have you rung your mother back? She may be ill?'

'Yes, yes, and no, she is not ill. I feel so tired that I have made up my mind to come back early. They don't really need me here. I am just here to make up the numbers. I am going to see about it on Monday.'

'Better get onto it then.' He hung up. He was too angry to keep talking to her. Best wait 'til they are face to face.

'Shitttttt!' Phoebe let the word come out of her mouth in an almost guttural cry. She knew she had to play it smart with Josh. He was clever, much too clever to try and deceive. After all, he had survived in Canberra for a long, long time. He could spot bullshit a mile off, the result of working with politicians on a day to day basis. No, she needed to tread carefully, not only for her sake but for his and her sister's family. Dropping her phone, she covered her face with her hands and sobbed until she could cry no longer.

***

Twenty-four hours later, she was sitting in a small room of a pathology service not far from her office.

'This will sting just a little.' Phoebe looked into the eyes of the smiling nurse taking her blood. She noticed that they were a jade green colour enhanced by her ash blonde hair. She was young, pretty and, so it seemed to Phoebe, full of life, full of sparkle, even joy. Everything she felt she was not. Compounded by the way she felt, utterly exhausted, it made it very hard to answer or be cordial in any way. A small half-smile was all she could do to reply to her assurances that it wouldn't hurt.

'There, all done. Can you check your name on the vials, please, just to make sure we have the right person?' Another broad smile. Phoebe picked up each one and, in turn, checked her name and date of birth. There seemed to be a never-ending line of vials, and she wondered if she had any blood left in her at all.

'Your doctor sure is giving you the works.' Still cheerful. Again Phoebe replied with a half-smile.

'All done, have a lovely day.'

To say 'you too' as she walked, or dragged herself out, took all her energy, but she felt she owed it to the young woman who had tried but failed to initiate any kind of chitchat between them. She just wished some people had a better radar for picking up on the emotions of others and acting accordingly.

Back in her car, she slumped over the steering wheel. What the hell was going on? Could she be pregnant?

No, she'd had a period a fortnight ago, and besides, she was on the pill.

A terrible thought struck her like a lightning bolt—if she was, it could be Pete's! No, she assured herself that was not the reason for her feeling like a truck had reversed over her a couple of dozen times.

Another thought struck her. It could be the remnants of the drug that Pete had put in her drink. Maybe she should have asked if her blood could be checked for Rohypnol. That would have given her some proof. She quickly googled it. Damn! It only lasts up to six to eight hours and then is undetectable. Deflated, she realised it must be something else. She had enough to worry about. Her hands gripped the steering wheel tightly. Work, stress, anger, worry, not eating correctly, the need for a holiday were much more reasonable answers for her ill-health than—*being sexually abused*. For now, paradoxically, even though she was terribly unwell, she needed to go back to work to make sure Pete thought everything was okay, and wait for the results of the blood tests. There was nothing of any substance that she could do until her head cleared and she regained some strength.

Exactly what she was going to do was something she had yet to work out. But rest assured, she told herself, she would, she bloody well would.

***

'You look like you are working hard.' Phoebe had not spoken to Josh since he had hung up on her a few days back. She hadn't the energy to think about much else other than how bad she was feeling. She lifted her head and tried to focus on him.

'Jean told me you didn't want to be disturbed, but that was because I thought you were working hard and deserved a break, not that you were having a break and not working hard.'

'Josh….' All the emotion she had been holding in gushed up, and tears welled in her eyes.

'What's wrong?' His nose for trouble was never far from seeking out the truth, 'what happened on that blasted trip?'

It was crunch time. If she told him, only trouble lay in front for them all; for her, him and her family. If she didn't, he would be so mad that he would, in all probability, not see her again. He had his pride, and keeping secrets from him was one of the great sins in a relationship with him. And she would carry the shame, guilt, and anger by herself.

He came over to her, and she dropped her face towards the desk; tears fell. He bent over her, her auburn hair next to his black crown, and he kissed the side of her face. He knew something terrible had happened, something awful, and he wanted desperately to understand. But she would have to tell him willingly. He knew that if he pushed her, she wouldn't. He knew her well enough to know that. Thoughts raced through Phoebe's head. What to say? What to say to make it all go away?

But she knew that this was something that was not going to go away. She sucked in her breath.

That gave him the signal to ask, 'What's wrong, Pheebs?'

She didn't want him to know the real reason, not yet at least. She must tell him a half-truth, tell him something that was indeed worrying her but not the real reason for her distress. That way, she would not have to worry about keeping the story straight—to lie, she was no good at—but to survive in this place, she knew that was a skill she would have to develop and quickly.

'Oh, I have just been to get my blood done…' she lifted her head to look him in the eye. She wanted him to believe her. 'I am a bit worried about what the results will show, that's all. I'm sure it's nothing, but you cannot help being a little on edge about it, especially as I have not been feeling great.'

Josh stood up and looked down at her as she looked him in the face with tears staining her flushed cheeks. It was plausible, but he was not sure this was the real reason for her distress. He felt it in his bones that something, something had happened on that blasted Tasmanian trip, and she was not going to tell him.

She read his thoughts. 'Josh, please, that's all there is to it.'

He let out a sigh and looked around her office, disgruntled but determined to let her have her way for the moment. 'You know; you really haven't settled in here, have you? Not a pot plant or a photo of any of your family. Makes me wonder just how much you do enjoy your job—eh?'

'I am too busy for such sentimentalities. Besides, whose picture from my family would I put up? My mother? Please, she annoys me enough with never-ending phone calls…'

'Which you never answer.'

'I do when I think I should. Besides, you have no photos in your office.'

‘I have no family, well none that I am fond of, I suppose. I would only want your photo on my desk, and we both know that would be courting trouble.’ They both let out a little laugh, although Phoebe’s was tinged with sadness.

‘Hey,’ he said. ‘I have an idea seeing as the cat is away. How about we escape the four walls and the artificial light, grab a ridiculously unhealthy meal and eat it by the lake?’

‘That sounds like the best idea you’ve had in a long time.’

# Chapter 21

'Well, did you have a good time with that girl?' Danielle was sorting through paperwork on the PM's cluttered desk and looking at him out of the corner of her eye.

'Didn't taste like a girl to me,' he replied and in the next breath, 'at the cabinet meeting this afternoon, what do you think I should say in regards to the Tasmanian trip and any type of policy that will keep the Feminazis' off my back—eh?'

She was always amazed at how he did not give a damn about anyone or anything. Once he had what he wanted, he moved on to new conquests without so much as a blink of an eye. She chuckled. He responded with 'what?'

'Nothing, you are just quite something, aren't you?'

'Yes, I would agree with that.'

She kept looking for the paperwork she was after.

'Well?'

She stopped. 'Oh, you want me to give you a good policy statement or something of the sort just because I am a woman? I don't know why you are worried about the cabinet anyway; you don't have any women in it for a start.'

'True, but the government has a few scattered here and there; MPs and backbenchers who will be after my blood. So anything, anything at all that you may have at the back of your head.'

'Haven't you got a women's policy advisor for that?'

'Yes, I have, but I doubt whether she would want to help me at the moment. She is too caught up in being the victim when we both know she was just as much up for it as I was.'

Danielle doubted it. In fact, she was quite sure that she had not, but her loyalty, even if he was pushing it to its limits, was to Pete, so she would never let on that she felt that he had indeed taken advantage of her.

'You know working women, mothers—that sort of thing.'

'Well, I have always been a working woman but never a working mother, so I cannot give you an insight into the needs of working mothers.' His questioning of motherhood issues took her a little off guard. She'd had an abortion, and it was the only time she had fallen pregnant. She had told herself she had not wanted a child, but deep down, she had done it to keep Josh. She was so sure her pregnancy had come at an inopportune time; he didn't want a kid, his career, and hers was too important to both of them; she would ruin all they had. She did not want to put him through the agony of making such a decision; life or death. She made the call, and now she was living with the consequences. She lost him.

'You know Pete; it's a little too warm in here. I've found what I wanted. I can't help you with policy advice right now. Talk to your ministers and advisors for a change maybe.' Her voice was a little higher than usual.

'Being a little reactionary today, aren't we?'

'Get stuffed,' she mumbled under her breath as she was leaving.

'You know Danielle, you and I are kindred spirits. We get what we want when we want it. Can you bring me a coffee? Thanks.'

She closed the office door behind her and looked around casually to see if anyone was hovering in the corridors or into their glass framed offices. Seeing that the coast was clear, she let out a silent scream, and she almost ran to her office and slammed the door. Stuff him and stuff his bloody coffee.

'So tell me, what was Tasmania really like?'

Her mouth was half stuffed with lamb kebab and a few hot chips. She gestured to him to let her finish; conveniently, this gave her time to clarify her response in her head.

'It was fine,' she said as she gulped the last vestiges of what she had been chewing. 'We had a press conference, and Pete made a few noises about helping women, refugees, and domestic violence, but apart from that, it really was just a junket: dinner, drinking and mingling with people that you would rather not be mingling with. I came back early because I was not feeling well.' She looked over the lake towards Capitol Hill. They were sitting on a bench outside the National Museum. They had taken a ComCar, and the driver was waiting patiently for them in the driver's seat as they finished their lunch. Josh was inclined not to believe her story or at the very least thought that she was leaving something rather important out.

A cool breeze ruffled their hair. She knew what he was thinking as he stared at her. 'Josh, can we just enjoy this?' She pulled that light blue scarf that she was wearing around her neck a bit tighter. The weather was getting cooler by the day, and being from further north, the chilling bite it held was a bit of a shock to her.

'Okay. If you're cold, how about we finish this and grab a coffee from inside?' Josh said in defeat. 'And if you are worried about the driver, we will buy him one as well.'

***

As Pete entered the cabinet meeting, he sneered at Danielle as she held the door open. She sneered back as she watched a small troop of men, all in suits and ties, make their way self-importantly into the room. She knew that they thought they had a say, but in reality, they were only there to make up the numbers. Pete had the last say: nothing they said was even considered. Women played no role in decision-making; even though a handful of them littered parliament, they were there to make the political parties look like they were all for equal opportunity. As she shut the door behind her and headed back to her office, she wondered why the electorate put up with it. It seemed as though everyone was too caught up with blogging, "X", and Instagram to really care about how they were governed, least of all who was governing them. Keep them entertained and distracted, and they won't notice what is really going on around them. She knew that was in the history books somewhere and never had more exact words been spoken.

As she sat at her desk, fielding calls for the PM and allocating his precious time to meeting and greetings, she thought about Phoebe, and to her utmost surprise, she felt a tang of pity for her and a touch of guilt about her own role in the sordid affair. After all, she had let it happen. She would never have thought in a million years she would be a party to anything of the sort that had happened in that hotel room. Intimidation, bitching and slander, yes, but allowing another woman to be raped!

How had she come down to this level? She was jealous of her, yes, but did that give her the right to let her go through what she had? No. She thought of herself as a tough cookie, but her tough exterior was tempered with a small amount of compassion and understanding, characteristics she always tried to conceal.

And due to them, she now felt positively criminal. Pete had raped her and threatened her family and Josh. It was all getting way out of hand. She knew she had to make some tough choices. If she kept supporting Pete, she knew she was defending a monster: God knows what else he was willing to do to satisfy his over-bloated ego. If she backed down and withdrew her support, she was in genuine danger herself. She had not shed a tear since the day of her abortion. But now tears dropped onto her desk, wetting the papers spread out before her. Years of regret and trying to hurt a man she had once loved passionately had caught up with her. She had painted herself into a corner: a corner that would prove very difficult to get out of.

***

Back in her office, Phoebe was uneasy. She needed to check on her family. They must not, under any circumstances, be dragged into this mess; she phoned Sarah. No answer. She tried again. On the last ring, Sarah answered. 'Sarah?'

'Yeah.'

'It's Phoebe.'

'I know, your name came up on my phone. Doesn't your phone do that?'

Phoebe ignored the dig. 'How are you all, the kids?'

'What's up?'

'What?'

'I said, what's up?'

'Nothing, can't I ring my sister to see how she is and how her family is going?'

'Well, yes you can, but this is the first time you have done it in, let me see…2 years, so you can imagine that I am a little taken aback by this sudden interest in me and my brood. So, I will ask again, what's up?'

'How are the kids?'

'Good, they are all in the backyard with water pistols. I can't be very long; otherwise, a fight will break out and then it will be chaos.'

‘Okay, okay, look, I am sorry that I have been slack. I will try to do better.’

‘Fine,’ Sarah replied, a little worried. What was going on with Phoebe?

As soon as Phoebe hung up, Sarah rang their mother. Not too long after that, Phoebe was on the phone with her mother, trying to explain her sudden interest in her sister’s life. The one comfort she got from that phone call was that her brother was overseas travelling in Asia. At least he was out of harm’s way. She would just have to be careful to keep everyone safe. Before she knew it, Jean popped her head in the door to let her know she was heading home.

‘Okay, see you soon,’ Phoebe replied, lost in thought as to how she would carry on. Just how would she keep up the charade? She knew one thing for sure—she was exhausted. Then she remembered that she had to go back and see the doctor about her blood tests. The surgery had rung to ask her to make an appointment, but it had slipped her mind. That was over a week ago. She would do it in the morning.

***

As she sat and waited to see the doctor, she felt as if she was there for no reason. She felt fine. She looked at all the other patients who were waiting. On the surface, most seemed okay except for the old man in the corner who looked to Phoebe to be a few hours away from death and those one or two who were sneezing into their hankies and tissues. If she didn’t have the flu now, she knew she would once she got out of here.

‘Mrs Cavanagh.’

She heard the name but didn’t take much notice of it. ‘Mrs Cavanagh, Phoebe.’ Oh, she was jolted out of her thoughts; she had not heard herself called by her married title for a long time. She was used to being called Phoebe. No one she worked with called her anything else. She stuffed her phone into her bag, got up from her seat and straightened her black pencil skirt. As she walked towards the doctor, she mouthed 'sorry' as he directed her towards his room. He gave her a small smile as she walked past. He followed.

As she sat, she said, 'Look, I feel like a bit of a fraud, I feel fine today, and if you don't mind, I am going by my maiden name now, Peters.'

'Okay, just change it with the girls out front on your way out. Now, let's go over your blood works.'

'Okay.'

The doctor sat in front of his computer and scanned her results. 'Everything looks fine. You have nothing much to worry about—'

Phoebe interrupted, 'That's good.'

He went on, 'But your iron is a bit low. Maybe you need to eat more red meat, and you may even consider taking some iron supplements, maybe two a day.'

'Okay. I will.'

'We will see how you go and if you don't start feeling better on the iron, we will do further tests.

'Alright, I told you I feel like a fraud.'

The doctor shook his head in a way to say it was fine. She smiled back.

'If you have any more problems, don't hesitate to make another appointment.'

She crossed the road and headed back to her car. It was a relief that everything was fine and all she needed to do was pop an iron pill or two to feel better and far less tired. She wished everything was so easy to fix. She slid into her seat and braced herself for a long and stressful day back at the office. However, she didn't stop herself from having a chuckle as she drove back, 'Miss Peters,' she thought. Why had she registered her married name? She could not even begin to understand. Maybe it was just a habit yet to be overcome. 'Oh, well,' she giggled a bit more. It was the first time since her attack that she had had any semblance of a laugh. It felt good.

The day seemed to muddle along like she was stuck in the mud with wellington boots on. Try as she might to power through the day, she just couldn't pick up any sort of reasonable pace. The trees outside swayed back and forth in the light breeze, and the backlog of papers that sat in her in-tray diminished at a prolonged rate. But before she knew it, she had worked through lunch, and it was rapidly heading towards 2 PM. She wondered why Jean had not popped her head in. She always made sure she ate or at least had a lukewarm coffee on her desk. Her stomach growled. She hadn't heard from Josh since last night; he had not stayed over as she had told him she needed space. This, however, was not true. She feared that in a moment of repressed anger, which often bubbled up when she least expected it, she would blurt out what had happened. She couldn't risk it. She could see in his face that he was taken aback that she had asked him to stay at his own place. He hadn't done that for a while. Now, late in the day, he had not rung. She knew he would be sulking.

She needed something sweet to make her feel better. Something with sugar and cream and maybe some delicious strawberry jam—cream bun! Comfort eating was called for, and she didn't give a toss. She may even have two cream buns. This was becoming a bit of a habit of late, and as she headed towards the café, she noticed that her skirt was just a little bit tighter than it usually was.

Two cream buns demolished and a trip to the loo later, Phoebe was back at her office, coffee in hand.

Jean came in. 'Hi, just letting you know I am back.'

'Oh, I didn't know you were gone.'

'Sorry, I thought I emailed you. Umm. Well, us office girls had a little celebration lunch for Sue, she is getting married next week and then she is off for a whole month on honeymoon.'

'Good for her.'

'Yes, yes, nice to see her so happy,' She stressed the 'so,' annoyingly.

'Boy, I am full. The Thai food on the main road is to die for.' Phoebe's face dropped, and Jean cut the conversation short. She asked. 'Can I get you a coffee? Phoebe...'

'Yes...oh, yeah, that would be great.' 'Oh, you have one already?'

'Silly me.' She took a swig. 'It is nearly empty, so another wouldn't go astray.'

'Okay, it's your heart rate.'

Phoebe didn't want another coffee. She felt wounded that she wasn't invited to the meal with the girls. She got on well with them all, and they often laughed together. She felt right at that very moment that she didn't fit in anywhere. Not with her peers or the girls in the office. A loner. 'Don't be silly. It's not office etiquette to invite the boss, so to speak.' She knew that they would feel unable to relax with her around. She didn't think she gave them that impression of being above their station in life. But she must. Could she feel any worse?

Jean appeared with her coffee.

'Phoebe, please, if I am interfering, feel free to tell me.' She held the coffee with two hands nervously. 'I'm just a little worried about you. I would like you to know that I am here…if you need to talk.'

She handed Phoebe the coffee and smiled. Phoebe could see her face full of concern. She was in no mood for sympathy and mistook her kindness for wanting to know the gossip so she could inform the girls.

'Thanks, but there is nothing wrong,' she replied a little tartly.

The words stung. Jean just looked at her in puzzlement and took her leave. Phoebe watched her close the door behind her.

'Wow, how to win friends and influence people,' she muttered to herself. She was right not to disclose anything to Jean. She was well known as the gossip of Parliament House, and that is not a mean feat in a place filled with them. No, she was learning that there are not many in this place that can be trusted. It's a hard lesson.

Her hunger was still not satisfied. Phoebe decided that she would go and grab something more to eat. Cream buns are excellent, but she needed something with a bit of green in it. She thought of going somewhere discreet but then thought better of it. She headed straight for the pigpen; she would not hide away in some little obscure coffee house hidden from all and sundry. After all, she hadn't done anything wrong. No, it was time she got herself back together and make a conscious effort not to be overlooked anymore. She wanted people of this great house to see her, and she would be seen, and she would be heard. She was not going to let Pete win.

# Chapter 22

Just as Phoebe was finishing off her late lunch of the biggest and sweetest doughnut on offer, Danielle walked past and spotted her. Danielle had her hands full of folders filled with papers for Pete to sign. Some of them were urgent. Pete was sending her on a bit of a goose chase, so she had given up trying to find him and was just going to dump it all on his desk. The sight of Phoebe scoffing a doughnut stopped her in her tracks. She had avoided her as much as she could since the incident, as she called it. No matter how hard she tried to justify or explain it away, she could not help but feel that Pete had crossed a line and one that should never have been crossed in the first place.

Much of her internal torment was driven by her love and loss of Josh. However, she found that the intense feelings that flowed out of the wretched relationship were ebbing. It was like she was riding a tide of emotion, sometimes it hit her hard, like a wave, and at times she was calm and not tossed around by how she felt. Mostly, however, she was more inclined to be calm. Things she would have tolerated and indeed instigated due to anger and resentment seemed to have lost their appeal. What had happened to Phoebe had shaken her to her core. It was a wake-up call. Politics and position should never allow for physical assault, and just because you are powerful, it should not make you untouchable. Phoebe did not deserve what happened. As she stood and watched Phoebe finish her last mouthful of the doughnut, Phoebe looked up and saw Danielle staring at her through the glass panels of the pigpen. Danielle was taken aback by being caught staring. All she could do was smile.

Phoebe smiled back nervously and watched Danielle disappear down the corridor.

'Shit,' Phoebe mumbled, 'what is she up to now?'

Danielle dumped the files on Pete's desk and decided she needed to talk to someone impartial. She couldn't explain it, but her involvement with the incident was eating her up. She hadn't seen her psychologist for over 12 months, but she needed to talk to her again, and soon. She made an appointment for the next day.

As Phoebe was walking back to her office, she got a call from Josh. 'Hey'

'Hey,' she replied.

'Can I stay tonight? I miss you.'

She thought for a second. She really couldn't keep putting him off.

'Only if you bring dinner with you. Okay?'

'Deal, what do you want?' 'Surprise me.'

'Okay.'

'And bring chocolate.'

'Wow, you have really developed a sweet tooth in the last few weeks, haven't you?'

His voice held back a bit of a giggle. 'Yep, got a problem with it?'

'No, no, I will bring chocolate. See you later.' 'Bye.'

It was only sugar that seemed to keep her going lately. Coffee just didn't cut it anymore.

***

Just as Josh hung up the phone, Danielle came into his office. She looked flustered, and he steeled himself for some sort of talking down. But to his surprise, she walked back and forth, agitated and somewhat flushed. She stopped and sat on the desk that was situated under the only window his office had. She faced him and swung her legs back and forth. Josh studied her. She was making him nervous, very nervous. There were not too many times in her life where she was lost for words in front of him. The last time was when she tried to hide the abortion. For her to be here meant she wanted to tell him something, but that something was going to be something she didn't really want him to know, but something that he should. He could still read her body language. What he couldn't make out was why she just didn't come out with it; there was no love lost between the two of them. It had been a long time since she had considered his feelings. He was anxious. She knew it.

'I've never noticed how pretty this little garden is outside your window.' Her gaze lingered on his face and not on the lilac African Lilies outside.

Josh stood. 'What is it you came to tell me, Danielle?'

She smoothed her navy skirt and pulled at the matching jacket. As usual, she was immaculately dressed. Not a hair out of place. Together, they looked like they had both just stepped out of a Vogue shoot.

'Josh,' she slid off the desk and back onto her feet. 'I am getting to a stage in my life where I don't want any drama. You may find that funny, but I mean it. I am getting less inclined to intrigue and, well, you know to backstab…'

Josh screwed his face up, as he had little evidence of why he should be inclined to believe her. 'What has happened to make you do such a U-turn?' He wasn't having any of it. She was playing him.

'Not so much…Ummm, it's been a buildup, you could say, over the years.' She paced back and forth. In truth, it was the shock of her role in what had happened to Phoebe, but she had to tell him something. 'I can't put my finger on it. Truth be told, I am tired. I am sick of being the bitch. I just want to get on with people and do the right thing for a change: to find some peace.'

'Peace, peace. You thrive on the chaos and drama, so don't give me that—something is up, so stop pussyfooting around. You have never been concerned about anyone's feelings in your life. Why start now?'

Danielle knew he was right, she did thrive in this place, but something had shifted. She couldn't understand it herself. All she could put it down to was that the incident with Phoebe has shaken her to her core. It was one thing to throw verbal barbs, to backstab and undermine, but to rape! She shook her head. He had to know. He had to, but what would be the outcome? Disaster, she knew it. All their careers would be down the tube. However, she was past caring. She stopped pacing and stopped him walking up to her by turning and facing him.

'Josh, please, what I am going to tell you will devastate you.'

'You have a habit of telling me such things. Well, what is it?'

She stood looking at him for a minute. Now that she had the opportunity, she found it hard to get the words out. She shifted her feet and looked past him. Could she do it to him again? Give him terrible news and watch his face crumple in grief as she had seen it do once before.

When she walked into his office, she had intended to tell him the nuts and bolts of it all. Now, as they stood face to face, she couldn't do it. She would ask him to talk to Phoebe.

'Something happened in Tasmania, between Phoebe and Pete.'

His face dropped, and he responded slowly. 'I knew it! What happened?' His voice rose with an alarming vigour, full of anger and concern.

‘That’s all I am prepared to say. I think you need to talk to Phoebe. And do it soon.’

She pushed past him to walk out the door.

‘Hey, now you just wait a minute.’ He grabbed her arm. ‘You have got to tell me what happened. Don’t expect to leave without telling me.’

‘Talk to Phoebe.’ She pulled away from him. ‘Has she slept with him?’

’Just talk to her.’

He wanted to shake the living daylights out of her, but he refrained as he knew it would not solve anything.

As she left and headed back to her own office, she heard him yell, ‘I hope this gave you a little bit of pleasure. Hey no, I don’t have to hope, as I am very sure it did.’

He sat down and picked up his phone. His first instinct was to call Phoebe. All he could think about was the two of them in bed together. It was too much. He slumped over his desk. This was a trick, surely? Phoebe wouldn’t do this to him. Would she? He was doubting her and hating himself for it, but he had to find out what had happened on that blasted trip.

Josh grabbed his phone, keys, and wallet off his work laden desk. He almost ran down the corridor fumbling with his phone trying to contact Phoebe. He needed to find out. He needed to know what had happened. He couldn’t help but think the worst, but he needed to hear it from her. Had she betrayed him with Pete? She hated him. How could that be? Phoebe was not in her office and not answering her phone. He headed for the office of the hated protagonist, but he wasn’t there either, which was lucky as he would have throttled him. He thought they could be together. His thoughts were getting the better of him.

***

For her part, Phoebe had skipped out for a coffee after getting an annoying phone call from her mother, telling her that her sister was once again pregnant and then from her sister to rub it in. Pete, Josh remembered, was at a taping of a news interview. He had arranged it the other week. He had put him in the government car this morning—he had forgotten entirely. Why hadn't Pete wanted him to go with him? He usually accompanied him to such forays—was Phoebe with him instead? He turned back down the corridor and headed for Jean.

'Jean, Jean, where is Phoebe?'

The older woman looked up, startled to see Josh looking so agitated and threatening. He didn't look refined and gentlemanly as he usually did. The veins in his neck protruded, and his face was a mix of pale white and rosy red. Jean swallowed before she answered.

'Ummm, she was in her office not long ago. I think she just went to get another coffee. Getting quite an addict,' she joked, but Josh wasn't laughing. He turned and quickly made his way to the pigpen, where he knew she would be. She had often told him that even though she didn't like the clientele, they did make the best coffee in the place.

He saw her sipping on a coffee and staring into space. Everyone else is chatting and laughing. She, in stark contrast, is alone and silent. Josh could tell by her face that she was tormented by something. Her face had lost some of its lustre. He hesitated at the doorway. He wanted to know what happened, but then he didn't. He couldn't stand the thought of her leaving him – and for Pete! No! It couldn't be. She loved him. She had told him time and time again. What the hell happened? What the hell?

He straightened his purple satin tie and headed her way. She looked up and saw him striding towards her. Her face said it all.

Tears welled up in her eyes. She stood and walked past him, and he followed. In the hall, he grabbed her by the arm and turned her to face him.

'I need to know what happened in Tasmania.' He implored. She could only shut her eyes and let the tears roll. They could not stay in the hall; the ladies room was just a few metres away. He directed her towards it. As they entered, he called out, making sure no one was in the cubicles. He didn't want anyone overhearing them. She was at the sink looking in the mirror and at her face, which was strewn with runny mascara, and patches of stained foundation. She was a mess.

They were alone; he leant back onto the entry door to stop interlopers.

He just said:

'Tell me.'

'I…I don't know how.'

'I don't care how—just tell me.'

She couldn't face him directly. She addressed him by looking at him through the large mirror that adorned the restroom.

'I had too much to drink, well I think I did, I must have…I thought that I was finally being accepted as an important part of the team. I thought, I thought…I was drinking with Pete and Danielle; they gave me Bloody Marys. Next thing I knew…' She looked down into the basin as a tear fell from her face. She fell forward, her hands secured on the basin to hold her up. She looked deep into it and not at him.

'He, he took me up to my room, and he raped me.' The words were out. He knew.

Josh stood up and walked towards her. Just as he did, a woman ventured into the loos.

'Out,' he yelled. The interloper scampered with a look of sheer horror on her face.

'He did what?'

'Don't make me repeat it. Please.' 'You didn't...I mean, it was rape?'

She slowly looked up at him through the mirror again.

'What?'

'I didn't mean what you think I do. It's just that I thought that you and him...I had no idea. No idea.'

As the realisation of what had happened to her hit him, anger rose in his face. 'Josh, we must handle this sensibly.'

'I'll kill him. I will!'

'Please, Josh, please. I have to deal with this; you can't make it better. I need to work out what I am going to do.'

'Why didn't you report it? There would have been evidence, surely?'

She tried to take what he had said in the way he meant it and not be offended by his tone.

'Josh, he...' 'What?'

'He threatened to have my sister's children taken off her. He said he would. And he would get her husband sacked. I can't remember what else but...'

'That absolute bastard,' he headed to leave the toilet and face off with what he now knew was not a man but a monster.

Phoebe ran and grabbed him. They struggled as he tried to make his way out. She couldn't restrain him, and she fell to the floor a blubbering mess.

'Josh, Josh, please...'

He came back and stood over her.

'Please, this has to be done my way. We have to be sensible, we can get him, and we will. But not like this. Not like this.'

He bent down and scooped her up into her arms. Never in his life had he wanted to kill someone so much as he did him. He cried with her. Their bodies huddled up against the door, ignoring the knocks and the calls of, 'are you alright in there?'

After a short while, they managed to get up, tidy themselves up a bit and head out of the toilets. They made up the excuse that 'Phoebe was not feeling very unwell and needed some space' to the crowd who had gathered around the doorway. All eyes were on them as they walked very quickly towards Phoebe's office; Josh did all he could to keep from exploding. Phoebe could feel his anger penetrating through her as he followed. Jean looked up as they passed her desk. She wanted to greet them but, by the looks on their faces, thought better of it. She looked down and made out she was busy with a pen and paper.

Once they had closed the door behind them, Jean got a phone call. 'Come back here, news to tell!'

'Be right there.' The phone call was from one of the new girls in the back office behind the wall. She took great delight in the office gossip so fitted in well with most of the others. As Jean walked towards her, she could see that she was buried in conversation with the other new office assistant. She looked up as Jean approached and left her offsider to focus her attention on Jean. Her short blonde bob shone under the lights of the office. Jean also noticed that her blue eyes were bright with the anticipation of letting her know the news.

'You will never guess, never ever!'

'What won't I guess?' Jean was a little bemused by her excitement.

'Phoebe and Josh, they were both in the womens' toilets, down the hall. They were arguing. They could be heard right to the end of the hall. Someone said that it has something to do with the PM.'

When Jean heard this, she pulled the young girl by her arm towards her and warned her to keep her voice down.

She then pushed her towards the old stationery cupboard at the back of the office and opened the doors. She manoeuvred the girl into the cupboard as far as she could so that the doors on either side protected them from prying eyes and ears.

'What are you talking about, Sophie?'

'Just what I said...Phoebe and Josh were fighting in the toilets, and someone heard the PM's name. Something is going on...' Her eyes were bright, but she was also a little apprehensive because Jean seemed to be a little on edge about the news. Usually, Jean enjoyed a little gossip. This was not the case now.

'Right,' Jean said. 'Not a word to anyone, you hear? Not a word.' 'But...'

'If you value your job, not a word, not one word.'

'Okay...but Jean...'

'You heard me. Back to your desk and get your work finished.'

Jean watched as the young girl went back to her desk and took her seat. She could see the girl was a little deflated and reluctant to get on with any work when there was a mountain of gossip to indulge. Jean also saw that Sophie knew something was up, and all she wanted to do was talk about it to anyone who would listen.

This would not only be dangerous for Sophie but for anyone caught indulging in other people's business—because this wasn't anyone—this was the PM.

Jean had a feeling that something was wrong, very wrong, and this was no ordinary run of the mill gossip. She knew Josh; he always kept away from trouble. For him to be involved, and so publicly, meant something, something terrible was brewing. Her brow creased as she remembered Phoebe and Josh's faces as they sought refuge in the office. Their muffled voices was another sure sign that something was wrong. Well, whatever it was, is, or will be, she didn't want any part of it. Nothing, not gossip, not taking sides, not a thing would be traced back to her. Her most important job now was to make sure that the new girls did not fall into the trap of being drawn into the intrigue. The new ones, the ones with little political know-how, were the ones that would get you hung. She looked at both of them. Sophie was distracted, only looking at her work but not seeing it. However, Grace was deep in thought and reading whatever was in front of her.

Jean knew she would have trouble with Sophie. Thank heavens, Grace was less inclined to gossip and only got involved so as not to be seen as the outsider. Jean was grateful for that. No matter how determined she was to stay out of it, Jean could not help but wonder what had happened. As she sat at her desk, she glanced over at Phoebe's door. There was no noise, all was quiet, but she could tell they were both still in there. Their silhouettes could be seen against the frosted glazed window that faced the hall. It seemed that Josh was pacing around the office, but Phoebe was sitting down. They had not emerged by the time Jean was ready to head home. She didn't say goodbye but left them to themselves. Whatever had happened, it was not going to end well. Her gut told her that. Besides, she had enough to worry about. Her granddaughter was ill, and they had yet to find out what was wrong. Nothing was more important to her now than that.

# Chapter 23

'You know; they are all straining their necks to know what was going on in that toilet.'

'You think I don't know that.' Phoebe was still shaking. 'Did you see Jean's face when we walked in?'

'How could I not?'

'Phoebe, I am going to kill him.' 'No, you are not, Josh.'

The anger in his face scared her. Even though they were speaking with soft voices, she could see and hear his hatred of the man.

'Josh, you have been around here for a while. You must have seen foes taken down by political backstabbing.' He looked quizzical.

'What can we do to get him out of power? Get the bastard so that he is no longer a threat to us or everyone else he comes into contact with, anything, please give me some ideas.'

Josh's face hardened. She had never wanted to 'get at' anyone before. She could see on his face that he didn't like what had just come out of her mouth.

'Pheebs, I am so sorry for what he has done to you…don't become like them, those who seek to fulfil their lives by destroying the lives of others. That is not you, but, but I can understand, leave it to me…I will bring the bastard down. Me and only me!

'No, Josh. No. I want to do it. I don't want you drawn in.'

'Phoebe, don't you see? I am in. I am. I love you and what he has done; well, he needs to pay for it. He can't rape and then blackmail you into keeping quiet and continue parading around as a moral and upright Prime Minister. I won't let you do this. I will get him.'

'No, Josh. We will do this together or not at all—okay? I don't need you to swoop in like a knight in shining armour to rescue me, we will do this together, and you must give me the ability to take revenge for myself. After all, it was me who he raped.'

He begrudgingly nodded his head in agreement. Standing now, one arm on the window frame, the other on his hip, he looked into the courtyard. He took some time to think.

She was distracted by her nails. They were chipped and looked awful. She hadn't had time to re-do them since her trip. She would when she got home. Although, when she thought about it, she was dog tired. Maybe too tired to care about them or anything else for that matter. She drifted off into thoughts that were miles away from the topic at hand.

'Phoebe, Phoebe, are you listening to me?' He was facing her once again.

'Umm?'

'What are we going to put about as to why we were in the toilet together? And how are we going to cover it up?'

'Not sure.'

'Shit.'

'What?'

'He just texted me. The vote is on. I didn't even hear the bell. He wants me to meet him in his office after it. Did you hear it?'

'No, no, hear what?'

Josh put his head out the door. To his relief, the office staff had left.

'Jean and the crew have already gone, thank God.' He went back in and looked at Phoebe.

'This gives us a little time to think of what we need to say about the toilet. I will come around tonight, and we will discuss it, okay?'

Phoebe realized that he would come face-to-face with Pete for the first time since he found out what had happened. She stood up, walked around her desk, and grabbed both his hands.

'Josh, for goodness sake, keep your cool. He hasn't won. He hasn't. We will make sure of it. Okay?' He nodded. She wasn't convinced. 'Please, Josh, I am relying on you. We must be clever about it.'

He knew she was right, but it was going to be bloody hard not to knock the prick out. They hugged, and he left.

When he arrived at the office of the PM, he wasn't quite ready to go in straight away. He walked up and down the corridor calming himself for the eventual meeting. He used to think this was only a job, and you get dickheads in all walks of life, no matter where you work. He never took anything personally. He always managed to let the crap flow over him, like a well-rounded stone, smoothed out by the flow of a river, with all the sharp edges taken off. Now, now it was bloody personal. He looked down at his jacket; he hadn't noticed that he had spilled some coffee on it earlier in the day. The brown stain was visible against the dark blue lapel, and some had even made its way onto his crisp white shirt underneath. It was not like him. The events of the day had completely absorbed him. Pete would notice. It would tell him that he wasn't on the ball. He had to keep his cool. He knew Phoebe was right. They must be smart about it, but it would take all of his self-control to appear as if nothing was wrong.

He gave a slight knock and went in.

'Josh, have you heard how the vote went?'

'Actually, no, I haven't.'

'For God's sake, go and find out and come back.'

Just as Josh was going to leave, Pete's mobile rang.

'Oh, for fuck's sake!'

'They blocked it?'

'Bastards! I can't believe it after all the wheeling and dealing. Some of them got some great stuff out of me. Josh, go and find out what happened and who stabbed me in the back. And for goodness' sake, go and clean yourself up.'

That was short and sweet, and it was late. Pete's demands could wait until tomorrow. Josh had more important things on his mind, like how to get rid of the bastard. He was glad Pete had suffered this defeat. The changes only benefited him and his cronies, which was the usual state of affairs. Someone had seen through it, however, and that someone who had not yet succumbed to the temptations of power had played him. They had better watch out. Their career was now in serious jeopardy. While he was thinking, it hit him how much more careful he and Phoebe had to be. If Pete would go after someone who just voted against a bill he wanted to be brought in, how angry would he be with those who sought to destroy him? The thought made him shudder, and he sucked in some air. They needed a plan that was foolproof and one that would see this monster's complete and utter downfall.

***

When she got home, Phoebe made herself a cup of tea. Rang her mum and her sister. She just wanted to be sure they were all okay. She prepared herself for the usual 'are you in trouble?' 'Gee, you are ringing me again? Three times in a month, what is going on?' Her mother was especially tricky.

Phoebe held the phone away from her ear and studied the mould patch in the corner of the room while her mother waxed on about how Mic still visits, and he brings the little one with him. And when are you going to find yourself a nice man?

At the beginning of her relationship with Josh, Phoebe decided not to let her family know anything about it. She was down here, and they were up there. What they didn't know wouldn't hurt them or her.

'Well, mum, I had better say goodbye. I am ravenous, and I think my dinner is burning in the oven.' Lie.

Josh knocked on the door. 'Hold on,' she yelled.

'Who is it? Have you got a visitor?' 'Bye mum, talk again soon.'

She hung up. As soon as she had got home, she had changed into a rather drab looking nighty. Its straps were a little frayed and the pattern, consisting of faded roses, did nothing for her complexion. But it was comfy, and comfort was something she needed. But now that Josh had turned up, she regretted it. Not that she wanted anything other than emotional support from Josh, she felt washed out and old. The nighty contributed to the feeling, and she didn't want him to think of her as being old.

She let him in. He didn't even notice what she was wearing. He just headed straight for the kitchen and the cupboard that stored his supply of scotch.

'Want one?' he asked.

Usually, she would say no and have a chardonnay, but tonight, with a tight chest and feelings that needed to be controlled, she agreed. One would help calm her nerves.

They sat on the beige two-seat lounge next to each other for a long time. He gulped his scotch, she sipped, but both stared into space.

The only noise was the humming of the air conditioner and the stream of cars that whizzed past the flat on the road outside. It wasn't until a truck of some description went past blaring its horn that they were both snapped out of their thoughts. Josh drained his glass and reached down, grabbed the bottle and refilled his glass. Phoebe declined; she was still sipping what was left.

After having had his first gulp, he asked, 'Well, what's the plan?'

Phoebe looked at him and shrugged her shoulders. She looked down at her lap. She was twisting her glass around and around in her hands, watching the remnants of her scotch swill around the bottom of the glass.

'You know something?' Phoebe looked at him. 'It was Danielle that told me that something had happened, you know. I am not sure why she did, though.'

She turned down her mouth. Danielle had told. Had she hoped to turn Josh against her?

'What did she say?'

'Just to ask you what had happened in Tasmania. That something happened there.'

'Do you think she is feeling guilty about it?' Phoebe wondered how another woman could let something as wrong as the rape of another be hidden and then cover up for the perpetrator.

'Well, if she does, she is not the Danielle I know. But, that being said, she did seem remorseful. She wanted me to know. She also knows that I will not let it go.'

'Do you think that she wants you to confront Pete? Cause once you do, you're gone.'

'I know. But…thinking about it now…it's not the vibe I got off her. She was irritated. It seemed as if she was really pissed about it.' He drained the last of his second glass of scotch.

'Maybe, just maybe,' he continued, 'she will be an ally.'

Phoebe looked down at her glass and sighed, she didn't think Danielle would be any such thing, but she didn't argue. Instead, she decided to make a start on their planning. 'I think we will have a coffee. We need clear heads to work this all out.' She stood up, 'it's all such a mess.'

Five minutes later, they both had steaming cups of instant coffee in front of them. But Phoebe was agitated. She got up and searched the cupboards for biscuits.

'Phoebe, I don't think we should eat biscuits right now—aren't we going to have some dinner soon?' She stopped looking and closed the cupboards one by one. She didn't feel like devising a plan tonight. Her head was thumping, and she was starting to feel exhausted. She must go back to the doctor soon; she couldn't remember if she needed to get more blood taken. She would ring the surgery in the morning and ask. She sat down next to Josh. He was supping his coffee and just staring straight ahead, lost in deep thought. She couldn't help it, but a tear ran down her face.

She had let him down. She had come gatecrashing into his life and turned it upside down. She leant back into the lounge and raised the coffee to her mouth, and blew it softly. As she did, she was transported back to a time when there was less stress in her life. She thought about family trips to the beach and the sound of the waves crashing on the shore. She hadn't been to the beach for a very long time. She longed for it, the rhythm, the blue of the ocean, the smell of salt.

She remembered being ill when she was younger and spending some time at the Royal Newcastle Hospital. She had had some type of operation, and recovery took a week or so. If you were going to be ill, it was the best place. The sea air wafted around the wards, and you could look out the windows and see the sea, and if you were bored, you could count the many coal ships that were scattered on the vast blueness that stretched out to the horizon. There is something therapeutic about the ocean, no better place to recuperate. Another thing she loved was the group of grey-haired ladies who volunteered their services, coming into the wards with trolleys full of an array of lollies and magazines. They appeared like angels from behind closed curtains and seemed to drift along on the polished floors. Just after her surgery, they had even washed her hair while she was in bed. They made a type of mini saloon at the end of the bed next to your head where they could shampoo and massage while you rested, and you didn't have to move, not one inch. This was one of the most beautiful moments of her life. Wow, she thought: her life, what a mess, when a moment like this seems like one of the best.

'Well,' Josh said eventually, 'should we get on with it?'

'I suppose,' she responded as if the fight had left her.

'How about we order some dinner? I won't be able to think on an empty stomach. What do you feel like?'

'I feel like pizza, something terrible, one with the stuffed cheese crust.'

'What? Is this the man I know and love?' She blushed when she said it. He hadn't said he loved her since he had found out what had happened, and she was desperate for him to do so. He pulled her close. She laid her head on his shoulder. She let out a long breath as she waited for his response. The long slow escape of breath blew past his ear. He pulled back to look into her face. Her eyes were filled with tears, and her nose was red. She was beautiful even so, and at that moment very fragile. He sought out her lips.

They hadn't had sex since before Tasmania; he missed her, all of her. She responded but not in her usual way. It was tentative and less ardent than before. He noticed that it was a timid response to his overture. He stopped and looked at her as tears rolled down her face; he murmured that it would be okay. He was here for her no matter what; they would get through this together. She allowed the floodgates to open, crying like never before. With his arms around her, she let all the rage, anger, shame and fear come spilling out. The pizza with its comforting cheese crust would just have to wait.

# Chapter 24

They decided that they would tell everyone their little episode in the toilets was to do with an illness of one of Phoebe's close relatives. Other than that, all was okay. Phoebe had got a bit emotional about it and needed to let off steam. Josh had sought to comfort her. With that as the only plan they had managed to devise late into last night, they put their heads down and got on with their day jobs. Jean popped her head in and said good morning. She fussed around Phoebe, asking if she needed coffee or anything, hoping she would give her more than just small talk and the reason, as mentioned above, for all the 'to do' in the toilets. Jean was reassured that what had happened in the toilets was nothing to do with the PM. Phoebe was quite upset that Jean had even mentioned that it involved him in any way, shape, or form. But Jean could feel it in her bones that it did. Phoebe was playing the game. Secrets and lies. Just what this place thrived on.

'Well, I'll leave you alone. Are you sure you don't want a coffee?'

'No, thanks, Jean. I just need to get onto this report. Pete asked for it ASAP.'

'Well, let me know if you change your mind.'

She was persistent. Phoebe would give her that; finally, she left her alone.

Josh had to face Pete. There was a meeting of MPs scheduled for the afternoon, and Pete wanted him to go over some issues with him, along with the treasurer, for most of the morning. How he would do it, he didn't know. Josh walked past Danielle's office and noticed she wasn't there. However, on entering Pete's office, he saw her hovering around the back of his desk, talking in muted tones to the PM over his shoulder. Pete looked as if he had a little smirk on his face. The treasurer wasn't there as yet. Pete looked up as Danielle greeted Josh.

'Come in, Josh.' It was all Josh could do, to walk into that office and face the man he hated most in all the world.

'The bloody treasurer thinks he has a part-time job, I am sure of it,' Pete grumbled at Josh.

Danielle shot him a look that said, 'Do you know? Have you asked Phoebe what happened?'

Josh tilted his head in a way that said yes. She pulled away from Pete's chair and walked past Josh. She didn't want to be in the office if the shit hit the fan.

'Well, take a seat. I am just going about this amendment – you know, about the vote that happened the other day? Well, once again, I am trying to wrangle more money out of the plebs to fund tax cuts for some significant donors. Got to get the details right with the treasurer before I get the whip involved.' Josh noticed that this statement was delivered with no shame, no recourse to the corruption it exhibited. No, to Pete, it was just business as usual. 'I have had to water it down a bit to get everyone on board. Hey, that reminds me, did you find out who quashed it in the first place?'

He didn't wait for Josh to respond. 'The treasurer doesn't like it, but he has to sell it to the voting public, so he can just suck it up.' Pete looked up from the paper he held in his hand.

'Not too talkative today, are we?'

It was all Josh could do not to strangle the bastard. He didn't know what to say but took the universal approach and stated that he had been very busy with a lot on his mind and…

'Well,' Pete replied, 'get it off your mind and think of how we can talk the treasurer into appearing on the news tonight to spread the good word about this bill. I need this passed. If he does a good job tonight, we might get it through in the next vote.'

Just as Pete finished the sentence, the treasurer walked in. He was not naturally disciplined in punctuality, in fact, he wasn't much disciplined in anything at all. He was a 'ring in,' a payback for Pete being where he was now. Even so, he wasn't a total waste of space. Pete had set him up. Pete also knew he didn't like the policy he had put forward, largely because it would make him look like a very bad treasurer, which he was. Pete had very cleverly put him between a rock and a tough place. But even though the treasurer didn't like it, he had not voted it down: he was a patsy, and Pete knew it. The treasurer also knew better than to cross the PM. Now, much to his total dismay, he would have to face the press and champion a tax change that he didn't like or want. That's why, as he walked into the office, his face looked like a slapped fish.

Pete grinned at the sight of him. Pete didn't care how much stress it caused. He wanted it resolved right away. What he wanted, he got, and he needed all his ministers on board this afternoon whether they liked it or not.

'You will make sure you talk to the whip right after you leave here. I need you to get everyone on our side, not just the conservatives.' The treasurer nodded his chubby middle-aged head, a little reluctantly, or so it looked to Josh. But for votes, you need enticements.

So Josh sat and watched the two men arguing about what concession would be delivered to the MPs who were capitalising on the situation.

For Josh, everything he hated about politics was encapsulated in these two men: greed, lust for power, narcissistic overload, lack of talent, corruption, self-interest, not one slice of compassion. It was a game; no one was there for the betterment of the country. No longer did politicians carry any altruistic intentions for the good of the people. He was ashamed to admit that he carried on as if everything was all right when it was so apparently not. He also had to ask himself whether most of the time he just did not care, and was only out for himself just like the rest.

But Phoebe had changed his view. She was so passionate about wanting to be in this God awful place to try and do some good. She was like a breath of fresh air. It was like his stale, shallow, boring life had been swept away. He had to face the fact that he was part of the wheel that turned the machinations of politics, and it had turned into a power play of self-interest and degenerative moral standards. He wanted to shout at the two of them. He bit his tongue as both the treasurer and the PM decided that the MPs would be an easy fix. Pete would just make a few threats, and that would be that. Pete also directed – no, *told* – the treasurer what he would say concerning the policy and the taxes to the press. Politically speaking, it all sounded okay. Anyway, the people were way too concerned about the latest Facebook update or Instagram star to really give a fig about policies. Pete knew that the modern-day citizen wasn't listening. And it was just how he liked it.

It was mid-morning when Phoebe noticed the rain. The gloominess outside only added to how she felt internally. Her extreme tiredness worried her and spurred her on to ring the doctors. No, she hadn't had her blood re-done. She would need another request form—there would be a charge involved, and she was happy to pay. She was sorry for the inconvenience. Yes, she would pop in to pick it up. Fatigue overwhelmed her. She could not go on another minute sitting in her chair—she needed to lie down. Jean poked her head through the door, 'Coffee?'

Phoebe just nodded her head, and she placed her head in her arms on her office table. She was always amazed at how Jean knew when she needed a pick me up. As Jean left, Phoebe drew on all her remaining energy to yell out, 'and a doughnut.'

Sugar would provide the energy boost she needed to help her get through the rest of the day. Her energy levels were so low that she had to resort to the worst thing she could possibly do – eat some "comfort" sweets.

As she dozed, waiting for her food and drink, she made up her mind that she would drop into the surgery and pick up her blood form and have them done first thing in the morning. She needed to get on top of whatever it was she had going on. She had given half a thought to menopause, but she knew she was way too young for that, and she wasn't pregnant—20 pregnancy test sticks had told her that. No, it was something simple, she was sure. Anyway, she would get onto it that very day.

***

On her way home, Phoebe picked up the form for her blood. She would do the task in the morning before work. Tonight though, she was alone. Josh had to attend some event that Pete had roped him into. He didn't want to go, but he had to keep up appearances and all that. In a way, she was glad. It would give her some time to think things over without Josh seeking to influence her thoughts all the time. Now, on her own, she could think about things calmly and rationally. This was something that Josh wasn't, as yet, able to help with.

Tiredness soon overwhelmed her, so thinking soon came to an end. She lay on the lounge in front of the TV, dozing and not paying too much attention to how to keep bugs off lettuce; her eyes were closed. A text jolted her out of her malaise. It was from Danielle.

'R u up?'

Sitting up and staring at the phone, it took a while to register that it was Danielle. She was at once suspicious. What was she doing texting her? Not once in the whole time she had worked in Canberra had Danielle made contact with her in any way. Phoebe got herself a glass of wine and took a few gulps before she decided what to do. She couldn't ring Josh; he was tied up with the PM. Another gulp of wine set her nerves to rest. She would answer her; she was just as much intrigued as to what Danielle could want, as afraid of what she would say.

'Yes,' she texted.

Sipping wine and staring at the phone, it took longer than she expected for the next text to come through. She had drunk almost a whole glass of red before it did.

'I want to help.' was the brief message.

Phoebe was taken aback. What? She wanted to help. Help with what? Had Josh spoken to her? How would she help? Phoebe decided not to reply. She didn't know what to say. She put down her phone and went to the toilet. Sitting there, she thought about all that had happened. She tried to work it all out in her head, but it was way too late, and she had consumed too much wine. Finally, after getting off the toilet, she washed her face and got into bed. The TV in the lounge was playing to itself, and she was way too tired to turn it off. She fell into a deep sleep.

If she had stayed up watching, she would have seen footage of the PM at an impromptu interview done on the run earlier in the day. The reporter was focusing on the plight of immigrants, but the camera was focused on Josh. His face was hard, and he stared at the back of the PM with such intense loathing that no one could miss. So, the headline the following morning was not about immigrants but the relationship between the PM and his chief of staff. Phoebe slept, not knowing that tomorrow would bring turmoil, and it was just as well. She really needed a good night's sleep.

***

The PM saw the headline and the look on Josh's face. He had got what he wanted, Phoebe. He had snatched it from right under Josh's nose. He knew he would get some blowback from him, a bit of angst, but that was all. No woman meant too much to Josh. He had been outmanoeuvred, that's all. He would take it like a man defeated at his own game.

But now that his face had been plastered all over the morning news, Pete realised that there was something running much deeper; something much more dangerous was bothering him. He had been in politics long enough to recognise loathing in one form or another. It needed to be resolved, especially now that the politics watchers had noticed a rift. If that couldn't be done, they would have to broker some sort of deal in which their relationship, on the surface, was seen as being amicable. Can't have a PM being offside with his staff, especially his chief of staff

they are meant to be seen as having each other's backs at all times. Josh saw the headline as he drank his first morning coffee.

'Shit,' he mumbled as he crunched his way through his Weetabix. He had let his anger and hatred for the man show, and it was a mistake, a big one.

He would have to turn it around. Make Pete think that he was just having a bad day and that the camera had just caught him at a wrong angle, his bad side, so to speak. His phone rang, it was Pete, he ignored it. He needed to talk to Phoebe and run some ideas past her, but she wasn't answering her phone. Unbeknownst to him, she was heading off to have her bloods taken.

***

As for Phoebe, she had not seen the morning news; she wanted to get to pathology early. She was fasting, which meant forgoing her much-valued cup of morning coffee, and she was starving. She sighed when she walked in, and the waiting room was full. Seemed like everyone had the same idea. Decision time. Would she stay and wait it out or leave and get some food and come back another day? It was tempting, but she thought she might as well get an indication of how long she would have to wait. She was told it should not be much more than half an hour. Too long, coffee won. She would get some at work.

As she walked towards a bus stop, with the cool of the morning enveloping her, she realised she had left her phone on silent, once again. Before entering the pathology centre, she turned it down as she didn't want it ringing while she had blood taken.

***

Sitting on the bus, which was travelling quite a speed around the London Circuit, she pulled her phone out from the bottom of her bag and noticed some missed calls from Josh. She rang him straight away, but this time it was her turn to be a missed call on his phone. Whatever was going on would have to wait until she got back to work and had some strong coffees. Why she took the bus, she would never know, and she reminded herself never to do it again as it took forever to get back to Parliament House.

Jean was waiting for her. Phoebe could see she was relieved when she saw her. 'Josh has been looking for you. He has been here a few times annoying me to bits,' she said, trying her best to make it seem trivial, but she was both annoyed and more than a little intrigued. Phoebe wondered if she had heard the rumours about the rift in the big office. Of course, she had. Phoebe remained calm. She knew something was up, but she didn't want Jean knowing she was anxious about anything.

'Thanks, Jean. I will get onto him as soon as I can.'

Phoebe walked into her office and put her brown briefcase on the desk, starting to take off her fawn overcoat with rather large cream buttons down the front. As she was removing her scarf, she noticed that Jean had followed her.

She looked at her directly in the eye.

'Coffee?' she asked, knowing that Phoebe was in no mood for idle chatter.

'Please.' Phoebe shot back.

Jean left without so much as a mention about how lovely her light green scarf was, which was unusual. Jean always made some sort of comment about her clothing or the weather. Phoebe sensed that Jean knew something. She rang Josh. All he said was for her to meet him at the Tomb of the Unknown Soldier in an hour. She couldn't for the life of her understand why he wanted to meet her there. But she would. Her coffee arrived along with a cream cheese bagel. All the animosity she had held towards Jean disappeared as she munched through it. She didn't have much time, and as she left, she told Jean she was going to the Parliamentary Library to do some research. As she headed for the basement car park to the taxi rank, she had no idea what she and Josh would do about their situations. She hoped Josh had some fantastic idea that would get them both out of the mess they were in. In fact, she was very much hoping that this was the reason for their secret meeting at the War Memorial.

She had a bit of a giggle to herself as she waited for a taxi to turn up. The last time she had been there, she was just a kid. She remembered that between herself, her brother and sister, they had managed to set off nearly every alarm in the place. They were also given a right telling-off for making too much noise at the Tomb of the Unknown Soldier. This memory made her feel a little nervous about meeting there. She wouldn't want to talk to Josh there for fear of being told off again. She knew it was a solemn and sacred place, and she appreciated that now. But when she was a child, it was just another place to have some fun. She wished that her parents had been a little more informative and told them the significance of the site rather than not understanding why they had to leave in such a hurry.

A taxi pulled in and she waved to indicate she wanted to get in. She wasn't in the mood for chatter with the cabbie, so she just looked out the window while he went on about the weather and the tourists who gave him the bloody shits. When they drew in, she saw Josh on the immaculate lawns that led up the two steps of the memorial, in all its majestic glory. He was talking on his phone, his magnificent head bent over, and his black hair was shining in the late morning sun, his long black coat sitting perfectly on his shoulders.

He was gorgeous; nothing could take that away from him. If he lost it all, he would still have his looks and his charm. That thought cheered her a little. On alighting, she met him with a kiss on the cheek. He held her hands and looked into her eyes to see what mood she was in. He didn't see anything that would tell him to tread carefully, but he would anyway.

‘Phoebe, we are not meeting alone—we have another person meeting with us. Now this someone is the last person you would ever think would be trying to help us…’

She took a step back from him and pulled her hands away. ‘Who?’

Trying not to lumber in, but to ease her into the idea of this other person. ‘Well, she…’

‘She?’

‘Well, yes.’

‘Don’t tell me. It’s Danielle?’

’Now, Phoebe, she has had it with Pete. She has told me so, and she wants to bring him down just as we do.’

‘I am sorry, Josh, but I don’t believe a word out of her mouth.’

She turned and looked up at the memorial and let out a sigh. He walked up and placed his hands on her shoulders, and pressed his face into her hair.

‘Please, Phoebe, let’s give her a go. I have never seen her so angry and so disgusted with anything other than what Pete did to you.’

She pulled herself away from him and turned to face him again.

‘But she was there. She allowed it to happen!’

‘And she regrets it. She really does.’ ‘I don’t know, Josh, I really don’t.’

‘Don’t you see; she is his Achilles heel. He relies on her for so much. Me, I am just a patsy. He wanted to rub it into the last PM’s face, disloyalty. That’s where he gets his kicks. He only lets me know so much, but she has insights into all his dirty and dark deeds, and she wants to use what she knows to get to him. Come on, what harm could a meeting with her do? Just don’t say much, let me do the talking…’

‘Is that because you don’t really trust her?’

'Better to be safe rather than sorry.'

Another sigh from Phoebe, but this time it was long and drawn out.

'Come on. She is in the café.'

The café was warm and welcoming. As they entered, they couldn't see Danielle straight away.

Eventually, they saw her in a corner. It seemed as if she was hiding behind a rather large lily plant that was next to the table. As they approached, she looked up at them. She didn't smile; she just nodded her head. Josh pushed Phoebe forward, almost propelling her towards the table. They sat and exchanged greetings. Phoebe tried hard to be pleasant. She was looking at Danielle and watching as she surveyed the room. Josh followed suit. Phoebe had to restrain a grin, as it was all a bit cloak and dagger.

Emerging from behind the plant, a waitress appeared. She noticed Danielle flinch a bit. Phoebe realised that Danielle was indeed very nervous, in a way she had never seen before—it unsettled her quite a bit to see Danielle so worried, when she was always as hard as steel and never showed any type of emotion—well, only hate, envy and just generally being a bitch; then she had every right to be downright terrified.

'Can we order some coffees?' Josh asked the young redheaded girl as she focused on cleaning the table next to them.

'Oh, yeah, but generally, you order at the counter.' Josh smiled at her, which put her out a little, 'but I will take it for you,' she said with the grin of a young girl suddenly struck with a crush.

'You sure?' Josh asked, and she melted.

'Course…umm what would you like?'

'Err,' Josh looked from one woman to the other. Both were so distracted about the situation they found themselves in that they stumbled over their orders. He encouraged them by guessing what they would want. 'One soy latte for Phoebe,' she nodded her agreement. 'And a...'

Danielle jumped in. 'A long black, please.'

'And I will have a short black with some milk on the side, thank you very much.'

'Would you like anything to eat?'

Once again, Josh looked at the women, and both shook their heads; no, they wouldn't.

'Okay, your order won't be very long.' She turned and headed for the kitchen.

The three of them sat in silence for a minute, after which Josh leant forward, more towards Phoebe, as he knew she was having trouble with the fact that Danielle sat opposite her. Phoebe, for her part, had trouble believing Josh's impression that Danielle wanted to help and get back at Pete. After all, it wasn't her who had been raped, and Phoebe held a sneaky suspicion that she had been party to it all.

'Phoebe,' Josh said. She looked at him, but Danielle interrupted, staring intently at Phoebe.

'I know you don't think I have any reason to be here, to be asking you to believe that I have become so disgusted with the man I work for that I would turn on him. But I have. It has probably taken me too long, way too long, to realise that he is not worthy of loyalty. I regret, bitterly, that I have, if you like, aided and abetted his vile behaviour. I have sought to cover up all his deals and misdeeds. I am so ashamed of myself. But nothing compares to what I let him do to you. All I can say is that I am disgusted with myself.'

All through this dialogue, Phoebe was looking down at her skirt. She watched as her tears dropped on it and melted into the dark blue fabric. She was almost paralysed with emotion, a state she did not want to display, as she didn't want to show this woman any vulnerability. But it was too late. She let the tears roll. Could it be true that the only way they could recover from this situation was to trust her? To trust Danielle?

The young waitress brought out the coffees. As she placed them in front of their respective owners, Josh grabbed Phoebe's hand and squeezed it. If the young girl was curious as to why one of them was so upset, she did not show it.

She glanced at Phoebe and then at Josh's hand on hers and turned away, saying, 'enjoy.' She had plenty to tell her friend in the kitchen from where they were both trying to hear what was going on. From the body language and the look on the faces of the people at the table, they both knew that this was no friendly catch up. They surmised that it was the meeting of a wife, mistress and a wayward husband. Deciding which woman was which took up most of their time.

Phoebe wanted to talk to Danielle, to tell her everything that had happened, how she felt and what she had lost, but she did as Josh told her and kept quiet. They all took a sip of coffee. Phoebe wiped her face with a tissue she had hunted out of her bag. A few minutes of silence ensued, then Josh's phone rang. He ignored it.

'Pete?' Danielle queried.

'Yes.'

'He is probably looking for me so that I can take to task the minister, who shall remain anonymous, for speaking out of line the other day to reporters. Idiot, he was just coming out of a wet lunch, so to speak, so we can't delay things much longer.'

'Look,' Danielle continued – they all knew full well who he was referring to, 'I know his weaknesses, and I am one of them. He trusts me implicitly. Bringing him down will not be as hard as you think. I can get things done that you can only dream about.'

'When do we start?' asked Josh.

'No time like the present,' Danielle said before she half-finished her coffee and stood up. 'Don't do anything before I contact you and let you know what to do, okay?'

She waited for both of them to give their assurances and left. Phoebe watched her go as she sipped her coffee. Josh just stared at the centre of the table. He was almost unbelieving of what had just transpired. He had hardly said anything, and Phoebe nothing at all. With all his heart, he wanted to believe that Danielle was going to do as she had said. But he remembered another time when she said one thing and then did another. He gulped his coffee and went to pay the bill. Phoebe followed suit, gulping the latte. She headed away from the café, and Josh soon followed.

The young girls at the counter spent the rest of the day trying to figure out what was going on. The redhead, by late afternoon, was convinced it was a love triangle gone wrong rather than a wayward husband.

# Chapter 25

The week dragged on, and Phoebe was glad to finally get home at the end of a long Friday full of ridiculous meetings and time-wasting discussions. It was cold, and she was looking forward to snuggling up with a blanket and sitting in front of the fire, even if it was only a tiny bar heater. Josh was not going to be around tonight. She was relieved, as she needed rest and comfort. She had filled her handbag with some chocolate bars from the little convenience store up the road. She had the taxi drop her there just so she could. On the way through the gate, she noticed a letter sticking out of her mailbox. She grabbed it as she walked past and glanced at the sender's address. It was from her doctor's surgery.

'What could they want?' She asked herself as she put the key in the door and let herself in.

Her apartment was dark and freezing. After turning on the lights, she put the letter down, went over to the heater, and turned it on, followed quickly by the kettle. As she did, she toyed with the idea of getting some Thai food delivered. 'Why not?'

As she contemplated what she would want to eat, she caught sight of the letter. She picked it back up and stared at it. She remembered how her mother did this, trying to see who had sent it by staring at it, rather than just opening it up. She chastised herself and tore it open.

*Dear Phoebe,*

*The doctor would like to see you and talk about the results of your last blood test. You can make an appointment on this number............................................He has also told me*

*to let you know that there is nothing to be concerned about. However, he would like to see you ASAP.*
*Regards Emma*
*Practice Manager.*

'Umm,' she said to herself as she re-read it, a little confused. She didn't get her blood done, did she? She had walked out the other day, not wanting to wait. How can results be back? She would ring in the morning and tell them about the probable mix-up. She flung the letter back onto the kitchen table, showered, and put on her warm, fleecy pajamas, the stripy red ones that she had bought on a whim in Myers a few weeks ago. Her Thai food arrived, hot and smelling wonderfully of lime and lemongrass. After she had finished her food, she noticed that she had spilled a big dollop of juice all over the letter.

'That's what you get for bringing me bad news.' Phoebe was convinced it was bad news. No doctor sends you a letter to come to see them unless it is. You don't hear from doctors if it is good news. No, they just let you get on with your life. No, bad news it was. After her food had settled, she felt a headache was coming on. She heated water for a hot water bottle and went to bed early. This solitary night hadn't turned out to be as comforting as she had expected, and now she was sorry she had told Josh not to come over. He would have been able to allay her fears; she was sure of that.

***

Across town, in a rather more expensive and exclusive area than the one Phoebe inhabited, Danielle faced a sleepless night. She had not felt so torn in many, many years. Not since she had gone behind Josh's back about the baby. She had stayed steadfastly loyal to Pete. But now her support, well, it was a lie. She liked power, just as much, if not more than Pete. They made a great team, and they had made it to the pinnacle of power. But power had taken over Pete. Yes, he had always been an arrogant bastard, but to do what he did to Phoebe... She had overlooked many an abuse of power, but she couldn't condone it anymore. No, he had stepped over the mark. She felt sorry for his wife. But she was a wife he didn't care for, and she doubted if his wife cared for him either. It would be the social embarrassment that would be tough on her. Danielle knew that she was happy to waft around being the PM's wife, but she was also glad to do it without him. She liked to be the centre of attention and did not like sharing the limelight with him. So instead of sleeping, she spent the night staring at the lights of the city and working out her next move. She needed to be strategic. She fell asleep counting all the people she would need to badger to turn against Pete. She felt it was time for her to abandon him.

***

Later the next week, Phoebe arrived at the doctor's surgery to find out the results of her tests. She felt a little silly as she argued black and blue she had not had any blood taken. Finally, after a 10-minute discussion with the young girl on the other end of the phone, she remembered that she had indeed had her blood taken. She had totally forgotten. She would come to understand this as brain fog, but for the moment, she just thought she was very forgetful. It worried her, but she tried not to show it. On hearing her name called, she picked up her bag, and as she walked towards the doctor who was smiling at her, she nearly fell over the walking frame that belonged to an old lady sitting up from her. She apologised and quickened her step. She was flushed from embarrassment. The doctor waited for her to pass and directed her to his room at the end of a dimly lit corridor. The fluorescent lights gave the hall an almost eerie feel. The office was much brighter, and she sat on the black seat opposite the doctor as he looked for her blood results.

'Ah, yes, here we are.'

'All good?' Phoebe managed to utter.

'Well, I am not sure as yet. You have an abnormality that I was testing for. You have a raised ANA. But your iron is fine due to taking the tablets, which I want you to keep doing, but your cholesterol is a little high.'

'Well, I know why that is. I have been indulging a bit in what you may call 'comfort' food. I have a very stressful job, and it's how I get through the day sometimes…'

'Well, I am not too worried about that at the moment. It's the ANA that concerns me, so I want to retest your blood.'

'What's an "ANA"?'

'It can be a normal variant, but may also point toward an underlying "autoimmune" disease. Are you still feeling tired? And you mentioned last time you were here that you had sore hands—do you still?'

'Ah, well, yes and yes but…autoimmune – what is that?'

'It is a very complex area, way too complex for me. Once we have double-checked for ANA, I will refer you to an immunologist, and we will go from there.

'Okay, but you are scaring me now.'

'Look, the tests will be done again; I am sure it may be nothing, but I want to make sure. Autoimmune can be many things. Most of the time, they are diseases that are controlled well through medication. I am just making sure all is well with you. If it turns out to be nothing, well, all good. Make another appointment with me once you have been to pathology, and we will take it from there. Oh, and try to lay off the junk food a bit and don't "Doctor Google" anything. Most of the stuff you find on there is rubbish.'

'Okay…ummm…okay. See you next time.'

'Don't forget your pathology referral.'

She had started to walk out without it. She took it from the doctor's hand; a little shell-shocked that she had anything of the sort going on.

As she walked out of the surgery and closed the door behind her, she pulled a face. She was annoyed by the obvious reference to her weight. She knew she was eating all wrong. She put it down to stress. She was sorry she didn't ask more questions. She was going to find it extremely hard not to Google it. But she made herself promise not to. It was going to be a long day. Thank God tomorrow was the weekend.

***

Danielle cancelled the social event she had planned for that weekend, lunch on Sunday with her dog mad sister. She wasn't sorry to do that. She couldn't be bothered with the fluff and the madness of a house full of neurotic dogs. Her sister wasn't too concerned, 'she would take them all for a long walk instead.'

'Fine,' Danielle responded to her lack of disappointment. The sisters got on well enough, but it wasn't a close bond. They saw each other more or less out of loyalty rather than any pressing need to get together.

Weekend or not, Danielle had strategies to work out. She would need some headspace and some time to think. She had been the power behind the man; she had used her political intuition to get Pete where he was. She would now have to use it to bring him down.

'Where to start?' Not the cabinet. No, she would have to white ant him, and she would have to do that from the peripheries of government. Get to those who are less than happy with him. It was getting on in the morning, about 10 AM—She was in her dressing gown and slippers.

She looked out her window and saw the Saturday morning traffic winding down the road. She made coffee and found a notebook. What was left of the morning and all afternoon would be spent listing names and positions held in the parliament. Selecting those she knew would turn on a pinhead to get Pete out of office and those who would be too nervous about doing so. She would have to come up with something to lure them in. After all, Pete still had over a year and a half 'til the next election, and shafting him would mean many of them could theoretically be in danger of losing their jobs if whoever replaced Pete didn't like the look of them. She needed an angle that would hook them. It was going to be a long day and an even longer weekend.

***

Monday found Pete in a mood. Danielle was nowhere to be seen, and Josh had rung to say that he would be in late. He had a cabinet meeting to attend this morning, and there was a press call later that day. Pete wanted Josh to help him run through what he should say. His press secretary was next to useless, and Pete let him know it at every opportunity. He needed his treasurer as well – they both had to be on side when it came to the cabinet, but all were AWOL; even Jamie, the one who was put in place to undermine Josh, had flown the coop. Couldn't stand the heat.

'For fuck sake!' He yelled at one of Danielle's underlings. She wasn't tough or hard-edged and was very intimidated by the

PM. Her facial expressions gave her away. To be anywhere near him, especially when he was in such a dark mood, was too much for her to bear. Particularly as she was pregnant and not feeling the best. He yelled at her to get Danielle on the phone. On her way out of the office, she fainted in front of the doorway.

'For Fuck's sake!' Pete yelled again as he stepped over her to find someone else to bark his orders out to.

Danielle hung back as long as she could. After all, she didn't want to make Pete too angry with her. She was in for the long game, and it was a game she would win. However, when she arrived back at her office, she found her pregnant girl in hysterics, on the floor being attended to by a couple of paramedics, and Pete nowhere to be seen.

'Danielle! Danielle!' boomed from the other room.

Danielle was surveying the scene in front of her and didn't, at first, hear her name being called with the urgency and emotion of a mother who had lost sight of her child at a funfair.

'Danielle!'

She turned to face whoever it was that was screeching her name. She saw the Minister for Women, Abby Stein. She'd been given the job in a reshuffle of the cabinet a few weeks earlier. Now, she held the dubious position of being the only woman in a room full of mouldy and stagnant old men who occupied the front bench. She had a job ahead of her, she thought. Danielle acknowledged her with a quick nod of her head.

Pete hated the former minister he tossed to the backbenches, replaced by the woman screaming at her through her very bright veneers. Danielle knew this one was more suited to the position as she was ruthless and unencumbered with kids; she wouldn't be taking time off for family events or emergencies. She had nerves of steel. But, at that very moment, she looked anything but calm; her face was white and stood in stark contrast to the dark coat and skirt she was wearing. Her pearls gleamed creamy white against her throat, which was red and held taut due to her concern for the young girl in front of her who was still sitting on the floor holding her stomach and making awful whining noises.

'Danielle, I was just coming over to see the PM…and I find this. Did she say something about the PM yelling at her, pushing her? Is it true?

'Umm, I am not sure. I have only just arrived myself. But I will find out what happened, as soon as I can.'

'Thank you.' The minister drew in a deep breath.

The paramedics indicated that they were taking the girl to the hospital to check out why she fainted and keep her in for observation. Danielle looked at her tear-stained face and felt sorry for her but was mostly annoyed at the trouble she was causing. Once placed on the ambulance trolley she was off to hospital. Danielle told her she would ring later and check how she was going. She tried to sound as concerned as she could without overdoing it.

'Well, after that little episode, I will …er, go back to my office. I will ring later to make another appointment with the PM.'

Danielle saw the look of disgust cross the MPs face as she turned and left the scene. Out of nowhere, a decidedly devious thought crossed her mind. This incident may just have provided her with an opening to get at Pete. In fact, it was a gift from the political gods. She couldn't have planned it better.

It wouldn't be long until word spread about the poor pregnant girl who got in Pete's way. He wasn't popular with any of his ministers, but he got them into government, and in government was where they wanted to stay. She knew she would have to find an alternative Prime Minister, one that everyone felt could keep them in power and maybe do a better job than Pete in the polls. That was a hard call. She needed to undermine his public persona and let the public see his real character, not the one polished up for TV. She would write a list of those she thought she could sway into being interested in the top job, who were popular within the party but she would need to do it in a way that didn't raise suspicion. The list would be ready for when the shit hit the fan.

But in the meantime, she would start on the PM by making him look incompetent. She would no longer cover for his outbursts. She would let the talk go and not seek to dampen it down. Most people knew what he was like, but she had always contained the conversation but not anymore. She would swear blind to him that she was doing her best. He would believe her, as she was his only true confidante in the whole of parliament. He ruled because he had the backing of the populace and her, but that would not last much longer, not if she made the right moves to the right people.

Danielle was deep in thought when Josh found her at her desk. Unusually for Danielle, a few meaningless things were scattered across it: paper clips, a pen, and a tiny ruler...Josh thought how unlike her it was to have anything on her desk she didn't need right at that very moment. Her face was white, almost sickly pale, and she was staring into space. He bent down so he could look into her eyes, and he waved his hand back and forth across her face.

'Oh Josh, what are you doing?'

'Just trying to bring you back from wherever you were...Problems?'

'Not really. Just something has presented itself to me that may provide an avenue for our adventures in politics.'

She brushed a piece of her light blonde hair back behind one ear, revealing a beautiful diamond stud that glistened under the harsh lights of the office. She started to put the bits and pieces on her desk back in the allocated spots.

Josh grinned as he asked, 'And what may that be?'

'Go to Phoebe's girls, especially Jean; she will know all about it by now. Ask her the latest on the PM.'

'Okay,' he drooled, interested, but not wanting to seem over-excited about the news.

'Oh, but don't make it too obvious; you just want to know what is going on as you heard something on the grapevine. As you are his chief of staff, you need to be aware of any indiscretions or rumours going around the place. She will love filling you in.'

He was about to leave when she realised he had come looking for her, so she asked, 'Ohh, did you want something?'

He spun around on his very stylish leather shoes, looked at her and said, 'You know what? I can't remember what it was.' He waved goodbye as he took off down the corridor towards Phoebe's office. He was surprised at how light he felt at that very moment.

Danielle stared after him. She watched him stride down the hall, his head of hair shining under the fluorescent lights, a pang of remorse struck her in the throat. She dismissed it, but it wouldn't leave her alone.

***

Halfway there, he spotted Phoebe walking towards him. He looked at his watch; it was getting on for lunchtime. Phoebe acknowledged him from a distance, and he stood and waited for her to reach him. He noticed that she seemed more serene than she had for the last few months. She was smiling, and her hair was tied back in a messy bun. She had a splash of colour on her outfit by way of a very burnt orange shirt against a dark blue, almost black suit. A pair of black shoes with a hint of burnt orange as decoration completed her look. He was impressed. She had taken his advice to get some nice clothes and look the part, even if she didn't feel it. She had to be seen to fit in. And, of course, she was aware she had Danielle to compete with.

'Let me guess,' he said as she reached him and he kissed her, European style on each cheek, 'you are going to lunch early.' She grinned.

'Yes, I am, but only so I can sit and think about the hullabaloo this morning. Have you heard?'

'Is it to do with the PM?' 'Yes.'

'No, I haven't.'

'But…how do you know it's…'

She shook her head. Instead of continuing with the question, she just pulled him along the corridor towards the café. 'Just wait till you hear what I have to tell you.'

# Chapter 26

Pete was in a foul mood. The incident with the young mother-to-be had soured his demeanour so much that he didn't want to be bothered by the meeting. He told all the attendees that what they needed to discuss would be done quickly, and there would be no stuffing around. The ministers all looked at one another. A couple had hoped to change his mind on a tax incentive that they thought would be popular and bring a little relief to those who were doing it tough. Since they had come into government, the economy had taken a bit of a whack and was not doing as well as it was before the election. They had, as a government, promised to bring in further economic growth and prosperity. Now, however, there had been an increase in uncertainty, primarily due to fears of war in the Middle East and consequent loss of stability in the markets.

However, Pete was not worried about that. To him, it was just another hiccup in the economy. Wars come and go; this one would fizzle out just like the others, although he had to agree that the threat of war had spooked a lot of people, and he wasn't sure exactly what to say. Usually, he could put a good spin on it and allay the peoples' fears. They just had to wait it out. The ministers who wanted to push for a little wage relief knew that today's meeting would not be the time or place to promote their idea. The meeting would be limited to going through the agenda in a matter-of-fact way: in other words, not kicking up too much of a stink about anything. Soon it was over. However, just as they were about to follow each other out of the room, one of them received a news update on their phone.

'PM pushes a pregnant woman to the ground. She is rushed to hospital.'

The Minister for Agriculture just stared at it. He couldn't believe what he was seeing. He looked up as other ministers pushed past him. Pete was gone. The minister didn't know what to make of it or indeed if he should show the update to anyone. If Pete was going to face trouble, there was going to be a lot of backbiting and bitching. He kept the information to himself, knowing that the rest of the cabinet and indeed the entire parliament would find out soon enough. They would have to go into damage control.

***

What the Minister for Agriculture couldn't understand was how this got out? Usually, anything Pete did that was questionable did not make the news. His close-knit supporters and fixers made sure of that. There was always a price for silence or a threat. Something had changed. Something had shifted, and he wasn't sure what it was. The joy of winning the election had worn off quickly. The fun was over; if he was truthful, it had been over for a while. But now, it seemed as if there was a whiff of doom in the air. Pete felt uneasy, very uneasy for the first time since taking up his position. His first task was to try to find out who had leaked to the press. The first cracks were beginning to show. He needed to find out who had breached protocol before the cracks turned into full-blown breaks. His job, and indeed the government, were in jeopardy if things started to spiral out of control.

***

Phoebe and Josh were enjoying coffee and a lovely bit of creamy cake as they talked about the incident with the PM and the young girl. Once this topic felt like it had been exhausted, Phoebe was going to tell Josh about her recent trip to the doctors. She was interrupted when some mobile phones went off in unison, including their own. Everyone in the café looked at their screens and the news update. Phoebe and Josh just stared at the message. A few in the café gasped in shock at what they were reading. A few politicians from the other side burst out laughing. Although the incident was not a laughing matter, it was almost too much for them to see their fiercest opponent get negative press. It was a first, that was for sure.

'I better get back and see how Pete is taking this,' Josh said as he rose from his seat.

He surveyed the room, and as he did, a few of the opposition members of parliament held up their coffee cups in mock salute. Phoebe noticed as well.

Josh looked at her.

'Danielle?' she queried; he shook his head in acknowledgment and left.

Phoebe almost couldn't contain her joy. It had started. His downfall had begun. Although she was concerned as to what the future held, she felt that this was a fight she was more than willing to be involved in. She felt sure that this leak was Danielle's way of showing both her and Josh that she meant what she had said. She was going to fight him and bring him down. This was the first shot across the bow of a besieged ship. She relished the rest of her cake, and as Josh had left half of his, she ate the rest of Josh's as well. She told herself she would need the energy for the fight.

***

Josh saw Jean hovering around the corridor outside Pete's office. She was white with fear. 'Oh, Josh, I am so glad you are here. Pete is livid, and Danielle is nowhere to be found. I don't know what to make of it all.'

'Josh, Josh it wasn't me who told the press. It wasn't me.' She burst into tears.

Josh was taken aback that she would think that anyone thought it was her. He placed his hand on her shoulder and tried to convince her that no one thought any such thing; she sniffed and said, 'I would never do that, I would never…'

'Jean, go and get yourself some coffee. I will see Pete and try to get to the bottom of it all. You don't need to stress about it. It has nothing to do with you.'

Grateful for his support, she turned towards her office to get her bag.

'Jean, will you make sure no one gets through to the PM? No calls, nothing. Tell the others not to let anyone through to my office or his, okay?'

She nodded her head and went to tell everyone what Josh had said.

Josh found the PM in his office surrounded by his press secretary and his staff.

'Josh, Josh what the fuck is going on?'

Josh had just walked in and noticed straight away that the PM was red with rage. He had been betrayed, and he would get to the bottom of it. The press staff looked as if someone had reached down their throats, pulled their innards out, then pushed them back in. Ralf, the PM's press secretary, was almost apoplectic with rage, so much so that he was having trouble speaking.

'We need to find the leak…we need…need to find them.'

'I know that, Ralf, if you can't be more helpful, then fuck off.'

The younger press staff looked at their boss in total confusion and embarrassment. Out of the three of them, two young men and one woman, or girl, as she seemed to Josh like she was here on work experience, all looked entirely out of their depth. If the floor swallowed them all up at that very moment, Josh was sure they would be very grateful.

'Everyone out except Josh. Go on, piss off.' The PM waved them out, much to their relief. The three younger ones couldn't get through the door fast enough. The press secretary, however, was a little taken aback about being asked to leave. After all, it was his job to make sure the PM got good press.

'I just wanted to...' Ralf started, but was interrupted.

'Just fuck off!' He turned, white as a sheet in rage, slamming the door on his way out.

Josh now faced the steaming rage of the PM alone.

'Now, now,' he started to say.

'Don't bloody "now, now" me. I want answers, and I want them now.' He hit the table with his fist.

'You will get them, but not by biting everyone's head off. Look, I know this is new territory for you, but believe me, it is not the first time a PM has been betrayed, and it won't be the last.'

'I know that, but it is the first time it has happened to me. The damage is going to be horrendous. The story is getting worse. The backbiters are saying I pushed her. I didn't. She's a piss weak little thing. She shouldn't be working here if she can't stand the pressure. Fuck!'

His hands went to the top of his head as he paced around the office.

Josh looked down at the computer screens which stood side by side on his desk. Both had the news plastered on all the networks. The TV on the wall had 'breaking news' updates on every channel. As Josh scrolled through the programs, he thought – Yes! Danielle had been given a gift, and she had used it well. Josh found it very hard not to smirk. The PM grabbed a bottle of scotch and poured himself a large drink. He indicated to Josh if he would join him, but he declined. Josh was thinking of his daydream about owning a bar on a beach somewhere. He wouldn't leave this place now, not when this bastard was going to get his just rewards for everything. The beach and the bar can wait.

'That bloody press secretary is useless. Where did we get him from?'

'Well, if I remember rightly, he is the son of one of your large donors.'

'He's qualified, isn't he?'

'Well, he wrote stuff for a student newspaper.'

'What the…why did we…don't answer that. Don't let him speak to anyone. I want you to do that. Sort it out, Josh, and sort it out now!'

'Well, I think Jamie hired him…'

'I don't care who did; glad that weak-willowed dumb arse left.'

Josh left the PM to his scotch. He wanted to find Danielle and then Phoebe. They all needed to play it safe for a while until the next phase could be instigated. Danielle had done very well. Josh just hoped that nothing could be traced back to her. He was dying to know how she did it. He thought about the poor young man masquerading as the press secretary. Danielle had been the one to keep everything from the press but at the same time made him feel like he was doing a great job. Now that she had withdrawn her services, he was in for a big fall. Josh almost felt sorry for him…almost.

Josh had no luck finding Danielle, so he went on the hunt for Phoebe. Jean told him that she had left a little early, but she was sure she had her phone with her. He didn't know why she had said that. Of course, she would have her phone. He had rung it a few times but still no answer. He went into her office and looked around. Desk clear. He looked out the window. It was overcast and trying to rain. It was only 4 PM, but it was already getting quite dark outside. He didn't know what to do. He resigned himself to returning to his office and speaking to a few people. Make it look as if he gave a damn.

***

Phoebe was back at the doctor's office. They had rung, the doctor wanted to see her as soon as possible. She didn't like the sound of it, but she wasn't too worried. Truth be told, her health was the last thing on her mind at the moment. The doctor called her in.

'Haa, Pheebs, sit, sit.' He pointed to the chair on the opposite side of the desk from him. She noticed that his chair looked new and quite comfy, but the one he was directing her to had seen better days. Its black plastic covering was a little ratty. The rest of the décor in the office was okay. She thought it was a little bit of bad form to give the patient the ratty chair.

She watched as he swivelled around in his seat and looked at her results.

'Now, first of all, how are you feeling?'

'Err, well...'

'Tired, have you any aches?'

'Well, yes, I am a little tired, and sometimes I feel so tired I don't want to get up, and I don't know why.'

'That is only...'

'Have you found out about the auto...what was it – Autoimmune?'

'Well, yes. Your results indicate that you have a raised ANA, not high, but it is there.'

'Oh, what does that mean?'

'Well, to tell you the truth, I'm not really sure, other than that it indicates that you have something going on with the immune system that causes you to feel below par.'

'Oh, so...what is the next step?'

'See a specialist in the field. I will write you up a referral. I know a very good immunologist, Dr Lock, who has a surgery in the middle of Canberra. Make the appointment to see her as soon as you can. Hopefully, she can get to the bottom of it, and you will be on your way to feeling better.'

He handed her the referral, and she headed out into the cool of the Canberra evening. She would make an appointment in the morning. She didn't fancy going home. The rain had eased off, so she decided to walk down the street to find somewhere where she could find a nice Thai dinner. She needed some "me" time, so curry and time on social media would make up for a pretty shitty day.

***

Danielle took a deep breath and put a false smile on her face as she walked into Pete's office. Fortunately, he wasn't there. She let out a sigh of relief. It would give her a bit of time to settle down and get her story straight. Back at her desk, she opened the calendar list for meetings that day; she looked at Pete's appointments. The minister for community welfare was coming in. Danielle knew that deep down he was not a fan of Pete, but that he had, like the rest, put his support behind him so they would get into government. She would ring and move the appointment forward half an hour so she could talk to him about some 'important' matters. She spent the rest of the time jotting down a few points of disagreement that he had long held with the PM. She would rile him up a bit before his meeting with Pete. She had no doubt that they would argue about it. The minister was more left of centre than Pete. He was also facing a backlash from his constituents regarding the somewhat arcane changes to welfare entitlements the government had just passed. He just happened to have a rather large number of people doing it tough in his electorate. Danielle knew he wanted the PM to backtrack on these changes. She also knew that Pete wanted to double down on them a bit more. She would, in a roundabout way, let the minister know this so that he was fully armed for the meeting. This meeting was going to take a rather swift change of direction, which she hoped would catch Pete off guard. Slowly, slowly, she would dismantle the whole edifice of this farce, of this PM.

***

Phoebe spent the morning in her office on Dr Google, trying to make sense of the results from her blood test. She had made the appointment to see the specialist – two months' wait! She wanted a few answers, and she wanted them now. Dr Google was suggesting that she could end up dead or with cancer, in stark contrast to what her GP had told her. After an hour, she decided that it really was not a good idea to seek advice from everyone who held pretensions of being a doctor from around the world. She closed the tab just as Josh walked in.

She looked up.

'Can't stay long. Just wanted to know where you got to last night. I rang you, but you didn't answer. What is more important than a phone call from me?'

She grinned as he walked towards her desk. 'Well, if you must know, a curry and a movie night.'

'Without moi?' He feigned shock that she did not want him to join her.

'Just needed some time to reflect and gain some strength back.'

'That's all'

She had decided not to tell him too much regarding her health. She didn't know what was going on anyway, so until she did, she decided to keep it to herself as much as she could.

'That's it?...I believe you. Thousands wouldn't.'

'Please, you sound like my mother.'

He screwed up his face, and as he did, she thought that no matter what he did, he was still handsome. Today, he looked rather well turned out in an Italian suit and dark plum shirt.

'Err,' she said. 'Have you got something special on today or what?'

'Or what?' He said as he left her alone again and closed the door behind him.

***

As he walked towards his office, he popped his head into Danielle's room to see if she was back. To his relief, she was. She nodded towards the door of the PM's office, and just as he looked towards it, he heard raised voices.

She grinned, and Josh knew that she had thrown the cat in with the pigeons. 'Ouch,' he mouthed as he made his way to his desk, where he decided he would keep his head down for a while.

The minister walked out of the PM's office in such a huff that Danielle didn't have time to say anything. The next thing she knew, she was being summoned into Pete's office.

‘What the hell just happened?’ he said with his back to her.

Before she could respond, he yelled, ‘Why the fuck weren’t you here yesterday? Eh?’

‘My sister’s…’

‘You can’t take time off. You know that. The whole place goes to shit when you do. So where were you?’

‘My sister, her dog…I mean, her daughter was ill, and she needed me.’

‘Your sister? You have never mentioned her to me before. Why not? Well, next time her kid gets sick, it’s not your responsibility, okay?’

‘Okay.’

He looked at her in a way that said she needed to sound more convincing.

‘Yes, I said, okay.’

She had never mentioned her sister to him because she had thought her life was a frivolous waste of time. Too much time was spent worrying about the welfare of her tribe of dogs and little else. Her sister fretted about the least little thing. Her children were grown up and moved away, and it wasn’t too far from the truth when she said she had to help her with her child. To her sister, her dogs *were* her children. One was sick, and her sister was a little too upset about it all. The dog only had an upset stomach, but she thought it provided her with an excellent pretext to go over and help her. The lie she told was not much of a lie. It was something she could truthfully say, but replace the dog with a child and look him in the eye, firmly. Her sister would say that she was there if anyone asked.

‘Now, go and see if that girl is okay. Go and see if you can shut her up, bloody do something.’

‘Okay. but how did your meeting go…’ ‘He can go to hell.’

She left him to the scotch he had poured himself. Danielle had never seen Pete so upset by an ugly but minor event before, nor like this. But she was sure she would see him even more so in the not too distant future. She used to enjoy being his attack dog, keeping him safe from most of the political fallout from his behaviour, but this, this was so much sweeter. And as she left him to ruminate over whether or not he would come out of this unexpected situation with any damage to his reputation, she felt a wave of barely containable exhilaration.

# Chapter 27

As the weeks rolled into months, rumours that generally remained hidden bubbled to the surface. They were small bubbles at first, then becoming more prominent, and they were all about Pete. They trickled out into the talking heads of the Canberra political morass slowly but surely. Tiny bits of salacious gossip doing the rounds gave people many hours of joyful time to debate whether there was any truth in any of it. Pete and his wife were less and less inclined to put up with each other. Not that they did before the talk emerged anyway. It was true, his wife had not been to any functions of late, significantly the Winter Ball, where she usually shone in silky taffeta and gold heels: indeed it was something no one missed, no matter how much they disliked their partner.

But that wasn't the end of it. Soon they were commenting on whether or not he had a bit on the side, another woman hiding in the darkness. This gave the political staff at least a month's worth of idle chatter as they went about their days running the country or simply shuffling papers in their boring little offices they inhabited on a daily basis. Pete, himself, was totally unaware of how much entertainment he was giving everyone. No one said a word to him about the rumbling gossip.

The only thing that could give anything away was the occasional sly wink of an eye as ministers, secretaries, senators, and janitors passed each other in long hallways, cabinet rooms, government meetings, offices, or any one of the eating spots in the building.

It seemed that, no matter what side of politics you were on, gossiping about the PM was a blood sport everyone was enjoying. All the while, some were whispering about a leadership battle. Pete's popularity in the polls was heading south, mainly because he had done stuff-all for the country since he was elected, and the opposition had put a younger leader in place, who was giving him a run for his money. It didn't help his image as an ordinary bloke to be caught talking about the revered Aussie battler in degrading tones, which was quickly uploaded to YouTube and broadcast on every Australian news bulletin whilst "shock-jocks" competed to express the greatest levels of outrage. His own ministers were only half-hearted in their defence of him. He was losing something, something intangible but genuine in politics, and that was relevance. He never had respect. He had started out as the new king but was quickly heading for the role of court jester. Ominously for him, this transition occurred before the juiciest gossip was let loose on the hoards who were now already sniffing blood.

***

Danielle had managed the slow leak of information very artfully. As arrogant as he was, Pete was not suspicious of her and still regarded her as a faithful ally. For the time being, it was all going as planned. Pete knew something was going on and that there was talk, but Danielle managed to throw him off the scent of any gossip originating from her department.

'Bloody disgruntled backbenchers. Are you sure you don't know who they are, got any hints?' Pete was getting more and more agitated as time went on.

'No, not at the moment. But believe me, I am getting close. They will soon be crying over their soy lattes. Don't worry. It's all just a storm in a teacup.' Danielle spent much of her days reassuring him it would all pass over.

'And who took that bloody video of me talking at the business council?'

'Not sure,' she replied.

She left him stewing behind his desk, but not before she put a large whiskey in front of him. She was ready to make her next big move, but she needed to catch up with Phoebe and Josh. They would initiate this next step, and it was something that may unnerve them, but she was sure that they would agree to it. They had played their roles well these last few months, and the tide of political goodwill had well and truly changed direction. She just needed a flood and a full moon to make his removal from office complete.

Spring was once again returning to Canberra. The late morning sun shone directly onto Lake Burleigh Griffin, making it shimmer as it burnt off the remaining morning mist.

***

Phoebe, sitting in the back of a cab, was feeling both exhausted and a little apprehensive. She hadn't heard a whisper from Danielle for the past few weeks, and now, all of a sudden, she wanted to meet up with her in a secret spot. She had gone to work early to catch up on some somewhat unnecessary paperwork. Pete had been storming around, throwing himself into being the PM rather than just playing at it. All the gossip and bad press had made him anxious. If he wasn't at cabinet meetings or sweet-talking ministers and senators over long lunches, he was storming around the offices in a mood, as he wanted everything done yesterday. Hence, she thought she had better show her face.

He asked Phoebe to research the primary needs of women in society—a rather broad undertaking. He wanted a policy that would help underprivileged women succeed but without costing the government too much. It must be a state policy, one that says the government cares and is doing something. Now that she had been given the task, she didn't much want it. It was all smoke and mirrors anyway, and she felt so tired she could have curled up under her desk and slept the rest of the day away once he left. But Danielle wanted to meet at 9.30, so she was on her way. She had never been to this place before; it was situated on the outskirts of Canberra, on a hillside, with 'red' in its name. The driver knew where she meant. It wouldn't take long, 15 minutes or so. Well, if they had gone in the right direction, it may have only taken five or ten minutes. She arrived to see Danielle looking out the big windows watching for her.

Once she was seated and greetings exchanged, Phoebe became overwhelmed by the view. Why hadn't she been here before, she wondered if Josh knew about it? Probably, but he was more inclined to dine at dark and secretive places late into the night. Enjoying coffee in very bright and breezy cafes, not located in the House; early in the morning was not his scene, not at all.

They made small talk until their drinks arrived. Phoebe desperately wanted something with sugar and cream but felt she shouldn't. Danielle was so exasperatingly skinny. The chocolate sprinkle on the top of her coffee would have to suffice. After a minute or two, Danielle put down her cup and looked Phoebe straight in the eye.

As she did, Phoebe looked down and noticed that Danielle had put on a rather stylish sky blue coat that didn't scream 'public servant' but rather 'a lady who does lunch.' Phoebe thought she should have done the same. But it was too late, and besides, wasn't it all getting a little bit too cloak and dagger?

As if reading her mind, Danielle said. 'You can't be too careful, Phoebe. This is playing with fire. We don't want to draw attention to ourselves. We've both appeared in the media.' Phoebe mused whether her attire lacked 'camouflage', but didn't say anything. She just nodded and wished that she had had the forethought to come in "disguise", so to speak. To be honest, she was barely able to dress in what she had on, pure public servant vogue. She couldn't even remember if she had changed her knickers before she put her stockings on this morning. Her brain was in a fog. She couldn't think clearly or remember much of what had happened earlier in the day. She couldn't wait to see the specialist.

'Phoebe,' Danielle's voice was low but strong. 'I know we have not always seen eye to eye, and you have been thrown headfirst into a cauldron of crap, so to speak. I am sorry that what you were seeking from this place has not come to be. It is a swamp where only the most deceitful, self-focused and arrogant seem to survive. I know that you held loftier goals, but that is the way it is. Now, I must ask you to become like those you despise. I need you to be deceitful so we can nail him. I know it is a big ask but hear me out.'

Danielle was looking at her so intensely that it made Phoebe very nervous. She shifted in her seat and waited for what was coming.

'We both know that he is keen on you. We need to use that to our advantage.' Phoebe tried to say something, but Danielle put up her hand to silence her. 'Please hear me out.' Just as she was about to continue, a young waitress, bright and bubbly, arrived at their table asking if they would like some more coffee. Yes, they both would, and Phoebe would have a jam doughnut as well. She thought she might as well because she sure was not going to like anything Danielle was going to say.

‘Phoebe, he raped you. He raped you and got away with it.’ Danielle watched Phoebe’s face flush with the memory. She knew that it was a wound that lay very close to the surface. ‘He can’t get away with it. He just can’t.’

Phoebe was confused and a little scared of what Danielle had in mind.

‘I want to set him up so that he…so that he feels that he can take advantage of you again and…’

‘What? You want him to attempt…’

Danielle’s face told her all she needed to know.

Phoebe couldn’t believe it. No, no way would she be part of it.

‘I can’t, Danielle, I just can’t.’

‘Phoebe please….’

Phoebe was now standing and looking Danielle straight in the eye. ‘No.’ She turned and left the café.

The young waitress was again heading towards their table and watched Phoebe go; confused, she asked Danielle if they still wanted their order.

No, they didn’t, but she would have the bill if you don’t mind. The young waitress returned the coffee and doughnut to the kitchen with a little laugh. She was happy that one of the perks of the job was eating food that had been ordered but no longer wanted.

Danielle sighed as she left and stared out over the view. She knew she had been mistaken. She didn’t know why the hell she had asked that of Phoebe. She watched as Phoebe flagged down a passing taxi and jumped in. She had believed that the fury of a man taking advantage of a woman and not being held accountable would be almost unbearable. She had let her heart rule her head. She knew she could get him any number of ways – she had just wanted him to pay.

If she had been truthful to herself, she would have realised that underneath her plan lay her own sense of betrayal and anger towards men in general. She had been hurt, left and abandoned, and she needed some sort of cathartic experience to release her from her torment. But this was not the way. No, she would be more prudent with her future plans. What she needed to do was to continue to use politics to strengthen her hand. She put that meeting down to having a brain fart, as the saying goes. She needed to maintain clarity and focus in planning for his downfall. She knew Phoebe would tell Josh what she had suggested.

It wasn't long, and her phone rang. Indeed, it was Josh. She chose to ignore it until she could explain her lapse of judgment in a way that would make it sound much less diabolical.

***

Josh was angry, so angry that Phoebe was unsure as to whether she should have told him.

'Keep your voice down. The girls in the office will be able to hear you.' He did not care at that very moment if the whole House heard him.

'She doesn't need to involve you in any way; she assured me she could bring him down just by...well, you know.' Phoebe had put her finger to her mouth, imploring him to be quiet.

He sat on the chair opposite her and looked at her over the desk. Her face was flushed, but she also looked weary, world-weary. He was worried about her.

'When do you see the doctor?'

'In a few weeks.'

'Can't come soon enough.'

'Yeah.' was all she could manage to say.

Later the next day, Phoebe noticed that Jean was upset and was trying very hard to mask it.

The office gossip issues had blown over a little, and Phoebe felt sorry to see Jean, not her usual happy self.

'What's up, Jean?...Do you mind me asking?'

Jean looked at Phoebe as a tear fell from her face.

'Come into my office.'

Phoebe shut the door behind them.

Jean had had bad news about her youngest grandchild. She might have serious childhood cancer. They were doing tests and trying to find out what was going on, but it was taking so long, and waiting for results was starting to get to her. She hadn't told anyone else, but she knew she could trust Phoebe. The younger woman spent the next hour or so consoling Jean, who was distraught. Phoebe told her that it was not certain as yet, and to try and stay positive even though she knew it was hard. Jean eventually dried her tears and decided that she would be better off going home. As Phoebe was seeing her out of her office, her phone rang. It was her sister. She answered it reluctantly, just in case anything had happened to her mother.

'Hey, sis, just rang to let you know your little brother is engaged—oh, and she is pregnant. Mum is over the moon. And of course, I am glad cause I'm not the only one with kids. I can gloat when they are up all night with croup, haha.'

Phoebe wasn't in the mood. 'Great, I am glad. When's the engagement party?'

'Ohh soz, Pheebs, we already had a family dinner. Didn't think you would have had the time…'

'Well, thanks for letting me know.' She hung up.

'Bitch.' Phoebe knew her sister just wanted to rub in her growing estrangement from the family. Their sibling-ship had always been a type of competition, particularly for her sister. She wanted to be the most loved, the most highly regarded. It seemed that Phoebe was a threat to her sense of self. If she could make Phoebe feel less about herself, she felt better. Love was not something either sister held for each other. Phoebe had come to expect little else from her, and indeed from her brother.

Phoebe happened to bump into Danielle later in the day, and they found an out of the way place to have a quick chat.

'What's new?' Phoebe asked, making sure to steer clear of Danielle's last ridiculous request; in fact, the less said about that, the better.

'Not much today, but I will keep my ear to the ground. I know there are some rumblings on the backbench, and what happened to that poor girl has made everyone a bit jumpy. She is suing him, you know.'

Yeah, she will need some good luck with that, Phoebe thought. 'What about you?' Danielle asked.

'No, not much. I have spent the last hour or so with Jean, whose granddaughter is ill. They think she may have cancer, a bad one. But they can't be too sure at the moment.'

'Bloody hell,' Danielle replied.

'Exactly.'

'Well, better keep going,' and with that, Danielle turned on her heel and left Phoebe to ponder the fate of Jean's granddaughter on her own.

Later that day, Danielle met up with the PM and related the news to him.

Ever the political opportunist, he quickly wanted to put a spin on it so it would make him look good.

'Is there any way we can help? Do they need anything?' What sort of political mileage can we get out of it?

Danielle thought for a second that he was genuinely concerned, but the ulterior motive crystallised.

'I'll see,' she said, quite dryly.

'Oh...and get me my press secretary and Josh. Thanks.'

She nodded her acquiescence and headed for her desk, knowing that he had forgotten the name of his press secretary.

After making her calls, she sat and thought of what the PM might do to help the child while making it all about himself. Some sleight of hand trick was needed, smoke and mirrors, that sort of thing.

She would ring Jean – see how they could help out. She knew that about 2 months ago, changes had been made to some Medicare provisions relating to cancer treatment and tests, such as MRIs, which cost a fortune. People now had to pay for many of them. They had managed to pass this in the House and the Senate by promising extra funding for nurses and equipment for public hospitals, but any such provisions had yet to materialise.

***

'Phoebe, Phoebe...Phoebe.' Jean was at her office door once again, but this time rather animated.

'You will never guess what.'

'What?' She responded as she looked up from her work.

'Well, we need to pay for a few things for my granddaughter now that the benefits have been changed. My daughter was worried about how she could afford it, but...but the PM has said that we don't have to worry and that everything will be taken care of. Can you believe it? I just don't know...' She turned and left her as she wanted to tell everyone who would listen to her good news.

Phoebe was shocked. She couldn't believe that Pete would be doing this out of the goodness of his heart as the changes he and his cronies had brought in left not only Jean but thousands of others out of pocket in a time of dire need. She had told him how she had felt, but of course, her opinion didn't matter. Phoebe couldn't believe that he would publicise this as it would show him as a hypocrite. She rang Danielle.

Danielle was almost delirious with delight at what she saw as a vast misstep by Pete. She couldn't have wished for a better development, and was so glad how often his ego clouded his judgement. She knew he wanted a "good news" story to cover the indiscretion with the pregnant woman. Usually, she and others would point out the flaws related to doing this good deed. But this time, no one was going to, and by the time he realised his folly, it would, hopefully, be too late.

Word soon got around as to what was happening. Of course, all were very sorry to hear of the plight that that had befallen Jean and her family. But there were others in this small enclave of the House, those behind office desks, cleaners, maintenance, and security who felt slighted: many had loved ones with similar traumas, and they couldn't help but feel diminished and marginalized. Why was one staff member being treated with free care while others were not? The pot was starting to simmer.

Danielle spoke to Pete later that day. She soon found out that the grand gesture to Jean was only for his house staff to know and not for public broadcast. All had been told not to leak any details; otherwise, they would be out of a job.

'Oh, okay. I thought you would want the world to know how benevolent you are,' she said with her tongue in her cheek.

'Now you know damn well that the general public has had that particular Medicare benefit cut. How would that go down? Not well, eh?'

'But...' she almost forgot and was going to tell him the consequences that inevitably would follow, stopping herself just in time.

'So, why Jean?' She changed the subject.

'She just happened to need the help, and I need to resurrect myself with people around here. I need their support after that stupid incident with that young girl.'

'Oh, you mean the pregnant one that you pushed over?'

He looked up at her from his desk, over the top of his black-rimmed glasses. He wasn't impressed with her comment.

'If I didn't know better, Danielle, I would think that you are angry with me.' She had had enough and turned upon her beautiful new Jimmy Choo shoes and left.

But before she went through the door, she said. 'Now, what makes you think that?'

He laughed. He was sure in his belief that she would always have his back. At her desk, she picked up her bag and took out her makeup. She looked at herself in the stylish silver embossed mirror that she had bought in a trendy store in London many years ago and examined her face. Truth be known, she was trying to think and wanted to look as if she was just tidying herself up. She brushed her cheeks with her blush and re-applied dusty pink lipstick to her long thin lips. She knew she would have to wait until Jean's granddaughter was having treatment, the very same procedure that was no longer paid for via a revoked Medicare benefit. A well-timed press leak about this politicised favour would no doubt add further to the PM's declining fortunes.

Danielle knew favours went on all the time in this place, but this one would surely prove to be a huge political misstep and would inevitably highlight the hypocrisy of the political class and bring him down. The healthcare cuts had not been favourable in the eyes of the public and indeed members of the House, but he had fought hard in parliament to get them accepted. Deals were made, and health insurance companies were given huge incentives to keep premiums down for at least 12 months. By then, everyone would have forgotten about the cuts. Private health was looming large on the policy horizon.

Medicare was becoming too expensive, especially in the wake of tax cuts to the wealthy, and politics, on both sides, was succumbing to the pressure of private health companies, both pharmaceutical and insurance, who coveted the economic benefit of the sick having to pay a high price for life-saving services. Well-funded propaganda had persuaded most of the public that health was not something that should be regulated by the government, and market forces and self-regulation were the antidote to utopian socialism. The healthcare industry would set their own price, knowing that people would pay anything to stay alive. Besides, social media technology had delivered the "Go Fund Me" alternative for those in dire need.

Danielle was going in for the kill. She would let a hostile backbencher know. On the phone, she could tell by the member's voice that she was quite surprised at a request for a meeting with Danielle. Danielle convinced her that the Prime Minister would appreciate it very much. Danielle knew that she had disagreed with the cuts and would be more than interested in the little arrangement he had come up with to save his bacon to make him look kind to his staff. The member was hard working and had an attitude. Pete didn't like her. She wasn't in the cabinet, or indeed the front bench, even though Danielle thought she belonged there. Indeed, Danielle often wondered why Phoebe didn't work with her more closely; they seemed like kindred spirits. That would be down to Pete. He didn't want too much on the agenda that was female-focused. Having a good looking policy advisor was politically an advantage, but it didn't mean he put much thought into women's issues. Putting them together would only lead to heated debates and tears. Amid his misogyny, he was incapable of realising the talents of both these women, indeed of any woman.

Finally, the time and date were set for the meeting. It was to be the day after tomorrow in the café at Questacon at around 10 o'clock. The MP was taken aback at why it had to be there, but Danielle told her that all would be revealed at the appropriate time. On leaving, the member gave a wry smile as if she was aware that some type of intrigue was afoot, and she was not sure whether she wanted to be a part of it or not, but its allure was almost impossible to resist. Danielle spent the rest of the day writing a plan as to how she was going to act out her sense of disbelief once the shit hit the fan.

***

Phoebe sat in the specialist office, waiting for her turn. She was lucky to have been rung up just as a patient cancelled.

'Phoebe…' She only needed to hear her first name to stand and walk towards the doctor's room. Once inside, the doctor indicated for her to take a seat while she scanned her blood results. Phoebe glanced around the room and read some of the basic medical information that adorned the white walls. It was a bit chilly, and she shivered involuntarily. The doctor seemed too young to be a doctor, let alone a specialist. Her hair was jet black. Her appearance gave away her Asian heritage, but she had a strong Australian accent. Her eyes were kind and welcoming, and Phoebe felt at ease with her.

'Now, Phoebe, tell me what has been going on with you?'

'In what way?'

'Well, why are you here?'

'I have been feeling drained lately, well actually for a while, and it is starting to really interfere with my everyday life and work…'

'What do you do for your work?'

'I work…I am a policy advisor to the PM.'

'Oh, impressive…must be a hard job?'

'Well, it has its moments.'

'Anything else going on that you have noticed?'

She wanted Phoebe to list her symptoms. Phoebe thought for a minute.

'Yes, I sometimes get aching hands, and a rash appears on my face, especially when I am fatigued.' Phoebe showed her a picture that she had taken of the rash when it was terrible for about a week.

The doctor nodded. 'That's what we call a butterfly rash, and by looking at your blood, I think you may have what we call an autoimmune disease, specifically Lupus.'

'I have never heard of it.'

'No, not many people have.'

'What is it exactly?' Phoebe was taken aback that she had anything at all, particularly a disease.

'Well, it is autoimmune. That means that your immune system is involved, and, in your case, it is over-reactive, so it attacks your body when it doesn't have anything else to attack. In your case, however, it seems that it mainly attacks your joints and skin. …'

'Oh,'

Phoebe rubbed her hands that seemed to throb with the unwelcome news.

'Now, stress is a major contributor to it. I think your job would be quite stressful?'

'Well, yes…it is.'

'Do you notice that you seem to get a flare when you are under a lot of pressure?'

'A flare?' Phoebe was confused.

'When you notice your symptoms are worse. You see, with this type of disease, it goes up and down. Sometimes you will feel okay. And at other times, you will struggle to get through the day. That's when your rash might flare up as well. Stress can cause you to feel very unwell. Now I will prescribe some tablets that I would like you to take...'

Phoebe wasn't only half listening,

'Is there any way you can decrease your work schedule, maybe take a break until we get on top of this?'

***

Phoebe found herself back in a taxi. She had missed a lot of what the doctor had said but knew that stress was a significant issue with what the doctor had called chronic disease. How do you not stress? Life is stress! Let alone a job with a bunch of sleazy backstabbing...Ohhhhhhh. What in the world was she going to do? She had basically been told that her job could be a cause for her symptoms getting worse. She looked at the scripts in her hand. She will get them filled tomorrow. There was just too much to take in, and she had to see the specialist again in a few weeks to see how she was getting on.

Only when she thought her life couldn't get any more fucked up, her phone rang. Josh was looking for her. She didn't answer. She needed time to take it all in...a chronic disease...she decided to take herself home and have a long hot bath. She told the taxi driver she had changed her mind and gave him her address. She rang Jean and told her she was going to work from home for the rest of the day—that was a lie, but one everyone used when they needed to get away from the suffocating work environment and lick freshly lacerated wounds clean.

She lay in the bath listening to the passing traffic. She heard her phone ring every 10 minutes or so --bloody annoying. She knew it was Josh looking for her. She ignored it as her skin drank in the warm bubbles. Why couldn't life be like a warm bubble bath where you felt safe, toasty warm and pain-free? Why was it all shit instead? She pulled herself up about being melodramatic. Relax. Her mobile rang again.

***

Josh was pacing the corridor outside of Pete's office. The MP who Danielle had leaked information to a few days before, was having words with the PM and their raised voices caused many who were walking past to raise their eyebrows at him. He shrugged his shoulders and gave a wry grin as if to say it was politics as usual. He needed to get onto Phoebe. He needed to tell her what was happening. Much of the backbench had heard about the intervention now, and they knew that if it leaked to the press—he was history. But it was all probably too late. Abby had leaked it to the media, and she was telling him just that. Pete was furious. He wanted to hit her, but that would only lead to making a bad situation even worse. The press would crucify him, and he would be up for assault.

It was all going to be out in the public sphere the next day. The vultures were already circling. The cabinet members were huddled on the other side of the building, trying to decide who to put up as a challenger. None wanted to fight in his corner. No one could agree on the person to take his place. However, nearly everyone acknowledged that Pete had to go, and the sooner, the better. His arrogance, the tales of his sexual misdemeanours, and his total lack of care for anything other than power made those who still held some vestiges of faith in the system ready to work towards his ouster. Some, of course, we're only hoping to better their place in the hierarchy. All of these competing motivations needed to be addressed before they could come up with someone to replace him.

***

In the meantime, Phoebe was blissfully unaware of what was happening. Finally, after many refills of hot water and when her skin was so wrinkled that her fingers looked like dried out prunes, she reached for a towel to dry herself. She put on her PJs and sought out her favourite tea in the kitchen cupboards. She picked up her phone and noticed all the missed calls from Josh. She felt a bit of a chill come over her; what if something terrible had happened to him. She rang him straight away.

'Hey, what's wrong? You okay?'

'Yes, fine. I could ask you the same question. Where have you been?' Phoebe didn't want to let him know the full extent of her diagnosis just yet. She decided to tell him a little white lie.

'Oh, I had a bit of a headache, so I decided I would be better working from home. But I will admit that I fell asleep, and I had my phone on silent.'

'Well, okay. You must know that the fan is going to be hit sooner rather than later. Our rogue MP has contacted the press, so everything will be in the papers tomorrow.'

'Oh…gee, that is unexpected…the backbencher? I, well, what do you think will happen?'

'All I know is that we both need to keep our heads down and try to make out we want to help him solve the situation. What we don't want is to be too caught up in it. Let the main players make the paper, not us.'

'Oh God, I never even thought of us being caught up in it. Being in the papers. Why would they do that?'

'Well, the press will get to anyone who is in his orbit of influence. That includes you and me.'

'Oh, that is all I need. My family will never let me live it down…oh God, what is happening?'

Not so much a question as an outpouring of tension and frustration.

Josh stayed silent on the other end of the phone. After a few minutes, she said in a voice that was almost on the verge of breaking, 'can you come over right now?'

He didn't answer straight away. He knew he was in for a big day tomorrow, and he wanted to spend the rest of the day getting his head around how he was going to handle Pete. But, the sound of her voice worried him. She needed him. Five minutes later, he was in a taxi and on his way.

# Chapter 28

Early the next morning, as he watched Phoebe sleep, he thought about their lovemaking. She had practically jumped him as he walked through the door. She made it urgent and intense. It felt like it was something they would never do again, and she wanted to make the most of it. He, in turn, had kissed her hard, and he now worried that he had left marks on her neck indicating their union. It was a warm day, and she could not cover them up with a scarf. It would be embarrassing for her to go to work looking, well, as if she had been molested. He tried to look at the other side of her neck, but she was in a deep sleep; it was almost as if she was in a coma. He wondered at her ability to sleep so soundly at a time like this. He got up to make coffee and fruit toast.

'Hey, hey, wake up. I have some coffee and toast. We have got to get moving, so come on, eat up.'

She groaned and rolled onto her back. Josh quickly looked at the side of her neck that had been hidden from view. Relief; nothing much to show for their night of passion. However, he was a little disappointed even if he knew the marks would not be a good look for her.

'What are you looking at?' she queried as she tried to sit up.

'Oh, nothing. Here, drink your coffee while it is still hot.'

'Okay.'

She fell back again.

'What are you doing?'

'I feel like I have just come out of an anaesthetic. Wow, really floaty and dog tired. I wonder if…'

She stopped herself. She was going to say if it had anything to do with her illness. Just in time, she remembered she hadn't told Josh the full extent of it as yet. With everything that was going on, she didn't want to burden him with anything else. She made herself sit up and drink her coffee. The toast was golden brown, and the fruit in it plump. Butter ran down her chin as she chomped on it.

'What were you going to say?' He was also enjoying their morning treat beside her in bed.

'Oh, I was just going to say if it is true that a piece of fruit toast is as fattening as a piece of pizza?'

'Well, I suppose that all depends.'

'On what?'

'On what type of pizza you are talking about.'

'True.'

'Thin and crispy with only a few toppings would not be as bad as a supreme with a thick crust.'

'Hey, have you seen those pizzas with the sausage in the crust?'

'Errr no, and no thanks.'

She laughed. She was glad they were not ruminating on work stuff just yet. There would be time enough for that in the coming days and weeks.

'So, can we go back to enjoying our fruit toast without worrying about what it may or may not be doing to our waistline?'

She took a big chunk out of her toast in response to his request.

He took a taxi to work half an hour before her. He wanted to pick up the papers and get a heads up as to what may or may not be revealed in the press about Pete's spontaneous generosity towards a staff member's family before he entered the danger zone.

Phoebe took another bath, a very rare luxury. She lingered in the warm depths feeling her joints get warm and felt comforted. She really didn't care anymore. What will be, will be. She needed a rest, both physically, emotionally and intellectually. As she lay in the warm bubbly water, she noticed the cob-webs on the ceiling. Was it a women's lot to see these things no matter what was going on in her life? She wondered if the very few women who held positions of absolute power did? They, she knew full well, would have cleaners. But, she held her position. She was confident that if a cob-web escaped the notice of the home help, they too would be debating to themselves, when in the bath, whether or not to get out of the tub and remove it or just try and ignore it. She couldn't, just like she knew they wouldn't either. 'Shit.' She got her towel and flicked it towards the web. It was now hanging by a thread from the ceiling. She needed to get out of the bath to be able to pull it down. She did.

'Go to work,' she chided herself.

Josh had seen enough of the papers to know that today would be historically momentous, a day to be talked about in political circles for many years to come. Even though it was a bit dreary due to a drizzle of rain, he had asked the cabby to pull over at the first newsagent. He was a traditionalist concerning reading the news; he still enjoyed the feel and look of the papers. In doing so, however, he risked mucking up his hair. Today, that was the least of his worries. The cabby, a new immigrant, spent the whole journey to the House with a broad grin on his face hoping Josh would take up a conversation with him any time so he could practice his English. That was not going to happen as Josh was buried in the papers. His face held hard as he read the numerous articles ripping the PM to shreds. It occurred to him that from one journalist, in particular, this was not just a political vendetta. It was personal, very personal. What could it be about? He noticed the name of the writer. Female. He bit his lower lip. 'I wonder…' he murmured to himself. He made a note on his phone to find her and persuade her to meet up. He knew that she would automatically think he was meeting her to defend the PM. It was a Sydney paper, so he knew he would have to fly there to make it as easy for her as possible. Suddenly the cab stopped. He noticed a few in the ministry walking with their heads down, trying to avoid the press, which was swarming around. Others, from the government, were trying their best to hide their smiles – the traitors, a group to which he belonged, but as yet, no one had any idea about it. He would work hard to keep it that way until the bastard was brought down. He took a deep breath, signed for his passage and handed the papers to the cabby. He was happy to take them as it would give him some reading practice while waiting on fares. As Josh got out and closed the door, he put on a face that showed that he felt that the PM had nothing to worry about and that it was all just a big misunderstanding.

The next few days were nothing less than deplorable. Deception, pointless negotiations, suspicion, and loathing filled the Canberra air with so much hate and anger that it was nearly impossible to breathe. Josh booked a plane to Sydney on the pretext of rounding up support for the PM from his MPs in the battlefields of Western Sydney. But, of course, he was not going to do any such thing.

He was going to see the disgruntled journalist. He tried to convince Phoebe to come, but she said she couldn't as she wasn't feeling too well. He was worried about her. She seemed to have slowed down and was less animated than when she first arrived to take on the world. He was worried it had worn her down; the backstabbing, the inflated egos of those who wanted nothing more than political fame and indeed fortune, and of course, the taste of battle. He wasn't surprised by it. She had been through hell. But he needed her to have a bit more fight left.

He flew off. Sydney looked magnificent from the sky. He loved to try and pick out landmarks—the Centre Point tower, the boats on the harbour. Water, that was the remedy. Life on a beach, a drink, and long lazy days making small talk to anyone who would listen. One day, he told himself as they came into land, one day.

***

'What do you mean he has gone to Sydney?' Pete was furious as he had utterly forgotten that Josh had taken leave for a few days, even if it was on political business.

Deep in thought and picking at her deep pink nails, Danielle had learned during her long association with the PM to tune out when he was ranting. Trying to calm him never worked, and reason, well, that was something for times that were in his favour. Pete knew he was in trouble and sinking fast. The press were relentless. His polling figures were almost the worst for any sitting PM in the history of the nation. To top it all off, there were rumours that his chief whip was making moves that would see him ousted as the leader.

'I told you I needed to remove that bastard before he put the knife into me.' He got no response from Danielle. She was still busy with her nails and a little cross as she had noticed one of them was chipped. Besides, she knew the ship was sinking. Josh was on his way to blast the last hole in the side. So, there really was no valid reason to assure him that all would be fine. It wouldn't. She waited till he had calmed somewhat and went to the little bar fridge hidden in a dark corner of the room. She pulled out an ice tray and a cool crystal glass, filled it with some of the finest scotch that money could buy, and dumped in a handful of ice. She handed it to him, and he drank it straight down in one go. He handed it back to her.

'So glad you are here, Danielle. I don't know what I would do without your continued support.' She grinned at him but said nothing.

'Danielle?'

'Yes?' The first word she had said to him in at least an hour.

'I will be okay, won't I?'

She smiled again.

'Of course. You will be fine. This will all soon pass,' she said as optimistically as she could.

His shoulders relaxed a little, and he headed for his chair.

She offered some advice. 'Stop reading the news and the Twitter-sphere. Rest for a bit. I am sure this will all be over soon.' He sat down. 'Yes, yes, I am sure you're right.'

She left and closed the door firmly behind her, leaning back on it, she let out a rather loud sigh. She looked over her shoulder. She hoped the PM was caught up in his own destructive thoughts, and he hadn't heard her obvious frustration. He hadn't.

It was too late to meet with the reporter by the time Josh got to the hotel. He quickly texted her and let her know that he could meet up with her anytime the following day. But it must be somewhere where they would not be noticed. She knew the perfect place and 11.30 in the morning would suit her. Done. Now he could relax just a little. He loved this hotel. The windows overlooking the old clock tower gave it a unique feel, and being in the heart of the city was always fun. Even though Canberra was Australia's capital, Sydney was the big smoke. Canberra was a country town in comparison. You could get lost here, and that was fine by him; he had escaped for a while. He was a little excited to be on his own in this playground. Should he grab a nice meal, or should he just order up room service? He looked out of the windows that overlooked the bustling city street below. It was 11.30 at night, and the streets were still full, full of life and adventure. He was enjoying watching the antics of the people in the street below when his mobile rang. It was Danielle.

He let it ring off. He didn't want to talk, not while he was enjoying his solitude. It rang again; he let it ring out. And again. 'Bloody Hell!' he yelled. What was it with this woman?' He knew what was wrong. She could never let anything go. She had to know precisely what was happening at all times.

That's what made her a good PA but a terrible partner. He thought back to the time when they were together. She kept tabs on him all the time, but she was a little more elusive, and he always had a hard time trying to find out what she had been up to if there was a hint of intrigue about. That's why she had been able to fool him...

He went to the bar fridge to get wine. She rang again. He knew that she would keep ringing until he answered. To not reply would mean facing a very petulant taking down once they come face to face in the coming days, and besides, he couldn't afford to get on her bad side. She was vital to getting Pete the boot. He picked up.

'Yes.' Was all he could muster.

'Can you please answer your phone the first time I ring?' A demand. 'Sorry, I was in the shower,' he lied.

'Bullshit.'

He rolled his eyes as she waited for him to agree. He didn't. He heard her sigh.

'What the hell is going on? Have you spoken to her yet?'

‘Nothing is going on, and no, I haven’t spoken to her yet.’

‘Well, what are your plans?’

‘We are meeting at a place she says will be private at 11.30 in the morning, okay?’

‘Don’t you get all antsy with me, Josh. I am in the thick of it here with his highness. God, he is pathetic.’

Josh knew she was copping the rough end of the stick, and he relented.

‘I know Danielle, sorry. I am just so happy to be out of that bloody place for 5 minutes. I was just going to go out and grab something…’

‘You must keep to yourself as much as possible. We don’t want anyone questioning why the PM’s chief of staff is wandering around Sydney on his own at this time of crisis, do we? And when you go out tomorrow, try to disguise yourself a bit so as not to draw attention to yourself.’

‘What the…’

‘Josh, it is important, okay. Get some room service, and I hope for God’s sake you booked in another name?’

He hadn’t, but he told her he did. This made him angry; he should have known better.

‘And that reporter…make sure she stays quiet about your meeting. Stress to her that if she really wants to bring the pig down, she must not say anything yet. I will let you know when you can tell her and when she can cut loose. Okay?’

‘Okay, okay.’

‘Josh, this is really important. Our futures are hanging on a fine balance. We must do this right.’

‘Got it, don’t worry, all will be fine.’

‘Make sure of it.’

‘Room service it is then.’

‘Good.’

She hung up.

He drank his wine while he perused the room service menu. It looked good, especially the pulled pork hamburger with extra bacon and cheese. But somehow, he had lost his appetite. She had made him feel nervous about the whole damn plan now. He knew that they were taking a risk, but for Danielle to sound uneasy, it brought it home to him what they were doing; bringing down a PM.

Even though Phoebe had been too fatigued to go to Sydney with Josh, she did manage to drag herself into work. The day was overcast, giving the whole place a sense of impending doom. She thought that even if it had been sunny, the mood wouldn't be any different. The grey skies just emphasised it. She walked past Jean's desk and wondered where she was. It was very unusual for her to be missing. She didn't overthink it any more until Jean popped her head into her office with the look of sheer distress on her face.

'What the hell is the matter?' Phoebe asked, concerned for her.

Jean couldn't manage to tell her. She just indicated that she needed her to follow. Phoebe was soon walking up the hall behind Jean. Many of those walking past the pair let it be known that they were less than pleased with Jean.

Pheebs noticed that she just kept looking forward and striding as fast as she could to where ever it was they were going. Phoebe realised that Jean was also a victim in this crazy situation. Not only was a beloved grandchild ill, enough to make anyone stressed, but she was at the centre of a political maelstrom.

'God.' Phoebe thought. 'The poor woman.'

Phoebe thought Jean would keep walking straight out of the building. She wouldn't blame her if she did. Suddenly Jean stopped in front of a room Phoebe had never been in before. It was the cabinet room. No one was in there. Jean went in, and Phoebe followed. Inside was a big oval-shaped table. Its décor was effortlessly stylish, and it made Phoebe feel a bit overwhelmed. Here in this room, decisions were made that impacted everyone in the nation. The imprint of many discussions, fights, reconciliations, and inflated egos also gave it a sense of gravitas. It was an impressive place. Jean, however, just wanted to use it as somewhere they could be away from everyone. The room was only used for cabinet meetings, and there wasn't one scheduled until the end of the week.

Jean sat. So did Phoebe. They were both at the most rounded end of the long table, the one nearest to the door. Phoebe waited until Jean was ready to talk, noticing that Jean had changed her hair. She had some very light red streaks in the front, which matched her red knitted cardigan, and Phoebe liked the new look. But, even with the new 'do, Jean was looking her age. Phoebe felt a pang of sympathy for her. Here was a woman that had worked hard and loyally all her life. She genuinely cared for people and took pride in her work. Now, she found that people often didn't return the favour, and her job had become a millstone around her neck. When Jean still had not found the ability to talk, Phoebe leant over and took hold of her hand.

Jean managed to look up at Phoebe. Tears rolled down her flushed cheeks.

Phoebe squeezed her hand.

'I…I just don't know what to do…I feel so responsible…'

'Now, just stop that. You are not responsible for anything. You are a loving grandmother who was worried about her grandchild. You did not cause the mess the PM finds himself in…'

'But.'

'No, no but's.'

A moment's silence.

Phoebe didn't let go of her hand as she knew Jean was devastated and felt terrible for her.

'I like the colour of your shirt. It suits you. What is it, peach?' Jean tried to sound happy, but in truth, she didn't know what to say, so she focused on Phoebe. She always did this when she was hurting. She didn't like to bother others. She felt terrible for dragging Phoebe away and showing vulnerability to her. She had always been the strong one. She was the big sister, the one the family turned to when things went haywire, the wife who her husband relied on, and a mother and grandmother. She was always strong. But not this time. She felt defeated.

Phoebe didn't respond to her question regarding her shirt. Instead, she looked Jean in the eye.

'Jean, Pete always has and always will have just one concern – himself. The way he has used your situation is deplorable. You must not blame yourself. Please.'

'They do; they all blame me.'

'They, as you call them, can't wait for his downfall. So don't worry about that. You keep your head held high. Pete has only himself to blame. He has many enemies, and they are just using this as a way to do him in, so to speak. Jean, promise me that you won't keep thinking it's your fault.'

The older woman shook her head in agreement. 'I will try, but I can't promise anything.' She sniffed.

'You know you only have to ask, and I will help with anything you need.' 'Thank you,' she whispered. They sat for a bit longer, both with tears in their eyes, holding hands. Jean needed a human touch, someone who wouldn't yell at her to snap out of it or to build a bridge. She knew Phoebe would be that person. That is why she felt she could let her in.

The events of the last few weeks lay heavy over the heads of both Phoebe and Jean. Phoebe was concerned for the health and wellbeing of Jean and indeed her poor little granddaughter. She was starting to wonder if it was all worth it, all this backstabbing and undermining of Pete. She had tried to talk to Danielle, but she was always busy, or she had just left her desk when she phoned. Danielle never returned her requests for her to ring back. Phoebe wondered why.

***

For his part, Josh had had a very informative meeting with the journalist. The meeting was held in a small dark café in the basement of a building with an ancient feel—all sandstone and dim lighting. All was intrigue and secrets. What she had to say and what he had to tell her, he felt for sure, would undoubtedly spell the end for Pete. But it was what Danielle wanted that worried him. She wanted to make sure Pete was done, not just relieved of political office, but out of it altogether, and with his reputation in tatters; he had to be—otherwise, they would all be political toast. Danielle insisted that there was only one way. Josh disagreed; in fact, he was adamantly against it. He couldn't let her do what she wanted. On the way from the airport, he stopped in at her place. Danielle was waiting.

***

A few days later and the toll had well and truly knocked Phoebe about. 'Now look, you really need to take some time out.'

She was sitting opposite her doctor, who was concerned about a recent flare of her symptoms. Phoebe was feeling so tired and inflamed that she was having trouble keeping her head up.

'You really need a break. Can I suggest you take some holidays?' The doctor was a little exasperated that she would put work ahead of her own health.

'Ummm, I can't right now. I was going to wait until...'

'Look, you are fighting a losing battle in regards to your health. Is there any way you can take some time off? Even if it's only for a few days. I also want you to increase your medication, for the time being, just to get you through this rough period.'

Phoebe shook her head, no she couldn't take time off, not right now, but yes, she would increase her tablets. She went straight home to bed. She told Jean she had an appointment and probably wouldn't be back 'til the morning.

Throughout the weeks that followed, there were many accusations of sexual harassment and assault by the Prime Minister—it was all over social media, and took up much news time and journalistic endeavour to weed out the rapidly-growing deluge of people with complaints. Phoebe read the stories and wasn't a bit surprised at Pete's hidden past. He, of course, denied all of it. The government had taken a defensive stance. The stories from the deep past, well, they just weren't right. It was a political character assassination, pure and simple. Early one morning, as she sat at her desk, one story grabbed Phoebe's attention. It was about the rape of an advisor that had happened in Tasmania about 12 months ago. There were witnesses. The victim hadn't, as yet, spoken out about it but was insistent that it was true. It had happened. One person very close to the PM was ready to tell all. The only thing holding them back was getting permission from the victim to go public.

Phoebe put the paper down as her face went white. She felt sick; she couldn't believe it. Who the hell had told? Permission, no one had asked her. Was it Josh? No, he wouldn't, but...she needed to get hold of him. She tried his phone, and he didn't answer. She kept trying. What the hell...why wouldn't he answer? She got up and looked out the doorway to see who was around. Jean was not at her desk. No one was visible, which was odd. It was all a bit too quiet. She headed for the café, her head spinning, to see if anyone was there and to find out what she could. She regretted that decision as soon as she walked in. There was a little more than a handful of people having an early coffee. All of them turned and looked at her. She noticed the papers in front of them. It was a bit of a quirk in Canberra that some still enjoyed the feel of paper, troglodytes they were called politely. But when you had to play in the dirt, there was nothing like dirtying your hands with ink.

One person stood and made a move to walk towards her. No, that would not do. She knew they all thought it was her! She turned quickly and left them staring after her. She started to breathe rapidly and was feeling quite faint by the time she entered her office. Jean followed.

'Phoebe, I had hoped to catch you before you got to your office...I was waiting at the front entrance for you, but you must have got here earlier than usual today...'

Phoebe's ears were ringing, and as she turned to face Jean, she wobbled, making the older woman put her hand under her elbow.

'Jean...what is going on?'

'The PM is asking for you. He doesn't sound at all happy. He sent around an escort for you, but you weren't here. I think you should see him and explain...' Her voice was high with anxiety.

'Explain? Explain what?'

'Well, that you didn't...'

'No, I bloody well didn't. So who did? Who did Jean?'

'Go and see him, explain.'

Phoebe was still lucid enough to find the situation ludicrous. She was the victim, but she had to explain to the perpetrator that she didn't rat him out. She would have to grovel. No, she wouldn't. She wouldn't do it. He can go to hell.

'Jean, if you could, please tell the PM that he can shove his job up, well you know where, and that I will not be coming back, ever.'

Someone had told the press. She would find out who. Not only had they taken away her right to keep it to herself, but they had also taken away her agency. It had happened to her and not the person who felt it was their right to tell to gain some political advantage. She was done, done with this place and most, if not all of the people who worked here.

What to do now? She picked up her belongings and put them in her bag. She shook Jean's hand, wished her granddaughter all the best, said she would miss her; she really would. Phoebe then walked away with her head held high, knowing that all the women behind the wall were looking and whispering. They would wait until she was out of earshot to spend the rest of the day in glorious gossip.

Later, in a taxi home, Josh rang.

'I take it you have seen the papers? he asked.

'Yes.'

'I am sorry…it shouldn't have happened…I tried to stop it.'

'What do you mean, you tried to stop it?'

'Danielle…well, she thought that the accusations of sexual assault would help, especially if your assault was known…and well.'

'So you let her leak it to the press?'

'No, no, Phoebe. I tried everything in my power to stop her. She wouldn't listen.'

Phoebe hung up on him.

‘Turn around. I want to go back…please.’

She was looking at the driver through the rear vision mirror, and he returned her gaze. He didn’t ask if she was sure. He could see by her eyes that she wanted to go back. He turned, and soon she found herself in Danielle’s office.

‘Shut the door behind you,’ Danielle told her. ‘I don’t want the PM to know you are here if he comes back from his myriad of press interviews. He is trying hard to overcome all this, but the story about you will be his death knell. Sit.’ Danielle glared at Phoebe.

‘No, thank you.’

‘Okay, drink?’

‘No.’

‘Well, yet again okay, so say what you came here to say then.’

‘How dare you, how dare you tell what happened to me to the press. I did not give you permission. He threatened my family…’

‘Oh, he always does that but as if he would do anything, especially now that his political backside is fried. If that is all you are worried about, relax.’

Phoebe was fuming.

‘No. No. That is not all I am worried about. Why didn’t you just go the whole hog and give them my name as well, eh? Let it all out.’

‘Well, I did think about it, but the press is pretty good at finding these things out for themselves. So, I gave them the bait, and they will chew it up and spit it out. Anyway, don’t just blame me. Josh was in on it too.’

‘What?’ ‘You heard.’

‘He told me he tried to stop you.’

‘You are lying.’

‘No, you are lying.’

'No. I am not. Josh is just as keen to get that bastard and felt that letting your story out would nail him to the wall. And it will.'

Phoebe wobbled. She reached for the chair that was in front of her and sat down. Her face was pale, and she felt as if she wanted to vomit.

Danielle was at the drinks cabinet pouring whiskey. She walked back over to her and said: 'Down this.'

She did. When she had finished, she looked up at Danielle who was looking at her with a smirk on her face. Yes, it was true that she didn't like what Pete had done to Phoebe, but she didn't like Phoebe either. This woman, this young, pretty, intelligent woman, had come and taken away the one thing she loved more than anything—Josh. She would not stand for it. She wanted her gone. And yes, if it meant hurting Josh, again, well, she was willing for that to happen. He would eventually come to know that she was the one for him eventually and not this blow in from the sticks. She would have him, and he would have her, and they would once again take on the world together. Josh would never be happy with Phoebe, not in the long run. He loved the rough and tumble of politics. Danielle had watched Phoebe over the last year and had concluded that she just didn't have the tenacity or the strength to handle the power, deception, and deviance of the political game. He would soon tire of her. She knew what he wanted, and she would make sure he got it.

'You are lying.'

'Am I? No, no, I don't think so.'

Phoebe watched as Danielle picked up her phone.

'Just listen to this.'

Josh's voice. 'Well, I don't think it is the right thing to do...but it would be the end of him, that's for sure.'

Phoebe got up, grabbed her bag and ran out of the office as fast as she could.

She needed to process it all and decide what to do next.

Danielle watched her leave. She had done what she had set out to do. The cost? Well, the downfall of a PM, a fragile government and the man that she loved being wounded for what she expected would be a very short time. She was happy. It was all coming to fruition. She downed a whiskey and went on pretending she had everyone else's best interests at heart.

***

Phoebe was done. She booked a flight. She made a random decision to fly to the next available destination. Singapore via Sydney. Perfect. Just what she needed, an entirely different environment. She packed quickly and ignored the phone. Josh was ringing and leaving messages every half hour or so, but she would not be drawn in. She would hand in her resignation later in the week if she felt like it. Or she may decide to just disappear into a void. On the plane, she drank. Although it looked quite appetising, her food sat on the tray in front of her, untouched. Her head spun the entire trip, and it was not until she had walked into her hotel room and the welcome air conditioning that she let her guard down. She cried until she fell asleep.

***

For his part, Josh was furious at Danielle. He had only agreed to her plan in theory. The last thing he had wanted was for Phoebe to be hurt yet again. He was also very concerned about her. She had left no indication of where she had gone. Even Jean had no idea. One day followed another, and still no Phoebe.

He found out during that week that Danielle had told Phoebe that he was in on the newspaper scheme. He couldn't speak when she told him. He wanted to hurt her, hurt her so much, but he turned away in anger and left her open-mouthed and calling for him to grow up.

'Unbelievable!' She screamed out loud. He heard her.

He fumbled for his phone. He must find Phoebe. He didn't care where she was. He had to find her. His world had crumbled. He didn't care what was happening in government. He knew Pete would very soon resign due to mounting pressure, but this gave him no satisfaction. The only thing that would help how he felt was to see Phoebe. The political world was falling down around his ears, and he could not give a flying fuck. Where the hell was she?

***

'Yes, mum, mum, yes I am fine,' Phoebe said this in the most positive way possible. She wasn't, but she wasn't going to let her family know what an absolute train crash her life had become. Her mother was only half listening as she was busy with her grandchildren.

'Where did you say you were, dear?' Phoebe had told her she was in Albury having a break from work.

Her mother would start asking awkward questions if she mentioned Singapore. She would want to know why the hell was she there, in a place like that. Albury was a much better option. Phoebe had never been to Singapore before. In fact, she had never been out of the country, but from what she had seen so far, she had quite liked it. It was hot, steamy hot, but the change from the weather in Canberra was welcome. She liked the busyness, the noise and the many, many people who crowded the streets. She liked the fact that she felt like she could disappear into the multitudes and not have to worry about bumping into someone she may know. Yes, she would stay a while and soak up the culture, the food, and anonymity. She could hear her mother telling off one of her sister's brood.

'Mum, mum, look, I have to go…mum?'

'Oh, before you do, I heard on the news this morning that your guy is going to resign. So he should, after what he did to that poor girl in Tasmania, and the other pregnant lass, tut, tut. Did you know the one he assaulted, the pregnant one?'

Phoebe was taken aback. Gee, a great time for her to get interested in my work, she thought to herself.

'No, mum, no, I don't.'

'That poor pregnant lass, what a jerk. I don't know why you would want to work for someone like that. Hope you are going to come home now…'

'Mum…I will talk to you later.'

Her mother was distracted by the kids yet again. Phoebe felt like an afterthought.

She hung up, wondering if her mother would even notice that she had.

The bright lights and the heat of the night beckoned. She had spent the last few days both in rage and quiet despair locked in her room, cooled by the air conditioning, darkened by the thick heavy dark blue curtains; she had felt safe cocooned within four walls, but the air had turned stale. She needed fresh air and to see people, people who were busy getting on with their lives, just being well, ordinary.

Amongst the crowds, she could lose herself, maybe even forget who she was. Food was first on her agenda as she was starving. She had not eaten much of anything since her arrival. She wanted something authentic, something she had never had before. She asked at the hotel front desk, and they gave her a couple of intriguing options. Finally, she decided on a restaurant about 500 metres down the road. Although the menu held some items very foreign to her, it sounded divine, just what she needed; food to nourish her soul.

She headed into the steamy night. As she looked around at a world so different from the one back home, busy, hot, with a myriad of languages and cultures swirling around her, she failed to notice the Caucasian man that was walking directly behind her. He kept a safe distance so that she would not become spooked by him, his face showing the joy of someone who had just caught sight of something they had been longing to see but had refused to believe it existed. His camera was slung over his right shoulder; he was sweating, so his white shirt short-sleeved shirt was soaked with sweat, and he was doing his best not to be noticed.

Phoebe looked cool in a blue cotton dress adorned with white flowers. Food stalls were huddled together under the bright lights of the buildings on either side of the road as far as the eye could see. Steam, full of rich aromas, wafted from the pans filled with all sorts of strange and familiar foods; eggs, chicken, noodles, crabs, dumplings, vegetables. She was mesmerised. She had never seen anything like it, so she spent a minute taking in the scene and chastising herself for having been too settled. She thought she just might become a vagabond, a traveller. Cut all ties and be free, damn them all. She ditched the restaurant idea and decided to walk the street in search of a bowl of something magical that would sweep her feelings to the back of her mind, even if it were just for a short while.

# Chapter 29

Back home, the nation was reeling from the sudden resignation of the PM. The press was having a field day. They had championed him, but now they were tearing him down. The cameras flashed. Josh watched the whole sorry episode on TV in his office. The events of the day had snowballed. Something had happened that had forced his hand. The general public was unaware of what it was. Josh knew, and he wished he didn't. The pictures of Phoebe in Singapore took over his thoughts. The press had found her. Josh and Pete knew it would only be a matter of time before she was hounded into telling her story. Josh knew Pete had no recourse, and that made him glad. The atmosphere against men who abuse women had turned into a rage in the wake of the #metoo movement. There was no longer any excuse, nothing he could say, no amount of money thrown to the masses would make it okay.

Josh sat, wondering if he should go after her. He wanted to, with all his heart and soul. But he knew she was keeping a low profile, and she needed time. Time to lick her wounds and think. He loved her, and the most challenging thing would be to keep away, but he knew she needed space. He just wished she would answer her phone. He needed to warn her of the coming storm. He was hesitant to send a text as most of the time, texts cannot convey what you need to say, and meanings can get misconstrued. He needed to speak to her. As he sat, he realised that the only way to get her to talk to him would be face to face. He booked the next flight to Singapore.

The next day, Phoebe woke and thought she might go sightseeing. There were so many things to see: Raffles, The

SuperTree Grove, Garden Rhapsody, that crazy hotel or whatever it was that looked like it had a ship sitting on top of it. For the first time in ages, she felt mentally okay. Physically, however, was another thing. She checked herself in the mirror. She was pale, and she felt a little weary, and her hands hurt, but she was not going to let it stop her.

She put on a dash of red lipstick, brushed her hair so that it shone and admired the lite summery dress she bought in the airport as she arrived. She realised as she disembarked and the steamy hot air hit her that she didn't have enough suitable clothes for the climate. So she added shopping to her list. If she was going to stay for a while, she needed a new wardrobe. She waved at the nice young girl behind the desk in the lobby. She waved back and tried to get her attention, but it was too late. As Phoebe walked towards the entrance, she was besieged by a mob of photographers.

'Phoebe, Phoebe, what have you to say about what the PM did to you…and his resignation…Phoebe…Phoebe.'

Light bulbs popped, and mics were thrust in her face.

She stood still, scared and confused. The concierge and a couple of other hotel staff came to her rescue. Someone grabbed her under the elbow and directed her back towards the lift. Several staff tried to form a barrier between her and the press. One of the photographers fell over. It was madness. At least 15 of them, shouting and taking photos; Phoebe was mortified. The nice young girl from behind the desk managed to keep them out of the lift with the help of a security guard. They accompanied Phoebe back to her room and made sure she was alright and if she needed anything. No, she assured them, she was fine. What she needed was time to take in what had just happened. She wanted to process what it all meant and what she needed to do next.

She now felt like a prisoner, scared and confused about what she could do. She was trapped. She had not, intentionally looked at any news coming out of Australia, but now, she needed to see what was happening and what was being said that had just precipitated her ambush. She trembled as she turned on Sky News. And there it was: across the bottom of the TV, a banner announced that the PM had resigned because he had raped an advisor who had fled to Singapore. There were independent witnesses, so it wasn't just her word against his. Her identity was revealed. She was stunned. She trembled and sat on the bed. She couldn't believe it.

Who were these independent witnesses? Who? How dare they…how dare they use her story to get their own way…Josh, she needed to speak to Josh. Was that a good idea? Danielle had told her he thought it was a good idea to drag her into this mess to get to the PM. But…could she really trust Danielle? She hadn't heard Josh's side of the story. Should she? Should she give him a chance to tell her his side? Her head was spinning. She didn't care how early it was. She needed a drink. She grabbed a straight scotch from the drinks fridge and gulped it down almost in one go. She would ring Josh. She would. What other options did she have? Not many.

She picked up her phone and searched for his number. She had little option but to seek his help. She found it hard to admit, but she missed him. He answered almost straight away. She told him what had just happened and before she could finish, she burst into tears. Josh told her to hold tight. He was just about to board a flight to be with her. Together they would get through this.

'Whatever you do, Phoebe, don't leave the room, sit tight, okay? Just sit tight.'

She hung up, relieved he was on his way and that together they could work it out. She held onto that hope as she spent the remains of the day laying down on the king-size bed, drifting in and out of sleep, trying not to overthink the chaos back in Australia and how the nation thought she was to blame for the downfall of the PM, 'popular legend' that he was. She would be branded a whore and a liar by the government's political allies and heralded as the 'woman' who got rid of a misogynistic leader by the opposition. No matter what side of the political fence people sat on, she would be blamed for the political upheaval due to being a woman. Her life in Australia would not be worth living. She would not return – *never*. Josh would have to understand. Her life as she knew it was over.

Hunger overwhelmed all her emotions. She had not taken any notice of her stomach rumbling, but now it was getting ridiculous. She needed food. The decision not to return helped ease her distress somewhat. She didn't know how she could not go back; she would miss so much about the country. But an adventure would help her heal. She dragged herself into the bathroom with its sleek, white, modern design and looked in the mirror, pushing her hair away from her face. Her hair was worrying her, among all the other stuff she had to worry about. Lately, her hair was so dry and lank, and the colour not as vibrant, it was a dull brown, not like its usual vivid brown with red hues, and when she brushed it, she could see lots of hair in the brush. She put it down to stress. She also noticed that a rash was bubbling up across her face. Fatigue was killing her. She ached all over. Indeed, what had the doctor said? Stress was a leading culprit when it came to her disease. How she would manage it and what was happening in her life, she did not know.

She had not taken her medication. She had forgotten in her rush to go sightseeing, and with the catastrophic events of the morning. She would do it now and order some food. Comfort food was a must. She rang the restaurant and placed an order for a mushroom pizza, wedges, and hot chocolate. She needed carbs. Not long after she had hung up, the phone rang. She knew it could not be Josh as he was still a few hours away. She was hesitant to pick it up, so it kept ringing. Finally, she decided she would but not say anything. She did just that. Holding the earpiece to her ear, she could hear a young female voice saying, 'Mam, mam, I am just ringing to check that you are okay. Please, mam?'

It was the lovely young girl from the front desk.

'Yes, yes, I am fine. Thank you for asking.'

'Okay. mam, please, if you need anything, let me know.'

'Thanks.'

She thought it was lovely of the girl to be concerned. After all, her troubles had nothing to do with her. She was now growing impatient for Josh to get here. Even though she was excruciatingly angry with him, she missed him and needed to see him. A knock came at her door. 'Room service.' She looked through the spyhole in the door to make sure it really was. She saw a young man waiting for her to open the door and looking rather bored. She let him in.

'Hello, mam.'

'Hello.'

'Where would you like me to put it, mam?'

'On the bed will be fine.'

'Okay.'

She followed him to the door, and he turned and smiled at her. She wasn't sure if he wanted a tip – she didn't know the protocol, but he turned and headed down the corridor.

She watched him enter the lift and then look the other way. No one was hanging around. She quickly shut the door and locked it. She gulped down the hot chocolate. She wanted to turn the TV on while she ate but was scared the news would be all about her and anxiety would rear its ugly head and bring her back down again. So instead, she opted to listen to one of her favourite true crime podcasts. The dulcet tones of Mike and Gibby would calm her nerves as they discussed murder and mayhem. She put on headphones and lay back. She didn't realise that she had fallen asleep until she was woken suddenly by her phone ringing. It was Josh.

'Hi, I have just landed. Look, I know this may sound a bit dramatic but don't answer your phone anymore. It won't be long until someone tracks down your mobile number.'

She didn't answer. 'Phoebe, are you there?'

She was processing how she felt. Could she trust him? She had little option but to.

'Okay. Okay. I won't.'

She heard him let out a sigh. 'I am on my way.'

After hanging up, she realised that she hadn't told him where she was, which hotel. Because she had not been watching the news as a way of self-preservation, she didn't realise that where she was staying was all over the networks. It was no secret. It wouldn't be long until the news was widespread. Her mother was sure to ring. But she would not answer. She couldn't deal with her anyway.

She paced the floor, waiting for Josh to arrive. She was counting the white flecks in the thick blue carpet as a way of keeping her thoughts in check when she wondered how he would get through the press? He mustn't be seen; he would get caught up in it all and...God, what a predicament. She knew he was a political player, and he would sort something out. He would come through the back door; she was sure of it. She rang the hotel lobby hoping to find the nice young girl. She was on a break. Phoebe would ring back.

She had no need to worry. Josh had the forethought to take one of the many back entrances. Years of political sneakiness gave him the upper hand, and soon enough, she was letting Josh into her room. At first, there was awkwardness. Stilted hellos and sideways glances. Finally, he just stood looking at her. He wanted so bad to rush to her and kiss her, but he knew this was neither the time nor the place for an overt show of affection. On the other hand, she wanted him to: Stalemate.

'Hey,' he said, 'have you managed to drink all the wine in the fridge yet?'

'No, no, not yet. Help yourself.' She smiled at him.

'Want one.'

'You bet.'

'Well, this is an outcome I would never have expected.'

They were sitting at the little table and chairs by the window, looking at the people below going about their business buying food and drink, chatting to friends and street stall sellers. They sipped their wine. They were careful to stay out of the way of prying eyes or indeed any wayward telescopic camera lens.

'Well, I wouldn't have envisioned ending up here.'

'Me either.'

He looked at her intently.

'You know Phoebe; I didn't leak your name. Granted, I did agree with Danielle that it would be a course of action that would nail Pete, but I did *not* say it should happen. I was against her using you for his downfall or as his *femme fatale*.'

Phoebe knew deep down that this was probably the case, but it helped greatly to hear it from him. She took a big sip of her wine, and she smiled, 'femme fatale?' They both laughed.

It was hard not to. It was like they were in some poorly written crime novel. Both were relieved that the tension had been released.

He relaxed into the back of his chair and let out a deep sigh. Both sat in thoughtful silence for a minute, and then Josh explained that Danielle was their common enemy. It had all been a game to her. She had hoped that with Phoebe out of the way, he would see the error of his ways and want her back. He left out the fact that she thought Phoebe didn't have what it took to thrive in the world of politics and that she was where she was only because of her looks, and now she had to pay for it.

Phoebe listened. Thoughtful and sad. She had let herself be manipulated and used. Not just by Danielle but by Pete and the whole political system as well. She had been a fool. But, she knew it was not entirely her fault; the system was broken. Sad. But that was how things were. She didn't want anything to do with it anymore. She knew she didn't want to go home with her tail between her legs. She didn't know what she wanted at all.

They both decided they were done with politics, and for now, Australia. What to do? They talked through the night. After another bottle of wine, they both agreed that they wanted to escape—but to where? Should they even go together? Was there still room for a relationship? Of course there was. The wine had further clarified that. Decisions needed to be made and now; but before they made any decisions, they rekindled their relationship with drunk sex. It was sloppy, fast and all-encompassing. The giant bed engulfed them. While in the throes of love, they confessed to each other that they couldn't live without each other and once finished, they slept till the early dawn. What they would do would be something to be thought about in the new future that now lay before them.

The sun streaming through the window contributed to Phoebe waking early. They had forgotten to shut the curtains before they went to bed. She padded over to close them and noticed a bunch of people standing around the entrance to the hotel with cameras slung over their shoulders. She stood looking at them for a moment in a sleepy fog. It didn't register straight away that they were here for her. She looked back at Josh, and it hit her. She hurriedly shut the curtains, breathing heavy. What to do? How would they leave?

'Josh, Josh…Josh.' He stirred.

'Josh.'

'Yeah.'

'There is a heap of press outside. We left the curtains open. Do you think that they could get photos of us? Josh?

'What?' He sat up, not registering what she was saying.

'Do you think that they could have gotten some shots of us, you know, in bed?'

'I…I don't know. What makes you think that?'

'Well, maybe curtains open, drones, things like that.'

'Well, if they did, good luck to them.'

'Josh, you are supposed to be making me feel better.'

'Sorry. Could you make us a coffee, or should we order some room service—wait, scrap that, they may have moles in the kitchen.'

'What the hell…you mean they may be checking on what we order? That's news?'

'Anything is news when it comes to a woman and the downfall of a PM.'

'Josh, if they do have some footage of last night, I mean when we were…I will never be able to go home. They will label me a whore. God, what if they do?'

'Now you are jumping to conclusions' Josh didn't tell her that some parts of the press already had done similar things before.

'But, it would give him ammunition against me. He could say that I was consenting and use the footage to make the claim that I was promiscuous—I am still married after all.'

Josh jumped out of bed and peered through the curtains. He knew she had a point. It was turning into a bigger mess. He wanted to protect her, but he would have no way to if what she thought was true. What next?

'Josh?' She was not happy with his brooding silence. 'We may have a problem, eh?'

He scoffed but without much conviction.

'Now you are really worrying me,' she said. She was slumped on the bed, seemingly defeated. He walked towards her and took her hands in his as he looked down onto her auburn head of hair.

'You know how I always said that I would like to have a small bar on a beach and spend the day chatting and entertaining tourists.' She shrugged in response, thinking he was less than serious.

'Well, I think it's time. And I want you to come with me.'

She looked up quickly into his face to see if he was joking with her or not. He wasn't.

'You mean run?'

'Run? No, no…nothing as exciting as that, just …relocate. Start again. Less stress, no egos to deal with. Sun, sand, and beach. What we both need more than anything is more freedom…and less…well…less bullshit.'

She could tell he meant every word. 'Ummm, what about my family?' 'What about them?'

'I won't ever see them again?'

'I am not saying that. We will lay low until the dust settles. But, seriously, it may be a few years. I can't say it won't. But if we go back, we will be in deep shit. No rest; our careers are now dust.

'Ha!'

'What?'

'What career? Mine had only just started.'

Well, that is how it goes sometimes. Women in politics are usually the first to get blamed when the shit hits the fan. Look, I am not saying that you can never go back and do what you want. All I am saying is that we need to lay low and let the stories in the newspapers die. And die, they will, and they will move on to their next victim. If you choose to go back, I will go with you and face everything head-on.'

They looked at each other for a few seconds, unsure of the future, when Phoebe said:

'I'm hungry.'

'Me too,' said Josh.

'I will ring the front desk and give our order to our young girl. She can write it down, take it to the kitchen, and tell them it's for another room. She can collect it for us. I am sure she would as she has been terrific so far. I need pancakes to think properly.'

The helpful young lady was happy to get their breakfast, and yes, the press was still in the lobby.

Phoebe and Josh showered and were soon eating a delicious array of pancakes and poached eggs on toast, washed down with Earl Grey tea and black coffee. The rest of the morning was spent talking about what to do next. Should they go away, or should they go back? The final decision was going to be Phoebe's; Josh was adamant about that. He would follow her back or take her away, and it would be her decision and hers alone. About midday, they turned on the international news. What they feared had happened. Drone footage had indeed caught them in bed together. But the footage was grainy, and it was hard to make out whether it was them or not. The press wanted the public to believe it, based on their insistence that it was.

'Phoebe? Josh asked as she stared at the news. 'Phoebe?'

'Um,' she replied, 'how about we go away after we have gone back and faced the press. I cannot leave with my name in the mud. What if we go back, put our point of view out there and then leave, and leave forever?'

Josh tried his best to dissuade Phoebe from taking such drastic action. No, he was sure it was best just to go, hide, and finally grab hold of the life he had dreamt of for so long. Where warm sea breezes welcome you to the day instead of freezing cold mornings. He wanted it now so bad he could almost scream at her to take advantage of the situation and go. Just as he was making another plea for her to see sense, the voice of Pete coming from the TV caught them both off guard.

'What the...?' Josh listened to him blather on about the women he was accused of assaulting being cheap, particularly his advisor, who, he added, had left her husband to have a fling with him. The rumours about him raping her were not to be believed. They had had sex, and it was consensual. You can tell by the recent tape that she enjoys it, sex, that is. She would sleep with anything that had a heartbeat. No, he will not resign. He will stay. After all, they had gotten rid of that stupid directive that politicians and staff could not enjoy relationships. He had done nothing wrong but be beguiled by a beautiful and wily woman. He was very sorry he had upset his wife and family, and he would do everything in his power to make it up to them.

The PM was shoring up his support now that he could use a tape of Phoebe and Josh entwined. He looked somewhat stronger again.

Josh looked at Phoebe and knew what she was going to say.

'I'm going back!'

'Look...I think you are being a bit rash...'

'Rash? Rash?' Her voice was high pitched and a little shaky.

He threw his hands up in the air and faced the TV, what he would give to be able to reach into it and strangle the bastard. He was sick of it. He was tired of the weight of it all. But then he stopped himself. It wasn't just his name that was being dragged through the mud—it was hers, and she was wearing the brunt of it. Of course, she needed to go back and try to make it right. Not just for herself but for her family. As much as she complains about them, she hated the thought of them thinking she had let them down.

He turned to see what she was doing. She was draining the last of the red wine from the bottle. 'To courage.' She laughed, a laugh that let him know that she was on the verge of tears.

'Okay, if you are going back, then I am coming with you.'

'No hiding?'

'No. Straight out the front door. You have done nothing to be ashamed of. You must hold your head high at all times. But, we must, we must make a plan of action. We cannot just go back without knowing how we are going to handle the situation.'

'Interviews?' she queried.

'Yes. But we must be picky as to who we do it with. No right-wing mags or newspapers. Let me think about who, and I will arrange it.'

'What about Danielle? What will she be doing? Do you think she has been sacked?

'Whoa, whoa, whoa, slow down, will you. I can't think with you carrying on.'

'Scuse me?'

'Sorry, but I need to think.'

She smiled at him. The whole thing was crazy, but she felt safe with him. She was so glad he was going to stick with her and not jet off into the horizon playing bar. Together they could weather the storm, and at the end of it, they would indeed take off.

He was relieved to see her relax a little. He felt his own tension lessen somewhat as well.

'No matter what has happened, Danielle is like a cat with nine lives, but rapidly consuming them! That being said, she is close to using them all up. But, no, we are not to worry about her. I will make a few calls and get a feel for the political climate back home.'

'Okay. I better ring my mum and sister. Bet I won't get a word in edgeways. But I must let them know I am fine and will see them soon.'

'Good luck,' he jested with her.

'You too.' She left him on the bed, thinking and looking up contacts. She went into the bathroom to have some privacy. She always felt awkward talking to family in front of other people.

The next day their flight home was booked, an early afternoon flight that would see them arrive in Sydney late evening, and then onto Canberra in the early morning. All they had to do now was get out of the hotel and into a cheap taxi to Changi airport. Fortunately, it was pouring with rain which had deterred most of the press. Only the most obstinate had braved the downpour and were dripping all over the foyer floor.

Josh and Phoebe decided that if they were going to face the press at home, they would do the same here. After a late breakfast, which Phoebe only managed to pick at, they grabbed their luggage and headed for the lift. The doors opened, and they faced a ragtag assembly of reporters soaking wet and down on their numbers. Both sighed with relief. This was not going to be as bad as they had suspected. Indeed, they just walked without much in the way of a push or a shove to their taxi, which they could see just outside the big glass doors of the hotel. The press that was there shouted at them and took lots of photos.

Phoebe wanted to hide her face, but Josh prompted her not to. She had nothing to be ashamed of, and burying her face would make it look like she did. They had checked out over the phone and left their keys in the room, so there was no need to see the concierge. Once safe inside the taxi, they relaxed a little. On the main road to Changi Airport, Phoebe looked over at Josh. She thought back to the first time they had sat in a car together like this. That time she was arriving alone. This time they were departing together. Where had the two years gone? He could still make her look at him in awe. His handsome face was always a delight to her. She had to admit, though, it had hardened slightly, but only a little. She was saddened at the thought that she may be to blame.

As they approached the airport, she knew that no matter what happened—the politics, the drama, the name-calling—he would be there. They would weather it together. She thought that they might well indeed end up running a little bar on a beach somewhere. Now, however, it was time to be strong, to hold tight and face the maelstrom that awaited them. She squeezed his hand. He did the same. She acknowledged to herself that she was tired, exhausted. But she would not let it stop her in her fight to clear her name. She was not going to let any sexist, egoist, lying pig of a politician get the better of her. She just wouldn't.